The Torontonians

a novel

The Torontonians

by Phyllis Brett Young

McGill-Queen's University Press
Montreal & Kingston • London • Ithaca

ISBN 978-0-7735-3324-0

Legal deposit third quarter 2007
Bibliothèque nationale du Québec

First edition published by Longmans, Green and Company

Printed in Canada on acid-free paper that is 100% ancient forest free (100% post-consumer recycled), processed chlorine free

McGill–Queen's University Press acknowledges the support of the Canada Council for the Arts for our publishing program. We also acknowledge the financial support of the Government of Canada through the Book Publishing Industry Development Program (BDIDP) for our publishing activities.

Library and Archives Canada Cataloguing in Publication

Young, Phyllis Brett
The Torontonians : a novel / by Phyllis Brett Young.

ISBN 978-0-7735-3324-0

I. Title.

PS8547.058T6 2007 C813'.54 C2007-904503-0

Quotation from the song "Stormy Weather," copyright 1933 by Mills Music, Inc., is used by permission.
Couplet by B.K. Sandwell is quoted with the kind consent of Mrs. Sandwell.

Contents

Studio portrait of Phyllis Brett Young, circa 1959, used for publicity and book jackets. Courtesy Valerie Argue

Foreword

PHYLLIS BRETT YOUNG

Phyllis Brett Young was born in Toronto in 1914 of English immigrant parents. Her father, George Sidney Brett, was head of the Department of Philosophy, University of Toronto; her mother, Marion Brett, was an avid reader and a talented woodcarver. Educated in both public and private schools, Phyllis attended the Ontario College of Art before marrying her longtime sweetheart, Douglas Young. The early, depression-era years of their marriage were difficult financially, but after World War II, Douglas began a successful career in personnel that led to a five-year stint with a branch of the United Nations in Geneva, Switzerland. There, their only child, Valerie, attended the International School, while Phyllis Brett Young had the freedom, and perhaps the perspective, to focus on her first two novels.

By the fall of 1960, after a two-year relocation in Ottawa, the Youngs had returned to Toronto and Phyllis Brett Young's writing career had taken flight. Between 1959 and 1969 she published four novels (*Psyche, The Torontonians, Undine,* and *A Question of Judgment*), a fictionalized childhood memoir (*Anything Could Happen*), and a thriller (*The Ravine,* published under the pseudonym Kendal Young). Positively received by readers and reviewers alike, her novels appeared in numerous editions and languages in Canada, the United States, England, and other European countries, while *The Ravine* was made into a movie under the title *Assault.*

Over the years, the Youngs lived in a variety of apartments and houses (both urban and suburban), eventually retiring to their country dream home near the town of Orillia, Ontario, where Phyllis Brett Young died in 1996, and her husband just eighteen months later.

THE TORONTONIANS, SOME REFLECTIONS FROM THE AUTHOR'S DAUGHTER

My mother was not a feminist. However, she undoubtedly would have been had she been born in 1944 instead of 1914. In *The Torontonians* one can see her attempt – played out through her heroine, Karen – to come to terms not only with post World War II materialism but also with the strong social pressure on a woman to find fulfillment as lady of the suburban manor. She was more successful in the former than the latter. Had she been born three decades later, she might have concluded her novel with a major role reassessment instead of just a change of life-style. But Betty Friedan had not yet published *The Feminine Mystique* (1963), and my mother, for all her intelligence and competitive spirit, was still the product of a culture in which married women only went out to work under extreme circumstances and of a society that expected that a devoted husband, healthy children, and a comfortable home to look after would be fulfillment enough. Early on in *The Torontonians* (page 9), Karen's husband, Rick, hits the nail on the head when he tells her that "one can't be content unless one is using, and really using, whatever talents or aptitudes one happens to be blessed with." Unfortunately, neither of them fully grasps the significance of this statement for Karen's life.

It is interesting to note that while the protagonist of the novel may not find the answer to some of her problems, the author of the novel, in the very act of writing it, is already working her way towards a solution, just as so many other women writers had done before her. Phyllis Brett Young's writing was not really a hobby, as she described it in several interviews following the publication of her first novel, *Psyche.* When people see their creative endeavours purely as leisure activities, they generally resist any attempt to market their wares. To do so would generate all kinds of pressure – to produce, to publicize, to succeed – and quickly drain their hobby of pleasure. My mother not only needed a creative and intellectually challenging pastime, she also wanted, as most writers do, to be published, read, and enjoyed.

Novelists constantly have to deal with questions about autobiographical content in their works. In the interest of protecting others (and probably also the mystique of their own creative process), they insist that all characters, events, etc., are purely fictitious. This can never be entirely true, as everything must stem ultimately from the mind and experience of the creator. (I don't think it would be revealing too many family secrets to say that although the home in question was not a renovated farmhouse, the wonderful story in *The Torontonians* about the buckwheat lawn is, in its essentials, entirely true.) The question is, does it really matter what the author's sources of inspiration are? It's the literary transformation that counts: a good novel always stands on its own. In the case of my mother, her Author's Note assertion that the participating characters in *The Torontonians* are, "in word, deed, and appearance," wholly the product of her imagination is, in a literal sense, a statement of fact. My father would never have gone hunting, I do not have a bossy, critical aunt, and not one of my uncles would ever have prefaced his remarks with "Let's face it"!

The Torontonians is not a *roman à clef* but a novel of manners in which the characters – although engagingly brought to life through deft description and the smart dialogue for which the author had such a good ear – are more recognizable as products of their background and times than as actual people. And while the book offers a personal perspective through the eyes of its heroine, it also provides a keenly observed picture of a whole generation of middle-class women throughout Canada, or anywhere else in North America, from the mid-forties to the end of the fifties (the reference to "the sixties" on page 25 is a rare typographical error from the original edition), caught in what Phyllis Brett Young describes as "a gilt-edged suburban labyrinth" (13), and ultimately, "an evolutionary *cul-de-sac*" (319). The frequent, and somewhat unusual use of the pronoun "you" draws the reader into Karen's world and at the same time suggests a collective experience – a particularly effective technique for her reflections on society and the times. Although the role of women was about to undergo a seismic change, and the hippie era to provide a brief respite in the headlong pursuit of material wealth, many of the issues dealt with in the book still resonate today, and the often amusing expositions of human foibles ring as true for me now as they did forty-seven years ago.

With the exception of a few places such as Rowanwood (the prototypical residential suburb) and Elmdale Avenue (representative of many old, residential streets in the Annex area of central Toronto), the author clearly identifies most of the settings for *The Torontonians,* "as an outer framework of fact for an inner core of fiction" (Author's Note). Flashbacks to Karen's childhood in the Annex provide glimpses of Toronto life between the First and Second World Wars: the sports, music, movies, and mores; the sights and sounds of the city's treed, residential streets, marred by depression breadlines and pleas for food. There is a wealth of topical references to post World War II Toronto to supply background and context to the story: from business to politics, from advertisements and magazines to a variety of household and other products – even the cost of buying a home, a fine example of the power of inflation!

My mother fought hard for the title of the novel. She wanted her readers to know that "Toronto the Good," long considered a dull, provincial town, was fast becoming a lively, cosmopolitan city. Longmans Green & Co. agreed and published it as *The Torontonians* in 1960. American and British publishers were not persuaded, however. In those days for a novel, or movie, to be set in Canada (and especially Toronto!) was the kiss of death for international sales. Thus over the next five years *The Torontonians* was published in the United States by G. P. Putnam's Sons and

Valerie Argue (Phyllis Brett Young's daughter), holding coffee cup, early 1960s. Courtesy Valerie Argue

Paperback Library Inc. as *Gift of Time* and in England by W. H. Allen as *The Gift of Time* and by Pan Books Ltd. as *The Commuters.*

It was not just Toronto and Torontonians but Canada and Canadians that Phyllis Brett Young wanted to put on the map, and in each of her works she tries to do just that. As she said in an *Ottawa Citizen* interview (7 April 1960), "I write because I love Canada and I wish more and more people would write about Canada as it is today."

After my mother's death, I reread all six of her books in chronological order. I was struck by the speed with which she developed her skills as a novelist. (Prior to *Psyche*, she had been submitting short stories to magazines but had decided her real interest lay with the novel.) She never took a writing class or joined a writer's workshop – useful as those can be – but built on a good English language education by the simple (or not so simple) act of writing, writing, and more writing, in the consistent and disciplined way of so many successful writers. *A Question of Judgment* (1969) was her last publication. After that, family needs took precedence over personal fulfillment, and unfortunately she never got back to her writing. Not for lack of inspiration, however. A born story teller, Phyllis Brett Young never stopped coming up with new ideas and plots as long as she lived.

Valerie (Brett Young) Argue
March 2007

About the Novel

A novel of manners, *The Torontonians* puts a Toronto suburban neighbourhood in the late 1950s under the microscope. Rowanwood is populated by upper middle-class couples who entertain one another with a round of cocktail parties and barbecue dinners. The novel focuses on a group of couples in immediate social orbit of Karen, the protagonist — her best friend Susan and husband Lewis, her childhood friend Barbara and husband Matt, and her flirtatious high school friend Fay and husband Roddie. On the periphery are couples with whom Karen shares only a Rowanwood affiliation: the cloying Betsey and Harry, as well as Millicent and her appropriately named husband, Biff. There's also Mrs Johnson, the one single mother in the neighbourhood, who works two low-paying jobs and still manages to send her son to the prestigious Upper Canada College, a paradox that fuels novelistic suspense as well as intrigue when it begins to embroil Lewis (whose enigmatic character makes him an ideal hero of the popular gothic romance variety).

During weekdays, with husbands at work in the high-rise buildings downtown, Rowanwood housewives perform the subtle rituals of gracious living. They know to enter one another's houses without ringing the doorbell, raise their eyebrows in mild bewilderment at the one wife who doesn't join her husband for breakfast before he leaves for work, but largely ignore the Polish count who takes up residence in the largest house of the neighbourhood – and with its large matriarch – and hone their aesthetic tastes to create a "gracious" life. The Rowanwood men also have finely tuned aesthetic sensibilities and are quite capable of recog-

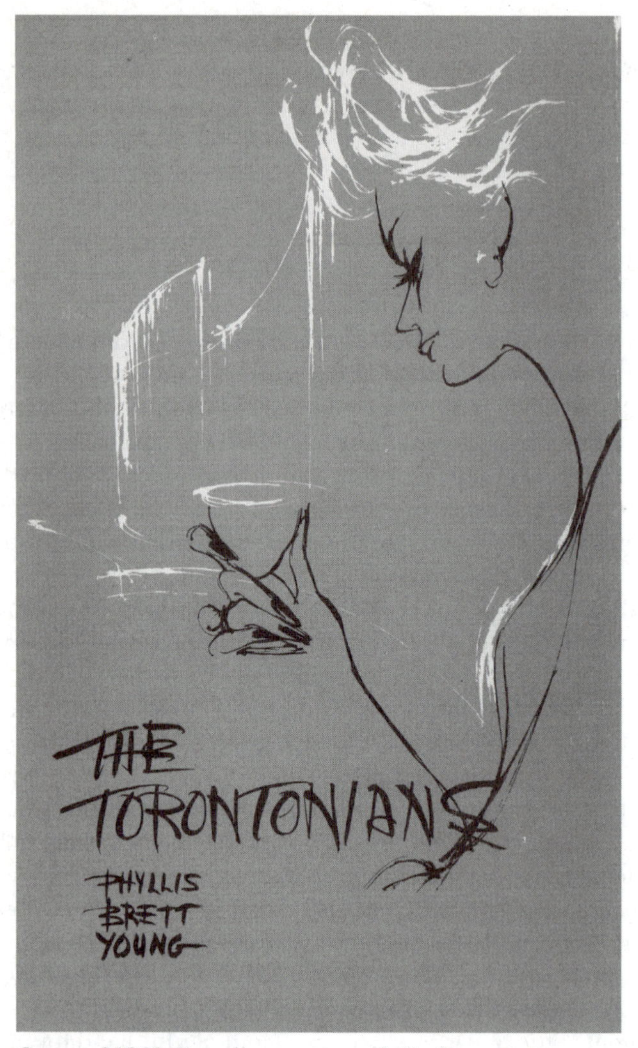

Cover of 1960 Canadian version of *The Torontonians* showing new Toronto City Hall and martini glass designed by Jean Miller.

nizing the need for a carpet of particular hue to set off a room just so, or outdoor lighting dimmed just enough to prevent it

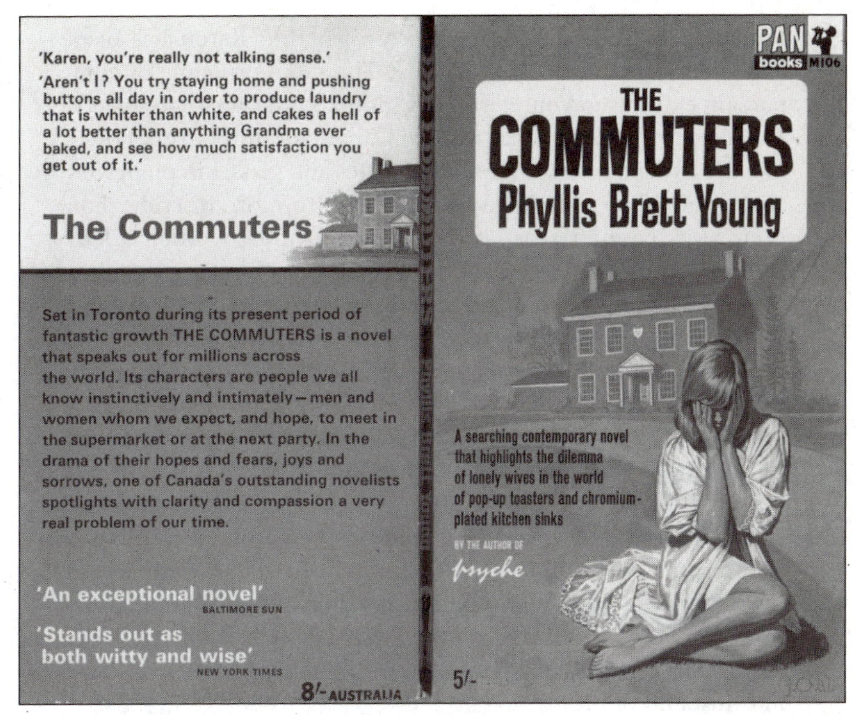

Cover of Pan Books paperback version of *The Torontonians,* retitled *The Commuters.*

becoming "*un peu Versailles*" or "if you prefer, *un peu* Bayview" (170). Rick, Karen's husband, tells her when she prepares for a stressful meeting downtown, "the way you dress could matter" – and she knows that he is right.

Young's readers quickly understand that each neighbourhood has its own particular codes for dress and behavior; Young describes Rowanwood's through a series of comparisons. Rowanwood is not Admiral Road, for example, where Rick's sister lives with her psychiatrist husband, Ned, holdouts among their contemporaries who have left the Annex for the lure of suburban lawns. Nor is Rowanwood like small-town Planesville, where the wives aspire to cosmopolitanism by dressing in pearls and cashmere, learning French in which to converse with their French-

Canadian help, and seeming to care whether Karen has been entertained at Buckingham Palace. The same principle of comparison extends to Young's observations about Canadian society. The narrator explains that refined Canadians don't drink liquor like the British, for example, with bottles and glasses in plain view above the table; that Canadian doctors are more discrete than their Swiss counterparts, as they would turn away, when a lady removed her glove to reveal a cut finger.

Not surprisingly in a world where she is so acutely aware of her social station, Karen also measures the progression of her life, putting each period in a neat package. There was a childhood on Elmdale Avenue, salad days in Geneva, the early years of marriage in Toronto on Gavin Street, and her current life in Rowanwood. The dilemma that fuels the story that Karen tells herself, which makes up the novel, is her current bewilderment. Despite her carefully nurtured ability to be absolutely punctual, to avoid the cracks in the sidewalk when she walks, to wear and say just the right thing, Karen, like so many women of her generation, has lost her balance. *The Torontonians* recounts Karen's attempt to regain that balance, with the help of her friends and her husband of twenty years.

Nathalie Cooke and Suzanne Morton
2007

Introduction

The Second World War and the 1960s are easily recognized as periods of intense social change. It would be a mistake, however, to assume that the intervening years were times of stability and concord – the 1950s was also a period of change. The ground was shifting and, like the characters in this novel, many Canadians were anxious and uncertain about their lives and their communities.

Production and consumption increased during the 1950s and the majority of Canadians benefited from a rising standard of living, with the national economy fueled by natural resource development; large infrastructure projects such as the St Lawrence Seaway, the TransCanada Pipeline and the Trans-Canada Highway; and a growing manufacturing sector in Ontario. Although per capita income nearly doubled between 1946 and 1960, the level of prosperity should not be exaggerated: gains were not evenly distributed and Canadians had a lower standard of living than Americans, and less disposable income. Sociologist John Porter, in his famous 1965 study, noted that during the 1950s the majority of Canadians belonged to what he defined as lower- middle class and working class groups.[1]

Nevertheless, in part as the result of new government income support programs such as Family Allowance and Old Age Security, more Canadians had access to better housing, food, health care, transportation, and domestic technology. This new standard of living was perhaps most visible in upper-middle class suburbs such as the fictional Rowanwood – itself a consequence of urban growth – but, as the novel points out, the two worlds of

Two images of Toronto: top, Osgoode Hall Law Courts, with Canada Life Assurance Building on left, 1930s; bottom, Toronto skyline from the harbour, circa 1940s.

Toronto and small town Planesville were not as different as was sometimes imagined.

There were anxieties and uncertainties in the political realm. While Canadians saw themselves having emerged from the Second World War as a "Middle Power" with international prestige and influence founded on past military success and influential allies, the emergent Super Power status of the United States posed particular challenges to English Canadian nationalism. The Cold War, increased defense dependency on the United States, and recognition that the Soviets would soon have the hydrogen bomb pushed Canadians to promote a multilateral model for North Atlantic security, leading to the creation of NATO in 1949 to balance the weight of its neighbour to the South. But the influence of the US was not only through its military might: *The Torontonians* provides many examples of a North American culture influenced by American musicians and celebrities and both of Karen and Rick's daughters were living, at least temporarily, in the States. Nor did English-speaking Canadians consider themselves quite as British as before, as shown in the description of the trip to England where Karen is appalled by the London snobbery of a Canadian-born friend. Canada's break with Britain over the Suez Crisis in 1956 marked this change in external relations, a transformation that was mirrored domestically by the adoption of a new flag – without the Union Jack – in 1964. If American popular culture was omnipresent and English-speaking Canadians no longer identified with Britain in the same way, what did it mean to be Canadian and how were differences from the US to be maintained?

The Torontonians provides a vivid picture of English Canadian interest in nationalism and Canadian identity during this period, referring to Canadian popular culture through sports heroes, orchestras, and high cultural celebrities such as author Robertson Davies, editor B.K. Sandwell, and photographer Yosuf Karsh. The fictional walls of Lewis Preston's downtown Toronto office contain landscapes by Canadian painters, presumably somewhat akin to the Group of Seven. Published just ten years after the federal Royal Commission on Arts, Letters and Sciences (commonly referred to as the Massey Commission), *The Torontonians* can be seen as a nascent example of burgeoning nationalist pride and confidence in the cultural realm.

This interest in what it meant to be Canadian occurred at a moment of rapid population growth, the result of both immigration and natural increase. Between 1946 and 1962, 1,761,505 documented immigrants arrived in Canada, playing a significant role in the overall population increase from 12 million to 18.5 million people. These "New Canadians" were almost exclusively European or "White" emigrants from former British colonies and dynamic large communities of Italians, Greeks, Portuguese, Poles, and Yugoslavians began to change the essentially British character of cities such as Toronto.[2] Throughout the Western World, the period 1946–61 is associated with "the baby boom" as those in marriages delayed because of the depression and the war began producing children at the same time that the age of first marriages dropped and general birthrates increased. Every year between 1952 and 1961 saw at least 400,000 babies born as the population grew from 14 to 18 million people. (One quickly realizes the significance of these numbers if they are compared with rates today. In 2004, with the Canadian population at 32.6 million, almost twice that of the period under discussion, only 337,000 babies were born in Canada.)[3] One of the consequences of early marriage is seen in *The Torontonians:* at the age of forty, Karen has two daughters who have already left the family home.

Families were not only starting sooner and growing, they were also changing in structure. While the model was the father-led democratic family, with the father's authority connected to his responsibility for the economic support of the family and the mother remaining at home, taking responsibility for domestic tasks and child rearing,[4] in actuality, the number of married women working outside the home was increasing during this time. Part of the explanation for this change was a desire to participate in the expanding consumer economy. Washing machines, electric stoves, Mixmasters, and automobiles were redefined as necessities, not luxuries, but in 1960 very few Canadian homes boasted chest freezers, dryers, or dishwashers.[5]

Even in the well-off suburb of Rowanwood, where the only wage-earning woman was a single mother, Karen's unpaid labour in household renovation and helping to seed a buckwheat lawn was necessary to achieve and maintain a standard of living beyond what was possible based on what her executive husband was earning.

It was also the ideal that every nuclear family live in a separate home with a private yard – a housing form that became possible with the upsurge in automobile ownership, which permitted families to move outside the periphery of major cities into areas where land was available for new developments.[6] With such housing, as in this novel, men commuted downtown to work and suburbs became female spaces during the day. Amid the conventional wisdom and platitudes portraying this as a good life for women, the ambivalence and discontent of women like Karen has been recognized by historians such as Veronica Strong-Boag and Valerie Korinek who, like the protagonist, complicate our understanding of postwar suburbs, seeing them as simultaneously a site of alienation and superficiality as well as community and meaning made possible through neighbours, morning coffee breaks, afternoon bridge parties, home and school associations, and garden clubs.[7] Second-wave feminism did not emerge full blown in the 1960s or with the publication of landmark classics such as Betty Friedan's 1963 *The Feminine Mystique. The Torontonians* had such an immediate impact on so many of its readers because it resonated with something they were already feeling. Karen is clearly looking for something more, something to give her life purpose and meaning outside family and consumption, but she has not reached the point where fundamental gender role change is imaginable. The ambivalence identified by scholars is at least temporarily resolved by Karen and the novel, with self-scrutiny posited as the key that allows Karen to acknowledge the dangers of an increasingly materialistic society and ultimately calls for the reassertion of core human values as a necessary antidote to the threatening alienation and malaise of mid-twentieth century suburban life.

Widely read and reviewed both within Canada and abroad, *The Torontonians* was an instant bestseller when it first appeared in hard copy on 21 October 1960. Two years later Donald Goudy of the *Star Weekly Magazine* described its author as "snugly and securely settled in as Canada's bestselling woman novelist" and estimated that Phyllis Brett Young had reached 10,000,000 readers with her first three books.[8] In other words, Young was nothing short of a literary sensation – Canada's answer to Grace Metalious, American author of the 1956 blockbuster *Peyton Place*, and a forerunner of Britain's J.K. Rowling in the present day. All three writers appealed to popular audiences by pushing the boundaries of expectation. Rowling took the gamble that young readers were not only capable of slogging through countless pages but also willing to deal with fearful villainy and the even harsher truths of ageing and mortality. Metalious shocked her readers by taking aim at dearly held assumptions about New England propriety. *Peyton Place*'s impact in the year of its publication should not be overlooked. As Ardis Cameron reminds us in her introduction to the 1999 reissue, it was more often found stashed in the kitchen cupboards and under beds than on bookshelves because it not only exposed the sex and scandals of a fictitious New England community but also served as a sexual primer for countless women and dared to depict female sexual pleasure.

Largely ignored, because reframed in the hugely successful television series, was *Peyton Place*'s depiction of women's potential to empower themselves and support those around them.[9] This same potential for change and ability to enable change is understated in Young's *The Torontonians* as well. The novel revolves around the possibility of three life-altering events that threaten to upset the status quo but are ultimately resolved. Its innovation is, however, not so much its exposure of the secrets behind suburban doors as its insistence on locating actions at a precise moment in time and in a place that had yet to be seen as a locale worthy of novelistic scrutiny – late 1950s suburban Toronto. Explaining that *The Torontonians* was about "right now" and about "the immediate past," Young went on to explain in a radio interview taped in Moncton, New Brunswick that, "No novelist or historian in future years will be able to capture our way of life as we who live it."[10] But the risk of using Toronto as a setting was not insignificant for an author aiming to reach audiences outside Canada. One must remember that this was decades before such Toronto novels as Michael Ondaatje's *In the Skin of a Lion* or Margaret Atwood's *The Edible Woman, Life Before Man,* and *Robber Bride.* Atwood's *Cat's Eye,* of course, would bring international attention to the neighbourhood depicted here as Rowanwood.

Young's project involved two gambles. Would audiences in Canada and abroad appreciate close scrutiny of her particular place and moment in time? And would close scrutiny of a suburban Toronto setting support an extended exploration of the mores and manners of mid-twentieth-century suburban society? The novel's wide appeal was quickly confirmed by reviews appearing across the US, in the *New York Times* at one end of the country and the *Los Angeles Examiner* at the other, as well as in the *Baltimore Sun,* the *Washington Post and Times Herald,* and the *Berkeley Daily Gazette.* To the first question, Canadians Robert Fulford and Margaret Laurence both gave a resounding yes. "The book in its best moments is an exercise in acute local nostalgia, and for people (like me)," admitted Fulford, "who maintain an uneasy love affair with Toronto, Mrs. Young's approach will be fascinating."[11] Laurence honed in on the same vignettes, praising the "warmly evocative descriptions of the city 30 years ago, when the voices of the peanut man, the ice man, the strawberry man and the knife-grinder echoed along shady Elmdale Avenue."[12] (One wonders whether the preference she voiced for the novel's passages of nostalgic reminiscence over those of sociological analysis prompted her own novelistic method in the 1969 housewife novel of the Manawaka series, *The Fire Dwellers.*)

However, the most scathing criticism of the novel – and a most revealing one – also came from Fulford's review. *The Torontonians,* he grumbled, "is an altogether unimpressive example of romantic commercial fiction. It has all the up-to-date touches, including the most fashionable sort of anxiety, but at heart it is strictly from *Ladies Home Journal*."[13] At first this seems jarringly at odds with the critical consensus, which focused on the novel's "wit" and "appeal," "perception" and "tenderness." Ken Carnahan of the *Berkeley Daily Gazette* wrote, "[*The Torontonians*] is a perceptive story ... The characters are all well drawn and the prose is warm and enjoyable to read."[14] Florence Crowther of *The New York Times* wrote, "In a growing catalogue of books that have been probing the sweet life of suburbia, Mrs. Young's stands out as both wise and witty."[15] Discussing "Toronto Snobbery" in the *Toronto Daily Star*, Lotta Dempsey described "[a] highly sophisticated novel on the lines of higher-ups (with considerable forays into the existence of the rest of us) ... with echoes of the past 30 years of manners and mores which formed the present."[16] In a similar vein, Augusta Gottleib in the *Sunday Saint Louis Post Dispatch* attested to the novel's wide appeal and concluded that "Young has written a witty and nostalgic novel with perception and tenderness. It will certainly appeal to many people – because in a light, deft way she is talking about most of us."[17]

What distinguished Fulford's grumble was his frank admission that the novel just did not speak to him. By classifying the novel's prose as "strictly from *Ladies Home Journal*," he assigned it to a category of fiction that neither appealed to nor catered to him. While he intended the remark to be damning criticism, it is actually a concise appraisal of the novel's project and target audience: to lead Canadian women to reflect upon the ways they might script their lives in late 1950s Canada. That Fulford reviewed the novel at all is testimony to its impact.

But what was "the prose of *Ladies Home Journal*"? Women's magazines actually brought together a wide range of lifewriting genres, from the highly contrived to the seemingly unmediated transcription of daily life, from the prescriptive rhetoric of marketers and professional specialists to missives from women trapped in the trenches of domestic life. *Ladies Home Journal* was the most successful of the American mass-circulated periodicals – collectively dubbed "the big six" and including *Good Housekeeping, Woman's Home Companion, McCall's, Delineator,* and *Pictorial Review* as well – that had an enormous presence in Canada, moving untaxed across the border.[18] However, one Canadian women's magazine, *Chatelaine,* outlasted all its Canadian competitors and even maintained circulation numbers well above those of the two national Canadian magazines, *Maclean's* and *Saturday Night.* Its popularity resulted from its ability to acknowledge regional diversity and, under the editorship of feminist Doris Anderson, its brave coverage of social issues – including abortion, employment equity, even lesbianism – unparalleled in its American counterparts.[19]

Indeed, in the 1960s *Chatelaine* explored the very issues at the heart of Young's novel – the roles and choices available for women in a changing world and the possibilities and anxieties caused by change – in a number of formats within each issue. It was thus the ideal venue for Young's *The Torontonians,* which made its debut in *Chatelaine,* a condensed version appearing in three installments in the October, November, and December issues of 1960.

Looking at those issues now, through the lens of the twenty-first century, one is struck by the magazine's probing scrutiny of woman's roles inside and beyond the home. Anderson's editorial comment in October 1960 focuses on gender inequities in the workplace and deplores the absence of women in executive positions and the difficulty women were experiencing in being considered for salary increases or promotions. The "Features" section contains some frank admissions of maternal ambivalence. In "Confessions of an Unwilling Mother," for example, the author finds the news of yet another pregnancy as "welcome as the income tax."[20] In "The Baby Who Almost Wrecked a Marriage," the director of casework for the Neighborhood Workers' Association tells June Callwood that the first baby is no magic solution for a rocky marriage.[21] The first of three excerpts from *The Torontonians* appears in the "Fiction" section, alongside a short story by Gabrielle Roy. The accompanying illustration shows a romanticized side profile portrait of an attractive young woman wearing a discreet negligee with sweetheart sleeves. The byline explains that "*Chatelaine* is pleased to introduce The Torontonians, which we predict will be one of the most talked-about Canadian novels of the year." Although the story of Karen Whitney is clearly framed as fiction, it serves a function similar to many of the other articles and features of the issue in scripting a woman's life. This parallel is emphasized by a text box that appears within the novel excerpt:

> HAVE YOU A STORY TO TELL?
>
> You, like most women, probably can remember a particularly dramatic, inspiring, or revealing event in your life. "What a story I could tell!" you sigh.
>
> Well here is your chance to tell it. ...
>
> Type it out and send it to us. For satisfactory pieces we will pay you our regular rates.[22]

Examples of such "life stories" appear in the "Features" section, mirroring their fictional counterparts. In December, for example, in "I'm Glad I Died a Little," writer Patricia Young describes her battle with a brain tumor and offers a vignette of her despair and very momentary thoughts of suicide that bears an uncanny resemblance to the opening scene of Young's novel.[23]

Chatelaine, like other women's magazines, took pride in excerpting fiction by celebrity authors. Nevertheless, *The Torontonians* was an unusual choice. Of the eleven novels excerpted in 1960 and 1961 – *Rose* by Elizabeth Shenkin, *Speak of Love... and Murder* by Mignon G. Eberhart, *The Inn of No Yesterdays* by Brysson Morrison, *Death Comes to the Island* by Florence Ford, *If She Should Die* by Forbes Rydell (one of the pseudonyms for Doloris Stanton Forbes), *My Love, My Enemy* by Jan Cox Speas,

The Secret Gift by A.E. Johnson (a pseudonym for Americans Annabell and Edgar Johnson), *Honey for Tea* by Elizabeth Cadell, *Claws of the Cat* by Florence Ford, and *The Beloved Son* by Cecil Maiden – it distinguished itself by being the only novel set in Canada, written by a Canadian, and focused on ordinary rather than extraordinary circumstances. For the most part, novels serialized in *Chatelaine* fell into the categories of mystery or popular romance. (Cecil Maiden's entry in the December issue is the other exception to the rule, a nativity story appearing in honour of the Yuletide season.) *The Torontonians,* despite Fulford's idea of it as commercialized romance, actually overturned the conventions of the dime store romance by focusing on Karen's life twenty years after her wedding, her refusal to accept an invitation to have an affair, her renewed commitment to marriage, and, more generally, her disillusionment with romantic idealism. Although more conservative than feminist in its insistence on a return to the status quo of marriage, *The Torontonians* mirrors Doris Anderson's editorial comments on women's rights and responsibilities more than the other serialized fictions included in *Chatelaine.*

Although more realistic than the other novels serialized in *Chatelaine, The Torontonians* still provided a highly mediated transcription of life in mid-twentieth-century Toronto. Its formal elements include the three choices typical of fairytale plotlines: carefully delineated and balanced comparisons and contrasts between the novel's locales, couples, and characters; controlled use of flashback for character development and foreshadowing; and the assumption of a sympathetic reader called into existence through use of second-person address, as noted in this volume by Valerie Argue in her Foreword. As today's readers approach the novel, the wry sense of humour and tongue-in-cheek irony are so striking as to make some sequences of the novel read like camp. However, contemporary audiences also noted the satiric stylization of the novel. "Mrs. Young has a perceptive wit, a nice sense of balance on the thin edge that separates satire from irony," wrote Joan Walker:

> Don Quixote tilted at windmills, Phyllis Brett Young tilts at the sacred cows of suburbia, poking fun at the ranch-type bungalow, the bigger and better electrical appliances, the strange tribal customs of the natives such as the barbecue and the "inverted snobbery [that] dictated that servants did not belong to the Good Life ..." All these things are satirized with a lively sophisticated touch, and in this category the book is excellent, even if the suburban pack will be in full cry after Mrs. Young, anxious to nail her hide to their knotty pine walls.[24]

Mordecai Richler once explained that his role as novelist was to capture his moment to the best of his ability. As he wrote in 1970, "No matter how long I continue to live abroad, I do feel forever rooted in Montreal's St. Urbain Street. That was my time, my place, and I have elected myself to get it right."[25] In *The Apprenticeship of Duddy Kravitz*, Richler brought Montreal's Main to life in the mid-century. Young did the same for Toronto's Leaside and the area along the ravine (fictionalized as Rowanwood), the Annex (Elmdale), and one much-admired buckwheat lawn of the late 1950s. With this reissue of *The Torontonians*, we bring them to life once again.

Nathalie Cooke and Suzanne Morton
2007

SOURCES

With thanks to: Elaine Yarosky of McGill Libraries who enabled us to pick up the trail of one of Canada's popular writers after it ostensibly disappeared in 1981; Lorna Hutchison and Ryan Hendrickson, assistant director for manuscripts at Boston University, who helped us begin the search; McGill research librarians Karen Nicholson and Kendall Wallis, as well as Matt Doyle, Andrew Clelland, Kim Corry, and Gillian Jackson for their successful sleuthing; Jennifer Garland for her research on and insights into the history of women's magazines; Shirley Tillotson, who shared the novel in the first place; the Social Sciences and Research Council of Canada for funding the contextual research; and, of course, Valerie (Brett Young) Argue for her valuable insights and support for this initiative.

Phyllis Brett Young's papers can be accessed through the Phyllis Brett Young Collection in the Howard Gotlieb Archival Research Center at Boston University.

FURTHER READING

Clark, S.D. *The Suburban Society*. Toronto: University of Toronto Press, 1965.

Dummitt, Chris. *The Manly Modern: Masculinity in Postwar Canada.* Vancouver: University of British Columbia Press, 2007.

Fahrni, Magda. *Household Politics: Montreal Families and Postwar Reconstruction.* Toronto: University of Toronto Press, 2005.

Kuffert, L.B. *A Great Duty: Canadian Responses to Modern Life and Mass Culture in Canada, 1939–1967*. Montreal: MQUP, 2003.

Owram, Doug. *Born at the Right Time: A History of the Baby Boom Generation.* Toronto: University of Toronto Press, 1996.

NOTES

1 John Porter, *The Vertical Mosaic: An Analysis of Social Class and Power in Canada* (Toronto: University of Toronto Press, 1965).

2 Alvin Finkel, *Our Lives: Canada after 1945* (Toronto: Lormier, 1997), 47.

3 Statistics Canada, "The Daily," 31 July 2006, http://www.statcan.ca/Daily/English/060731/d060731b.htm; accessed 20 May 2007

4 John R. Seeley, R. Alexander Sim and E.W. Loosley, *Crestwood Heights: A Study of the Culture of Suburban Life* (Toronto: University of Toronto Press, 1956).

5 Joy Parr, *Domestic Goods: The Material, the Moral, and the Economic in the Postwar Years* (Toronto: University of Toronto Press, 1999), 243.

6 Richard Harris, *Creeping Conformity: How Canada Became Suburban, 1900–1960* (Toronto: University of Toronto Press, 2004).

7 Veronica Strong-Boag, "Home Dreams: Women and the Suburban Experiment in Canada," *Canadian Historical Review* 72, 4 (1991): 471–504; "Their Side of the Story': Women's Voices from Ontario Suburbs," in Joy Parr, ed., *A Diversity of Women: Ontario, 1945–1980* (Toronto: University of Toronto Press 1995) and Valerie J. Korinek, *Roughing It in the Suburbs: Reading Chatelaine Magazine in the Fifties and Sixties* (Toronto: University of Toronto Press, 2000).

8 Donald V Goudy, "The Case of the Reluctant Writer," *The Star Weekly Magazine*, 24 February 1962. This jaw-dropping estimate of audience size presumably included readers introduced to her work through excerpts serialized in magazines, but still seems incredibly high. Her first novel, *Psyche*, was excerpted in *Woman and Beauty*, for example, and her later novel *Undine* in the German magazine *Sterne*.

9 Ardis Cameron, "Introduction," *Peyton Place* by Grace Metalious (Boston: Northeastern University Press, 1999).

10 Quoted. in Jane Reid, "Writing Is Good Excuse." *The Moncton Transcript*, 21 May 1960.

11 Robert Fulford, "Lament for a Dead Toronto," *Toronto Daily Star*, 25 October 1960: 18.

12 Margaret Laurence, "Sociologist's Methods Mar Novelist's Art," *The Vancouver Sun*, 5 November 1960: 5.

13 Fulford, "Lament for a Dead Toronto."

14 Ken Carnahan, "The Bookshelf; Magic of the Past," *Berkeley Daily Gazette*, 10 June 1963: 13.

15 Florence Crowther. "Status-Symbol Living," *New York Times*, 23 July 1961: BR20.

16 Lotta Dempsey, "Toronto Snobbery Something Special?" *Toronto Daily Star*, 13 February 1960.

17 Augusta Augusta, "Novel about Suburbia," *Sunday Saint Louis Post Dispatch*, 23 July, 1961.

18 Mary Ellen Zuckerman, *A History of Popular Women's Magazines in the United States, 1792–1995*. (Westport, Connecticut: Greenwood Press, 1998): 6; Mary Vipond, "Major Trends in Canada's Print Mass Media," in Carole Gerson and Jacques Michon, eds., *History of the Book in Canada*. v. 3 (Toronto: University of Toronto Press, 2007): 244.

19 Korinek, *Roughing It in the Suburbs*; Valerie Korinek, "'Don't Let Your Girlfriends Ruin Your Marriage': Lesbian Imagery in Chatelaine Magazine, 1950–1969." *Journal of Canadian Studies.* 33.3 (1998): 83-109.
20 Shirley Wright, "Confessions of an Unwilling Mother," *Chatelaine* 33, 10 (October 1960): 25.
21 Violet Munns as told to June Callwood, "The Baby Who Almost Wrecked a Marriage," *Chatelaine* 33, 10 (October 1960): 52.
22 *Chatelaine* 33, 10 (October 1960): 150.
23 Patricia Young, "I'm Glad I Died a Little," *Chatelaine* 33, 12 (December 1960).
24 Joan Walker, "She Ridicules Suburbanities," *The Globe and Mail,* 22 October 1960:16.
25 Quoted in Robert Fulford, "Mordecai Richler: An Obituary Tribute by Robert Fulford, *The National Post,* 4 July 2001.

Author's Note

The participating characters in this book are, in word, deed, and appearance, wholly the product of my imagination. The residential suburb, Rowanwood, does not exist and never has existed. There is no such school as Waycroft, and no such building as the Preston Trust. Neither Gavin Street nor Elmdale Avenue appears on any map of Toronto that I have ever seen, nor is there any Holton Street which crosses Yonge.

Geneva, as I present to you, is geographically precise. Its streets, its hotels, and its restaurants are there for you to visit. As with Toronto, the names of public figures, of actual periodicals, of stores and buildings have been used as an outer framework of fact for an inner core of fiction.

P.B.Y.

The Torontonians

1 The exact size and shape and colour

Early morning sunlight warm against the thin, smooth contour of one cheek, Karen sat in the breakfast-room and thought about suicide.

The thought was a toy she now played with too often when she was alone, but it fitted in size and shape and colour into the appalling emptiness inside her. In her mind's eye, she saw it as a grey cube, opaque, polished, its surface a tactile pleasure to which fingers clung in spite of what was hidden within its six-sided facelessness. A child's block, fashioned in hell, with no need for any outer marking. That she should look on it as a toy made it no less evil, did nothing to disqualify it as a companion for the despicable tears that had recently become part of the pattern of her nights and days. So far, she had been able to confine the tears to those times when she was by herself. There was that, at least, to be thankful for. So far, she had not wept in front of anybody else, not even Rick.

Her gaze wandered from her half-filled cup of coffee to Rick's empty one, to his table napkin neatly replaced in his silver ring, to the morning newspaper he had put down less than two minutes earlier. Breakfast had been very pleasant. As long as Rick was actually with her she could keep her perspective fairly straight, even though—or rather because—they had had twenty-one years together. Rick, unlike herself, had no private devils, no frustrations with which he was incapable of dealing.

While finishing his coffee, he had said, "It looks as if the United Nations has really taken hold this time."

"That's good," Karen had replied, but what the United Nations did, or did not do, was only another facet of a civilization that now struck her as completely futile. She thought of the question children had asked one another when she was small. "If you could push a button and end the world, would you do it?" At ten years of age, she had cried, "No! Never!" Now she felt she might quite easily push the button.

"Rick," she said, "I wish you had been a milkman."

"For God's sake," he said, but he was smiling, "why a milkman?"

"Well, it wouldn't necessarily have to be a milkman. I was just using that as a symbol."

"As a symbol of what?"

"Of an uncomplicated existence," Karen told him. "I just meant, why couldn't we have been simple people, leading a simple life. People who didn't feel forced to keep up with anything or anybody."

Rick laughed. "Where did you get the idea that milkmen don't try to keep up with other milkmen? I'll give you five-to-one odds that if our milkman hasn't got a TV set he wants one, and not just because he likes to watch TV."

"Do you really believe that?"

"I do."

Briefly Karen was aware of the size and silence of the rest of the house. For some curious reason, in hot weather it always seemed even larger than it was. And the silence, when Rick left, as he would very soon, would become in itself an almost tangible presence.

"If I sound cynical," Rick was saying, "then I have expressed myself badly. What I was attempting to say was that it is unrealistic to think that any one level of society is more contented than any other. I am, I hope, reasonably easy to live with?"

"You're marvellous to live with."

Rick really did have a particularly attractive smile. "You exaggerate. However, even you, wildly prejudiced as you appear to be, would find me hell on wheels if all I had to do was tote milk bottles by the light of the moon."

Although much more serious than she had allowed herself to

appear, Karen could not help laughing, because the picture he had evoked of himself was so utterly ridiculous.

"They don't deliver at night any more," she told him.

"Don't they? I must be behind the times. But that doesn't alter the point I'm making, which is that one can't be content unless one is using, and really using, whatever talents or aptitudes one happens to be blessed with."

What he is telling me, Karen thought, is that a milk wagon, a loaf of bread, and thou, would *not* be paradise enow. And it is no denial of his love for me, because I know precisely how he feels. Much too precisely.

She took a cigarette from the package lying beside the bowl of golden nasturtiums in the middle of the table. "It's supposed to be different for a woman, isn't it?"

"In what way, sweetheart?" he asked, but she knew from his tone that his thoughts had already begun to move away from her, that metaphorically he was already on his way downtown. He would not be wholly hers again until the end of the day. A day in which she might or might not play with her deadly toy. A day in which she might or might not weep.

Almost, but not quite, she began to say, "A vacuum cleaner, a new car, and thou, is supposed to be—" But, the cliff's edge of her despair close in front of her, she had retreated from it as she had so often in the weeks just past, because she could see no way of putting it into words without some apparent criticism of Rick himself. And Rick deserved no criticism of any kind.

So, instead, she said, "I just mean that, given the right circumstances, most women would, I think, be perfectly satisfied with a milk wagon built for two. A nice simple one."

"No white-wall tires?"

"No, darling, not even white-wall tires."

If he had not been thinking of the office, he would have known at once that she had evaded his question. He would have recognized the qualification inherent in the phrase 'given the right circumstances'.

Standing up, he said, "It's time I left, sweetheart."

"I'll miss you, Rick. Have a good day."

He had kissed her, and she had subdued a wild impulse to cling to him, to beg him not to leave her defenceless against the emptiness. "Take care of yourself, darling."

"Don't get up," he told her. "I'm going to move fast now. By the way, the carpet comes to-day, doesn't it?"

"That's right."

"Well, be sure you get the men to put it down. Don't try to do it yourself."

"No, darling," Karen had said. "I won't try to do it myself."

The carpet was, and had been for years, a symbol to them. A Chinese carpet, thick and soft, the clear translucent green of a tropical sea. Window-shopping, when they had had scarcely enough money to eat properly, they had promised each other that some day they would have a carpet like that. Looking into the future, they had seen it as the final touch, the outward and visible proof of success. When they could afford a carpet like that, they would have "arrived".

Alone with the coffee cups, Karen asked herself—arrived where, and why, and what in hell does it do for us?

She reached for a cigarette, and thought, I smoke too much. And so what? As that doctor in England had said, the one who was doing cancer research, there was something a little silly about giving up a pleasure in order to move from one mortality group to another. Which brought her very neatly, altogether too neatly, back to the thought of death again. Julia and her husband Ned would say she was morbid, a word they were very fond of. They would be wrong. They usually were. She was not morbid. She was defeated. Which was, in many ways, a great deal worse.

Although she and Rick never said so outright, because Julia was Rick's only sister, Julia and Ned could be quite extraordinarily irritating.

Not long ago, Julia had said, "The trouble with you, Karen, is that you are much too materialistic. Much."

Julia always told everybody what was the matter with them, and it was incredible how consistently wrong she could be. You would have thought that the law of averages alone would have given her a better score. The trouble with Julia, herself, was that she was compensating for so many things. For not having money. For having produced two children who were, to put it kindly, not too bright. For failing to have any sex appeal. Objectively, you could sympathize with Julia. But not, if you were at all human, when she was telling you what was the matter with you.

Ned Mason was a psychologist on the staff of the university, which might have made him more perceptive than Julia. It had not, which on the whole was probably fortunate.

Julia and Ned, who were permissive parents, had not approved of the way in which Karen and Rick had brought up their two daughters. Since there had been nothing specific to criticize, Ned had pronounced Carol and Peg "abnormally normal". Ned had a habit of saying things like that. He had also talked, when Carol and Peg were restrained as his own children were not, of the importance of "liberating the infant psyche." Yet when both Carol and Peg had been allowed, without protest, to leave home while still in their teens, Julia and Ned had behaved as if this ought to be taken up with the Children's Aid Society. They had been quite blind to the really terrible self-discipline implicit in letting children go when the time arrived to do so.

And yet, Karen thought, as she watched slow smoke curl upwards from her cigarette, she had not cried when either of them left. Even though bits of her heart had been cut away, she had not cried, because eight months ago she had still been the person she had always been. And that was a person to whom tears were as foreign as temper.

Carol had gone first. Then Peg.

They had, Karen remembered, been quite gay, Rick and Peg and herself, on the October evening when Peg had boarded the train for New York. They had supplied themselves in advance with large white handkerchiefs, waved them at absurdly close quarters, and, refusing to say "Good-bye," had said instead, "See you at Christmas."

Afterwards, she and Rick had had coffee at a place across from the Union Station, and later driven up Yonge Street, something you would never have thought of doing before the subway was built.

Karen had always liked Yonge Street, even in the days when it was congested with street-cars. The lights and stir of this main artery never failed to stimulate her. Here she could feel the heart-beat of what was very much her city, although there was no denying that as far as convenience went, it had grown much too rapidly. Toronto had been quite different when she was a child and lived on Elmdale Avenue, a street shaded by trees that were not, of course, elms.

It had been a cosy city in those days, and when you lay in bed at night you had been more aware of the measured hoof-beats of the mounted policeman's horse than of the occasional car that passed. You had known with absolute certainty that it was the policeman's horse, and not the milkman's, because the rhythm was entirely different.

That every rhythm was now different might, Karen was beginning to see, be an underlying cause of what could not be as sudden a personal disorientation as she had at first thought. All she had to do was look at some of her friends to see that it was far from easy to keep your balance when the rhythm changed.

After the First World War there had been a lot of talk about a lost generation. If "lost" were to be translated as "disoriented", then the generation most lost was her own, because the years when you needed a stable, unchanging background were the years between eight and eighteen. Until you were eight you accepted most things as natural phenomena. There was no such condition as a startling general change, because up until that age it was all news to you. It was when you were adolescent that you needed to be free of the complications of general change. So much about yourself was changing then that it was just about all you could handle. After eighteen, your equilibrium was—or at least ought to be—stabilized to a point where you could assess change as part of a progression belonging to many millenniums, and therefore nothing to get upset about.

But if you did not have the opportunity, in those early years, to adjust within a more or less fixed framework of living, there was a better than fifty-fifty chance that you would have difficulty in catching up with yourself, let alone with your era.

The Industrial Revolution must have caught a whole generation off base.

For that matter, the discovery of the wheel must have thrown quite a few people for a loop.

You had marvelled at the way in which your parents' generation had been able to accept a mechanized world. Now you saw that, secure in themselves, they had watched rather than belonged to the innovations that had reshaped man's entire existence. Your own generation had had no time in which to watch and consider. It had been part of the maelstrom, and had had little choice but to move with it, too fast. Much too fast.

You did not at the time realize what was happening to you, because when you were really young, rather than "still young" as all the magazines now put it, you were resilient. Incredibly so. It wasn't until much later, when you found yourself thinking of death as a restful state, and saw your friends leaning on barbiturates, whiskey, and tranquillizers, that you began to understand that, somehow, mechanical evolution had outstripped any social evolution as it might apply to you and most of your generation.

Which, Karen thought, is all very interesting. But where does it get me? Exactly where I was ten minutes ago. Caught in a gilt-edged suburban labyrinth from which I see no satisfactory avenue of escape; yet which, if I go much farther into it, will, I think, destroy me utterly.

Her grey eyes sombre, she stared out of the open window at the lawns and trees and flower beds of a large garden which, in June, was always at its best. All the gardens in Rowanwood were large. Theirs was no exception. Everybody was always saying that if you lived in Rowanwood it was just like living in the country, which was, of course, quite untrue. It was not like living downtown, but neither was it a damn bit like living in the country. Which was sad, because it really had been the country when she and Rick had bought an old, dignified brick farmhouse with no intention at the time of turning it into a show place.

Suddenly the too easy tears were there again, pricking against her eyelids. Tears which, if the telephone had not rung, would have spilled over in a torrent she would have been incapable of controlling.

The telephone was in the front hall. It was cool in the hall. The breakfast room, flooded with sunlight, had become uncomfortably warm.

"Yes?" Karen said.

It was Millicent who replied, and as usual she wanted you to do something for a Cause. This time it was an afternoon bridge, the proceeds of which were to assist New Canadians.

You could trace the history of the world back across a good many years just by remembering Millicent's brief but forceful enthusiasms. The Koreans, the Israelis, the evicted Egyptians, the Hungarians. Without even looking at a newspaper, you could be quite certain that things were relatively quiet in foreign parts if Millicent could find nothing more alarming with which to concern herself than the difficulties, if any, of New Canadians.

"I'll buy four tickets," Karen said, "but don't expect me to play bridge in the afternoon."

Millicent was a big woman, and she had a big voice. Since she lived right across the road, Karen sometimes wondered why she bothered with the telephone at all when she could probably have made herself heard without it.

"I can't sell tickets to you on that basis," Millicent said. "It wouldn't be right."

"What wouldn't be right about it?" Karen asked.

"You wouldn't be getting your money's worth," Millicent told her.

"Do you think I would if I came? And anyway, isn't it the New Canadians who are supposed to be getting some profit out of this, if anyone is?"

"Certainly. But I'm not asking you to *give* your money away."

"Why aren't you?" Karen asked. "It might work."

"Don't be difficult, Karen," Millicent said. "You know perfectly well how things like this are always done."

"Yes, I know how things like this are always done. I'm simply suggesting they might be done differently for a change."

"Karen," Millicent said, "have you thought of seeing a doctor recently?"

Memory of the sharp pain, which had been bothering her off and on since early spring, momentarily deflected Karen's attention. Could the pain be in any way responsible for her present state of mind? It did not seem likely that the answer could be as simple as that. In fact, it seemed highly unlikely, even though the pain, when it struck, could be very bad.

"Karen? Are you still there?"

"Yes, Millicent, I'm still here."

"Well, are you going to take a table, or aren't you?"

"I'll buy four tickets, but don't expect bodies to be included in the price. I'm sorry, Millicent, but that's the way it is. Or, if you prefer it, the way I am. Good-bye."

Listening to the echo of her own voice, Karen was shocked. What a bitch I was, she thought incredulously. I'm never like that. Oh, God, what is the matter with me?

Almost without thinking, she began to dial a number as familiar to her as her own. There was very rarely a day when she did not either talk with Susan on the telephone, or see her, or both. Susan was now all that made Rowanwood even remotely bearable. Susan who was more a part of her life than anyone she knew, aside from Rick. Susan whom she had first met, not in Toronto, but during her year at school in Switzerland, and who because of this was the only one amongst her friends ever to have known, or even to have heard of, Cyr.

Susan would still be in bed, but she would be awake and she would have had breakfast. In her mind's eye, Karen could see the big bedroom with the plate-glass wall overlooking the ravine, and Susan, in a devastating negligee, lazily reading philosophy, her hair and face as perfectly groomed as they might have been if she had been on the point of going out. Susan and Lewis never had breakfast together, something which caused a certain amount of comment in Rowanwood.

In general, Rowanwood liked to pretend that just because you had money there was no reason to think that you were different from anybody else. In Rowanwood you were supposed to find the same homely virtues (such as wives breakfasting with their husbands) that you might find anywhere else. A Good Life, as they were fond of saying in Rowanwood, did not depend on money. Of course they were fortunate, they were not trying to deny that, but their good fortune must not be assessed in terms of anything as coarse as high-bracket incomes. There had been a time when they had called themselves privileged rather than fortunate. The terminology had changed because the word privilege presupposed the antonym under-privileged, and such a thing was not to be tolerated in a proper democracy. You could think vaguely of the "less fortunate" with an easier conscience, it appeared, because of course they had their own Good Life.

"Hello?" Susan said. Even her voice sounded lazy.

"I've just been a perfect bitch to Millicent," Karen told her.

Susan laughed. "Millicent can be very provoking."

"She was. But that's no excuse. I'll have to go over and apologize to her."

"She'll enjoy that," Susan said. "In a perfectly nice way, of course. She'll tell you that you ought to see your doctor."

"She already has."

Still laughing, Susan said, "Well, she'll tell you again, darling."

"Why in the devil does Millicent always have to be running things?"

"It's probably because she lives with Biff. If I lived with Biff I would be driven to something worse than running things."

For a moment Karen was tempted to say that she thought it had driven Millicent to something worse, too. Instead, she said, "Susan, are you and Lewis doing anything tonight?"

"Not that I know of," Susan replied. "Why?"

"Julia was trying to get you yesterday. She's going to call you again this morning. She and Ned are having one of their 'small informal get-togethers'."

Susan said exactly what Rick had said when Karen had told him about this. "Oh, my God!"

"I know what you mean."

"I have never," Susan said, "been able to understand why the Masons ask Lewis and myself to these things."

Karen found herself smiling. Even the thought of Lewis at one of Julia and Ned's parties was really very funny. "Glitter of rich bourgeois, if you must know. Although that is certainly not the way Julia and Ned will have put it to themselves."

She could talk like this to Susan, because Susan understood that it was no contradiction of the fact that basically she was really quite fond of Julia and Ned. Though just why she should be, she really didn't know, because either singly, or together, they nearly always managed to annoy her. Susan was inclined to be amused by them, but then Susan was not related to them.

"Look, Susan," Karen said, "I should go and make my peace with Millicent before the carpet comes."

"Does the carpet come today?"

"It's supposed to."

"Good," Susan said. "I'll be round this afternoon to see it."

As she put down the receiver, Karen found herself thinking of Lewis with his cool, speculative blue eyes, his perfectly tailored double-breasted grey suits, and his thick grey hair brushed back from a broad forehead. President of the Preston Trust, owner of the Preston Building, and director of half a dozen companies, Lewis Preston had a charming smile and charming manners, but he never gave away anything of himself. After knowing him for more than fourteen years, Karen often felt that she still did not know him at all.

As she rose from the telephone and turned toward the front door, an almost forgotten conversation came back to her, disturbing her as it had not at the time.

On that occasion, she had made some casual remark about Susan's popularity with men.

"Glad Rag Doll," Susan had said, and she had not been smiling. "The party girl in person. But it's your kind they marry. I'm the brunette they think they can make in a parked car."

"But you're not like that!"

"Tell a few of the boys, will you?" Susan had said. "They don't seem to have your insight."

"But take Lewis—"

"I did take him," Susan had said, and had changed the subject.

It was true that Susan, with her height and her slightly tip-tilted nose, was eye-catching in a particularly provocative way. But nobody with any sense, Karen felt, could look at her amused, intelligent brown eyes and make a mistake about the kind of person she was. Nobody other than a man at a party, she amended to herself. A man at a party was not always noted for his perspicacity. However, it was not what Susan had said which now disturbed her, so much as what Susan had *not* said. Susan, she was realizing fully for the first time, nearly always changed the subject when Lewis's name came up. Neither she nor Susan was given to the kind of intimate discussions that so many women indulged in, but the manner in which Susan avoided, whenever possible, any reference at all to Lewis—his opinions, his likes and his dislikes—was decidedly unnatural.

Reaching the front door, she opened it, and closed it behind her without locking it. In Rowanwood, to lock your door during the daytime was considered inimical to togetherness, if not downright hostile.

For a moment she paused on the doorstep between the white pillars which, together with the fanlight above the door, and the magnificent pines across the end of the back garden, had first attracted them to the house.

Her growing dissatisfaction with the house, and the way of life it now represented, did not extend to the pines. Or even, for that matter, to the long row of Lombardy poplars that separated their property from that of Betsey and Harry Milner, who owned the ranch-type bungalow to the east of them.

The poplars had been a very good idea, because Betsey and Harry were too basically Rowanwood in their outlook for you to want to see much of them. Betsey and Harry would never be able to understand why Karen and Rick should spend so much time sitting in their garden after dark when they could have been inside looking at TV or listening to hi-fi. Betsey and Harry had the kind of hi-fi set-up that involved loud-speakers all over the place, so you could hear the percussion from here and the strings from there. All that Betsey and Harry ever used it for, however, was off-colour stories and Presley. To be able to hear off-colour stories and Presley from several sides of the room at once did not seem quite worth the expense necessary to make this possible.

Pleasantly conscious of the warm caress of sunlight on her bare arms, Karen did not hurry as she walked around her own circular driveway and through the western gap in the cedar hedge, in order to cross over to Millicent and Biff's cut-stone residence on the other side of the unpaved road.

Millicent and Biff's house was one that you could only think of as a "residence". It would have been difficult to find a sharper contrast to the small frame house beside it. Dunnington Grubbe had "done" the grounds around Millicent and Biff's house. "Undone" was the only word for the Johnson property, the single holding in Rowanwood to beat the local restrictions by what had had to be accepted, with rancour, as squatter's rights.

Glancing to her right between the trunks of the old elms bordering the road, Karen saw that the yellow blind was still drawn down in the upstairs room that she knew, by inference, to be Mrs. Johnson's bedroom. She also saw young Pete Johnson's bicycle lying across the steps of the wooden porch. It must have broken down again, she thought. I'll ask Rick to help him fix it. There was no Mr. Johnson. It was even possible that there never had been. Not as such.

The Johnson house had become known in Rowanwood as the Blot on the Landscape, or more simply as the Blot. When you came right down to it, however, there was nothing much the matter with it other than that it could never be advertised by any real-estate agent at fifty thousand dollars, was devoid of such necessities as picture windows, dining terrace, and basement recreation room with built-in bar, and was suspected of having only one bathroom. Though this last was generally considered as scarcely possible.

When the Johnson house was discussed at the monthly Rowanwood community meetings, everyone was always quick to say that there was nothing personal, nothing personal at all, in their attitude toward the Blot. It was entirely, they said, a matter of protecting investments. After all, you had to be realistic in these matters, and though they individually and collectively would be the last to say that sentiment didn't have a place in their scheme of things, this just wasn't the place for it. To be quite brutal, although they were not in the habit of being brutal, the county ought to do something about an eviction. Lewis, who never attended the meetings, had been asked to use his influence. He had refused, and you had gathered indirectly that his refusal had been more positive than was thought altogether necessary.

Democratic freedom of speech at these meetings was unhampered either by the presence of Mrs. Johnson, who conveniently worked the four-to-twelve shift in a downtown restaurant, or by that of thirteen-year-old Pete.

Environmental rebellion had, Karen realized, been the first bond between herself and Pete, with his irresistible smile, straw-coloured hair, and huge chip on the shoulder.

They had been sitting in the sun on her front door step one day, when Pete had said, "You know, Mrs. Whitney, you've shown me something. What I mean is, you've shown me that a person can be smart and have lots of money without being a louse."

"Pete!"

"Well, all right," Pete had said, "but you take that Mrs. Barret." He was referring to Millicent. "Who does she think she is to be always telling a guy off? All I got to do is to put one foot on her lousy—I mean on her lawn, and she comes out and acts as if I was a juvenile delinquent, or something. Why, I bet I could tell you things about her that—"

"But you're not going to, are you, Pete?"

His smile was there, as she had hoped it would be. "Heck, no. Why should I bother telling things about a dame like her?"

There was no doubt about it. Pete had come a long way since he had found a welcome in one house in Rowanwood. There was also no doubt that people who lived in cut-stone residences should pull down their blinds.

As she turned into Millicent's driveway, the sun warm on her back, Karen wondered if there was a tactful way of saying this to Millicent.

She stopped to look at the roses, banked along the front of the house, and it occurred to her that, full-blown and handsome, they were not unlike Millicent herself. In an earlier era, Millicent would have been looked upon as a Fine Figure of a Woman. By present-day standards, there was, frankly, just a bit too much of her. Everything to do with Millicent was a little larger than life size. Including a husband called Biff.

Biff was both taller and larger than Millicent, an accomplishment in itself, and he had, of course, been a football player. Fortunately their living-room was enormous, because when Biff replayed some of the Toronto–McGill and Toronto–Queen's games of the thirties, complete with tackle and touchdown, he needed space. To re-enact the North African Offensive, it was necessary to go down to the recreation room.

They had two children. The boy took after Biff. The girl took after Millicent.

Boris was the discordant note in a household otherwise typical of its kind. Boris was a Polish Count, a quite genuine one. What he lived on was a mystery, and where Millicent had picked him up was another mystery. It had probably been during a 'help Poland' campaign. Boris drove an ancient Packard, never had any ready cash, and was at Millicent's house whenever Biff was not, and sometimes even when he was. It was a situation that Rowanwood found highly amusing, and, because it was Millicent who was involved, it had so far not occurred to anyone to find it other than amusing. The idea of Millicent as a romantic figure was one that beggared the average imagination. Pete, Karen was morally certain, and herself were the only ones up to the present to have guessed the truth.

She rang the doorbell once, and walked into the front hall. In Rowanwood an inverted snobbery dictated that servants did not belong to the Good Life, and there were those who had hinted that Lewis, who did have servants, might be better off over on Bayview where, it was suggested, he belonged. Betsey and Harry were amongst those who said this kind of thing. Betsey and Harry thought that everybody should live in ranch-style bungalows and be just like themselves.

"Hello, Millicent!" Karen called.

Millicent's voice came from upstairs. "I'll be right down. Go on into the living-room."

Millicent came down in pink mules, and a pink dressing-gown, and she had not yet done up her mass of dark hair. She looked, as she did in almost anything she wore, like something out of a Wagnerian opera of the pre-Pons era.

"Oh," she said, "it's you, Karen. I thought it was Fay. Fay has agreed to take two tables."

Karen was aware of the familiar tightening of the nerves that always assailed her whenever Fay's name was mentioned. It had been the same as far back as when she and Fay were at school together. Annoyed, she told herself that Fay wasn't always in a mess of some kind or another, that to worry about her all the time was absurd. But in her heart she knew it was not absurd, because there really never was a time when Fay was not either in trouble or looking for it.

"Millicent," she said, "don't you think you're running things a little close?"

She had seen Biff's yellow convertible pass her house just before she left it, and now, looking across the centre hall to the dining-room, she could see Boris already installed at the dining-room table. The only reason she had not noticed his car in the driveway was, she supposed, because it had become such a fixture there.

"I don't know what you mean," Millicent said.

"Don't you?"

"No, I don't. Will you have some coffee? It's still hot."

Feeling curiously trapped, Karen accepted. Even in the pink dressing-gown, Millicent was imperious.

Millicent went into the dining-room, and came back with a cup of coffee. Boris, with the morning newspaper under his arm, slouched in after her, took one of Biff's cigarettes from a solid-silver box, and, with a slight bow toward Karen, slouched out again.

"It's going to be another hot day," Millicent said.

"Yes," Karen replied. "It's going to be another hot day."

"Is your coffee the way you like it?"

"Perfect, thanks."

This is hopeless, Karen thought. Millicent is cross with me, and I am cross with her. But with Boris practically in our laps, I'm damned if I'm going to apologize.

"M-o-th-er!"

Karen looked inquiringly at Millicent.

"It's Arlene," Millicent said. "She's home with the flu." She raised her voice. "Boris?"

"*Chérie?*"

"Will you go upstairs and see what Arlene wants?"

"*Volontiers.*"

Karen watched him pass across the front hall, and start up the impressive stairway. Suddenly she felt genuinely sick. It had been one thing to suspect that Boris was very much at home with Millicent. It was another to find him more or less *in loco parentis*. Biff was, in many ways, a big oaf, and he had undoubtedly been involved in more offensives in North Africa than those headed by General Montgomery. But even he did not really deserve this.

"Millicent," Karen said. "Don't go on with it."

Millicent must have heard the funny catch in her voice, because, instead of telling her to mind her own business, she said, and she did not sound at all like herself, "I can't help going on with it."

"You frighten me," Karen told her.

"I can't help that, either."

"Millicent, it isn't like you."

"How do you know whether it's like me, or not? How could you know? You weren't born six feet tall, looking like Pallas Athene straight out of the forehead of Zeus."

Karen had never heard Millicent talk in this way before, and she never did again.

"You've got it both coming and going, Karen," Millicent said. "You're as strong as a steel cable, and you look like Dresden china. Men want to look after you. I'm nearly forty, and this is the first time anyone has wanted to look after me. I've never been treated the way every woman wants to be treated. I've always been Good Old Millicent. Well, it isn't that way with Boris. He's gentle. He doesn't make me feel as if I were being tackled on a rugby field. Do you know what Biff said to me the first time?"

Karen shook her head. It was not something she would have been likely to know.

"He said, 'Well, old girl, we certainly made yards that time, didn't we?' "

It would have been very funny if it had not been so pathetic.

Karen stubbed out her cigarette in a brass ash-tray that had been recently polished. And, as she stood up, one part of her mind was as surprised as always that Millicent, who seemed to spend all her time running things, should be such an excellent housekeeper.

Briefly, she laid her hand on the big woman's arm. "Be as careful as you can," she said. "Good-bye, Millicent."

"Good-bye, Karen. I'm glad you came over."

Karen was already out on the front walk when she heard Millicent calling to her. "Karen!"

Karen turned. "Yes?"

"Have you decided to be sensible and come to the bridge for the New Canadians?"

This was Millicent as she had always known her. This was the Millicent who, if she refused again, would almost certainly tell her to see a doctor. This was the Millicent who made it virtually impossible to believe there could be any other, and certainly not one with tears in her eyes and passion in her voice. Perhaps this would continue to be a sufficient protection for her.

"Yes," Karen said. "I'll come."

As she walked slowly along the empty road in the increasing heat, she realized that, whether she liked it or not, Millicent was now a friend in a way she had not been before. This made her feel responsible for Millicent's welfare, and it was a responsibility she did not want. Did everyone have to have troubles? she wondered. Was there no such thing as an uncomplicated existence for anyone? If Biff ever stumbled on the truth about Boris, there would be absolute hell to pay. Biff was one of those men who still carried a double standard, complete with pennants. Probably in his university colours, blue and white. Biff, in short, had even more muscle in his head than he had elsewhere.

She stepped off the road to let a grocery truck go by, and then waited a moment for the dust to settle. The road needed oiling again. There was rarely a time when it did not need oiling. It was believed in Rowanwood, and probably with some truth, that the county was trying to force the issue of paving, with the resultant increase in county revenue which this would produce. But so far, Rowanwood had clung steadfastly to the country-in-the-city atmosphere that, people felt, was one of its distinctions.

As she moved back on to the road, a man who had been walking behind her caught up, and for one crazy moment she thought it was Cyr. The man passed, a complete stranger; but during that brief moment when their feet had fallen into an accidental rhythm, she had once again walked a dusty Swiss road near the French border.

Breathing unevenly, she watched the stranger as he increased the distance between them—a tall, loose-knit man in a white shirt and grey trousers, whose broad shoulders rolled to his easy, slightly rolling gait because he walked with his hands in his trouser pockets. It was Cyr's walk. But it was not Cyr. Neither was it Switzerland in the thirties. It was Rowanwood in the sixties. That other had been long ago. So long ago that when she closed the front door of her house, and picked up the letters that had been delivered while she was out, she did not recognize his writing.

2 | Nothing serious, I hope?

Karen always thought of her life as being principally divided into four parts, the divisions created by changing environments rather than by elapsed time. Environments each of which had its own special aura.

Her earliest memories belonged to the big, old house on Elmdale Avenue when Barbara, living next door, had been more than a substitute for the brothers and sisters she had never had. She and Barbara had done everything together until her last years at school, when, in the backwash of the Jazz Age, she had spent so much time with Fay.

The year she spent at school in Geneva stood apart as unique in itself, even though it was in Geneva that she had met Susan, who became, and continued to be, the closest friend she was ever to have.

Then there had been the apartment on Gavin Street where she and Rick had first set up housekeeping. This had been an important period in her life, because it had encompassed Carol and Peg as babies, and the foundation of what she and Rick now shared. It was a period, however, to which she returned in memory only in relation to its purely personal aspects, because the aura of Gavin Street had been the aura of war, of emotional and physical stress. They had, it was true, stayed on in the dingy apartment on Gavin Street for several years after the war, but not from choice.

Lastly, there was the present and Rowanwood, where she had continued her friendships not only with Barbara and Fay, but with Susan.

Nothing was ever really a coincidence. You could, by working back, nearly always trace a quite reasonable interplay of cause and effect. Even so, it was odd that all the most important skeins in her life should have found some representation in Rowanwood.

That Barbara and Matt should have gravitated to Rowanwood was something so predictable it left no room for speculation. Barbara, once she had grown out of the tomboy stage, was a girl who could scarcely have helped doing what was expected of her. Karen's mother had always approved of Barbara, and the reasons for this were quite obvious. Blonde, serene, and very pretty, Barbara had, even when she was small, the clean look that goes with perfect health and a clear conscience. To meet Barbara was to trust her. To know her was to like her.

The same could not be said of Fay. Although Karen's mother had never said in so many words that she did not like Fay, the inference had often been there.

"I don't see what you and Fay have in common, dear," she would say. "Not that she isn't a sweet girl, of course. But you just don't seem to have much in common."

Probably the only thing that Karen and Fay had ever really had in common had been that neither of them had had any School Spirit. It could be quite a bond, not having any School Spirit. Particularly when you were surrounded, six hours a day and five days a week, by hundreds of healthy, hearty, games-playing girls so soaked in School Spirit that you wondered why they didn't have a special smell.

Fay and Roddie had built in Rowanwood—not, as Barbara and Matt had done, because it was the correct thing to do, but because Fay would always be looking for something that she would never find. Rowanwood, with its spacious lawns and rich outward tranquillity, had, Karen knew, appeared to Fay as a kind of promised land where she would be all right in spite of herself. When you thought of Fay you thought of Greek tragedies; and you felt that it could probably never have been stopped, the inexorable progression of events that had led her into marrying a man like Roddie.

Fay's judgment had always been terrible, but what involved

thought processes had made her believe that if she married Roddie she would be safe from herself, Karen would never know. She was safe from Roddie—that much was certain. Which left her—and God alone knew why she shouldn't have foreseen this—if anything less safe from herself than she had been before.

Afterwards, Karen saw that she had been sent to school in Geneva because her parents were determined to get her right away from Fay and Fay's friends. She had, in her parents' phraseology, "got in with the wrong set", and they would have done almost anything to get her out of it. What they had not seen was that they were attempting to remove her from the era into which she had been born, and that such a thing was quite impossible.

Although historically the Jazz Age ended with the stock-market crash in 1929, actually its influence spread across another five or six years. To be sure, bootleggers tended to go out of business; the flashier speakeasies closed down; and a great many prominent people exchanged Forest Hill Tudor for something more medieval in the way of décor, living under these conditions at His Majesty's expense. But these were changes that affected only a certain age group; and Karen, when she had begun dating, had stepped out into a world that, for her generation, still revolved around hip flasks, roadsters with rumble seats, and the conviction that any party that ended before dawn was a failure.

It was a restless, and in many ways rather frightening, period in which to be to some extent on your own for the first time. You could not help being aware of the bread-lines downtown. And, as often as not, when you answered the door bell, it would be to find a shabby man begging for a sandwich and a cup of coffee. What frightened you was that many of these men were young, not much older than you were yourself. You ached for them in their defeated hopelessness, and even on a sunny day shivered in the fringes of a long shadow from which there was no guarantee that you yourself would escape.

So, in order not to think, you looked for diversion, and on the whole you had a good time.

You danced to the music of Guy Lombardo, Benny Goodman,

and Duke Ellington. You had breakfast at Child's in the middle of the night. You drove at ninety miles an hour at sunrise on the lake-shore highway. Mae West, Joan Crawford, and Ronald Colman became as much a part of your life as a great many of your own friends.

Although you knew nothing about boxing, you listened to the Schmeling–Louis bout in which Schmeling scored the surprise knockout in the twelfth round. Much in the manner of the old lady who bet on a horse because it had a kind face, you won five dollars on that fight simply because you rather liked the Germans at that time. You had met, and been impressed by—as Hitler had intended you should be—one of the good-looking student "ambassadors" he had spread through the English-speaking countries. It was not until some years later that you understood the reasons behind the reserve that had made Kurt such a satisfactory date but such an oddly unsatisfactory person. Going out with Kurt had been rather like acting out an evening on a perfectly appointed stage. As long as the evening lasted, you felt wonderful. When the curtain went down, when the evening ended, *auf Wiedersehen* was a mockery because you were left with nothing at all. As Hitler had intended you should be.

When the leaves were turning, and the air was as sharp and dry as a good Chianti, you went to the intercollegiate football games and cheered madly for the University of Toronto. Later in the year you cheered even more madly when Red Horner tangled with big Ching Johnson, and the Toronto Maple Leafs scored the goal that defeated the New York Rangers in their battle for a place in the National Hockey League play-offs.

You read Warner Fabian, Havelock Ellis, F. Scott Fitzgerald, and Viña Delmar without realizing that you were clinging to the bright skirts of a vanished era. In retrospect, you were not particularly proud of the reading you had done at that age; but when, years later, you found Peg buried in the pages of *Moulin Rouge*, already weighted with the knowledge of how sordid the world could be, you wondered whether it had been so bad after all. And you could certainly be everlastingly grateful to Havelock Ellis for having put you straight about sex, something nobody else had seemed inclined to do.

Yes, she had a good time, but this did not prevent her from being curiously dissatisfied, from feeling as if she weren't really getting anywhere and that time might already be running short. So, when it was suggested that she go to Geneva, she didn't object to the idea. She could see that it might have its compensations, even though she did not know that she was going to meet Susan there. That she was going to meet Cyr there.

Also, although she would have died rather than admit it, she didn't mind getting away from Fay for a time. Ever since that horrible night in March she had realized that her mother had been at least partially right in saying that she and Fay didn't have much in common.

Sleet was hissing against the storm-windows when the telephone rang that night.

Karen, sitting in front of the library fire with her parents, laid down her book, and got up. "I'll take it," she said.

In those days, even in a doctor's house, you did not think of having more than one telephone on each floor, and the plug-in extension was something that the Bell Telephone Company had yet to put into mass production.

So Karen went out to the front hall, which, as it turned out, was just as well.

Fay's voice, at the other end of the line, was scarcely recognizable. "Is that you, Karen?"

"Yes. Is anything wrong?"

"Can you come over?"

"Now?"

"Yes," Fay said. "Right away."

"What do I say to my parents?" Karen asked.

"Tell them I'm alone in the house," Fay said. "Tell them I'm nervous and want you to stay the night. Tell them anything you like, but for God's sake come, and as soon as you can. I can't get down to let you in. The pantry window may be unlocked. If it isn't, break open a basement window. And, Karen?"

"Yes."

"Hurry up, will you?"

"Fay!" Karen said. But the line was dead. Fay had rung off.

Biting her lip, Karen went back to the library. "That was Fay," she said. "She wants me to go over there. Her father's out, and she's alone."

A small line of protest showed between her mother's delicate, arched eyebrows. You always noticed her eyebrows because they were so dark by contrast with her red-gold hair. Other people, Karen thought absently, probably noticed her own eyebrows for the same reason.

"It's terrible weather," her mother said. "And it's already late."

"Just after nine," Karen said. "It's not really late. It's just after nine."

Without looking up from the evening paper, although he was always saying that it was a rag, her father said, "Don't forget your tooth-brush." This was his way of telling her that she could go if she felt she must, but that he would miss her. He wasn't really thinking about her tooth-brush at all.

"I hate to leave," Karen said. "It's not that I want to go."

"You had better wear your fur coat," her mother said. "And your overshoes, not your rubbers."

Her mother actually was thinking about overshoes. Which did not mean that she cared any less. It was just the difference between them, and Karen recognized it as such.

"You'll be sure to wear your overshoes?" her mother said.

"Yes," Karen said. "I'll be sure to wear my overshoes."

She kissed them in turn, and went upstairs to pack a small overnight suitcase. In addition to the usual things, she put in a flashlight, and a bottle of sleeping tablets taken from the shelf where her father kept advertising samples. The drug companies were always sending him samples of something or other. Quite why she should have taken the sleeping tablets, Karen could never have said. Probably it was because there had been something in Fay's thin, taut voice which made her feel that she must do something out of the ordinary, and she could not, just then, think of anything else.

As she walked to the nearest street-car stop, her head bent against wind that cut like a knife, she made no attempt to think ahead to what might be expected of her when she reached the large, sombre house in which Fay had lived with her father and a succession of housekeepers since she was a small child. If you had any imagination at all, you never entered that house without thinking "poor Fay". Fay, who always had money to spend. Fay, who could come and go as she liked, night and day. Fay, who had never known what it was like to be told to be sure to wear her overshoes. If you were small, and dark, and had a heart-shaped face and no willpower whatsoever, you needed someone to tell you about your overshoes. You needed more than a father whose vision blurred if focused on anything other than a law book; more than housekeepers who either spoiled you silly, or grumbled about their feet. Poor Fay.

Karen, her mind firmly closed against speculation, was always able afterwards to recall the physical details, sharp and unforgettable, of that journey across the city.

The Italian fruit store, against whose window she sheltered from the sleet, was dark and silent, no echo left of the hysterical, garlic-tainted good humour that filled it by day. Whenever Karen went into that store, she felt that there were more Minellis than customers in it; but there was no doubt they were doing a land-office business. Two cars in the family, and the two younger boys at St. Michael's, were proof enough of this. A far cry, their future, from that of the ancient black-clad grandmother who had passed a peasant youth amongst the bare hills of the Udine.

The red and yellow street-car, travelling fast, braked to a grinding stop as she stepped out onto the road. Its folding doors opened and closed with no time wasted as she quickly climbed the two steep steps.

She dropped a purple ticket in the box beside the driver, still vaguely astonished that she should have graduated from the orange scholars' tickets that she had been able to use until her sixteenth birthday. During her fifteenth year she had very often had to produce a proof of age. This had been annoying, and, for no good reason, somewhat humiliating. After all, it was not a crime to be fifteen, but the Toronto Transportation Commission had somehow contrived to make her feel that it was.

When she sat down, she was in a bright, humid oblong peopled with passengers so used to this method of travel that, with no more than four feet between opposing rows, they were able to ignore one another's existence completely. It was an art that Karen had never been able to master, and she was, as always, at a loss where to fix her gaze. In the newer street-cars, the ones with air brakes and double seats facing forward, you were not exposed to this problem.

For a time she stared at the dark-grey composition flooring, where runnels of water from motionless wet feet washed first up, and then down the crevices between the ridges.

Then she looked up at the coloured advertisements above a row of heads that jerked and swayed in unison. Dunlop's Tires. Zam-buk. Wrigley's Spearmint Chewing Gum. Winchester Cigarettes. Murine. Pepsodent Tooth Paste. The old Italian grandmother had lived most of her life without these so-called necessities. Karen, depressed by the weather, the anonymity of her surroundings, and her formless fears about Fay, thought that she herself could get on very well without them.

Even then—although for a time she was to forget this—the multitude of "things" with which people burdened themselves bothered her quite a lot.

One day she had said to Barbara, "I'd like to throw away damn near everything I own."

Barbara was inclined to take what people said very literally. Her blue eyes thoughtful, she had said, "Well, why don't you?"

It was a good question. Why didn't she?

She changed street-cars at Bloor Street. The Bloor car was crowded and she had to stand, wedged close against strangers in an enforced intimacy it was better not to think about. The point of an umbrella jabbed her ankle. The mixed fumes of stale whiskey, cheap perfume, wet rubber and sweat made her wrinkle her nose in unconscious disgust. A man's hand came to rest on her hip, and lingered there, but there was nothing she could do about it.

"Jarvis!—Sherbourne!" The conductor's hoarse voice called the stops with the monotony of a machine capable nevertheless of exasperation.

Using her small suitcase as a battering ram, Karen forced her way through to the centre doors.

A green traffic light to the east gave her right of way as she walked across Sherbourne, and then, on a changing light, turned north across Bloor to the old Sherbourne Street bridge, its steel girders arching high above an unlit, storm-tossed well of darkness. What kind of night had it been when Fay's mother jumped to her death? There had been others before her, and others after her, but it was always of Fay's mother that Karen thought whenever she crossed the bridge. Fay did not remember her mother at all. Perhaps it would have been worse, rather than better, if she had.

The bridge was deserted, and without conscious volition Karen quickened her pace, even though in those days residential Toronto was a comparatively safe place after dark. At the farther end of the bridge she turned right onto a street lined with trees so ancient and so large that their leafless branches met in a heavy canopy overhead. Here and there a lighted window broke the darkness beyond the pale glimmer of ornamental street lamps, but for the most part the cumbersome, mid-Victorian houses were no more than bulky shadows looming above surrounding shrubbery.

When she reached Fay's house, it was to find the front at least in total darkness, something which for a moment unnerved her. She went quickly up the long walk to the front door, tried it, found it locked, and without perceptible hesitation circled the house by a cement foot-path. With the help of her flashlight, she found the pantry window unlocked as Fay had said it might be. She pushed her suitcase inside, heard it land on a linoleum floor, and climbed in after it, liking the thick darkness inside the house no better than the darkness outside, if as well.

In the centre hall, she switched on a light, and called softly, "Fay!"

There was no answer, so she took off her coat and overshoes, and went up a staircase carpeted in heavy, faded Oriental red.

Six doors, and a corridor which led to the servants' stairway, opened off the second-floor hall. Only the bathroom door stood open. The house had been built in an era when seventeen rooms and one bathroom had seemed like a perfectly reasonable arrangement.

Karen never knew why she crossed to that open door before going to Fay's room on the opposite side of the hall. It was one of those things you do without really thinking.

Years later, when she told Rick about it, she could still see the blood on the grey tiled floor as clearly as when she actually saw it.

"There was blood everywhere," she told Rick. "And under the washbasin there were two of those big white bath-towels soaked in blood."

"I always thought Fay was unstable," Rick said. "What did you do?"

"I was sick," Karen told him. "Just like that. After all, I was pretty young, you must remember. It didn't take long, and at least I didn't do it on the floor."

"No," Rick said. "You wouldn't, darling. You don't have to tell me that."

"You see," Karen said, "I thought she'd tried to commit suicide. I thought of her mother, and I could just picture Fay lying in her room, perhaps with her wrists slashed, perhaps dead. It wasn't the blood itself that made me sick, but the thought that she might possibly be dead."

She never told anyone else about that night, but even telling Rick was a mistake, because he never felt quite the same way about Fay again. Rick was not prudish, far from it, but he had certain standards. As a matter of fact he felt much the way Karen did, herself. It wasn't what you did, but how you did it, and with whom.

By the time she opened Fay's door, she was all right. "Fay?" she said. "Fay?"

Fay's voice was almost normal. "Karen? God, am I glad you got here! I thought you'd never get here."

Fay looked even tinier than usual in the big mahogany bed. There was blood in here, too, but it didn't show up as much on the Wilton carpet.

"I came as fast as I could," Karen said. "Fay, what in the name of heaven have you done to yourself?"

"The usual thing," Fay said. "But the worst is over. The only trouble is that I'm too weak to clean up the mess."

"What do you mean, the usual thing?"

Fay had sounded almost cross. "Don't be so dense," she said. "You know the facts of life as well as I do."

"Oh, my God!" Karen said. "When did you have it done?"

"This afternoon," Fay told her. "The damned woman told me everything would be fine if I just kept quiet for a couple of days."

"You'll have to have a doctor in," Karen said. "And the sooner the better."

"Karen," Fay said, "either make sense, or go home."

It had not sounded like Fay at all. It wasn't like Fay to be either angry or positive.

"Who told you where to go?" Karen asked.

"Lou."

"Then why didn't you call Lou instead of me? You must have known how I would feel about this."

"Yes," Fay said, "I knew how you'd feel, angel. But you're someone who can be trusted. Lou isn't."

"If you want my opinion, Lou is a tramp. But since she apparently knows already, what difference would it have made if you'd called her now?"

"Lou doesn't know a damn thing, and she never will, if I can help it. I'm going to tell her I made a mistake and didn't need her lousy address."

"You made a mistake, all right," Karen said. "Several of them, if you ask me. What do you want me to do?"

"Clean up before my father gets home. He's at the Bar Association. He'll be late. You're an angel, Karen. I'll never forget this."

On her knees, scrubbing the bathroom floor, Karen knew that she wouldn't forget it either. And the worst thing, then and later, was wondering whether she shouldn't have called a doctor, anyway, no matter what Fay said.

Fay always claimed later that the reason she and Roddie didn't have any children was because they didn't want them. This might or might not have been the truth. You could never tell with Fay. She was very sweet, but she was an awful liar. Certainly a child would have helped to make her marriage seem, to her and to everyone else, less of a farce than it actually was. And less of a tragedy. Farce and tragedy, both elements were there in Fay's marriage. And it wasn't that Roddie wasn't likeable. He was, very. He was also very good-looking. He was just someone no woman would marry if she were in her right mind. It was a question whether Fay, as far as men were concerned, had ever been in her right mind.

When Karen went into the bedroom to work on the carpet in there, Fay was smoking a cigarette. She looked better than she had, although she was still very white.

"Would you like something hot to drink?" Karen asked.

"No," Fay said. "No, thanks, angel. But when you've finished with that filthy job, a brandy wouldn't hurt. You'll find a bottle in my stocking drawer, right at the back. That damned woman. There should be a law."

"There are laws."

"Don't be like that, angel."

It was hard to tell where the blood left off and the carpet pattern began. The light, coming from one of those old-fashioned ceiling fixtures, was not good. If Fay had been a girl who ever read anything, she would have had a lamp in the room. There were plenty of lights in the house that she and Roddie built later on in Rowanwod, but they were concentrated on such things as built-in bars and glass-topped dressing-tables. Nobody in Rowanwood saw anything odd in this. On the contrary, it was Susan with her philosophy books, and Karen and Rick with their large library, who were considered odd.

Karen stood up. "I don't think that will show now."

"You're an absolute angel," Fay said.

"Have I time to take the towels down to the basement and wash them?" Karen asked her.

"Don't bother," Fay said. "Throw them out."

That was typical of Fay. Once she stopped worrying about something, and she did this very easily, she ceased to think.

"You can't just throw out towels in that condition," Karen said. "The cook and the garbage-man would make something of it between them, and the next thing you knew the police would be round digging up the garden and looking for bodies. And I'm not being funny."

Fay actually giggled. "Yes, you are, angel. Anyway, they wouldn't find any bodies."

"How do you know they wouldn't?"

Fay lit another cigarette. "You have a perfectly horrible mind, angel. I'll never enjoy being in the garden again. Throw the damn towels on the cupboard floor, and I'll look after them. There are two glasses in the bathroom which you can get for the brandy. You could probably use some, too."

"Yes," Karen said, "I could use some, too."

To look at the bathroom, you would never know that anything had happened. It looked just the way all bathrooms looked in those days. Dull. Functional but dull. The only bathroom in Rowanwood that looked like that was one in Betsey and Harry Milner's house. It was their idea of a joke, complete with pull chain and a bathtub with claw feet. Their downstairs bathroom had a music-box in the seat of the toilet.

In the morning, Karen looked in on Fay and found her asleep. Without disturbing her, she went down to have breakfast with Fay's father in a dining-room as large and cold as a baronial hall.

Mr. Wilcombe might be a rotten father, but he was a nice man.

"Ah, good morning, Karen," he said. "I didn't know you were here."

"Good morning," Karen said. "I came over last night."

"It was a nasty night."

"Yes. It was."

"Fay not coming down?"

"No," Karen said. "She's not feeling well. She's sleeping. She wasn't very well last night."

"Help yourself to bacon and eggs, my dear. Nothing serious, I hope?"

Karen felt like saying, no, nothing serious. Just a small abortion. Not the infectious kind.

"No," she said. "It's nothing serious."

"Well," Mr. Wilcombe said, "tell her to look after herself."

The one thing Fay never had been able to do, and never would be able to do, was to look after herself. What she needed was somebody to look after her. But there was no point in trying to say this to Mr. Wilcombe. There was nothing he could have done about it, because he needed looking after, himself.

Mr. Wilcombe drove her to the street-car stop on the other side of the bridge. He had a green Hupmobile, and it had an engine knock. But there was no point in telling him this either.

"Sure I can't run you up to school, my dear?" Mr. Wilcombe asked.

"No, thank you," Karen said. "There isn't any school today. It's Saturday, Mr. Wilcombe."

"So it is. So it is. How stupid of me," Mr. Wilcombe said. "In that case, won't you permit me to run you home?"

"No, thank you," Karen said again. "It's very good of you, but I'm in no hurry. You can just let me off here, if you will."

"Well, just as you say, my dear," Mr. Wilcombe said. "And if you have the time, you might give Fay a call later on and tell her to look after herself."

Yes, though she would have died rather than admit it, Karen had not minded getting away from Fay for a time. She had not really minded the idea of going to Geneva.

3 | Were you happy in that place?

When both Waycroft School for Girls and Geneva had become a part of her past, Karen could see that there were worse ways of preparing for a year abroad than going to a school like Waycroft. She could also see, as she had not at the time, that her lack of School Spirit was due to an already rooted dislike of conformity for conformity's sake.

She had worn the school uniform of green middy, navy-blue gym skirt, and long black cotton stockings because she had to: but she had not worn it with the belligerent pride of those who had real School Spirit. And she had insisted on pinning her middy around her waist rather than down around her hips, something which drew a great deal of unfavourable comment from the Right Sort. At Waycroft you were not supposed to have a waistline. In fact, you were not supposed to have anything belonging to a normal figure. The ideal was to flatten yourself both fore and aft in direct contravention of all natural laws of anatomy. However, nothing as insignificant as a natural law was allowed to interfere with traditions known in sum as the Waycroft Way.

Karen from the beginning aligned herself with a minority group that offered a stubborn, passive resistance to everything connected with the Waycroft Way. A group that refused any effort on the games field beyond the absolutely compulsory; that did not "go out" for things like the School Choir, the Dramatic Society, or the Extra Art Classes; that remained dry-eyed when the School Song was sung in the main auditorium at term endings.

Afterwards, Karen sometimes wondered if things would have

been different if Barbara had gone with her to Waycroft. Barbara really liked conformity. On the whole, though, she did not think that even Barbara could have persuaded her to find much virtue in anything as alien to her temperament as the Waycroft Way.

The greatest disgrace that could befall a Waycroft girl was to have her school pin taken way from her. This was a gold emblem that you—armed with a note to the effect that you were worthy —obtained at Birks for the sum of five dollars. Karen never had her pin taken away, because hers were sins of omission rather than commission. The time when Fay's pin was taken away became part of the school's history.

Mr. Wilcombe, coming out of his parental fog for the first and last time in Karen's memory of him, arrived at Waycroft looking exceedingly dignified, and, with a sound knowledge of the law to support him, gave the Head the choice of returning the pin or handing over the five dollars that had been paid to Birks for it. The Head, Mr. Wilcombe said, had no legal right to dispossess his daughter of property rightfully hers, without making proper restitution. The only proper restitution that he would recognize, Mr. Wilcombe said, was coin of the realm in the sum of five dollars.

What happened after that was merely rumour, because the prefect who had been eavesdropping—something a Waycroft prefect was not expected to do—had had to move away from the door in a hurry. However, Fay's pin was returned to her, and it was a solid fact that from that day on no Waycroft girl was ever asked to surrender her pin. It had something to do with the Board of Governors and the budget, you were told.

This was a story that, many years later, amused Susan very much when Karen happened to tell it to her. Anything about Waycroft seemed to interest and amuse Susan, who had, herself, been sent away to school in Virginia. And one day when they happened to be driving past Waycroft, Susan asked her to stop for a minute so that she could take a really good look at it.

It was odd, Karen thought, how little it ever seemed to change. The ivy-covered stone building looked as if it had been there always, which of course it hadn't. And as if it would be there for ever, which, despite all reason, she felt it might be. The trees surrounding the playing-fields appeared to be the same height. The grass, thick and close-cut, might never have known any seasonal change at all since the days when, reluctantly, she had rushed to and fro across it, to no very great purpose, with a lacrosse stick.

The only thing that had changed were the cars parked along the curb outside the yew hedge. The cars were really startling, because when she had been there, only one or two of the girls had had cars of their own, and the rest were a handful of beat-up jalopies belonging to boys who, for the record, were always somebody or other's brothers. The jalopies had such remarks as "Bored of Education" painted on their rusty sides. The Head, personally, had come out to order that one of them, bearing the legend "Hoo're you doing?" be removed at once. The Head had not been quite as out of touch with certain realities as her demeanour and appearance generally led one to suppose.

"It's a beautiful building," Susan said.

"Yes," Karen said, "it's a beautiful building."

"Do I get the vaguest whiff of money?" Susan asked.

"It's quite noticeable," Karen said, "when the wind is right."

"What was it like, going there?"

"What do you want to know?" Karen asked. "Shall I tell you about how Mary-Anne Bellevue broke the Waycroft record for the quarter mile? Or would you rather hear Jill Conover's poem about how Waycroft girls are born, but never, never made?"

Susan laughed. "It was like that, was it?"

"Yes," Karen said. "It was like that. Most private schools are."

Susan took a cigarette case out of the grey alligator bag Lewis had bought for her the last time they were in New York. "It looks like the kind of place where everybody falls in love with the School Captain. Were you one of the entourage?"

"No," Karen said, "I wasn't. The only time I fell in love while I was at school was with a policeman."

"Good God!" Susan said. "How did that happen?"

"He directed traffic at a corner I used to pass every morning."

Susan laughed again. "Would it be too intimate to ask which corner?"

Karen laughed, too. "It was the corner of Avenue Road and St. Clair, if you really must know."

"Did he ever speak to you?"

"No. But he picked my books up for me one day when I dropped them."

"Oh," Susan said. "Not only an officer but a gentleman. Had you dropped them on purpose?"

"I can say quite positively that I had not. But if Ned ever heard about it, he would say that it *was* on purpose. He would claim that it was a subconscious manifestation of the mating instinct. Both Julia and Ned would have a lovely time with the subject."

For two years the policeman had been the only good thing about going to school. Getting up in the morning, wishing she hadn't read so late the night before, and knowing that she was going to get polite hell for not having done her algebra, the chance that she might see him had been the single bright spot on her horizon. It was a possibility that sustained her through porridge, which she detested, and the inevitable last-minute hunt for her rubbers—because, in memory at least, it was always raining when she set out for Waycroft.

"He was just as aware of me as I was of him," Karen said. "You can usually tell about a thing like that."

Susan blew a perfect smoke ring. "Yes," she said, "you can usually tell." She nodded her head toward the school, "Were you happy in that place?" she asked.

"Not particularly," Karen said. "But at the time it didn't matter too much because I didn't really think about it."

Actually, if she had really thought about it, she would not have sent Carol and Peg there. Because both she and Rick had gone to large private schools, they hadn't considered any other possibility, even though at first it had been all and more than they could do to pay the fees. That was one of the things that going to a good private school did to you; it tended to make you feel that anything else was quite out of the question. It blinded you to the fact that in exchange for a good education you ran the risk of becoming, or continuing to be, a worshipper of inherited privilege. For there was no doubt that the Waycroft Way was most easily travelled in a Cadillac bought with money your grandfather had earned.

"Were Carol and Peg happy there?" Susan asked.

"Carol was. I'm not sure about Peg."

Peg had been seven when they entered her, and because she had had flu she had started late in the term. Karen had taken her in to see the Head first. Then they had gone to see the Head of the Junior School, who had said that Peg could print very well for her age, and that she would be put into the Junior Second. The Junior Second was having gym, so, for no very good reason, they were taken to the gymnasium.

The gym mistress, recognizing Karen immediately, had been very warm in her welcome. The whole thing had given Karen the most extraordinary feeling. It was as if all time was existing simultaneously. It was as if she were one of the scrubbed little girls in middies and skirts sitting on the board floor, their legs crossed tailor fashion, looking with awe and envy at an Old Girl, while all the time she *was* the Old Girl. The transference had made her actually dizzy.

"Girls," Miss Jergens had said, "this is Mrs. Whitney, and her daughter, Peggy. Peggy, you will be happy to hear, is going to be one of us." None of the little girls had shown any marked exhilaration at this prospect, but then it was not the Waycroft Way to give evidence of unseemly emotion. "Mrs. Whitney," Miss Jergens had continued, "was formerly Karen Holbrook, as some of you no doubt know. Karen is an Old Girl of whom I have always been particularly proud—"

At this point Karen had ceased to hear what Miss Jergens was saying. Instead she had heard the same voice saying something very, very different. It had been in the room near the gym where you were weighed and measured at the beginning of each term. Under the piercing gaze of Miss Jergens and her assistant, Karen, who had been fourteen at the time, had been attempting to Stand Up Straight. At Waycroft they made a fetish of Standing Up Straight.

Miss Jergens had turned to her assistant, Miss Crombie. "Miss Crombie, do you see what I see?"

"Yes," Miss Crombie said. "I'm afraid I do, Miss Jergens."

"It's distressing, isn't it, Miss Crombie?"

"Yes," Miss Crombie said. "You've put it very nicely, Miss Jergens. It is distressing."

"It doesn't look like one of my girls at all, does it, Miss Crombie?"

"No," Miss Crombie said. "I'm sorry to say that it does not look like one of your girls, Miss Jergens."

More than two decades later, Karen could, if she had wished, have repeated this conversation to Susan verbatim. That she did not do so was because, although there were many occasions when you could be grateful for having been to a good private school, what you had felt at the time was an entirely different matter.

"Karen," Susan said, "I think I understand now why you and Fay became friends. I've never been able to see before what you and Fay could ever have had in common."

Putting the car into gear again, Karen said, "That's more or less what my mother used to say."

"Did she?"

"Yes," Karen told her. "I might never have gone to Geneva if my mother had not felt that Fay and I had very little in common."

Waycroft had been a block behind them before Susan had asked a question she had probably thought of asking before, but never had.

"By the way, darling, have you ever heard from Cyr?"

"No," Karen had said. "I wouldn't expect to."

4 | A pop-up toaster would be quite unsuitable

The letters she had picked up on her return from Millicent's held carelessly in her left hand, Karen turned toward the breakfast-room with the intention of clearing away the dishes, and possibly getting them washed before the carpet came.

As she turned, she caught her own reflection in the mirror beside the living-room archway. At that distance, and in that light, she might have been no more than twenty. To move closer to the mirror was to see a montage of pictures of herself, slowly superimposed one upon another. It was rather like looking through an old photograph album, and seeing herself as she had been when she was at college; when she had married Rick; when they had lived on Gavin Street; when they had moved into this house, at that time a derelict set amongst the fields that were so soon to become Rowanwood; and as she was now—executive's wife in a fresh blue cotton dress, its utility denied by a wide collar and a frivolously full skirt.

At close quarters, the illusion of twenty, twenty-five, or thirty, was gone, but the mirror continued to lie by denying any real proof that she was forty. She was, she noted, as slender as she had ever been. And her face, thanks to the care she gave it, had yet to fall victim to all those awful things that the magazines were forever telling you were lying in wait for you when you reached forty. The magazines knew how to make a few lines in your face seem more disastrous than bubonic plague. In your grandmother's day growing older had been looked upon as a natural and, in its own way, satisfying process. Your mother's generation had been permitted to "grow old gracefully". Now you weren't allowed to grow old at all. You became, instead, progressively "less young", which was neither a natural nor a satisfying process, but simply a losing battle with Helena Rubinstein as your first lieutenant and the *Reader's Digest* as your chief medical officer.

I look, Karen thought bitterly, as if I had just stepped out of Vogue. A cardboard doll cut out of nothing. I am a success. I have conformed to the pattern, and I wish to God I hadn't. How have I let this thing happen to me? When did it begin, and where? Can I make a fresh start now? Would Planesville really be the answer I think it might be?

The people in Planesville had approached Rick tentatively as long ago as February. Two weeks ago, at the beginning of June, they had been more specific in their suggestions. Plant superintendent and general manager of a chemical plant that, up until the present, had been a purely family concern. Compared with outfits like C.I.L. and ChemCon, where Rick now worked, it was a small concern; but, as the people in Planesville had pointed out, it was expanding rapidly, and with government contracts coming their way, they were well within their rights in being optimistic about their future growth. Certainly the possible salary they had mentioned to Rick showed no lack of confidence in their future.

So far Rick had refused to comment on the offer one way or the other, beyond saying, "Big frog in little puddle? I don't know."

"Is it such a little puddle?" Karen had asked him.

"No," Rick had said, "as far as the company itself is concerned, I don't think you could call it that. But the town is certainly a little puddle. In a place as distant from any large centre, you'd be out of touch."

To Karen, being "out of touch" sounded wonderful. So wonderful that she had been very careful not to say so. To try and pressure Rick on anything really important could not help but be a mistake. Basically this must be his decision. But there was nothing to stop her hoping.

Karen had never been to Planesville, but she knew that part of eastern Ontario fairly well, and could imagine what it was like. Especially after Rick had told her the population. There were,

Rick had told her, approximately two thousand people in Planesville. And, he had added, most of them were dependent on the Planesville Chemical Company for a living.

There would not be more than two streets with stores, Karen thought, and these would intersect at the centre of the town. They would be lined with small, old-fashioned stores rather like those which her family had patronized back in the days on Elmdale Avenue. There would be three churches—the Anglican, the Roman Catholic, and the United. There might or might not be a movie house, and if there were, it would be tiny. There might or might not be a Woolworth's. There would almost certainly be an Eaton Mail Order Office, an immediate link with the familiar red and navy-blue delivery trucks. And there would probably be one of those small Loblaw's stores, scarcely recognizable as such, where you could never find anything.

There would be no postal delivery, and you would have to go to the brick post office to get your mail out of a box with a number on it. The bank, also brick, would either be next door to the post office, or right across the street from it. There would be a town hall, probably also brick, where you would go to vote on such essentials as a new snow-plough to keep the roads open, and not, as you did in Rowanwood, to listen to fresh schemes to get rid of the Johnsons because they didn't have a recreation room with built-in bar, and had only one bathroom. In Planesville there were probably houses that had no bathroom at all. From certain, if not all, points of view, this was a refreshing thought.

There would be a little red school-house—it would be brick too—and a "new" high school for the older children. Neither place would remind you in any way at all of Waycroft, any more than the dignified frame houses would remind you of the houses in Rowanwood. The houses in Planesville would have plenty of space around them, not because their owners were trying to prove anything to anybody, but simply because there *was* plenty of space. They would be painted white, something you could do yourself; in the country nobody would think you were doing it because you couldn't afford to have it done for you. In the country you didn't do-it-yourself to be smart, either; you did it because that was the way things were done in a small place—simply, and without ostentation. And on summer evenings you could sit on a wide front porch without explaining why you weren't inside watching TV. Luxuriating in what really was the Good Life—a far cry from the Good Life as Rowanwood envisaged it—you probably wouldn't even listen to more than one radio newscast during the evening.

It might, Karen thought, be almost as satisfactory as living in Toronto the way it used to be before it had become the fastest-growing city in the world. They said it was growing even faster than Los Angeles, and you could well believe this. They also said that a third of the cars in Canada were in Toronto and area, and you could well believe this, too. It had once been called a city of beautiful trees, beautiful churches, and beautiful policemen. Now, she felt, it could better be described as a city of big cars, big TV sets, and big business men.

If her mother had still been alive, Karen might, in the strictest confidence, have discussed the Planesville possibility with her. Her mother, although you would never have known this, had been born in a small town. When Karen's father died, Karen had half expected her mother to go back to that little town. At one time and another her mother had talked a great deal about her home town, and with real nostalgia. But she had not gone back.

"You can't go back," her mother had said.

Karen had never seen quite why you couldn't. Although, in her own case, it was different. She had nowhere to go back to, except Elmdale Avenue, and it was only too obvious why nobody would want to go back there. As she had known it, Elmdale Avenue simply did not exist any more.

It had been a mistake to show Susan the house on Elmdale Avenue. Susan, very naturally, had seen exactly what there was to see, a row of large, dingy boarding-houses with garbage cans at the kerb. It was odd how you could tell, just from looking at the outside of a house, that it was a boarding-house. Even the maples, which had once been so lovely, were now too big for the street and cast a perpetual gloom over it even at high noon. She had tried to tell Susan what it had been like in the past, but it had been no good. Susan had understood that it had been unlike what she saw, but that was as far as her understanding could go. Even memory, clear as it was, wavered in the face of that drab scene, and Karen herself had avoided Elmdale Avenue after that. This was not a difficult thing to do, because she no longer knew anyone who lived in the Annex. Anyone, that is, except Julia and Ned, who said they lived there because it was close to the university.

Karen's mother, when talking about her home town, had said, "If one could go back, there would be something to be said for it. If I lived there, I would in time become 'Old Mrs. Holbrook'. In a small community age is not the barrier it is in a big city. Whatever your age, you know everybody and everybody knows you. Here, in the city, I will eventually become an ageing cipher visited out of pity, if at all."

"What a horrible idea!" Karen had said. "Do you see that as my future, too?"

"No," her mother had said. "You are city-born, and city-bred. You have an orientation to big-city life which in itself will support you. Here you will always be amongst people who remember the same things you remember, even if they are strangers to you now. It is very important, as you grow older, to live where there are people with whom you can share memories. Not just specific memories, but the general impressions of changing decades as they have affected a certain kind of background.

"Your father, for instance, was never very interested in baseball, but one day I heard him talking to a man of his own age about Babe Ruth, and really enjoying the conversation. You see, he was remembering not so much Babe Ruth as an era when everybody, whether they were interested in baseball or not, tended to look on Babe Ruth as a kind of hero. But when I say 'everybody', I mean those people who belonged to a sphere wide enough to encompass happenings outside of their own small concerns. In the country, where I was brought up, we were more interested in prize cattle and the time the Town Hall burned down. If you, for example, had been brought up there, you might not have known who Humphrey Bogart was."

"Are you," Karen had said, "trying to tell me that Humphrey Bogart was a hero to me?"

Her mother had smiled. "Well, wasn't he?"

"All right," Karen had said. "Perhaps he was."

"Well," her mother had said, "the point I'm making is that some day it is going to mean quite a lot to you to know people to whom you can say, 'Do you remember Humphrey Bogart in *Casablanca*?', and to find that they do."

Why, Karen thought with irritation, do I have to remember that particular conversation now?

She put the letters down on the breakfast table without looking at them, and began to stack the dishes. If she and Rick moved to Planesville, she told herself, they would gain much more than they would lose. And anyway, it was not as if they were already in their dotage. There would be plenty of time in which to make friends with whom they could share memories. It had nothing to do with anything that Humphrey Bogart was already dead. That he was, like Elmdale Avenue, behind a door that could now be opened only by memory.

It was not until the letters were the only things left on the table that Karen really looked at them. She was not like Rick, who always opened a letter immediaely.

The three letters were all in business envelopes, a circumstance that to Karen practically guaranteed that they would all be equally uninteresting.

She picked up the top one, and began to slit the envelope with her finger-nail before she saw the return address on the back of it. Her knees suddenly unsteady, she sat down, thinking, no—— no, not now. I won't go now. Later, when I'm not so busy. But not now.

Dear Mrs. Whitney:

This is just to remind you that you are due for your yearly check-up, and that, subject to your convenience, Dr. Lowe will see you at two-thirty in the afternoon, June nineteenth. If this suits you, would you be good enough to confirm the appointment.

Sincerely,
Audrey Bolton (secretary)

The routine check-up was something she had instituted for Rick, and the children, and herself, when Carol and Peg were small. Rick had protested mildly at first, but he had gone along with the idea because it was a sensible one. In theory, just as in the case of your regular visits to the dentist, you would anticipate any serious trouble before it actually did become serious. You would always be perfectly relaxed about going to see the doctor.

This had been all very well when she fitted it between shopping and picking Carol and Peg up at Waycroft, confident in the knowledge that her heart and blood pressure were normal, and that an ingrown toe-nail was undoubtedly the only thing wrong with her. And even the toe-nail not really ingrown. But now that she had this recurrent pain that turned her grey when it struck, she found that the last thing she wanted to do was see the doctor. She was ashamed of herself, but this did not alter the fact that she infinitely preferred ignorance to knowledge that she was afraid to face.

She had not told Rick about the pain. To have told him would have been to attach an importance to it that she had been steadfastly denying. After telling Rick everything for so many years, there suddenly seemed to be rather a lot of things that she felt she could not tell him.

When they were first married, Karen, always healthy, had nevertheless worried quite often about perfectly imaginary ills. She would come across a bone in her hand that, it seemed to her, had not been there before. Or it might be a gland in her neck that did not seem quite right. On these occasions, even while she knew she was being an idiot, it was very helpful to be able to examine Rick and reassure herself that, since he apparently had the same peculiarity, it could not after all be so very peculiar.

In the beginning Rick had been amused. He had said, "If you

look very, very carefully, darling, one of these days you're going to find that I have some things you haven't got."

"Rick," Karen had said, "stay still, and don't try to be funny. This is serious."

He had not stayed still, and he had gone on laughing.

Finally, however, he had flatly refused to be a guinea-pig any longer. He had said, "For heaven's sake, sweetheart, why don't you buy an anatomy book and discover yourself all at once and get it over with?"

He had not been annoyed with her. He never was. But she had not bothered him in that way again. Neither had she bought an anatomy book. When there actually was something the matter with you, you did not need an anatomy book to tell you that this was so.

With the letter from the doctor's office in her hand, Karen knew that in order to preserve some small measure of self-respect she would have to keep the appointment. It might be the last thing on earth she wanted to do, but in her present frame of mind it was the last thing on earth that she could afford not to do.

The second letter was addressed to Rick, and across the stamp she saw what she had not seen before, a blurred cancellation bearing the name Planesville, Ontario. That a robin should choose that moment to start singing in the garden seemed, absurdly, like a good omen. With quick excitement, Karen thought: they're forcing the pace. Rick will have to make up his mind very soon now. There was no imprint on the envelope, which meant that it was a personal letter from Paul Holmes, the president. Unopened, as it must remain until Rick came home for dinner, the long white envelope was like a sign-post just too far away to read, that might, when approached more closely, say, "This is, neatly packaged, the answer to all your problems. This is escape from sham, from materialism, from Rowanwood and all that it stands for. This is the way to what is truly the Good Life."

Her glance falling on the chromium-plated pop-up toaster that Millicent and Biff had given them for Christmas, she thought: if we do move to Planesville, that toaster will top the list of things we will *not* take with us. In Planesville a pop-up toaster would be quite unsuitable.

Impatient now for the day to be over, impatient to know what the letter from Planesville contained, Karen looked at her watch, and thought: where are those damned men who were to have delivered the carpet at nine? A pity that she and Rick hadn't bought the carpet from Eaton's. Eaton's were so reliable about times. They had been very nice about unpaid bills, too, when she and Rick lived on Gavin Street. In return for this niceness Karen never bought anything without first seeing if Eaton's had it. She felt very loyal to the T. Eaton Company. It might seem strange to some people to be loyal to a department store, but when you read the newspapers these days you wondered just what else there was to be loyal to, except possibly the Atomic Energy Commission.

She picked up the third letter, and saw that she was looking not at the address but at the imprint—Sheraton-Mount Royal Hotel, Montreal, Quebec. She turned it over, and there was her own name and address written in a careless, slanting hand that meant nothing to her. It's probably an advertisement, she thought, and should have been addressed to Rick. If those men don't come soon I won't get out to Loblaw's before lunch.

It was very convenient having the new shopping plaza only three blocks away, but if you didn't get there well before noon you found so many cars ahead of you that you had to walk nearly a block to get to any of the stores. On Sundays, when the great asphalt apron with its neat white lines lay empty and deserted, it was quite impossible to imagine that you could ever have difficulty in parking. During the week, however, if you didn't get over there early you were lucky if you could get in at all.

Basically it was a good idea to have a representative selection of stores all in one spot; but, like so many good ideas, in practice it had overreached itself. In trying to offer too much, the architects of the plaza had re-created the very problems they had set out to overcome. At the moment everybody was sold on the idea, but it seemed to Karen that before long the housewives would probably start drifting back to Yonge Street. There was, of course, a real parking problem on Yonge Street. But on Yonge Street you didn't feel so regimented. You felt as if you had been left a little initiative of your own.

The unopened letter from Montreal still in her hand, she left the breakfast-room, went into the kitchen, turned on the electric dish-washer, and then went to the living-room windows to see if there was any sign of the carpet truck.

The street lay deserted in the summer sunlight. The blinds were still down in Mrs. Johnson's bedroom. Pete's bicycle still lay across the broken board steps. Boris's car still stood in Millicent's driveway.

If you had been a stranger from another planet, you might have wondered if Rowanwood was inhabited at all. You would not have understood the phenomenon of mid-morning doldrums. You had to live in Rowanwood to know that the men had all left the boxes in which they lived for other boxes in the business section downtown; to know that the women were either hidden inside cleaning the former, or had gone off in smaller mechanized boxes to the shopping plaza. These things explained to you, you, the stranger from another planet, would still fail to understand why the women should spend so much time shut up in their boxes. You would, if you had come equipped with any knowledge of the civilization you had invaded, wonder how on Earth women had allowed themselves to be hoodwinked into believing what the manufacturers wanted them to believe—that they had never had it so good.

Wherever you went you heard it. The radio blared it. Television played it up. The newspapers devoted whole pages to telling you how lucky you were to be a woman now, rather than at any other epoch in world history. You were constantly reminded that you were fortunate in the possession—on time payment or, which was less likely, for cash on the barrelhead—of a hundred and one gadgets expressly designed to make your life easier, more leisurely, and—that last awful word which no advertising man seemed able to resist—more "gracious".

In Karen's opinion, if there was one adjective in the whole

English language that could not be applied to the middle of the twentieth century, it was the adjective gracious.

And as for life being continually easier for women in a continually more mechanized age, this was complete nonsense, particularly if applied to women in the income brackets where labour-saving devices were likely to be sold in the greatest quantity. For what everybody seemed to overlook was the fact that most of these women had not been brought up to expect that they would do any housework at all.

"Never has it been so easy for you to polish your floors." Twenty years ago, and no more than that, someone was paid to polish your floors for you. You had a laundress who came every Monday to do your washing for you. You did the dishes on Wednesday and Sunday nights only, when the maid was out. If you had two maids, you didn't do that much.

In this connection, people who talked about "freedom from drudgery" made fools of themselves. No maid you had ever known had worked half as hard as you, with all your labour-saving devices, now worked. Or, for that matter, half as hard as a maid today, who charred by day and did her own housework in the evening so that she, too, could defeat herself in the possession of the many things that were supposed to improve her lot so miraculously. You and your sister of the working class were led up the same garden path, where the roses, by any brand name, still smelled. Tempted by newer and shinier gadgets, enticed by advertisers who knew only too well how to do their job, you took on more and more and more. Finally, run ragged by all the easier work you had undertaken, you had little or no time left for anything other than tending your machines.

Nuts, Karen thought savagely. Nuts to the Bendix, to the electric dish-washer, to the Frigidaire, to the multiple-sectioned vacuum with which you could—and, damn it, did—paint walls. To the power mower, to the home freezer, to all the things that made it just possible for you to keep up an establishment infinitely larger and more complex than was justified by your needs, whether you lived in Toronto, or New York, or Chicago, or Montreal, or anywhere else on the North American continent.

It didn't much matter where you lived in the United States or Canada, if you or your husband had any take-home pay at all, you were, whether you recognized it or not, caught in a maze similar to that in which scientists put white mice to see if they had sufficient intelligence to find their way out. If the mice were not intelligent enough to solve the puzzle, they ran round and round and round until they went out of their minds.

Recently Karen had seen a double-page spread in a magazine, entitled "All the Things You Are!" And there you were: chauffeur, laundress, wife, cook, nurse-maid, mistress, mother, hostess, teacher, house-painter, and gardener. In all these roles you were faultlessly dressed and invariably smiling. You were looking very pleased with yourself because you had discovered how to be more than "just a woman", and had yet to discover that there was a fair chance you would take this achievement with you to some nice quiet Rest Home. They weren't called Mental Homes any more, because the word "mental" didn't look well in an advertisement.

The dark-blue panel truck with the red lettering on it must have come from the road around the ravine, because it was in the driveway and had braked to a stop with a spurt of gravel, almost before Karen, lost in thought, realized it was there.

Two men got out of the truck. One was short and dark, the other was burly and dark. They were both in their shirt-sleeves, and she could see patches of sweat on their backs. When she had lived on Elmdale Avenue delivery-men had always worn uniforms and, for the most part, looked very smart in them. You were told now that it was not democratic to wear uniforms. If you said, what about the army? Isn't the army democratic?, you were told not to be difficult.

There had been other changes, too. You were proving your democracy, rather than your lack of breeding, when you called out of a window.

"Bring it to the front door, will you, please!" Karen called. "I'll open the front door for you!"

"Okay, lady!"

That was another change. When you lived on Elmdale Avenue

you were treated like a lady, but you would never have been addressed in that way. Now you were called "lady", and treated as a cross between the girl-next-door and Mom. You almost expected to be slapped on the back. It had never happened yet, but you felt it might at any time. Whether, if it did happen, you ought to react as wife, mistress, chauffeur, or cook was something you had been unable to decide.

The carpet was very large and sagged heavily between the two men. As she opened the door for them, she hoped they would avoid knocking over the hall table, the one she and Rick had bought in Paris.

"It goes in there," she said, gesturing toward the living-room arch. "You'll be careful of the table, won't you?"

"Don't you worry, lady," the big man said. "Don't you worry about a thing."

The table rocked, but did not go over. The letter from the hotel in Montreal, which she had put down when she went to the door, slid over the table edge and onto the floor. It was Karen thought, a good thing that she had moved the Burmese vase. The letter didn't matter. She could pick it up later.

"You want we should lay this carpet, lady?"

"Yes, please," Karen said. "Square it with the fireplace at the far end. Leave about three inches between the fringe and the fireplace tiling. I'm afraid you'll have to lift that big couch in front of the windows, and probably the smaller one, too."

"Nothing to it," the big man said. "Nothing to it at all."

"Well," Karen said, "it's good of you just the same."

"Nothing to it," the big man said again.

Silently she watched while they unrolled soft green velvet pile that brought the rose and grey and green chintz alive, that gave a harmony to the room that the old carpet had never done. Objectively she saw that the effect was going to be wholly perfect, that it would be difficult now to find a more beautiful room, not only in Rowanwood, but anywhere.

Figuratively what she saw was an unrolling of all the years that she and Rick had been in the house, the years that had led to this moment of empty indifference instead of happy achievement. And she thought, when the carpet reaches this archway where I am now standing, it will have caught up with me. The years will have caught up with me and I will be alone again with the question of where I am going, and why.

And she wanted to weep because the present was such an apparent negation of the happiness she had known during years when there had been no time for questions, no time for anything but a vital struggle that was now over. When you were on the way up, you concentrated on the climb itself. You knew where you were going. You even thought you knew why you were going there.

And if at times a small voice attempted to check you, to make you look more closely at what you were doing—well, you silenced it, because you were so busy making two dollars grow where there had been only one before. Although they hadn't thought of it like that, this was exactly what she and Rick had been doing when they planted the buckwheat lawn.

The patches of sweat on the men's shirts were larger than they had been. The big couch, the one done in rose damask, was, as she had thought it would, making it difficult to get the carpet down evenly. And it was a very hot day.

She would get them some ice-cold beer when they had finished. They would probably appreciate that. She and Rick must have drunk gallons of beer during the summer when they had put in the lawn.

5 | There's nothing like a buckwheat lawn

They had bought the house in the fall of 1948. Mr. King had just announced his resignation as Prime Minister, and nobody was as yet quite used to the idea of Mr. St. Laurent in his place. The Ford Motor Company had launched its first new post-war model, and people were not sure they liked that either. It won't last, they said. Some people even said the same thing about Mr. St. Laurent.

Captain Glenn Miller's recordings were selling as well, or better, than Artie Shaw's, because Captain Miller had chosen the right time to die. U.S. money was beginning to pour across the Canadian border in a golden stream that was still a long way from reaching high tide. And Toronto was a boom town where, with the easing of the liquor laws, you could at last buy a drink in public. That is, a real drink; something stronger than four-point-four beer. A cocktail in a place like the Cork Room, or the Silver Rail, cost you three times what it would have cost you at home, but you went to the bars in spite of this because the bars represented glamour and novelty. Also, if you did not go, you might lose your chance. The bars, like Mr. St. Laurent, might not last.

It was on a Sunday that they actually decided to buy the house. A Sunday that began like any other Sunday, very pleasantly, with breakfast in bed. Carol and Peg, in their pyjamas with the Mickey Mouse design on them, had prepared the breakfast. They were given extra pocket money for doing this, and they did it very nicely. Rick was inclined to think they should do it for nothing. Karen, however, did not agree. It was, she said, their day of rest, too. If they were asked to undertake an extra chore, some recognition should be taken of this. And it wasn't as if they didn't make their beds, and set the table for dinner, just as they did through the week. In as far as possible, however, Sunday should be regarded as their day off, too.

"What about Saturday?" Rick asked. "They have Saturday."

"They go back to school for games on Saturday," Karen told him.

"You mean they're supposed to go back for games."

The gym mistress had phoned up from Waycroft more than once about Carol and Peg not being at school on Saturdays for games.

Karen told Rick just what she had told the gym mistress. "Carol and Peg have both had so many colds this fall, that they haven't been able to go. You know how many colds they've had, darling?"

"Having colds didn't stop them from going to Massey Hall with us last night," Rick said.

"But that was to hear Rubinstein. If they had gone up to games in the morning, they couldn't have gone to hear Rubinstein."

Rick smiled broadly. "I give up," he said.

Beacuse it was Sunday, they all had a double orange juice, and they all had corn flakes with cream. Rick always had corn flakes with cream, but during the week Karen felt she must support Carol and Peg by eating Quick Quaker Oats.

More than once she had said to Rick, "I would never have got married if I had known it would lead me back to porridge for breakfast. I always thought that porridge for breakfast was something you escaped from when you got married."

"Shall we go back and do it all over again differently?" Rick would ask.

"No," Karen would say. "Not today. I'm too busy today."

And they would look at each other, and know they would neither of them ever want to change anything that had been between them. Anything they shared, simply because they shared it, was better than anything else ever could have been. For better, for worse. For richer, for poorer. In sickness and in health. Whatever else might change, this never would.

Carol and Peg sat on the end of the big bed, as they always did, and the trays were arranged on tables beside the bed so that they could all four reach what they wanted.

Karen often said afterwards that the larger bedroom was the only decent room in the apartment on Gavin Street, in spite of the flowered wallpaper. It was the only room you could feel at home in. The reprint of Tom Thomson's "Northern River" looked pretty awful against the wallpaper, but it did help to distract you from the flowers.

They used the large percolator on Sundays, so that when they were finished with corn flakes and toast and marmalade, Karen and Rick could go on drinking coffee while they smoked and looked through *Time* magazine, *Saturday Night,* and the *New York Times* Sunday supplement. Carol and Peg devoted themselves to the *Star Weekly*.

Whenever any one of them came across anything that was amusing, everyone of course had to listen to it.

"Well, my loves," Karen said, finally, "it's time we got dressed. Who's going to be first in the bathroom?"

"What's the hurry?" Rick asked. He sounded very contented and very lazy.

"Have you forgotten?" Karen asked. "We're supposed to be at Julia and Ned's at half past twelve."

Rick almost swore out loud. Almost, but not quite. In front of the children he always pretended that he enjoyed going to Julia and Ned's.

"It doesn't happen often," Karen said. And then because this sounded specific rather than general, she added, "I mean, we aren't often disturbed on Sunday."

"Except when we go to church," Peg said.

"Going to church does not come under the heading of disturbance, and I would like that to be quite clear," Karen said. "Now will you both go and get washed while I clear away the trays. And don't dawdle."

When Carol and Peg had left the room, Rick said, "I suppose we have to go?"

"You know we do, darling."

"Will their children be there?"

"Of course."

"Oh, my God," Rick said.

The Mason children, Molly and Frankie, were so absolutely intolerable you felt they probably had some chance of eventual rehabilitation, because nobody outside of their home would put up with them as they were.

When refused something, Molly and Frankie whined. If this didn't work, they howled. Either way, they always got what they wanted.

They had, from the beginning, been brought up to Express Themselves Freely. If, as Brock Chisholm had once so incautiously disclosed, there was no Santa Claus, at least nobody could ever say there wasn't a Dr. Blatz. Certainly not Ned, a psychologist who asked nothing better than to follow in the footsteps of the master. That he should have lost his way some time ago was his own fault rather than that of Dr. Blatz.

Ned had been one of the first to adopt those dark, heavy eyeglass frames designed to make a man appear at one and the same time scholarly and virile. Ned was tall and thin, and, since his hair had started to recede, he did have a somewhat scholarly look. He had never at any time appeared virile, a lack he attempted to offset with a forceful manner and an annoying habit of prefacing most of his remarks with the phrase "Let's face it." Even the way he said this was annoying. It was as if he alone, back to the wall, clear-eyed, clear-minded, were facing Vital Issues as yet uncomprehended by the idiot multitude.

Ned had once, quite by accident, been invited to one of the Prime Minister's receptions while in Ottawa as a member of a minor commission. There was no doubt that somebody had got him mixed up with R. E. Mason, the economist; but you could never have made Ned admit this. Until he died he would continue to embroider on a theme whose central motif, flanked by lion and unicorn, was, "As MacKenzie King said to me——"

Julia and Ned's house was one of those old, three-storey houses on Admiral Road built at the turn of the century when everybody had been so certain that residential Toronto would, following a tradition established by the ancient Egyptians, grow westward towards the prevailing wind. That Toronto society should instead have climbed the hill that cut across the city from east to west was a blow to a great many people who had overlooked the fact that social climbing is not necessarily limited to metaphorical heights.

Julia, as dark and thin and almost as tall as Ned, kept her house painfully tidy under its superficial layer of pseudo-Bohemian disorder—a disorder composed of volumes of Freud and Jung, copies of the *Financial Post*, and the latest French novels, their leaves never entirely cut.

On occasion, when Julia and Ned had one of their "informal get-togethers" it was really interesting, because Ned, *ex officio*, knew some pretty bright people. When this was the case you could forget the arty-academic atmosphere. You could forget the poorly reproduced Dufy prints, the ugly Picasso ash-trays, the Spanish shawl over the piano, and the curtains with the batik design that Julia had done herself.

Nothing, however, could lighten the tedium of a family get-together in that house.

On this Sunday when, though they did not know it, Karen and Rick were to find their house, things were going just as badly as usual. Julia, chiefly because she considered it unintellectual to prepare a decent meal, was a rotten cook, and the dinner had been horrible. Carol and Peg had eaten what was put in front of them. Molly and Frankie, exhibiting a discrimination equalled only by their bad manners, had thrown most of their food on what was, fortunately, an uncarpeted floor.

Now, the children having gone upstairs, Karen and Rick were sitting in the living-room with Julia and Ned, drinking native Ontario wine and wondering how soon they could escape.

We'll make Susan and Lewis our excuse, Karen thought. We'll say we're expected at the Prestons' quite early. What a lovely day it is outdoors. Oh, Lord, how can Ned talk such drivel.

"Let's face it," Ned was saying. "Truman is one of America's biggest mistakes. No man who says that his suit fits too soon should be permitted to run a country."

"Even the United States?" Karen asked.

Irony was always completely wasted on Ned. "Even the United States," he said.

"You're making me feel very uneasy," Rick said.

Julia frowned at him as she had probably frowned at him when he was a little boy. "You ought to be uneasy," she said. "The trouble with you, Rick, is that you never take anything seriously."

"No man," Ned said, "who wears a bow tie should ever be allowed to take public office."

"Churchill wears a bow tie," Rick said.

"Churchill," Ned said, "is a great man. Wearing a bow tie is just part of his strategy. Churchill is not really the bow-tie type. Truman *is* the bow-tie type."

By the time they finally got away it was after three-thirty, but the afternoon was still astonishingly warm for late September, and it was particularly nice to be going to Susan and Lewis's because, although actually they were not very far out, their house on the edge of a wooded ravine commanded a view of fields and trees.

Perhaps because of its wide-spread tracery of ravines, Toronto still had a surprising number of untouched pockets of land at that time. It was a state of affairs which, in the face of a post-war building boom that was gathering momentum daily, was unlikely to resist change much longer.

In theory this was something that Karen knew perfectly well. In practice, as they drove from formal city streets on to a winding country road, she simply could not imagine this small oasis in the midst of an encircling development as ever being anything other than an oasis.

Susan answered the door herself.

"The kids not with you?" she asked, as she led them through to the flagged terrace that seemed to be suspended over the ravine. Out there the sunlight fell through a screen of leaves now turned to red and gold and bronze. Gavin Street might have belonged to a different world. In certain rather important ways, it did.

"No," Karen said. "We dropped them off at the apartment. They wanted to come, but they had homework to do."

Lewis, who had been doing things with a silver cocktail-shaker, came across the terrace to greet them. "Karen—Rick," he said, "it's good to see you."

"Sit down," Susan said. "And be sure and say something nice about the chairs. Lewis just bought them."

"I noticed them at once," Karen said. "They're very good-looking, and marvellously comfortable."

"I don't," Lewis said, "see any reason why one should not be just as comfortable outdoors as one is indoors."

When you considered how wealthy Lewis was, there was no reason at all why he should not be as comfortable outdoors as he was indoors, but Karen did not put it exactly like that. "I quite agree with you," she said.

"Manhattan or martini?" Lewis asked.

"Whichever you have," Rick said.

"He has both," Susan said. "He always has both. And they're equally good."

"In that case," Karen said, "I'll have a manhattan, and love it."

"Martini for me, thanks, Lewis," Rick said.

Lewis's cocktails were invariably excellent. You could not imagine Lewis doing anything that was not done perfectly, any more than you could imagine him dressing in anything other than a faultlessly tailored double-breasted grey suit.

"My brother-in-law," Rick said, "thinks that a man who wears a bow tie is not competent to hold public office. Adopting this thesis, one is expected to find Mr. Truman incompetent."

It was quite safe to say this to Lewis, because you knew that Lewis never had worn, and never would wear, a bow tie.

Lewis smiled. "It's an interesting thought," he said. "Did you mention Lester Pearson?"

"No," Karen said. "We thought of Churchill, but we didn't think of Pearson."

"I believe," Lewis said, "that Roosevelt also wore a bow tie on occasion."

"Oh, Heaven!" Karen said. "So he did. I hope Ned never thinks of that. I really don't think I could bear it if Ned started talking nonsense about Roosevelt. Anybody else. But not Roosevelt."

"It almost looks," Lewis said, and he was still smiling, "as if the reverse might be true. As if it were almost necessary for success in public life to be a man who would wear a bow tie."

Susan laughed. She had a lovely laugh. "Do any of you feel that you are making any sense at all?"

"No," Rick told her. "Not much."

"Does it matter?" Lewis asked.

"No," Susan said, "I really don't think it does."

Their cocktail glasses were by no means empty, but Lewis got up and refilled them.

"You don't feel too cool out here, Karen?" he asked.

"No. It's heavenly out here in every way," Karen told him.

Susan and Lewis had not been married long at that time, and they had only been in their house for two years. Whenever Karen saw them together, she always thought how well they seemed to get on. It was quite ridiculous to feel, as she sometimes did, that she would just as soon not have been the direct cause of their meeting one another. Because it had been by her invitation that Susan had gone with them to the hunt-club dinner where they had all three met Lewis for the first time.

She pulled her thoughts away from a direction in which they had been given no reason to wander, and fixed her attention on a conversation now concerned with land taxes. The taxes on Lewis's house had apparently just been raised.

"The county," Lewis was saying, "has applied the tax increase to this whole area in order to get me. And they've got me."

Lewis was quite right in what he said, because, apart from his own beautiful but rather overpowering split-level, the only other houses in that area were the empty brick house with the fan-light, and the small frame house across the road from it. For no other reason than that the small house was the single inhabited one anywhere near Susan's, Karen knew that a Mrs. Johnson, who was a widow, lived there with her little boy. Karen had seen Mrs. Johnson quite often, but she had never had any occasion to speak to her.

"The tax won't really hurt us," Susan said. "But it will probably be hard on Mrs. Johnson."

Lewis gave her a look so noncommittal, even for Lewis, that Karen found it odd. "Yes," he said, "it will be hard on Mrs. Johnson."

Without wishing to, Karen found herself weighing the possible implications of that look. Could Lewis have any interest in Mrs. Johnson? No, quite impossible. You had only to think of Mrs. Johnson's hard face and brassy hair to know that such an idea was utterly fantastic. And yet there was something there, although Susan did not seem to have noticed it.

Karen looked at Susan, at ease in a lounge chair. Susan was wearing a lime-green linen sheath that went well with her deeply tanned skin. Susan never fussed about clothes, but "sophisticated" was the first word you thought of when trying to describe her. If you had searched for a second word, your probable choice, if you knew her at all well, would have been "kind".

No man who had Susan would ever look at a Mrs. Johnson.

Nevertheless, it had not been her imagination. Lewis's face and voice had changed with the mention of Mrs. Johnson. Why? Some time she would know. Perhaps not for a long time. But some time she would know. Because she would not forget the incident. Rick often said that she noticed too much, and remembered too much.

When Karen and Rick left, they said good-bye to Susan and Lewis in the front hall. When Lewis was at home, you always said good-bye in the front hall. When Susan was alone, she came out to the driveway with you, no matter what kind of weather it was.

"Rick," Karen said, when they were in their car, "darling, it's too lovely to go straight home. Let's take the longer way, and go past Mrs. Johnson's and that beautiful old house."

"What about the kids?"

"They'll be all right. It isn't as if it were getting dark yet. And I happen to know that Carol wants to surprise us with something for supper that she read about in a magazine."

"We'll be poisoned," Rick said.

"No, we won't," Karen told him. "You know perfectly well that we won't. And you mustn't forget to be surprised. We have at least an hour before supper-time, and it's so lovely around here."

Rick put the car into gear. "All right, darling," he said.

"Drive slowly," Karen said. "I like to look at the trees."

"There are trees on Gavin Street."

"I know, but they're not the same. Somehow, they just aren't the same at all."

Rick did have a point there, however. That there were trees nearly everywhere was one of the nice things about Toronto. Even on streets like Gavin Street, there were trees.

Karen saw the "For Sale" sign before Rick did.

"Look!" she said. "Look, it's for sale. The house. The old house. Oh, darling, let's stop and go in!"

"We can try, if you like," Rick said. "But it will be locked up."

"It might not. It won't hurt us just to try the door."

Rick turned the car into the overgrown circular driveway, and stopped in front of a white-pillared portico from which the paint hung in weathered festoons. Seen at close quarters, the surface condition of the house was not nearly as good as it had appeared from the road.

When they came out at dusk an hour later, however, it was with the conviction that the house was basically sound in every way.

Rick, paying little attention to views from windows and the lay-out of rooms, had tested good oak flooring, examined chimney flues, and tracked rustless copper plumbing to its source in a basement cluttered with ancient refuse.

Karen, wearing the introspective look of someone who sees something that isn't really there, had wandered from room to room, placing imaginary furniture, hanging imaginary curtains, and allocating space as though they already owned the house. Six rooms upstairs. The big one next to the bathroom, with windows facing out across the road and through the branches of a huge maple, would be lovely for Rick and herself. The two south rooms would bring hours of sunlight into Carol's and Peg's days. The east rooms could be turned into a study and a guest room. And the small room at the head of the stairs would make an excellent sewing and hobby room.

Downstairs, she saw the front hall not as it was, dingy and papered in something that reminded her of old pond scum. She saw it with polished woodwork, a delicate crystal chandelier, and a gleaming waxed floor on which their small, richly coloured Bokhara rug would, she thought, look very well. They did have a few nice things, and the Bokhara rug was one of them. Clean the fanlight above the heavy front door, possibly re-lead the panes, distemper the walls in soft rose, and you would have a beautiful link between the large living-room on the left, and the panelled dining-room on the right. The panels, she realized vaguely, would have to be scraped down to the original wood to be fully recognizable as such.

The old-fashioned pantry at the back of the front hall and next to the kitchen could be made into a delightful breakfast-room, and there was space under the stairway where a second bathroom could be put in.

The kitchen was indisputably a horror, with its ancient sink somewhere around knee level, and cupboards that for the most part could only be reached with an extension ladder. But even here Karen was undismayed, because large windows looked out toward pine trees, open fields, and the ravine where she could see a corner of Susan and Lewis's house.

Meeting Rick in the front hall, absently brushing cobwebs out of her hair, she said, "It's divine, isn't it?"

"It's sound," Rick said.

"But don't you love it, darling?"

"That might be putting it a little strongly," Rick said.

"You're not a woman."

"I think somebody once pointed that out to me before."

"How much do you think they might want for it?" Karen asked.

"More than we could pay," Rick told her.

"We don't know that."

"Look, Karen my darling, we are only just out of debt for the first time in our married life. Don't talk nonsense."

"That's just what I'm getting at," Karen said. "We haven't any debts, so we're all right. You have a good job and could raise some money. From the bank, and the insurance, and things."

"All I'm likely to raise is hell, if you go on talking like this."

Karen smiled. "I like you when you raise hell, darling," she said. "Once we had the house, we wouldn't have to spend much. We're both pretty good with tools and paint-brushes."

It was getting quite dark in the empty hall. Much darker than it would have been if the fanlight had been clean.

"Do you really think you would be happy here, Karen?"

"I don't see how I could help it."

Ten days later they owed the bank $3,000 with interest at 5 per cent, and repayable at $50 a month. They had borrowed to the hilt on their life insurance, paying another 5 per cent for this privilege. They had assumed a $4,000 mortgage at 4½ per cent, principal payments and interest to amount to $32.18 monthly. By the time they had had the title searched, and had paid the lawyer who drew up the deed of purchase, they had something less than $200 in their joint account with which to face the winter.

But they had the house.

If Rick had any reservations as to the wisdom of what they had done, he kept them to himself. Karen, for her part, regarded the house as a talisman strong enough in itself to ward off all evil.

She never knew exactly what thing, or combination of things, had made Rick take the plunge. At the time, she was wise enough not to probe. Later, when she asked him, he quite honestly could not remember. Unlike herself, once he had come to a decision, Rick never went back to re-examine or question his motivation.

It might have been his own dislike of the dark, cramped apartment on Gavin Street, and his recognition of the hard fact that, somehow, he had to make his living conditions a better match for his job if he were to move ahead as he expected to. It might have been because Karen wanted the house so much. Or it might have been because he wanted to give Carol and Peg something better than a slit of a room scarcely big enough for one child, let alone two.

One thing, however, was quite certain. It was blind luck, rather than financial acumen, that led them to make one of the shrewdest real-estate deals of that year. For, although neither they nor anyone else guessed it at the time, they had bought a house and property that was to double its value within the year, and more than quintuple it in the succeeding ten years, during which Rowanwood became one of the wealthiest and most exclusive communities in the metropolitan area.

The snows were particularly heavy during that first winter in the house, but in spite of this Susan dropped in nearly every day. She could have come over in the station wagon, but she preferred to walk. Dressed in ski slacks, knee boots, and an old raccoon coat, she said she felt like one of those pioneer women. She kept looking over her shoulder, she said, to see if the covered wagon was keeping up with her.

Karen worked like a slave day after day, painting, carpentering, and scrubbing. She never allowed Susan to help her with any of these things, but after Susan left she always found that the beds had been made, and that there was a casserole in the refrigerator.

In March, when the snows were melting, Karen drove with Susan to Buffalo to buy drapery materials in the mill-end stores there. And it was Susan who found the chandelier for the front hall in a second-hand store on Queen Street. Susan liked second-hand stores and auction sales, and her advice was very useful.

With the coming of spring they went to work on the outside of the house. Karen was not fond of ladders, but she spent a great deal of time on ladders during that spring and summer. The house had been built with the kind of yellow brick that used to be so cheap, and later became so expensive. They decided to leave the pillars of the portico, and the window-frames, white, and to do the front door and the shutters in that dark blue that looks so well with yellow brick. It did look well. The effect was, in fact, very striking, and people driving past on Sundays would stop just to look at the house.

"I don't think I've ever been so happy," Karen told Rick. "We've got everything here, and Carol and Peg simply love it. I don't think I've ever been so happy."

During that period the house was Karen's life. Everything outside of it receded, became vague and of no particular importance. The cold war was like something she had read about in a history book. Mr. Abbot's refusal to do anything about personal income tax was only what she had expected, anyway. It was nothing to get excited about. Downtown Toronto was a foreign country which she invaded only when she had to, and then only because she needed something for the house. She noticed that they were at last widening Poplar Plains Road and Bathurst Street. She found stop lights at intersections where she did not expect them. And she saw that the city was acquiring a new dimension composed of ever-thickening TV aerials. But none of these things really meant anything to her.

Friends dropped in, of course, amongst them Barbara and Matt and their three children, and Fay and Roddie. One day Fay and Roddie brought a couple with them whose last name she forgot because she had been invited at once just to call them Millicent and Biff. They weren't, anyway, the kind of people she would ever be likely to know well.

Julia and Ned came out and disapproved of everything. The trouble with Karen, Julia said, was that she had run away. Later on, Julia told her that her trouble was a compulsion to mix with the Best People.

"Let's face it," Ned said. "Too many people have read *Mr. Blandings Builds His Dream House*."

The wonderful thing about the house was that it was not at all like Mr. Blandings' house. Architecturally perfect, it lent itself with beautiful docility to everything they wanted from it. It produced no hidden weaknesses, and gave them no headaches. The brick did not need pointing. The fireplaces, both in the living-room and in the upstairs study, drew beautifully. The basement was dry. And the woodwork throughout, put in when builders had consciences and did not use green lumber, was all that they could have hoped it would be.

If they had run into unexpected expenses, necessary ones, Karen did not know quite what they would have done, because what with the mortgage, and the bank debt, and the taxes, they were running very close to the line.

They took no holidays away from the house that summer, but they didn't mind this at all because things were going so well they felt they might, with luck and care, be able to afford the second bathroom by the following spring. And, anyway, they all thought that picnicking under the pines at the back of their property was just like a holiday. Once clear of the heavy twitch grass between the house and the pines, you could set up deck chairs and a folding table on a firm carpet of pine needles. To call this sea of twitch grass, which actually surrounded the whole house, a garden, was a euphemism that amused rather than disturbed them.

"It's heaven not to have to bother with a lawn," Karen said. "Just one of the wonderful things about living here, that we don't have to bother with a lawn."

The first bulldozer appeared a hundred yards up the road on a morning almost a year to the day after they had moved into the house. Shattering the quiet, greedily burrowing into soil that had lain undisturbed for decades, the compact yellow monster was in a great many ways the most horrifying thing Karen had ever seen.

She despised tears, and cried only very rarely, but she cried on that morning as she did not when, later, she could count as many as a dozen bulldozers at work on what were now the carefully measured lots of a subdivision which, they were told, was going to be called Rowanwood. At the same time they were told how lucky they were to have bought property in the middle of what was going to be such a desirable residential area.

Later they were told how lucky they were to have anything as solid and substantial as Millicent and Biff's cut-stone residence across the road from them, and Betsey and Harry's big ranch-style bungalow right next door to them on one side, and the Willoughbys' California redwood on the other side. Not that all the houses in Rowanwood, always with the exception of the

Johnson house, would not be in the same category, but they were particularly lucky in having the close neighbours they did, because they were the kind of people who would take a real interest in their grounds, who would have everything nicely landscaped almost before their houses were ready to move into. You could count on these people to keep up their hedges and their lawns.

Rowanwood grew like a bed of mushrooms after a heavy rainfall. It had to be seen to be believed.

Houses, hedges, lawns, even full-size trees, sprang up more or less overnight. Biff had two Japanese maples put in that must have been over thirty feet in height. Biff worked for a brokerage firm on King Street, and when Biff wanted trees, he got trees. It might take, as it did, nine men, two trucks, and a derrick to put in his trees, but he got them. It was all, he told you, a matter of getting the ball. Once you got the ball, he said, you just carried it for a touchdown. He said the same thing when he arranged to have a quarter of an acre of lawn laid in a single day. It was, he said, merely a matter of getting the ball and carrying it for a touchdown.

Everybody, which meant Millicent and Biff, and Betsey and Harry, and Fay and Roddie when they built, and half a hundred others, said how marvellous it must have been in Rowanwood when it was still just fields and cows and things. But they didn't mean it, any more than they meant it when they looked at Karen and Rick's half acre of twitch grass and said how nice it was to have some of the original atmosphere still left in Rowanwood.

The snows of Karen and Rick's third winter in what they now, as everyone else did, called Rowanwood, were melting under a hot spring sun when they sat down one evening to discuss a situation they could no longer ignore.

As long as the snow held, they knew they had nothing to make excuses about. The house, polished, painted, and waxed down to the last quarter inch, compared more than favourably with any house in Rowanwood, if you didn't count Susan and Lewis's house, which was in a class by itself. The second bathroom had been in for over a year. The converted pantry was a breakfast room whose whole south wall was composed of windows. The lined, floor-length curtains that Karen had made for every room were as good as anything you could get done by places like Ridpath's. They could, perhaps, have had more furniture, but what they did have was good. As a matter of fact, the house itself, apart from the living-room carpet which could have been better, had a charm denied the houses that had had to rely chiefly on money to lend them character.

As long as the snow held, everything was fine. When the snow went, and it was going fast now, everything would not be so fine.

For a time the twitch grass had not mattered too much, but the preceding summer Karen and Rick had, in spite of themselves, grown more and more uncomfortable about it. It was not that anyone had actually said anything. People weren't even talking about the original atmosphere any more, which was in itself a bad sign. Mr. Willoughby and his wife, who lived in the California redwood, never had said anything. Mr. Willoughby was a retired banker who belonged to the old school; he said nothing, but put in a hedge of Chinese Elm between their place and his. Chinese Elm, as everyone knew, was just about the fastest-growing thing you could get.

With the curtains drawn, and a fire in the living-room fireplace, Karen and Rick went over the seed catalogues for what could quite easily have been the fiftieth time.

"Darling," Karen said, "what in the hell are we going to do?"

"Damned if I know," Rick said.

"We could move," Karen said. "We could go somewhere else where we didn't have to try so hard."

"Do you want to move?"

"No," Karen said, "of course I don't. You know I don't, darling."

"I didn't think you did."

"We can't let ourselves be beaten by anything as futile as a lawn," Karen said. "Not after we've managed everything else."

"There's the office to consider, too," Rick said. "They've taken quite an interest in this place down at the office. They seem to think I've proved something or other by getting this place. Only the other day J. L. told me that he didn't use to think I was sufficiently money-conscious. He said that in business you have to be money-conscious, if you want to get on. He said it was a state of affairs that he, and Mrs. Syerson too, deplored, but that you couldn't get away from it."

"Oh, God," Karen said. "I can just see them over there in that no-period castle of theirs on Bayview, deploring it. It must give them something to do when they run out of amusements like counting the Georgian silver and fighting their way through the broadloom."

Rick laughed.

"All right," Karen told him, "laugh if you want to, but you can't tell me you feel so differently yourself."

"No," Rick said, "I don't feel any differently. But I don't wear myself out battling aspects of civilization that are here to stay, for the present at any rate. I can't change the face of North America, and I'm not going to try."

"As far as I can see," Karen said, "we can't afford to change one half acre of it, let alone the whole."

"Well," Rick said, "let's see where we stand again. Buying sod is out of the question. That much is definite."

"We might just afford to sod the section in front that's circled by the driveway," Karen said.

"Which would leave us without enough money to buy seed for the rest."

"And what good would seed do us, anyway?" Karen said. She flicked the edge of a catalogue with one finger. "There doesn't seem to be a grass seed so far known to man that will grow properly in solid clay. That's why everyone else around here has had sod put down. If you don't count people like Biff and Lewis, most of them would have used seed, at least in back, if they had thought it would take. Rick—darling, what are we going to do?"

"We'll think of something," Rick told her. "Like me to freshen up your drink for you?"

"No, thanks," Karen said. "A second one only depresses me. I'm depressed enough without that. Anyway, liquor costs money."

They were sitting on the big couch that they placed in front of the fireplace during the winter months. Rick reached over and took Karen's hand in his. "Don't worry so much, sweetheart. We'll think of something."

"You always say that, Rick."

"Well, we always have, haven't we?"

He was quite right. They always had. And they did this time, too.

It was the following morning when Karen, washing the breakfast dishes, thought of buckwheat. Without even waiting to dry her hands, she went to the telephone and called one of the seed stores.

Yes, the man at the seed store told her, it was quite feasible. People didn't usually go about a city lawn in that way, but it was certainly quite feasible. As a matter of fact, he said, if you went to the trouble of putting in buckwheat first, your soil, no matter what it was composed of, would become even more friable than if you used one of those new chemicals that were so extremely expensive. Also, though he wouldn't want to be quoted on this, he personally was still a little dubious about the chemicals. There had been a good deal of talk about the possibility that they might, in the long run, upset Nature's Cycle. Personally, he did not think a lawn was a sufficient justification for this.

As far as buckwheat was concerned, he said, you could do a lovely job with it, but it would involve some labour. The ground would have to be ploughed over before the buckwheat seed could be planted. Then when the buckwheat came up, it would have to be scythed, leaving a three-inch stubble, because it was the roots that did the job. Then the ground would have to be turned over again, so that the chemicals contained in the roots, and the earth they had affected, were spread in an even topsoil. Once you had got that far, he said, there was nothing to do but put in the grass seed, roll it well, and keep it constantly watered until the grass came up.

Yes, he said, you could do the whole operation in one season, if you started early enough. The buckwheat, planted early, would be ready to harvest in the beginning of August, and the lawn proper would be up before winter. Producing a buckwheat lawn, he said, certainly involved some labour, but if you cared to do it, you would have a better lawn than you could get in any other way. It would, he said, be like one of those English lawns you heard so much about.

"I don't know what made me think of it," Karen told Rick that evening when he came home. "I was doing the dishes, and I suddenly remembered hearing about buckwheat lawns. I don't know where I heard it, or when. It will come back to me later. Look, darling, go on into the living-room and say hello to the kids, and I'll be with you in a minute and tell you all about it. I just have to look at the roast."

"It sounds like one hell of a lot of work," Rick commented after she told him.

"It will be," Karen said. "But we haven't any choice."

"No," Rick said, "I don't suppose we have."

"You were right as usual," Karen told him. "We did think of something."

"Yes," Rick said, "but did it have to be this?"

Although Carol and Peg, still in their Waycroft uniforms, were lying on the floor in front of the fire, reading, Karen and Rick felt free to discuss their problem quite openly. Simply because they were making no secret of it, neither Carol nor Peg would pay any attention to their conversation. It was odd, Karen thought, that the four of them should live together and be as close as they all were, and still face such very different personal problems.

"Daddy," Peg said. "Daddy, what is 'an old bag'?"

"What is that child reading?" Rick asked.

"*Moulin Rouge*," Karen told him.

"I thought we agreed the kids shouldn't see it?" Rick said.

"That's right," Karen said. "It isn't our copy."

"Where did they get it, then?" Rick asked.

"From one of their friends," Karen said.

"What kind of friends have they? Why don't they spend more time with kids like Barbara's kids? You wouldn't catch any of Barbara's kids reading that sort of thing at the age of twelve."

"No," Karen said, "you're quite right, darling. You certainly wouldn't catch one of Barbara's kids reading that sort of thing, but only because they read it under the blankets at night. It was one of Barbara's kids who lent it to Peg, if you must know. It was Kitty."

"Can't you do anything about it?" Rick asked.

"No," Karen said, "I can't. Since they are obviously going to read that kind of thing, anyway, I prefer that they do it in a good light rather than under the blankets with a flashlight."

"You consider their eyes more important than their morals, I take it?" Rick said. But he was smiling.

Karen laughed. "You know that isn't true. But I'm not going to try and fight a whole era, any more than you are going to save J. L. from smothering in his own broadloom."

Carol raised her smooth dark head from *Treasure Island,* but she made no attempt to look virtuous, because they all knew that *Treasure Island* was part of her homework. Instead, she supported Peg by picking up the diversion Karen had created.

"Mummy," she said, "why should Mr. Syerson smother in his own carpet?"

"For the same reason that Daddy is going to plant a buckwheat lawn," Karen told her. "Because that's the way things are, and it would seem that we can't do anything about it. Now, are you satisfied?"

"No," Carol said.

Karen smiled. "I didn't expect you would be. But then who is? Come on, my loves, your dinner is ready."

Afterwards, whenever Karen and Rick talked about that summer, they referred to it as hell. Complete and unadulterated hell. But they were inclined to laugh when they said it, because it had had its amusing aspects.

At first it didn't really seem as if they had undertaken anything too overwhelming. In the beginning of May, they had a man plough in the twitch grass, both at the back and at the front of the house. Then they spread the buckwheat seed, raking it carefully to make sure it was even. It rained rather a lot during May, and in June the bare ploughed earth was covered with a delicate, pale-green shadow. The buckwheat, rather to their surprise, was coming up. And Rowanwood was taking an intense interest in it. Which did not surprise them.

"People are beginning to ask a great many questions," Karen told Rick one evening.

"Tell them to mind their own goddamned business," Rick replied.

"That," Karen said, "is exactly what we must not do. In fact, we must encourage them to ask even more questions, so they will go away with the answers we want, instead of answers they have been allowed to think up all by themselves. They mustn't get the idea that we are doing this because we are too broke to do anything else."

"Well," Rick said, "it's the truth, isn't it?"

"A truth which will do you no good at all downtown," Karen told him. "Give me a cigarette, will you, darling? This has got to be like Tom Sawyer and the fence. People have to be persuaded that it's a good idea, and that we would never have considered doing anything else. From now on we have to pretend that we believe in a buckwheat lawn the way an insurance salesman believes in twenty-pay-life."

"Are you being funny?" Rick asked.

"No," Karen said. "Unfortunately, I am not."

"When shall we two meet again? In buckwheat, hypocrisy, and in vain."

"There!" Karen said. "That's exactly what I mean. That's exactly the sort of thing you mustn't say, darling. You mustn't even think it."

"I think I'll go out and cut my own throat, in that case. It seems to be the only solution."

Even for Karen, it was not entirely easy to carry out the policy she had advocated. Too many people were taking too close an interest in the buckwheat. Nearly everybody in Rowanwood dropped by at one time or another to look at it—even people they had never spoken to before. As time went on, she began to feel like that man who showed you around out at the Dale Nurseries. Or that nice man from Sheridan's, Mr. Brown, who talked so knowledgeably about compost heaps and bone manure.

"Yes," she would say, "it is a bit unusual, but then that's probably because there are so few people who know that there's nothing like a buckwheat lawn. And then, too, in order to ensure the best results, you really have to do it yourself, and not everybody wants to do that. You really have to be on the spot all the time. To ensure the best results, you have to stay right with it."

The question she was most often asked, was, "Wherever did you get the idea?"

Very fortunately Karen had remembered where she got the idea.

"Where did we get the idea?" she would say. And she would say it very casually, as if this side of the project was relatively unimportant. "Oh, from an acquaintance of ours. Perhaps you know him? T. R. Ashton, president of Onoto Refining."

After hearing this, nobody ever questioned the good sense of the undertaking. Very few of them actually knew the president of Onoto Refining but they had all heard of him, and most of them had read about him in *Saturday Night*, on the "Who's Who in Business" page.

"T. R. Ashton is essentially a simple, friendly man," *Saturday Night* had begun. "A man who prefers to be known as Tom, even amongst his two thousand or so employees. Tom began life as a farm boy on a rocky Muskoka farm. Not far, as it happens, from the fifty-acre estate where he now spends his well-earned vacations with his wife and three children. You may wonder when a man of his achievements finds time for vacations. We wonder, ourselves. . . ."

What *Saturday Night* had very wisely refrained from mentioning was that this "Canadian son of the Canadian soil", who had accumulated his first million before he was thirty, had spent three years in the hands of a psychiatrist. It was during this period that he had planted and brought to fruition his buckwheat lawn. Though whether this had been a symptom of his disease, or occupational therapy as prescribed by the psychiatrist, Karen had never been able to find out.

After the early rains in May, that summer turned into one of the hottest and driest on record. Under a scorching sun the lawns in Rowanwood became sere and yellow, and every night after dark you could hear sprinklers going on all sides of you. The sprinklers were turned on only after dark because, in order to prevent a water shortage, the county had decreed that they should not be used at all. You saw buckets ostentatiously set out in front of the houses, but you never actually saw anyone using them. You just heard the sprinklers going like mad as soon as it became dark. The county must have suspected what was going on, because one day they shut the water off completely. They made the mistake, however, of turning it on again in the evening, so nobody minded too much. They just made jokes about having had to wash the baby in Haig and Haig, and set out their sprinklers as usual.

The only thing not adversely affected by the drought was the buckwheat. It thrived to such an extent that you felt you could almost see it growing. It went up by leaps and bounds, until toward the end of July Karen measured one stalk over four feet in height.

"Isn't it marvellous?" she said to Rick.

Rick, who had once spent a summer on a farm, was not at all sure that it was marvellous. "It's doing too well for our purposes," he said. "If it goes on like this that man won't be able to get his scything machine through it."

"Of course he will," Karen said. "Don't worry so much."

The man, when he came to scythe the buckwheat, took one look, and said, "Lady, I could no more get my rig through that stuff than I could get it through a brick wall. I ain't never seen nothin' like it. That stuff will have to be hand scythed. I never seen nothin' like it."

"Well, will you do it by hand, then?" Karen asked.

The man said he would not, and he said it in no uncertain terms. He had never, he said, worked with a hand scythe, and he was not going to cut off his leg at his time of life.

When she told Rick about this, she said, "It looks as if we will have to do it ourselves. Can you get a scythe somewhere?"

"I could, but I won't," Rick told her. "I'm not going to cut off my leg at my time of life."

"Then what are we going to do?" Karen asked.

"Spit on it," Rick said. He was getting pretty tired of buckwheat.

"I suppose we'll have to use the hedge clippers," Karen said.

"That's a hell of an idea," Rick said.

It was a hell of an idea, but they were unable to think of a better one. Clipping, clipping, clipping, three inches from the ground as you were supposed to do, Karen thought sometimes that her back would break in two. At nights they were both so stiff they could not sleep. And the continuing heat was no help. How little help it was, they realised fully only when they began the soul-destroying job of spading over the roots. Under cloudless skies, the clay soil, stripped of its protective fronds of buckwheat, presented a surface with a consistency very like that of iron. To go on pretending that they liked what they were doing was almost more than Rick and Karen could manage. The fact that once a clod was broken free, and turned over, the under-soil was invariably soft and crumbling, was very little comfort at that juncture.

Susan, dropping in one day, and finding as she usually did that Karen was at work spading, said, "Darling, for God's sake, how do you stand it?"

Methodically uprooting buckwheat stubble, Karen said, "I don't really know." With Susan she could be perfectly frank. "I think of that thing with peasant women in a field. The one Millet painted. I try to be sorry for them instead of for myself. You know the picture I mean."

"You mean 'The Gleaners'?" Susan asked.

"Yes," Karen said. "That's the one."

"Look," Susan said, "why don't you let me send the gardener over?"

"It's a nice idea," Karen said, "but unfortunately us peasants have our pride."

"Nuts," Susan said. "I'm serious, darling. Let me send him over. He's sitting in our garden right now doing damn-all. He seems to spend most of his time just sniffing the flowers. He's like Ferdinand the Bull. I don't know what possessed Lewis to take on a full-time gardener."

Karen straightened her aching back, and aimed a kick at a loose clod of earth. "I do," she said.

"Well then, don't be so stubborn, darling."

"No," Karen said. "It's impossible. If this were just between you and me, I'd say send him over this minute, and all his progeny, bastard and otherwise. He could bring a tent, too. But it isn't just you and me. It's Rick. And Lewis. You can see, yourself, why it's not possible, can't you, Susan?"

"No," Susan said, "I can't. But if you say so, I'll take your word for it."

"Susan," Karen said, "it's the middle of the morning and I am going in to pour myself a stiff drink. I may never do such a thing again in my life, so you'd better join me. Susan, did I ever happen to tell you that there's nothing like a buckwheat lawn?"

One day the company president, J. L. Syerson, stopped by to look at what they were doing. If it had not been for this Rick would almost certainly have said to the devil with buckwheat lawns, and given the undertaking back to nature just as it stood.

J. L. had begun by being critical, in a polite way. Perhaps because it was Karen, rather than Rick, who happened to talk to him, he ended up by becoming really interested.

Karen knew how to convince J. L. that what she and Rick were doing was a very sensible thing to do, while at the same time making it clear that it would be a most unsuitable thing for a man in J. L.'s position to even dream of doing. She was able to make him see that, in spite of the work involved, she and Rick had too much discrimination to be satisfied with anything less than the best, no matter what it cost them. She made him see that there was nothing like a buckwheat lawn.

After that they had no choice. They had to continue with it because J. L. fell into the habit of cruising past in his new Lincoln to see how they were getting on. Their lawn, Rick told her, had become one of the topics in the directors' dining-room. In the directors' dining-room at lunch-time, Rick said, they were now talking about buckwheat lawns more often than they talked about farmers' daughters and travelling salesmen. It was, he said, just a matter of time before the two topics meshed. Before the travelling salesman and the farmer's daughter did what they always did, in a field of buckwheat rather than in a barn.

From then on they were able to laugh again.

The day they finished rolling in the grass seed, the day when there was nothing left to do but leave things to heaven and their sprinkler, they celebrated by drinking a whole bottle of champagne between them. Not, of course, the expensive imported kind. The domestic kind.

"Darling," Karen said, "it's hard to believe, but you know there was a time this summer when we almost lost our perspective."

"It's a question," Rick said, "whether we ever had any."

"You'll see," Karen told him. "You wait and see. Next spring we'll have the best damn lawn in Rowanwood. And all for fifty-seven dollars and ten cents."

"You're forgetting what we paid the man who did the ploughing for us."

"All right, darling," Karen said. "Sixty-seven dollars and ten cents."

"I'll believe it when I see it," Rick said.

"You'll see it," Karen told him. "Rick darling, have I ever told you how much I love you?"

The grass was showing thick and even that fall. By the following spring it was, beyond a shadow of doubt, the best lawn in Rowanwood. Not only the neighbours, but the Sunday drivers, would stop to look at it. And Mr. Willoughby next door, still without saying anything, had a man in to clip the Chinese Elm hedge so that when you were standing up you could see over it.

Later that year, some people went even further than that. In parts of Rowanwood, perfectly good lawns were torn up to be replaced by buckwheat lawns, because, as the people who did this explained to other people, there's nothing like a buckwheat lawn.

6 Right in the middle of Loblaw's

The carpet had reached the archway, and Karen stepped back. The years had caught up with her again.

"That the way you want it, lady?" the big man asked.

"That's perfect," Karen said. "Thank you so much. It's really perfect."

"Nothing to it," the big man said. "Just as long as you're satisfied."

"Would you like some beer?" Karen asked. "I have some beer on ice if you'd like it."

"Don't mind if I do." He looked at the smaller man. "How about you, pal?"

"A beer would go good," the smaller man said. He seemed to have sweated even more than his companion had. It really was fiendishly hot. Almost as hot as the summer when they had done the lawn.

The men came to the kitchen for their beer. They seemed more at ease there. "This is a nice lay-out you got here, lady," the big man said. "Lot of people, they'd give their eye-teeth for a lay-out like you got here."

Tell them to bring their eye-teeth around, Karen thought. We might arrange a deal. "I'm glad you think so," she said.

"Yeah," the big man said, "you've got it good in this here Rowanwood. Like you might say, you've got everything."

Everything and nothing, Karen thought. Everything and nothing. "Will you have some more beer?" she asked. "There's lots."

"No, thanks, lady," the big man said. "We got a truck-load to get rid of before noon. Thanks just the same, though."

"Thanks," the little man said. "Good day, lady."

"Good day, lady," the big man said.

"Good-bye," Karen said. "And thank you again."

"Think nothing of it," the big man said. "That there carpet, if I may say so, looks real good in there. It is, like you might say, the finishing touch."

As she closed the door behind them, and turned back to the archway to look at the carpet, Karen thought, he put it very nicely. He probably doesn't know it, but he put it very nicely. It is, as he said, the finishing touch. It is the end of something, without being the beginning of anything else.

I suppose I had better run the vacuum over it. Rick will guess that I'm not too interested in it, if I don't clean off those bits.

Automatically she fitted the parts of the vacuum together, the one the salesman had said would do her work for her. In a sense, the salesman had been right. The vacuum did do a great deal of physical work which she had once had to do herself. But in doing this it robbed her of the extra initiative demanded by mop, and broom, and duster. It left her mind completely empty. It made her into a robot which might just as well have been one of the chrome and rubber fixtures of the machine itself.

It was the same with the Mixmaster. "Just put all the cake ingredients into the bowl at once." You no longer had to remember that butter and sugar should be blended before adding the eggs and the balance of the sugar, and, after that, milk and sifted dry ingredients alternately. "Anyone can bake a superb cake." This was perfectly true. Neither the makers nor their sales staff had anything with which to reproach themselves. Anyone could bake a superb cake. You were saved labour. You were saved time. And for what? So that you could go down to the basement and do laundry which, if you had had any sense, you would have sent out. It wouldn't have cost you any more to send it out. In fact, if you were a victim of psychological obsolescence where household appliances were concerned, it would in the long run cost you less to send your laundry out.

Rick had been so pleased when they could finally afford an electric washing machine, and soon after that an electric dryer.

Instead of soaking and scrubbing, and lifting wet masses of clothes from one tub to another and back again, you just threw it all in the Bendix, pushed a few buttons, and—presto—it was all done for you, fluff-dried, much better than you had ever seen it before. It had, as the manufacturers had told you it would, saved you a great deal of time and effort. For what? So that you could go back upstairs and bake another superb cake? If you didn't, you would do something else very much like it, because to be "All the Things You Are" you really had to keep moving. You couldn't afford to waste all the valuable time you were saving on anything as futile as just being yourself.

There, Karen thought, as she looked the carpet over to make sure she had missed no particle of dust, that's done.

She stooped to pick up the vacuum, and was aware of the pain in her side again. Biting her lip, she thought, I am not going to tell Rick about the appointment with Dr. Lowe. When he asks if there was anything interesting in the mail today, I'll just tell him about the letter from Planesville, and the one from Montreal. What had she done with the Montreal one? She had had it in her hand when the men arrived with the carpet, and then—now she remembered. It had fallen behind the table in the hall.

She had to move the table to get at it. This meant stooping again, but this time there was no pain. Briefly she considered leaving it for Rick to open, since she was sure it was no more than a follow-up letter after their last stay at the Mount Royal Hotel. Then, shrugging, she opened it because it was, after all, addressed to her.

There was only a single sheet, and Karen, reading it in a glance, sank slowly on to the chair beside the telephone. Cyr—she thought. Cyr. It can't be. But it is.

If there had been any doubt about the signature, the content of the letter would have effectively banished that doubt. It was typically Cyr as she had known him so long ago. Undated, unplaced save for the printed letter-head, the note—for it was no more than that—was brief to the point of curtness. There never had been any hearts and flowers in Cyr's rare letters. Their value had lain solely in the fact that he had bothered to write at all.

Will be lunching at the corner of Holton and Yonge next Monday at twelve noon. Do you want to see me?

Cyr

Just that. After more than twenty years. No "Dear Karen". No "I hope you are well", or "I am well". Just "I will be lunching . . .". In effect, take it or leave it. Its value lay solely in the fact that he had written it at all.

As slowly as she had sat down, Karen stood up and went to the kitchen for her shopping list and her purse. Her heart might, for an instant, have stopped beating, but that was no reason why her day should stop. Even with Cyr's letter in her pocket, she still had to go to Loblaw's.

Rick had run the car out into the driveway for her before he left. Twice a week he left the car at home and went downtown with Barbara's husband, Matt.

When she got into the car, she turned all the windows down. Rick had parked it in the shadow of the big maple, but even so it was like an inferno inside. With a detached portion of her mind she noted that Boris's car was still outside Millicent's house, and that Mrs. Johnson was apparently going to stay in bed all morning. Which, on the whole, was sensible of her since she worked in the evenings. Pete, who had started at Upper Canada the previous autumn, did not come home to lunch as he had done when he attended the school in Rowanwood.

That Pete should be at Upper Canada College at all was something that Rowanwood could not quite believe. There had been a great deal of speculation about how Mrs. Johnson could afford to send him. Various answers had been put forward, not all of them kind, and some of them frankly libellous.

Karen drove the car out of the driveway and on to the road, while she tried to evoke a mental picture of the corner of Holton and Yonge. In this she was only partially successful, because since the subway had been built it was a part of Yonge Street that she rarely saw. It seemed to her that she had noticed a restaurant, a fairly new one, on the north-west corner, but its appearance persisted in remaining vague. It was not one of the chain restaurants; she was certain that if it had been a Child's, or something like that, she would have remembered.

Annoyed, she thought, why in the devil couldn't he have given the place a name? Why couldn't he have chosen somewhere like Town and Country, so that I could have felt oriented? Almost immediately she saw several reasons why he had not done this. He had chosen, in so far as was possible without any knowledge of her habits, a place where she would belong as little as he did, and where they could meet—*if* they met—on neutral territory. He had also, in all probability, tried to select a place where she would not be recognized. This, of course, was ridiculous, because naturally if she accepted the invitation she would tell Rick about it in advance.

The plaza parking area was, as she had expected, crowded. To cruise up and down the lanes directly outside Loblaw's, as most people did, was to waste time. With a slight shrug, she backed the car into an empty parking space not far from the road, but she did not immediately get out of the car.

How, she wondered, would she introduce the subject of the letter from Cyr? It should, she thought, be done very casually. She could, for instance, say, "By the way, Rick, I had a letter from a man I once knew, inviting me to—" No. That wouldn't do.

She might say, "I had rather a surprise this morning. One of those things you hear about, but don't expect—" That did not strike the right note either, and invited speculation as to just what you did hear about.

"You probably won't remember my speaking of Cyr who—" Rick most certainly would not remember for the very simple reason that she never had spoken about Cyr. Rick would know this, too. So that was out.

"An old flame—" That, indubitably, was the worst of all. Apart entirely from the fact that it was self-conscious to a degree, it simply was not a way in which to describe Cyr. It was all wrong.

Both irritated and surprised, Karen began to see that it could not be done casually at all. The very circumstance that she had never mentioned Cyr placed a most disturbing emphasis on the omission, because at one time and another she had told Rick almost everything she could remember about anyone or anything.

There had, she remembered, been no difficulty in telling Rick three or four years ago who John Steinberg was, and explaining that he had been in Geneva at the same time she was. When John had telephoned, she had asked him up to dinner without a moment's hesitation, and it had been a very nice evening. Because John had known Susan, too, Susan and Lewis had come over after dinner and it had turned into a party.

Old friends did reappear out of the past. There was nothing odd about such a thing. With people moving about all over the world as they now did, it would be odd if it didn't happen quite often.

Could she perhaps use John Steinberg's visit as a parallel, and say, "Another old friend—" She knew she couldn't, because inevitably she would then have to explain who Cyr was. To explain Cyr to Rick, or to anyone else for that matter, would be quite impossible because, as Susan had once said, it had been the damnedest relationship.

Karen reached for the dashboard lighter, pressed it harder and longer than was necessary, and lit a cigarette. As a situation it was, or appeared to be, too trite. It had a *c'est la vie* Hemingway flavour that was a bit much. It made you think of lean, dark men, becoming grey at the temples, who had Never Forgotten.

Cyr might be lean and dark—he might even be grey at the temples, and he had quite obviously not forgotten, but as a description indicating a state of mind Karen was quite certain that it did not fit at all. He had undoubtedly changed since she last saw him, but he would not have changed that much.

It was, she found, one thing to tell herself that he must have changed with the passage of years. It was another thing to believe it. Until this morning, like a photograph catching a likeness destined to remain forever static, he had stayed in his early twenties, and had stayed in Geneva. Now, suddenly, he was nowhere—neither here nor there; and Karen almost, but not quite, wished that he had stayed where he was, securely anchored to the past where he belonged. The next time I look in the mirror, she thought, I won't be able to prevent myself from wondering if he would find me much changed.

Was she going to see him? As yet she did not know. What Cyr had said was, take it or leave it. There was a fair chance she would leave it. Her life was already complicated enough without adding further complications. And Cyr, any way you looked at it, was a complication.

She threw her cigarette, half smoked, out on to the asphalt because the car ash-tray was, as usual, full to overflowing. Then she reached over the back of the seat for her shopping-bag, and got out of the car.

She threaded her way in and out amongst parked cars, the movement of her skirt bringing an illusion of coolness to her bare legs. Cyr—she thought. Cyr. It had been, as Susan had said, the damnedest relationship. His letter today, though, was the damnedest thing of all.

She ran into Fay at the frozen-food counter. She had hoped to get through quickly, without meeting anyone she knew. But with the whole of Rowanwood doing its shopping at the Plaza, this was next to impossible.

Fay had dark circles under her eyes. She looked as if she had not slept much, and as if she probably had a hangover. Which she often did.

"Angel," Fay said, "will you come to a bridge for New Canadians?"

"I can't," Karen said. "I've taken a table myself."

"Oh, God," Fay said. "You're the fourth one. I took two tables. God knows why."

"Millicent probably knows why," Karen told her. "She probably talked you into it."

"She probably did," Fay said. "I don't know why I'm always letting people talk me into things."

Including into bed, Karen thought, as she picked out two frozen turkey pies. The pies would make a quick, light dinner before they went down to Julia and Ned's. Rick never wanted much to eat if he was going out afterwards.

"Oh, God," Fay said. "Did you notice if they had any canned

sweet potatoes today, angel? They're always running out of canned sweet potatoes."

"No," Karen said. "I'm sorry, Fay, I didn't notice."

Fay, she saw, had eight TV dinners in her wire push-cart. Fay never served anything in her house that was not pre-cooked. If it was not frozen, it came out of cans.

"They're always running out of canned sweet potatoes," Fay said again. "Karen, what would you do, if you were me?"

It was characteristic of Fay that she would choose to ask you what to do with her life while you were standing right in the middle of Loblaw's with people crowding past you from both sides. She was not asking what you would do if you were unable to get canned sweet potatoes. She was asking you what you would do if you had her problem.

Fay might be ready to discuss her private life in public, but Karen felt it was scarcely the place in which to tell Fay that drinking, and sleeping with other women's husbands, was no answer to anything. At one time, Karen had guessed that there was something between Fay and Harry Milner. She had been worried about Fay then, because Betsey was a woman who, if she had discovered this, would have crucified Fay in open court. Roddie, of course, would not have minded much. There was that to be said for being married to a man like Roddie.

"You've never thought of leaving Roddie, have you, Fay?"

"No," Fay said. "I couldn't leave him. He can be awfully sweet, Karen. You don't know how sweet he can be."

"Well," Karen said, "I can't help you. I wish I could, but I can't."

Sometimes Fay had the most extraordinary flashes of insight. "It was always too late for me, wasn't it, angel? It was always too late. Right from the beginning."

Karen felt very uncomfortable, and it was obvious that the stout woman beside them, the one who was choosing some fillet of sole, was listening. "Don't say that, Fay," she said. "Don't even think it."

"I don't often," Fay said. The bright, white, artificial light in Loblaw's made the circles under her eyes look almost black.

"Well, don't *ever* think it," Karen said. "In time things may work out."

"Yes," Fay said, "in time things may work out. In another twenty or thirty years, everything may be all right. That is if I don't bitch things up completely in the meantime."

"I wish I could help you," Karen said.

"You can't, angel," Fay said. "Nobody can."

There didn't seem to be any answer to this. It was true. The only way in which anyone had ever been able to help Fay was to get her out of a mess after she had got into it. You could never stop her beforehand, any more than she seemed able to stop herself. All you could do was hope that the mess would not be too bad a one.

"It isn't," Fay was saying, "as if I was in love with Matt, or anything like that. I'm not."

At first Karen was so shocked she could not speak. Then she said, "Oh, no, Fay! Oh, no! You can't be mixed up with Matt!"

"Didn't you know?" Fay asked. "I thought you knew. You always do know things. You knew about Harry. You never said so, but I was sure you knew."

The stout woman had moved off. For the moment there was no-one else close to them.

"Fay," Karen said, "you couldn't be doing a thing like that to Barbara. Even you couldn't do such a thing."

"That's what I keep telling myself," Fay said. "I keep telling myself that even I couldn't be that bad. But nobody knows about it. I thought you knew because you always do know things. But nobody else would know."

"You can't be sure of that."

"Don't hate me, Karen," Fay said. "Please don't hate me, angel. I don't think I could bear it if you hated me. It would never have happened if Barbara didn't go to Cape Cod for three months every summer with her kids. It's Barbara's fault for going to Cape Cod."

With Fay it was always somebody else's fault. Karen suddenly felt horribly tired. "Fay," she said, "if you go on with this, I will hate you."

"I won't," Fay said. "I won't go on with it, if you'll just promise not to hate me."

"I wish I could believe you," Karen said.

"Oh, you can, angel," Fay said. "Really you can. As I told you, it isn't as if I were in love with Matt."

Fay always had been an awful liar. You wanted to believe her, but you knew you couldn't. You knew, too, that you would never hate her. You felt sick on Barbara's account, but to have hated Fay would have been like hating a child for taking a piece of somebody else's candy. And you could see that, in part, it really was Barbara's fault for concentrating on her children to the exclusion of everything else, including her husband.

Looking back, you could see that Barbara had never, except in the early years of her marriage, been a wife. She had been, first and last really, a mother. You had considered her wrong in this, but you had thought Matt didn't mind it too much. Now that you knew he had minded, you could see how it had happened. Fay alone nearly every night. Matt alone all summer. And the two adjoining gardens with no fence between because Fay didn't care about a garden, and Barbara had wanted more space for her kids to play in. Matt had not wanted the fence taken down. He had said that he liked some privacy, and that the kids had plenty of space, anyway. But the fence had been taken down because Barbara wanted more space for her kids.

Matt had not seen why Barbara had to go to Cape Cod every summer. Rowanwood, he had said, was not, admittedly, the sea shore, but it was still a pretty good place for children in the summertime. After all, he had said, that was why they had built in Rowanwood, wasn't it? Because the kids could play in the ravine where there was a stream, and because they would have a large garden. Barbara, however, had felt there was a serious lack of iodine in the Toronto air, and that three months by the sea, where there was plenty of iodine in the air, was essential to the children's health.

"I must go," Fay said, "or there won't be any canned sweet potatoes left. You aren't hating me, are you, angel?"

"No," Karen said, "I'm not hating you."

Why, Karen thought, do I always have to see two sides to everything? Why do I have to see that Barbara asked for this? She doesn't deserve it. But she asked for it, because Matt was—and probably still is—in love with her. He would never have even looked at another woman if she had spared him a reasonable amount of attention. Is there any way in which I can get her to stay home this summer? I can't do anything with Fay. Nobody can do anything with Fay. Somehow, I simply have to persuade Barbara to stay home this summer, though right now I wish I never had to see either of them again.

"Well," Fay said, "good-bye, angel. It was nice seeing you."

"Good-bye, Fay," Karen said.

"And don't worry, angel," Fay said. "It only happens in the summertime, anyway."

She is, Karen thought, just like the girl who said she was only a little bit pregnant. She has always been like the girl who was only a little bit pregnant.

Karen, if she had not been lost in thought, would never have allowed herself to be caught next to Barbara in the same line-up for the same cashier's desk. Once she realized what she had done, it was too late to do anything about it. The stout woman who had chosen fillet of sole was already behind her, blocking any reasonable retreat, and Barbara, ahead of her, had turned and seen her.

"Karen," Barbara said, "how fortunate, darling. I was going to call you later. I've taken a table for the bridge for New Canadians, and I'm counting on you to play."

Karen laughed. It was a relief to be able to laugh just then. "Barbara," she said, "I'm sorry, but it looks as if the only people who haven't taken tables must be New Canadians."

Barbara made a face. She looked very attractive doing it, and very young. "Millicent always over-sells," she said. "Millicent never knows when to leave well enough alone."

"I think that's right," Karen said.

"And she doesn't spend enough time with her children," Barbara said. "She should spend more time with her children, instead of always selling things to people."

Even as far back as the days on Elmdale Avenue, you could have, if you had thought about it, seen Barbara's future pattern. Even when she was climbing a high board fence, with her smooth, blonde hair falling across her eyes, you could have seen that she was going to be a Mother.

"Very few people spend enough time with their children," Barbara said.

If Mr. Wilcombe had spent any time at all with Fay, it might have helped. Then again, it might not have, because Mr. Wilcombe, although he had been such a nice man, would not have had the slightest idea what to say to her.

"Barbara," Karen said, "are you going to Cape Cod again this summer?"

"Of course," Barbara said. "Otherwise the children would go short on iodine."

"Matt isn't too lonely without you?"

"Oh, no," Barbara said. "He has the garden. That keeps him occupied."

There were, Karen noticed, no canned goods in Barbara's cart. It was full of fresh vegetables and fresh fruits.

"Do you often buy those frozen pies?" Barbara was asking.

"Not often."

"I'm glad to hear that, darling," Barbara said. "They have no vitamins in them. Absolutely no vitamins at all. I would never dream of serving them to the children. Of course, with just Rick to consider now, it's a little different for you. Still, I wouldn't advise you to buy them often."

"I don't," Karen said.

"I'm glad to hear that," Barbara said.

Barbara looked as if she had had eight hours of dreamless sleep. There were no circles under her clear, blue eyes. She looked as if, in spite of the heat, she had probably done her setting-up exercises as usual. She often told you that she never missed her setting-up exercises because they helped her to keep up with the children at tennis and badminton. Matt, she told you, didn't do exercises, which was why he couldn't keep up with the children.

"By the way," Barbara said, "Julia asked us down tonight."

"That's nice," Karen said. "I didn't know she was asking you."

"Yes, she did. But I'm afraid we can't go. Tommie has the flu, and I don't think we should leave him. It isn't anything serious, but still you never know, and I don't think we should leave him."

"Couldn't Kitty look out for him?" Karen asked. "After all, she's eighteen now. She ought to be able to look out for him."

"Well," Barbara said, "she could. But you never can tell."

"Barbara," Karen said, "your children are growing up, you know."

"Yes," Barbara said, "I know. They're very companionable now."

Barbara had missed the point completely. She was busy laying her vitamins out on the counter. To anyone else they probably looked like cauliflower, carrots, asparagus, strawberries, and rhubarb.

Karen glanced over her shoulder, but she could see no sign of Fay. The canned sweet potatoes were near the back, and Fay was tiny.

"Barbara," she said, "are you sure Matt isn't lonely without you during the summer? Mightn't it be nicer for him if you found some place where he could join you at least on the week-ends?"

"He has the garden," Barbara said. And it was obvious that she was thinking of vitamins, and not about Matt.

She needs to be hit over the head, Karen thought. But I can't hit her over the head in Loblaw's. Not even metaphorically. Why did I ever come into this damn place this morning? Why couldn't I have had the sense to stay home with my own worries? But even while she thought this, and while she was looking for her change purse, she knew that she didn't really mean it. She knew that if she could do anything at all to save Barbara's marriage, she would do it. Barbara had been her friend ever since she could remember. Barbara had know Elmdale Avenue as she herself had known it. Elmdale Avenue not as it now was, a street of boarding-houses with garbage cans at the kerb, but as it had been when they were children. A street, well cared for, flower beds in front of the houses, where people lived a pleasant, leisurely life to which the adjective "gracious" could properly be applied.

When she got out to her car, and had tipped the man who had helped her to carry her groceries, Karen found that she was thinking of Elmdale Avenue, and a time when neither she nor Barbara had had any troubles that could not be forgotten between one day and the next. A time when their greatest anxiety was whether or not they could get out of the house without wearing their rubbers.

As she leaned forward to switch on the ignition, the letter from Cyr, still in her pocket, crackled slightly. But she did not notice it, because she was thinking about Elmdale Avenue.

7 | Everything was very personal in those days

Elmdale Avenue, when she and Barbara were children, had been a lovely street to live on. Toronto itself, in spite of what the rest of Canada seemed to think of it, had been a lovely city to live in. At that time nobody would have dreamed of calling it the New York of Canada.

Everything was very personal in those days.

You dealt at little shops where you were known. In a way, the people who kept these shops were friends. You would never know them socially, but you nevertheless knew them a great deal better than some of the people who came to Sunday tea. The chain stores, in defeating these small private enterprises, later robbed you of a whole stratum of society and a measure of shopping convenience you were never to know again.

Right up until nine o'clock at night, Mr. Minelli, or one of his boys, had been ready to run over with anything you had forgotten to order earlier, like a pound of butter, or that special English marmalade without which breakfast was not really breakfast. Mr. Scott, at the drug store, always kept a copy of *Good Housekeeping* for you, and when you started buying cigarettes it was unnecessary to ask him not to advertise the fact. Without being told, Mr. Scott knew perfectly well that you smoked them out your window at night after your light was off.

The Chinese laundry, which did your things when your own laundress was sick, knew just how much starch to use. And when, occasionally, you went in there, you experienced a pleasantly terrifying never-the-twain-shall-meet feeling. When you were very young, you hoarded scraps of paper with Chinese characters on them that could have meant anything. That they should represent merely a list of shirts and sheets and underwear was obviously ridiculous. Actually, Karen's father believed—and there was nothing to disprove this—that some highly uncomplimentary remarks were mixed in with the sheets and shirts and underwear.

In those days all the stores delivered right to your back door. Their small trucks and horse-drawn carts were a part of the life of the street. A life that finally disappeared overnight. Like the age of the dinosaurs, it simply ceased to exist, and for no reason that you could put your finger on. It did not move on to another neighbourhood, although vestigial remains could be found south of College Street. It simply vanished.

Afterwards, you wondered where they had all gone to, all those people who had been such an integral part of street life as distinct from the life of the houses that lined the street.

There was the banana-man, his two-wheeled hand-cart piled high with bananas and nothing else, who passed slowly up Elmdale Avenue on Tuesdays and Fridays. He never left the road. You went to the curb to do business with him, warned in advance of his coming by the strident call of "Bananari-i-ipe!"

In June there was a man whom you knew less well because his season was short. "Strawberryri-i-ipe!"

There was a knife-grinder with a whetstone operated by a pedal. Karen's father always said that he took too much off the blades, and that the knives should be sent downtown. They never were. In part because it was easier to take them to the curb, and in part because to have done anything else would have been traitorous.

Whenever he carved a roast, Karen's father would say, "That damned man takes too much off the blades."

Karen's mother would smile. "I know he does. I believe you've mentioned it before, dear."

"Then why not send them out?"

"In the future I will, dear," Karen's mother would say.

But she never did. And Karen's father never really insisted that she should. He would have felt traitorous, too.

You bought your firewood from the street as a matter of course. You knew that, as soon as the chilly weather began, the woodman would be along. You counted on him, and he never let you down. "Dry woo-oo-ood!"

Toward the end of September, when fallen leaves were drifting across the street, and it occurred to you that it might be nice to have a fire in the drawing-room or the library, the wood was always there in the house.

"Have we got something with which to light a fire?" Karen's father would ask.

"Yes," her mother would reply. "The man came last week."

"Dry woo-oo-ood!" He never let you down.

You even, in a sense, did business with the rag-and-bone man. He would take anything that the garbage-man refused to take. He would, in fact, take anything.

Perched like a bundle of rags and bones himself on top of an unsavoury mass of refuse, he would move slowly up the street, taking an occasional swipe at his spavined horse with a desiccated whip. You did not like the rag-and-bone man, but you tolerated him. He had his uses. And he was part of the life of the street.

Karen never felt that Carol and Peg had missed anything too essential in not knowing a banana-man, or a knife-grinder, or a rag-and-bone man. She did feel they had missed a great deal in being born too late to know a hurdy-gurdy man. "O Sole Mio" and "Santa Lucia" had a certain something, never captured in any other way, when they were ground out of a large green box by a swarthy little man with a monkey on his shoulder. A monkey who carried a small metal cup into which you were only too glad to put a few coppers. The hurdy-gurdy man had a big smile and even bigger moustaches and wore gold earrings. Years later, when you were in Naples, you were vividly reminded of him. But you never heard "O Sole Mio" played quite like that again. Even in Naples. Even Lanza never moved you in quite the same way that the hurdy-gurdy man had when you and Barbara put coppers in the monkey's little cup.

The peanut-man survived, much longer than most, an evolutionary tide that would in time sweep him away too. He announced his coming with a small, shrill steam whistle, peculiarly audible to the very young. You always heard him in time to run into the house and get a nickel from your piggy-bank. You were allowed to buy peanuts, but not the hot buttered popcorn, which, you were told, was very indigestible. Since you never had indigestion—perhaps because you were not allowed to eat things like hot buttered popcorn—you felt you were being most unfairly discriminated against. Barbara, who was not allowed to eat popcorn either, felt just the way you did about this.

Neither you nor Barbara could see why you were forbidden to do so many things that the kids on the other side of the street could do. At the time, you and Barbara did not understand that the only thing the two sides of Elmdale Avenue had in common was the life of the street itself. All you could see was that the kids on the other side seemed to have a lot more fun than you did. They did not, for instance, have to come in off the street when it got dark. From your bedroom window, you could see them playing jacks or hop-scotch under the street-lamps until after ten o'clock at night. Neither the boys nor the girls across the street had to change for dinner, the way you and Barbara did. True, they were not served little iced cakes in their back gardens at tea-time, from a table set with family silver and a Madeira lace cloth. Their fathers did not take them for Sunday walks in the country, and they were not treated to the Christmas pantomimes at the Royal Alexandra. But you were inclined to forget these things when you saw them stealing slivers of ice off the back of the ice-wagon, and hooking rides on the Eaton and Simpson carts.

The only thing you and Barbara were allowed to do was to give sugar to the policeman's horse. The policeman and his horse were both magnificent creatures, the embodiment of law and order, as they paced in slow majesty up Elmdale Avenue at mid-morning, and again at mid-afternoon. The policeman and his horse were so much a part of one another that, if you thought about it, you were forced to imagine them coming to your rescue as one. You saw them galloping up the verandah steps in much the way the young blades of the Georgian era galloped their horses up the steps of St. Paul's.

Perhaps because you and Barbara were the only kids of your age on your side of the street, you could spend the night with Barbara as often as you liked, either at her house next door or at your own. On these occasions you did not, of course, go to bed as you were supposed to.

In the wintertime you put a blanket across the crack under your door and turned on the light again so that you could read *True Romance* and *True Confession* magazines that you had borrowed from the maids.

In the summertime you put your light out because it was more interesting to watch the kids across the street than it was to read *True Romance*. And as you got older, you and Barbara began to understand that those kids were not quite as lucky as you had once thought they were. They were, however, even more interesting to watch, and to listen to, than they had been. And you still envied them. But not so actively as before. Until long after midnight you could hear the gramophone, the wind-up kind, playing on the Geralds' covered verandah. You could hear giggles and shrieks, and in the darkness the protesting creak of a verandah swing. And sometimes you would see a girl running through the pool of light under a street-lamp, a boy after her.

> Can't go on,
> Everything I had is gone,
> Stormy weather . . .

To you and Barbara, only a little younger than those kids across the street, it was all very glamorous, but at the same time vaguely frightening. It was as if shadows, darker than those cast by the maples that lined Elmdale Avenue, hung over the kids across the street. It was as if next time some of them ran, giggling, through the light under the street-lamp where they had once played jacks, they would go into a darkness from which they might not come back. And you felt that perhaps it had not been such a bad thing, after all, to be forbidden to eat ice off the back of the iceman's cart.

8 | Don't get so excited, darling

Because she had been thinking about Elmdale Avenue, the suburban quiet of Rowanwood seemed oppressive to Karen as she swung her car into her own driveway. A bluejay flew out of the maple, tearing the noonday hush with a cry as strident as his plumage was beautiful. But when he had gone, a flash of brilliant blue against a heat-struck sky drained of colour, there was nothing left to break the silence but the distant hum of a power mower.

She carried an armful of groceries into the house, and left the front door standing open because she would have to make two more trips.

Somehow, she thought, I must find a way of doing something about Barbara and Matt. It's none of my business really, but I can't stand aside, doing nothing, while she smashes up her life. If she does, she might just as well have eaten ice off the back of the iceman's cart. It won't have done her any good not to.

Susan might be able to help. She would, she decided, talk it over with Susan when she came around to look at the carpet.

Susan arrived a little after three o'clock. At the time Karen was waxing the upstairs floors. Because she now had an electric polisher, Rick no longer helped her. With the polisher, it really was a very easy job, but it still took time. Time in which you had to think about something, in which your mind, if you had one, could not remain utterly blank. She had put Cyr's letter away in a bureau drawer with the firm resolution that she was not going to think about it, or about him, for the time being. With nothing to do other than push the polisher to and fro, this was not easy, so she had concentrated on Planesville instead. Perhaps in Planesville it would be possible to find one of those old one-storey houses that had been built before the term ranch house had come into the language to stay. Of course those old houses usually had an attic, but you could ignore the attic except on rainy days when you went up there to look through stuff you should have thrown away. You certainly wouldn't polish the attic floor. In Planesville you would have more useful things to do with your time, like keeping chickens, or planting a vegetable garden.

"Karen?"

Susan, as you did in Rowanwood, had walked in.

"Coming," Karen called. "I'll comb my hair, and be right with you."

"Why bother?" Susan replied. She was standing at the bottom of the stairs. "It's only me."

That was what she had so often said in Geneva. Why bother, she had said, and she had not bothered to say it in French.

The last time Karen had seen Cyr, he had said, "If you ever need me—" Well, she never had needed him. She didn't need him now. And she was *not* going to think about him.

Susan had moved over to the living-room arch when Karen joined her. She looked cool and relaxed. "Your carpet is divine," she said. "The room was nice before, but it's perfect now."

"I'm glad you like it," Karen said.

"Rick will be crazy about it."

"Yes," Karen said. "I think he will."

"But you aren't," Susan said. And she wasn't asking a question.

"Of course I am."

"Do you want to talk about it?" Susan asked.

"About what?"

"All right, darling," Susan said. "If you don't want to talk about it, don't. It's never a good idea to talk about things until you're ready."

"Susan," Karen said, "it isn't that—"

"Skip it, darling. I just wanted you to know that I was around. If you need me any time, I'm around."

"Thanks, Susan. I won't forget that. And it does help, knowing you're around. Where would you like to sit? Inside or out?"

"Let's go out under the pines," Susan said. "And, darling, don't dislike your beautiful carpet just because it cost so much."

There were times, Karen thought, when she could almost wish that Susan weren't quite so perceptive. Her quick perception was one of the things she most liked about Susan, but to respond to it now was out of the question. She could not say to Susan that she no longer found life particularly worth living, that she had fallen into the dangerous habit of playing with a toy labelled suicide. This was not something she could say to either Susan or Rick. It would worry them too much. Which made it a problem that she had to deal with herself, by herself. And it was not a state of mind that would be cured by any blinding flash of understanding. It would be cured by a readjustment of values that had somehow become jumbled, that were, she was reasonably certain, simply out of focus rather than irretrievably lost. No one person, and no one event, could set things straight for her. It would take a combination of events, and she just had to pray that she would have the wit and the luck to find the right combination before it was too late. Wit and luck. She would need both.

Meanwhile, in so far as she could, she would distract herself with other people's problems. Fay's. Barbara's. Millicent's. Anybody's but her own, even though it made her uneasy to realize how many of her friends did have quite serious problems. There could be something other than simple coincidence in this.

"The chairs are already outside," she told Susan. "What would you like to drink?"

"Have you any lime juice?"

"Yes. Plenty."

"Good. Then let's take a jug out with us. With ice in it."

Karen was already on her way to the kitchen when she heard the front door chimes. Everybody in Rowanwood had chimes. More than once she had thought of having them taken out.

"Susan," she said, "will you see who it is? It's probably Pete Johnson. Nobody else around here would ring."

A minute later she heard Pete's voice in the hall.

"Hello, Mrs. Preston, how are you?" Pete was saying.

"I'm fine," Susan said. "How are you, Pete?"

"I'm fine, thanks, Mrs. Preston."

"Susan to you, my boy."

There was a brief silence. Then Karen heard Pete laugh. "Okay, Susan," he said.

"That's better."

She's done it again, Karen thought, without surprise. Susan could cross age barriers in a manner uniquely her own. In this instance, however, she had crossed something more than an age barrier. Karen did not think that she had ever heard Susan sound quite like that before. Not even when talking to Carol or Peg.

They were both smiling when they came into the kitchen, Susan and Pete. Pete's straw-coloured hair was, as usual, a mess, but it suited him.

"Hi, Mrs. Whitney," he said.

"Hi, Pete. Glass of lime juice?"

"That would be swell. Thanks."

"We were just going outside," Karen said. "Want to come with us?"

It was nice that she could suggest this. And there was no doubt that she could, because there was a sense of shared camaraderie amongst the three of them at that moment which was as pleasing as it would have been difficult to explain.

Pete hesitated, and then said, "Gee, I don't think I'd better. I told my mother I'd run the car out for her."

Mrs. Johnson's car was a very old Chev. It must, Karen thought, need repairing, if anything, more often than Pete's bicycle. How on earth did Mrs. Johnson manage to send Pete to Upper Canada College?

"Mrs. Whitney," Pete was saying, "would it be too much for Mr. Whitney to look in his garage and see if he had a piece of chain? The chain on my bike has gone again."

"I'll ask him, Pete. He won't have time tonight, because we're going out, but I'm sure he can tomorrow."

"Well, thanks a lot. Tell him not to worry about it. I mean, I'm not in a hurry. Well, I guess I better be going."

When he had gone, Karen said, "He's a wonderful boy."

"He seems like a good kid," Susan said, "but I very rarely see him."

She had picked up the tray, and turned toward the door. Karen, who would have liked to see her face while she was speaking, had not been able to do so. Susan and Lewis had no children. In general, Rowanwood thought that this was because they couldn't be bothered with children. It could be true of Lewis. It was not true of Susan.

Under the pines it was almost cool, and so secluded that you could, without too much difficulty, pretend you were anywhere. You did not have to remember that you were in Rowanwood.

"Susan," Karen said, "I heard something rather shattering this morning."

"You sound very serious," Susan said. With a glass of lime juice in one hand, and a cigarette in the other, she looked as indolent as only Susan could look. You had to know her very well to know that she was never as indolent as she appeared to be. To know that when she said, "Why bother?" she was not necessarily saying what she thought.

"It's Fay," Karen said.

"It usually is. What is it this time?"

"She has managed to get herself involved with Matt."

"Fay," Susan said, without any change of expression, "is a little tramp. To what extent is she involved? Or did Waycroft teach 'involved' as a specific expression?"

"It could very well have done, if they'd taught it at all," Karen said, smiling in spite of herself. "At any rate, in this instance you can take it as specific."

"You're quite sure?"

"Quite," Karen said. "It was Fay who told me. She told me this morning in Loblaw's."

"Which might surprise me, but doesn't," Susan said. "Fay, I think, is capable of doing anything in Loblaw's. She might even be capable of getting involved there."

"Susan, I wish you'd be serious for a moment."

"I'm serious enough. Does Barbara know?"

"No," Karen said, "she doesn't. She was in Loblaw's this morning, too."

"Almost a complete cast. It sounds as if all you lacked was a director. What excuses did Fay make for herself?"

It was obvious that Susan knew Fay very well.

"She said it only happened in the summertime. Which scarcely qualifies as an excuse," Karen told her.

"Scarcely."

Picking up a handful of pine needles, and letting them slip through her fingers, Karen went on, "She also said it was Barbara's fault for going to Cape Cod every summer."

"Which," Susan said, "to some extent it is. Not that that excuses Fay. Could Barbara be persuaded to stay at home this summer?"

"She must be. Though quite how it can be done, I don't know. I suggested to her this morning that Matt might be lonely without her. She told me that the children have to have their iodine, and that Matt has the garden."

"A garden with Fay in it," Susan said. "Eden complete with serpent. I like Barbara very much, but she is, in some ways, an utter fool."

"You're being too hard on her, Susan. She's simply suffering from the same thing that most of the women around here are suffering from. She has much too much to do, and at the same time much too little to think about. Her days are full to overflowing, but she never faces any real challenge any more, so she has chosen to think of her children as her challenge, her purpose if you like. Women like Betsey Milner can fool themselves into believing that the acquisition of a new car, or a new fur coat, is a worth-while purpose in life. Millicent chooses to run things. Mrs. Willoughby, next door, usurps the rector's duties at the church, or tries to. Barbara, just like these others, has followed what would have been a natural inclination anyway, and just like the others has overcompensated badly."

Susan set her glass down on the wicker garden table. "You

seem to have given this a great deal of very deep thought since you left Loblaw's."

I must be careful, Karen thought. If I'm not very careful, Susan will guess that I, myself, have no purpose at all.

"Of course I've thought about it," she said. "And I'm as worried as the devil, if you really want to know."

"I can see that you might be," Susan said. "But don't get so excited, darling. We'll work something out."

"I'm not excited. I'm perfectly calm, and you know it. But there are certain things that a girl like Barbara could never forgive, and Fay is one of them."

"You're quite right. She would be so disgusted she would walk out without even remembering to pack the tennis shoes. And she would not come back for them."

Karen could not help laughing. "Try and sound more upset about it, will you?"

"I don't," Susan said, and briefly she sounded much more like Lewis than herself, "see any point in getting upset. I see a great deal of point in straightening this mess out, however, and if you will leave it to me, I'll see what I can do."

"What do you think you can do?"

"Darling," Susan said, "I think it would be better all round if you kept clear of this from now on."

"There's nothing I would like better than to keep clear of it. But you make me nervous. You look as if you wouldn't have been at all out of place conducting intrigues at the court of Louis the Fourteenth."

Susan laughed. "Which do you see me as, de Maintenon or de Montespan?"

"Neither would be quite right, Susan, you really are making me nervous."

"Don't be. There isn't too much I can do, but remembering some of the things you've said this afternoon, it could be enough. If you are correct in assuming that Barbara's impossible preoccupation with her children is, in part at least, an escape from a world she never made, it may be possible to pry her loose from it. It all depends on how suggestible she is, and whether or not she is still in love with Matt."

"I think you can take that as read," Karen said.

It was nearly five o'clock, but the sun was still high in the sky. They were, Karen realized, getting very close to the longest day in the year. All days were long enough, without having one that was longer than any other one.

"Well," Susan said, "I must go now. I'll see you again tonight at Julia and Ned's."

"*Morituri te* . . . Though that's not very nice of me, is it? What about Fay?"

Susan stood up. "Fay," she said, "will probably go play in somebody else's back yard. At the moment we are not worrying about Fay."

"I always worry about Fay. It's a bad habit I picked up so long ago I don't suppose I'll ever get rid of it. No matter what she does, I can't help feeling sorry for her."

"I know. Sorry and sad. Because Fay is trapped, as we all are in one way or another, by her own inadequacies."

Startled, Karen said, "I didn't know you felt that way, too?"

"Didn't you?"

"I suppose I did. If only because we have always thought alike. Do you really have to go?"

"Yes," Susan said. "If I'm to change before dinner, I must."

Not everybody bothered to change for dinner. But Susan did, and Barbara did, and she herself did. Metaphorically, if not literally, the three of them lived on the same side of the street. It was the way it had been long ago on Elmdale Avenue. If you lived on the same side of the street, you not only behaved as the others on your side did, you also protected them, if you could, in any way possible. In so far as you were able, you proved to yourself and to everybody else that you had been right in not eating ice off the back of the iceman's cart.

9 | Neither here nor there

After Susan had gone, Karen took the tray in, put the oven on at four hundred, and went upstairs to shower and change.

She took off her dress, decided she could not wear it a second time, and put it in the laundry basket in the hall cupboard. Then she laid out fresh underwear on the end of the big double bed in the bedroom she shared with Rick.

In a house so large they could have done what a great many people in Rowanwood did, and had separate bedrooms. But neither she nor Rick had ever dreamed of doing such a thing. The time when they lay in bed and smoked a last cigarette after the lights were out was one of the best times in the day. What at first appeared to be total darkness would lighten, as they smoked and talked, to a dark twilight in which the furniture would again become dimly visible, and the windows would reappear as grey oblongs cut out of the night. They never drew the curtains across because Rowanwood was badly lit, and no actual shaft of light came into their room even though it faced the street. Occasionally, when a car passed, there would be a flicker of light on the ceiling. But this was quickly gone, and during the week there were very few cars after eleven o'clock. Mrs. Johnson's old Chev came in toward one in the morning, but this was usually all at that hour, and by then they were almost always asleep. Moonlight, which could have disturbed them, was never more than a pearly cast to the darkness because their room faced north.

Until the preceding April Karen had slept, as Rick did, deeply and without dreams she could remember on waking. But since early in April she had been sleeping very badly, and had fallen into the habit of getting up and sitting by the window, sometimes for hours at a stretch. Rick never woke, so he knew nothing of this.

Moving very quietly, she would put on a dressing-gown, pick up cigarettes and matches, and cross to the lounge chair by the windows. The pattern of light and shadow that was the sleeping street was now one that she felt she would never forget. There was a queer, indefinable sadness about the street at night. The dim radiance of widely spaced, unfrosted bulbs was no more than a feeble, pathetic thrust against the whole of outer darkness, emphasizing rather than dispelling the weakness of man's hold on the tiny corner of the universe he had taken for his own.

At night, even the square bulk of Millicent and Biff's house became dwarfed first by the heavy, overshadowing blackness of the elms bordering the road, and then by the dark, limitless bowl of the sky itself.

The loneliness of these night vigils would have been more than she could have borne if she had been alone in the room. Rick, even in sleep, stood between her and the danger of being overwhelmed once and for all by the knowledge that in the final analysis you were born alone, lived alone, and would die alone. By day, this was knowledge she could either face or forget. At night, half hypnotized by the sleeping sadness of the deserted stage that was the street, she could not forget it, and she could face it only because Rick was there, still within reach if she needed him.

Even now, in brilliant late afternoon sunshine, she was more sharply aware of being alone than was either normal or necessary. And as she laid out a white dress and heavy copper jewellery, the hot silence of the house seemed singularly oppressive.

With nothing more to do in the way of preparation either for dinner or for going out afterwards, she changed her mind about the shower, and decided to have a bath instead. It would be nearly an hour before Rick got home, because it now took a full forty minutes or more simply to get through the congestion in the downtown area. If the plant where Rick worked had been anywhere other than where it was, on the waterfront near the foot of Bay Street, he could have avoided the worst of the traffic. Rowanwood was, Karen thought, as she had thought so often recently, about as inconvenient for them in this respect as it very well could be. Almost due north from the centre of the city, Rowanwood could only be reached by fighting heavy traffic until you were past Eglinton Avenue. And even when you got beyond Eglinton, you found you were being held up as you had not been in the past.

Some of the men in Rick's office had moved into the new apartment houses they were putting up downtown. These men, Rick had told her, were able to get from home to office in something under twenty minutes.

Toronto, unlike New York and Chicago, had been slow in accepting the concept of downtown apartment houses, and in general Torontonians had yet to get used to the idea. In Toronto, the word home was still spelled h-o-u-s-e, and anyone who lived in an apartment by choice, and more particularly an apartment downtown, was considered eccentric if not unstable. On Park Avenue in New York, you were told, it was all right to live in an apartment. But in Toronto it was different. In Toronto, if you were stable, you lived in a house. Your Dun and Bradstreet rating was helped considerably if you owned a house, even if, as was usually the case, the mortgage company could put forward a much better claim to stability in this context than you could.

There had always been, of course, a few places like the old Alexandra Palace Apartments that used to be across from the General Hospital. Places where wealthy people lived out their declining years. There had never been any criticism of these people, perhaps because it was well known that most of them, prior to moving into the Alexandra Palace, had owned houses for as much as fifty or sixty years. After fifty years, even in Toronto, you had established your stability beyond reasonable cavil.

"John Swinnerton is in an apartment now, isn't he?" Karen had asked Rick.

"Yes," Rick had told her. "John and Rita got out of their house a month ago."

"Do they like living in an apartment?"

"They seem to," Rick had said. "It seems to work out very well. I drove him home one night last week, and stopped in for a drink. They seem to be well satisfied."

"Didn't it remind you of Gavin Street?" Karen had asked.

"Oh, Lord, no," Rick had said. "It's compact, but it isn't small. The living-room must be almost as large as the one we have here. And the view from the balcony is really something."

"Well," Karen had said, "I can see that it might be all right during the week. But what on earth do they do at the week-ends?"

"They have a place out near Whitevale. They go out there every Friday night, Rita told me, and come back in early Monday morning. They seem to be well satisfied."

Lying up to her chin in cool water, Karen thought, I must drop in and see Rita one of these days, otherwise I probably won't see the apartment until the fall. She never seemed to see John and Rita during the summer. It was curious the way you stopped seeing anyone connected with the office in the summertime. Soon after the middle of May, by tacit agreement, you withdrew into your own community. Between May and October you were unlikely to see anyone who had anything to do with the office, even if they were quite good friends. Rowanwood, although you had not planned it that way, became for five months virtually your only concern. At any time of the year Rowanwood was too great a part of your life, but during the summer it was to all intents and purposes the whole of it.

How had they gone wrong, she and Rick? When they had bought the house, they had envisaged a more comfortable, but still relatively simple continuation of the kind of life they had led on Gavin Street. They had thought that, once they were settled in, they would go to more concerts and plays, rather than to what amounted to none at all. They had talked about getting season tickets to N.H.L. hockey games, when the bank was paid off, but somehow they had never got around to it. They had even discussed at one time the possibility of owning their own summer place, but with the demands that the house made on them they had given up the idea as one requiring more effort than they were prepared to make. One by one, they had let these things go. But why, when they represented interests much more valid than those supplied by Rowanwood? Was Rowanwood, and the life it represented, a positive force against which they would never have an adequate defence? It couldn't be. Even with everything moving faster and ever faster, there was no natural law that said that you had to be trapped, as Susan had put it, by your own inadequacies. There was no point, however, in even trying to get out of your own particular trap until you had a very good idea of how you had proved yourself inadequate. It was rather like being on a merry-go-round that seemed unlikely to stop. You would get off without injury only by pulling the right switch.

I am, Karen thought, reaching the stage where I'm likely to pull the first switch I find, and to hell with what happens after that.

She sat up abruptly, reached for soap and wash-cloth, and told herself that she wasn't going to think about it any more just then.

She was, improbable as this might have seemed at any other time, actually glad that they were going down to Julia and Ned's. Julia and Ned would get on her nerves, as they always did, but this in itself would be a welcome distraction. And there might be someone interesting there, particularly since Ned's book had come out. The title of the book was *Psychology, the Present Trend*. Karen, after reading it, had felt that it should have been called *Let's Face It—We're All Psychotic*. Nevertheless, it had been well received, and Ned had lost no time in joining the Canadian Authors' Association.

At least, Karen thought as she stepped out of the bath and began to towel herself, Ned won't suggest writing games tonight if Susan and Lewis are going to be there. Ned's idea of a writing game was to subject unsuspecting guests to aptitude and apperception tests. But even Ned would not make the mistake of putting Lewis into the "unsuspecting" class. And he knew very well, or ought to by now, that neither she nor Rick would co-operate. They had already refused to do so on more than one occasion.

Ned had made it clear that he thought this proved something in itself. "Let's face it," he had said, "you two have hidden fears.

The bourgeois guilt complex. Not at all unusual, and nothing to be afraid of as long as you face it."

"You face it, old boy," Rick had said. "I'm tired."

No, Karen thought as she went into the bedroom to dress, there won't be any writing games.

She heard the front door open and shut, and then Rick's voice, "Hi, sweetheart, where are you?"

Immediately Karen was happier than she had been all day. "I'm upstairs," she called. "Be with you in a minute."

"Be with you in less than a minute!"

This evening, because it was a greeting and not a good-bye, she clung to him as she had not dared to do that morning. "Darling," she said, "I'm so glad to see you."

"And I'm glad to see you," Rick said. "I only saw it briefly, but the carpet looks fine, doesn't it?"

Karen put enthusiasm into her voice which she was unable to feel. "It looks marvellous. Even the men who brought it said it was the finishing touch."

"You're getting all dressed up. Are we going somewhere?"

"Julia and Ned's," Karen told him. "Had you forgotten?"

"Oh, my God!" Rick said.

"That's just what you said when I told you in the first place."

"Did I?"

"You did."

"I should learn not to repeat myself," Rick said. "By the way, was there anything interesting in the mail today?"

"There's a letter in the study that could be interesting," Karen said. "It's from Planesville. No letterhead. I put it on your desk."

"Right, I'll get it. Have we time for a drink before dinner?"

"Plenty of time."

"Good," Rick said. "Then let's have it in the living-room. My guess is that we'll be cooler there than on the terrace."

When they were sitting on the couch in the living-room, with their drinks on the coffee table in front of them, it took an enormous effort of will on Karen's part not to ask Rick immediately what was in the letter which, already opened, he had put down beside the cocktail tray. Her impatience to know what was in it was very close to being physically painful. She should, she knew, have been grateful that it had been so easy to suppress the existence of the two other letters. But with a possible answer to most, if not all, of her problems lying within reach of her hand, she could at the moment think of nothing else.

Rick stretched in a movement of perfect contentment and relaxation. "It makes the room come alive, doesn't it?"

"What does?" Karen asked.

"The carpet. What else, idiot child?"

"Sorry, darling," Karen said. "I was thinking of something else. Yes, it's quite perfect."

"Well, it looks as if we really have arrived, doesn't it?"

"Yes," Karen said. "Yes, darling, we have arrived." To sound glad about this was difficult, but she managed it, she thought, very well. At least Rick seemed to find nothing odd in her manner. To propose a toast of some sort would have been suitable, but this was beyond her. Actually, she was surprised that Rick had not done so. It was Rick who had bought the champagne when they finished putting in the buckwheat lawn. He was probably, she decided, distracted by the letter from Planesville. But if he was, he gave no immediate evidence of it.

"What do you suggest I wear to this damn gathering tonight?" he asked.

Karen picked up a cigarette, waited while he lit it for her, and then said, "Wear whatever you like, darling. It doesn't really matter because whatever you wear you're bound to be wrong. If you wear a sports jacket, they'll think you're being condescending. If you wear a suit like the one you have on, Ned will think you're putting too much money into clothes. You can't win."

"You said Susan and Lewis were going to be there, too, didn't you?"

"That's right," Karen said. "And Lewis, of course, will be wearing a grey business suit. As long as you're going to be wrong, anyway, you might as well keep Lewis company."

There was no need to conjecture about what Ned would wear. Ned would wear his red velvet smoking jacket with the black silk lapels.

"More?" Rick asked, lifting the cocktail shaker.
"Trace," Karen said.
"By the way," Rick said, "have we anything else on this week?"
"Just the barbecue here. That's day after tomorrow. Wednesday. I've told Susan and Barbara and one or two others about it. I'll be calling the rest tomorrow if the weather forecast is good."
"Well, just as long as we aren't tied up Friday," Rick told her.
"Why Friday?"
"We're going to Planesville on Friday," Rick said.
"Both of us?"
Rick nodded. "That's right. I'm going to look over the plant. You can look over the management wives."
I must *not* show what this means to me, Karen thought. Whatever I do, I must be casual about it. "Won't it be more a question of the wives looking me over?" she asked.
"Not from where I sit," Rick said. "They're after me. I'm not after them."
"Will we be staying overnight?"
"Yes," Rick said. "As a matter of fact, we've been invited to stay with the president, Paul Holmes, but I'm going to turn that down. As a house guest it's difficult to be objective."
"Can you turn it down?" Karen asked. She did not see how he could, without giving offence. But she did not say so. Rick usually listened when she offered advice, and quite often accepted it. In this particular instance, she felt too strongly about the whole thing to risk it. In a curious way, she felt that it would be tempting fate to thwart her if she took a hand in it at all. If they were going to get off the merry-go-round by pulling a switch labelled "Planesville", she wanted Rick to be the one who actually pulled the switch.
"Of course I can turn it down," Rick told her. "This is business, sweetheart, and that's how I want it kept. You won't mind staying in a second-rate commercial hotel for one night, will you?"
"Why should I?" Karen said. Still, it was a disappointment not to be going to one of those lovely old white clapboard houses on a wide, quiet street that couldn't possibly remind anyone of Rowanwood. The hotel would be nice, though, even if Rick did

refer to it as a second-rate commercial one. It would almost undoubtedly be right across from the brick post office at the main intersection.

"Rick," she said, "they want you to make up your mind now, don't they?"

"Yes," Rick said. "They want me to make up mind. They also, I should point out, want to make up their minds, too. The idea is that we go up there Friday afternoon or evening, and then Saturday I will spend the morning with Holmes going over the plant, and after that have lunch with him and some of his top management. Mrs. Holmes, I gather, will pick you up and take you to lunch with some of the wives."

"It sounds lovely," Karen said.

"Well," Rick said, "I wouldn't put it just like that. But it certainly gives us an opportunity to case things from several different angles."

Rick, Karen thought, I love you more than all the rest of the world put together, but there are times when you drive me crazy. He sounded, she told herself, just as he had sounded when they had first discussed buying the house, infuriatingly noncommittal.

"Look," she said, "I think it's time I put dinner on. If we don't eat soon, Julia will make some remark about the fashionably late."

"Do you know whom they've invited?"

"Julia said Robertson Davies might be there. He's in town just now."

"Do you believe her?" Rick asked.

"I believe Ned would ask him," Karen said. "I don't believe he'll be there."

It was quite obvious that Robertson Davies was not going to be there when, at ten o'clock, Julia brought in a tray with glasses and a wine decanter on it. Susan and Lewis were there, and a Dr. Thompson and his wife from the university, and a pleasant-looking man who had been introduced as an author—but not Robertson Davies—when Julia brought in the wine.

Both Julia and Ned, in common with a good many Canadians,

seemed to think that by decanting a local wine they could turn it into a Beaujolais or a Sauterne. Not that they went so far as to make any such direct claim, but Ned could always be counted on to refer to "the grape" and to make some mention of France. After his book came out, he had done one of those personal interviews for a Canadian wine company. It appeared in their advertising under the caption, "Why I changed to Wine". The inference was that Ned had changed from whiskey. The truth was that he hadn't changed from anything. Whiskey had never agreed with him.

Wine, and very good wine, had been a constant factor during Karen's year in Geneva, but she usually remembered it in particular as part of the only picnic she had ever gone on with Cyr. That he should have taken her on a picnic at all had been completely out of character, and she had had a feeling all day that he had been on the verge of saying something that he never did say.

They had driven to Annecy, and from there up into the mountains overlooking the lake. Lake Annecy, encircled by mountain peaks, was undoubtedly one of the most beautiful places in the world. The French were apt to irritate you with their universal conviction that anything French was better than anything anywhere else. With their *belle langue,* and their cuisine, and their *haute couture,* and their *paysage*—all, you were given to understand, *unique au monde*—they put a strain on your good manners that you felt was greater than it should have been. But where Lake Annecy was concerned they could use all the superlatives they liked and still remain well within the boundaries of fact, rather than those of national prejudice.

Cyr had parked the car on the edge of a sloping pasture high above sapphire-blue water. Then he had got out, stretched lazily, and lain down on his back on the short green grass. If he had not continued to chain-smoke, Karen would have thought that he had gone to sleep. She had picked an armful of blue and yellow and white flowers whose names she did not know, and had felt like a picture of Heidi that had hung for years on the wall of her room in the house on Elmdale Avenue. She had, she remembered, been very happy.

Without opening his eyes, Cyr had finally asked, "Hungry?"

"No rush," Karen had told him.

"We could eat here if you like."

"What would we eat?"

"You'll find some food in the back of the car," Cyr had told her. "If you don't like the look of it, we can go down to the Auberge de Savoie."

Mixed up with his old windbreaker and a crumpled copy of *La Suisse*, she had found a Gruyère cheese, one of those long French loaves, and a bottle of red wine. If it had been anyone else's windbreaker, she would *not* have liked the look of it, because of course the bread was unwrapped.

They had used his clasp-knife for cutting the bread and the cheese, and had taken turns in drinking from the wine bottle. The sky had been very blue, and there had still been snow on the tops of the mountains across the lake.

"Ah—the grape," Ned was saying. "Wasn't it Voltaire who said that wine was a companion in itself? Though that's neither here nor there."

Karen took a glass from the tray Julia was holding in front of her. So often you were neither here nor there. Ferney-Voltaire was only a few kilometres from Geneva. Briefly Ned had made sense.

"Now where was I?" Ned asked. "Oh, yes. The point I have just been making is that small bathrooms are definitely inhibiting. Nine out of ten people suffer from an unacknowledged sense of claustrophobia. It's unhealthy."

"What's unhealthy?" Rick asked. "Claustrophobia?"

"Well, that too, of course," Ned said. "But you see what I'm getting at, don't you?"

The party, Karen noticed, seemed to have divided into two groups. She was now with Rick, Lewis, and Ned.

It was Lewis who answered Ned. Lewis never drank anything but martinis or scotch-on-the-rocks, but he seemed to be enjoying his wine. Lewis had beautiful manners.

"No," he said. "Personally, I don't quite see what you're getting at, Ned. Perhaps you could explain your point a trifle more fully."

Ned, when he answered, sounded a little condescending. An intellectual humouring a not too intelligent bourgeois. The funny thing was that he quite honestly thought he was a great deal brighter than Lewis. All Karen could hope was that this was not as obvious to Lewis as it was to her.

"My point," Ned said, "is that the modern home is completely out of balance space-wise."

"You mean we should have smaller living-rooms and bigger bathrooms?" Karen asked.

Ned nodded approvingly. "That's the idea, exactly. Let's face it. An entirely revised architecture."

"It would be less expensive if you just interchanged the furniture," Rick said.

"I don't follow you," Ned said. "Interchange what furniture?"

"You know," Rick said, "from one room to the other. Instead of tearing all the houses down, just shift the furniture. We could certainly do with a few more inhibitions in the modern living-room."

"You people never know when to be serious," Ned said. "You aren't prepared to face your problems frankly." He sounded more than a little annoyed.

"Frankly," Rick said, "I wasn't aware of having any problems."

"Exactly what I mean," Ned told him. "Lack of awareness is one of the greatest ills in the North American home of today."

"Don't," Rick said, "forget claustrophobia."

It was, Karen thought, on the whole fortunate that Susan chose that moment to join their group. Even under a stark overhead light that did nothing for Picasso ash-trays or the works of lesser Canadian artists, Susan looked very attractive. "What are you talking about over here?" she asked.

"Bathrooms," Lewis said without inflection.

Susan looked at Karen and then looked away again. "How fascinating," she said. "We've been arguing about whether Dali was mostly mad when he painted cows on top of grand pianos, or mostly sane because he made so much money out of it."

Karen glanced across the room, and saw that the author was already saying good-bye to Julia. She wished she had had more opportunity to talk with him.

"Rick," she said, "I'm afraid it's time we were leaving. Ned, it has been a most interesting evening."

Everybody stood up then, but it was another ten minutes before they actually left. Which, as Rick said later, was nevertheless par for the course.

At night Admiral Road looked as if it had not changed at all within her memory of it. Even when she had been a little girl, Karen had noticed how old the trees were on Admiral Road. This apparent changelessness made the cars at the kerb, their own Buick, and Lewis's Lincoln, seem anachronistic. Looking back across the years, she remembered friends of her grandmother's, the ancient Miss Smiths, sitting white-gloved in the back of their electric car behind an equally ancient chauffeur. And she felt that the Miss Smiths, if they had still been alive, would have fitted into the scene with more conviction and grace. Admiral Road had once been a very fashionable address, something now easier to believe at night than in the cold, clear light of day.

She was, she found, standing on the sidewalk with Rick, Susan and Lewis, and Dr. and Mrs. Thompson, in one of those awkward regroupings which happen so often after you have already said your good-byes. The Thompsons apparently had no car.

"Can we give you a lift?" Rick asked them.

"Oh, no, thanks," Dr. Thompson said. "We're just a block or two from here."

"We like walking, anyway," Mrs. Thompson said.

"You're sure?" Karen asked.

"Oh, yes, quite sure," Dr. Thompson said. "Thanks just the same. Well, we'll be off now. We've enjoyed meeting you."

"We've enjoyed it, too," Lewis said.

"I hope we'll meet all of you again," Mrs. Thompson said. "It has been such a nice evening."

"It was a nice evening, wasn't it," Susan said.

It looked very much as if the things that had already been said inside were going to be said all over again, and it was a relief when the Thompsons actually did move off.

Rick and Lewis both had their respective car keys in their hands.

Rick grinned. "I wouldn't start moving the furniture directly you get home, Lewis. I'd sleep on the idea first, if I were you. With four bathrooms in your house, it will require some careful planning."

Lewis really had a very nice smile. "Blood is thicker than water," he said.

"I wouldn't know about that," Rick said. "But it's nice of you to see it that way. It's certainly thicker than Ontario wine, anyway. I will admit that much."

I wish I knew Lewis better, Karen thought. I don't really know him any better than I did the first time I met him. Even though I see him often, I don't know him. I wonder if even Susan really knows him?

Rick waited for the Lincoln to pull away from in front of their car, and Karen, sitting quietly beside him, felt as if she were in the middle of a dream. She and Barbara had had friends on Admiral Road back in the days when it was still a good address. And for a moment Karen found it difficult to believe that her real self was not still twelve years old, and playing tag in a summer dusk that meant that very soon both she and Barbara would have to run all the way back to Elmdale Avenue in order to get there before nine o'clock. If they were not home by nine, they were not allowed to go out to play the following evening. The rules were the same for both of them. Their mothers always got together on things like that.

Even the shadows of the trees, cast across the empty road by the street lights, looked just the same as they had when she was twelve years old.

"Any choice as to the way we go home?" Rick asked.

"No," Karen told him. "None at all, darling."

She regretted having said this almost immediately, because he chose to cut across Lowther to Avenue Road, and another and far less pleasant memory was forced upon her. It was something which she had once told Rick about, and in telling it she had made it sound very funny. At the time when it had happened, however, it had been far from funny.

When you are seventeen, there is nothing even vaguely amusing about making a damn fool of yourself.

10 | Your mother wouldn't mind, would she?

It had happened toward the end of March during her last year at Waycroft, and not long after Fay had got into trouble.

There had, quite conceivably, been other people somewhere in that large, gloomy house on Lowther Avenue, but at the time Karen had had no proof of it. Since she never did have any proof, there might not have been, which made the incident one she would have forgotten entirely if such a thing had been possible.

When Fay had asked her to dinner on that Friday night, she had not been particularly anxious to go. She would never be able to visit Fay's house again without seeing blood on the floor. This was something she could not very well say to Fay, so she agreed to go.

Mr. Wilcombe had gone out soon after eight o'clock, and she and Fay had settled down to the one thing they did have in common, a discussion of what they did not like about Waycroft. It was a season of the year when it was difficult to think of anything you did like, so this was a fairly satisfying occupation. March might be pleasant enough in some places, but in Toronto it was a time of sleet, cold rain, and colder winds. Even the huge living-room in Fay's house seemed a relatively cosy place to be in March in Toronto. And because Mr. Wilcombe gave her all the spending money she wanted, Fay had some excellent recordings.

They were listening to Tommy Dorsey when the telephone rang.

"Oh, hell!" Fay said. But she didn't waste any time in going to answer it. Fay was always too restless to want to stay still for long.

She came back almost at once.

"It's Lou," she said. "She wants us to go to a party."

"She wants you," Karen said. "She doesn't want me. Go ahead, and I'll go on home. I honestly wouldn't mind in the slightest."

"She wants you, too," Fay said.

"Look," Karen said, "Lou doesn't like me, and I don't like her."

"I'm not going if you won't," Fay said.

Lou, a big brunette with prominent eyes and the morals of an alley-cat, was at the Shaw Schools taking a course in stenography. She shared rooms with another girl on Bedford Road just off Lowther. Rooming-houses, even in those days, had begun to creep across the Annex. Just how and where Fay had ever met Lou, Karen had never been able to discover.

"Fay," she said, "you can perfectly well go without me. I really don't know why you would want to go there again, but if you do, you can perfectly well go without me. We'll take the street-car together as far as Bedford, and then I'll just walk home while you go up to Lou's."

"We'll talk about it on the street-car," Fay said.

As Fay had known, Karen had been unable to argue on the street-car. She had not been brought up to argue on street-cars. And by the time they started to walk up Bedford, Fay had somehow managed to make her feel foolish if she persisted in her refusal.

The party was just the kind of party Karen had known it would be. All Lou's parties were the same. There was only one bedroom, but this did not stop it from being occupied almost immediately by four people. The hall was small, but not too small with the lights out for another couple. After that, the kitchenette was taken over, also with the lights out.

Karen, feeling most uncomfortable, very quickly found herself alone in a badly over-furnished living-room with someone called Carl who would, she was sure, at once begin to make the sort of approach one could expect at Lou's.

Karen had, twice before, come to Lou's simply in order to look out for Fay. Why she had let herself be persuaded into coming when there was no longer any real point in doing anything about Fay, she did not know.

Since the next few minutes were almost certainly going to be unpleasant, she decided to get them over with as quickly as possible.

She stood up. "I'm sorry," she said, "but I'm going home now."

"Do you really have to?" Carl said.

"Yes," Karen said. "I really have to."

"Then will you allow me to see you home?" Carl asked.

Karen was so taken aback that for a moment she did not know what to say. Manners of this kind were the last thing you would expect from any friend of Lou's.

"You mustn't misunderstand me," he said. "I don't want you to go. I don't want that at all, because to tell you the truth I was feeling kind of lonely when Bob called and asked if I would like to go to a party. But this kind of party—well, it just doesn't seem like your kind of party any more than it's mine."

For the first time, Karen really looked at him. He had light brown hair and direct blue eyes, and seemed as nice as he sounded. He looked quite a lot like Barbara's fiancé, Matt, and Matt was one of the nicest boys she knew. She would not, she thought in passing, have got so involved with Fay if Barbara had still been free in the evenings. Since Barbara had become engaged to Matt, she didn't seem to have time for anything or anybody else. She was completely absorbed in him.

It was reassuring that this man should remind her of Matt.

"Then you haven't been here before?" she asked him.

"No," he said. "And I don't expect to come again. Any more than I expect that you will come again."

Relieved that she did not have to explain the reasons for her own presence in a place she would never have chosen to visit, thinking him very perceptive to have seen this for himself, Karen said, "You're quite right. I'll never come here again, either."

"Your coat is probably in the hall, isn't it? Let me get it for you while I get mine. I can clear the way at the same time."

Karen flushed. "Thank you," she said. She had not liked the

idea of going into the hall. Almost anything might be happening in the hall by now.

With a quick smile, he said, "Just leave it to me."

He really is nice, Karen thought. If he had been feeling lonely, it was a pity that it had turned out to be such a waste of time for him to come up here.

He returned very soon with their coats, helped Karen into hers, and led the way through a hall in which the lights were now on again.

On the way down the stairs from Lou's apartment to the front door, he said, "I hope you won't mind my telling you this, but you remind me of my only sister."

"Of course I don't mind," Karen told him.

"It's not so much the way you look," he said, "although she had the same marvellous hair. It's more the way you are. Easy to talk to, and just—I don't quite know how to put this—just, well, easy to be with."

"Why did you say 'had'?" Karen asked quietly. "Your sister—she isn't—?"

They were just inside the front door by this time. He pulled out a package of cigarettes, offered it to her, and when she shook her head, lighted one for himself. Karen would have liked a cigarette, but Waycroft girls were not supposed to smoke, which meant that Waycroft girls did not smoke on the street.

"Yes," he told her, "my sister's dead."

He avoided her eyes, and concentrated on lighting a cigarette, but she saw the faint tremor of his hand, quickly controlled.

Anything more, and she would have been suspicious. Anything less, and it would have been ineffective. It was quite a performance. Laurence Olivier would have had no need to be ashamed of it. None of which ever made Karen feel any better afterwards about her credulity. Afterwards, she was morally certain that he had never had a sister of any kind, alive or dead.

"Which way do you live?" Carl asked, as they came out into a blustery night with bare branches like cold castanets overhead.

"We can go along either Lowther or Bernard," Karen told him.

"From here, it doesn't make much difference. I imagine Lowther is actually the quickest way."

"Good," he said. "As it happens, I live on Lowther, myself."

"Oh, do you?"

"Yes," he said. "I seem to be kind of lucky tonight. Look, do you mind if I talk to you about Linda, my sister?"

"No," Karen said. "Not if you'd like to."

The streets were deserted. It was not the kind of night when anyone who did not have to would have thought of going out.

"Linda was two years older than I am," he said, "but we did everything together. We just got on well, I guess. I don't quite know how to explain what Linda meant to me. But I'm sure you understand, without my going into it. I remember when I was seven—"

He talked steadily.

Linda had always been there when he needed her, until—well, she had always been there. She had been right there with him when his cocker spaniel was run over. Then there had been the time when she saved him from drowning. When she was thirteen, she had shared her new bicycle with him. And when he was old enough to have a bicycle of his own, well, then they had gone on long hikes into the country, just the two of them, because they were both so crazy about the out-of-doors. And when he had started going out on dates, well, he didn't quite know how to put it, but Linda had set him straight about a lot of things.

Karen could not have seen it all more clearly if it had been in Technicolor. She felt like crying.

Just when he had started to hold her hand, she could not have said. But when she realized that this was what he was doing, she did not draw her hand away. To do so would have been cruel. And it was obviously a help to him to talk it out like this.

"Linda took marvellous photographs," he said. "I wish you could have seen some of them. If she hadn't—well, I know I'm prejudiced, but I think she would have been as good as Karsh. Some time perhaps you could see some of her pictures."

Karen's voice was naturally husky. She was glad that it enabled her to sound as compassionate as she felt. "I'd like to," she said.

"Would you really?"

"I really would," Karen told him.

"Well, maybe I could give you a ring some afternoon, and if you were free, you could come over."

"That would be nice," Karen said. When you thought of afternoon, you thought of sunlight, and afternoon tea, and yourself—in blue, probably—bringing comfort on a highly spiritual level. He stopped suddenly. "Listen," he said, "we've just passed my house. It's just a couple of doors back. Could you come up for a minute now? It's still awfully early. Just after nine o'clock. Your mother wouldn't mind, would she?"

If he hadn't, Karen told Rick two years later, put in that bit about her mother, she would have refused at once. It was, really, because she was seventeen that she felt unable to refuse. When a girl is fifteen, she told Rick, she is usually more or less resigned to the fact that her mother will have to know just about every damn thing she does, and where, and with whom. By the time she is nineteen, she is old enough to realize that what has in fact become a myth can be almost as useful as having her roller skates along. Even the worst wolves seem to falter before a sentence beginning "My mother—". But when a girl is seventeen, the last thing she wants anyone to think is that she is in any way tied to her mother. To be perfectly honest, she would just as soon that nobody knew she had a mother at all.

I don't think, she told Rick, that he had any real intention of asking me up that night when we left Lou's. I think he intended that it be an afternoon, as he had suggested. I was just too naïve then, too Waycroft if you like, to see that from his point of view the time of day didn't matter. That whereas I was thinking in terms of tea and sympathy, he was thinking of something quite different. Don't laugh, she told Rick, but I honestly didn't believe that anyone ever did that kind of thing until after dark. Why, even Hollywood was waiting until after dark. I wouldn't be surprised if, in the future, it was referred to as one of the Dark Ages.

Karen saw no reason for telling Rick that it was not only the reference to her mother that did the trick, but also the expression on Carl's face. They had paused under a street lamp, and Carl's expression had been such a mixture of boyishness and manfully controlled sorrow for his departed sister, that Karen had simply not had the heart to turn down his suggestion. Anyone who could have refused such a spontaneous plea would have had to have a heart of stone. Either that, or know her way around a lot better than she, Karen, did at that time.

The only comfort she ever found afterwards was in the realization that there were things you had to learn sooner or later, and that on the whole it was a good thing that it be sooner.

"Well—" she said.

"Just for a minute or two," Carl said. "It's so early, and the way you remind me of Linda—well, I just don't want to let you go without showing you one or two of her things. It's silly, I know, but it would—well, it would sort of bring her back a little. Just for a minute or two, will you? There's this one she took of two little kids picking wild flowers. In a way, it's kind of simple, but—well, it does things to you. You don't need to stay and see any of the others this time, but you must see this one of the two little kids."

Waycroft, Karen told Rick later, was absolutely soaked—drenched if you like—in jokes about etchings during her last year there. And some of those jokes smelled even worse than the lockers full of black gym stockings that nobody ever took home to have washed. You would think, this being the case, that she would have made the connection between photographs and etchings with most of her brains tied behind her back. That she didn't just proved that, in spite of the jokes, most of the girls at Waycroft were "nice" girls. He might not know it, she said to Rick, but the reason why so many nice girls told such crude jokes was simply because they didn't really understand them. If anyone had ever drawn them a diagram of something other than birds and bees, she told Rick, those girls would have died of mortification before they would have told any of those jokes. But nobody ever did. It was not the Waycroft Way to admit that there were any propagating forms of life other than the birds and the bees.

"You will come, won't you?" Carl said. Even his voice was boyish, although he must have been at least twenty-three.

"All right," Karen said. "But just for a minute."

"Oh, good. I just couldn't wait."

And *that* was the truth, Karen told Rick. If he had been able to wait, things might have been a lot more difficult than they were.

We went back, she told Rick, to one of those tall, narrow, frantically dismal houses on Lowther near Bedford. There was a dim light on in the front hall, but the rest of the house was dark. I didn't much like that. I liked it even less when we got inside and I realized that it was another rooming-house. I had somehow got the idea that he lived with his family. Don't ask me how. You would have to ask him. He could have told you, I'm quite sure.

If I could have backed out then, Karen said to Rick, without feeling as if I would be acting like a ten-year-old, and without cause, I would have done it. Believe me, seventeen is a hell of an age for a girl to be under circumstances such as those were. She would rather die than behave like a child. She doesn't usually know how to behave like an adult.

Well, he said his apartment was just at the top of the stairs, and so we started up the stairs, with me going first because he had such good manners. It was a three-storey house, but there wasn't a sound in it anywhere, and just that one light in the front hall. It made me think of the house of Dracula. It didn't, of course, look the slightest bit like any house Dracula would have condescended to, but that's what it made me think of just the same. Which is probably why I turned around just as I reached the first-floor landing.

When she told Rick about it, she was even able to make the next part seem funny, which was really quite an achievement.

Her hand was still on the bannister when she looked backwards, and saw the face of the man called Carl as she would not have seen it quite so soon if she had not caught him unawares.

All trace of boyishness had vanished. The direct blue eyes were bold and calculating. His mouth was tight in a half-smile that was a very unpleasant combination of anticipation and contempt.

Frozen, Karen stared down at him where he had come to a halt several steps below her, her expression telling him quite plainly that any effort on his part to regain his initial advantage would be a waste of time.

He finally broke the silence. "Well?" he said.

It was only one word, but it disposed of cocker spaniels, near deaths from drowning, and little kids picking wild flowers, just as effectively as several sentences might have done.

Karen's first reaction was that she was going to be sick. Her second, following almost immediately, was that if necessary she would see them both dead before she allowed him to come one step closer to her. The stairs, as they were in most of those old houses, were long and very steep. These stairs happened, also, to be uncarpeted, as was the hall below.

"You're not going to be difficult, are you, baby? I don't like girls who are difficult."

In the silence Karen heard the sharp intake of her own breath, but when she spoke her voice was perfectly steady. "If you move up one more inch," she said, "I'm going to throw myself down at you so hard that we will both go to hospital, if one or other of us isn't killed."

"Don't be such a damn little fool."

"I was a fool," Karen said. "I'm not now."

"You can't stand there for the rest of the night."

"I can stand here," Karen told him, "as long as you stand there. I could scream, but I prefer to do it this way. And don't make the mistake of thinking that I don't mean what I say. If you want to take a chance on being killed, come on up. If you don't, you had better start backing down these stairs right away."

If she screamed, she could quite easily shatter a self-control that was her only real asset, and to which she was clinging by a very thin margin as it was. With no assurance that anyone would hear her, it was something she simply could not afford to do, and she knew this.

For a moment he did nothing. Then he shrugged. "All right. Have it your way, you little bitch. Though where in hell Lou ever found anything like you, I'd give a lot to know."

Very slowly, he backed down until he stood beside the front door which was directly in line with the stairway.

Her hand damp on the bannister, her knees weak, Karen knew that she had still to win a complete victory. Time enough later to start hating herself as much as she hated him. Now she must concentrate on nothing beyond getting out of that house.

Without a word, she sat down on the top step, aware of the thick, soundless darkness behind her, a threat in itself which made the skin at the back of her neck contract.

"What in the devil do you think you're doing now?" he asked.

"Waiting for somebody to come in," Karen told him. "You aren't the only one who lives here. Somebody will come along sometime."

His answer was unprintable. It added up to his telling her to come down and get out of his sight as fast as she could.

This, Karen thought, is something I will never quite be able to forget. She shivered.

"If you want me to go," she said, "you'll have to open the front door, leave it standing wide open, and cross over to the other side of the street. Otherwise I stay right here until somebody comes along."

He looked as if he would have liked to strangle her. How, Karen wondered, could she even for a moment have thought he resembled Matt?

With a muttered obscenity, he flung the door open and walked out.

A cold wind, caught by an up-draft, pulled at the edges of Karen's coat as she stood up and came slowly down the stairs, never shortening the distance between them, but never letting him be cut off from view by the top of the door-frame.

He was across the street, as she had told him to be, when she stepped down off the outside steps. Even so it took courage to do this. In the shadows mid-way between two street lamps, he seemed more menacing than he had when she had been able to see him clearly.

I ran then, Karen told Rick. I didn't really need to, but I couldn't stop myself. He wasn't a pervert, or anything like that. He wasn't going to chase me on the street. But I ran, anyway. I ran for three blocks. I just couldn't help it.

On their way home from Julia and Ned's, they had already passed Upper Canada College before Karen could get rid of a picture of herself running blindly through that long ago March night.

"I hope Peg is all right," she said.

"Why shouldn't she be?" Rick asked.

"No reason," Karen said. And there *was* no reason, because Peg had not been brought up by housekeepers any more than she had herself. Still, things could happen to girls, in spite of their having had two parents on the job, rather than, as in Fay's case, no parents at all. Because Mr. Wilcombe, although he had been such a nice man, had certainly been a rotten parent.

"It's not like you to worry about either of the kids," Rick said. "And if you're thinking that New York is a more dangerous place for Peg than Toronto, I doubt if that's true."

"I wasn't thinking that," Karen said. "And I'm not worrying. Not really."

"Well," Rick said, "as long as you're not worrying."

They were on their own street by then, and as they swung into the drive the headlights swept across the front of the house. At times Karen still found it difficult to believe that this house belonged to them. After an evening in the Annex where they had lived for so long, it was almost impossible to credit the fact that they had come so far and so fast. Too far, and too fast.

Rick brought the car to a smooth stop in front of the garage. "You'd better get out here, sweetheart," he said. "I haven't shifted the mower yet. We really need a larger garage."

Six months earlier, Karen would have said easily and unselfconsciously that they didn't need a larger anything. Now she said nothing, because she knew that if she did she would be too positive.

As she got out of the car, the pain in her side was there again, a swift, unexpected agony. Her face drawn, she caught her lip between her teeth to keep from crying out as Rick manoeuvred the big car into the garage. Oh, God, she prayed silently, make me one of those people with their appendix on the wrong side. Oh, God, don't let it be anything worse than an appendix.

By the time Rick had pulled down the overhead garage doors and joined her, physically she was all right again. Emotionally she was not.

"Rick," she said, as they walked toward the front door, "we've always had a wonderful time, haven't we?"

"We always will, sweetheart."

"Rick, darling, whatever happens, don't ever forget that I love you. Really love you."

He put his arm around her, and drew her close to his side. "That's very nice to hear. But you make it sound a little like a last will and testament. You didn't realize it, but that's rather the way you made it sound."

Karen managed to laugh. It was a surprisingly natural laugh. "Did I?" she said. "What an awful thought."

As he unlocked the front door, Rick said, "You're pretty tired, aren't you, sweetheart?"

Karen nodded. "A bit."

"Well, we're not getting home too late as these things go. We should get a fairly good sleep."

Karen, still unable to sleep at three o'clock, got up as she was now in the habit of doing nearly every night, and established herself in the arm-chair by the windows.

The windows were wide open, but there was no sound anywhere apart from Rick's even breathing in the room behind her. And no movement at all, other than the restless turmoil in her own mind. With only the sleeping sadness of the deserted street to keep her company, she fought a concrete fear of death even while she caressed the grey image of a long peace from which there would be no need ever to waken again.

I must stop this, she thought in quiet desperation. I must stop it, stop it, stop it! I'll get a cigarette. I'll plan the details of the cook-out.

But she did neither of these things. To get up and find cigarettes seemed an effort not worth making. And with futility the apparent beginning and end of her life in Rowanwood, a Rowanwood cook-out was futile beyond any possible present consideration.

Without a sound, she turned her face against the back of the chair, and wept, also without a sound.

11 | Personally, I recommend the gin

In a community like Rowanwood you had to ask the neighbours in once a year. It was one of those unwritten laws which, if you had any perception at all, you did not need to have explained to you. It was tribal custom, just as, back in the days on Elmdale Avenue, it had been tribal custom to have at least one really large Sunday tea every winter, with the whole household upset for weeks in advance, and all the best silver and lace brought out, right down to those antique silver teaspoons of your grandmother's that were never used at any other time, and were always black with tarnish when found where nobody could ever remember having stored them.

The Sunday teas had been for the doctors, and their wives, with whom Karen's father was professionally associated. Amongst them there had been some real friends; but generally speaking the guests had been, as were the people whom you felt obliged to invite once a year in Rowanwood, no more than acquaintances.

At the Sunday teas the conversation had nearly always been about golf, and Florida, and the state of the stock market. It was not considered correct for a doctor to talk about his medical interests at a tea, any more than it was correct for wives to discuss their children and the Domestic Problem. Such subjects as the children were, in those days, reserved for morning telephone conversations. And nobody would have dreamed of discussing the plumbing at any time, except with the plumber.

Even in your early teens you had been sensitive to the difference between the yearly tea for the doctors and their wives, and other occasions when you were asked, for instance, to be sure that a Mr. Harold Macmillan was looked after, because Mr. Macmillan was from England and would not know too many people. In addition to passing cucumber sandwiches and little iced cakes from the Swiss Bakery, it was part of your duty to see that Mr. Macmillan didn't feel lonely. On these occasions you always enjoyed yourself, because the conversation would revolve around books and music and art. You had not felt, even then, that golf and Florida and the state of the stock market would play a very large part in your future. But books and music and art were different, and you really enjoyed talking to someone like Mr. Vincent Massey, who seemed to be quite well informed on these subjects. You even suspected that he might know more than Miss Kenwick at Waycroft, although this was not really something you felt in a position to judge accurately.

Dr. Banting, of course, always came to everything, because Dr. Banting was an artist as well as a doctor. Just how good an artist he was, you had never been able to decide. If he had not discovered insulin it might have been easier. The fact that Dr. Banting had discovered insulin tended, although it ought not to have done, to confuse the issue where his painting was concerned. Later, you were to find yourself in the same quandary with regard to Mr. Churchill's paintings. Mr. Churchill, too, had done things that confused the issue.

When Karen and Rick had lived in the apartment on Gavin Street, they had had The Gang in for beer parties where everybody sat on the floor and, because they still clung to the fringes of the Higher Education they had picked up at college, talked in necessarily general terms about Schopenhauer, and Freud, and transcendentalism. The sum of these discussions had always been that the world was going to hell in a basket. There had, Karen remembered, been a gloomy satisfaction in knowing that you were going to hell in a basket. A satisfaction that had failed to survive the morning-after mess, and the painful knowledge that since you had not been able to afford the party in the first place, you would be living on hamburger for the balance of the week.

In Rowanwood, in order to be a member of the tribe in good

standing, you had to give either a large cocktail party during the winter months, or a barbecue dinner during the summer.

The first time that Karen and Rick had come face to face with the inescapable fact that, whether they liked it or not, Rowanwood had become a community of which they were a part, they had sat down and worked out the relative costs of these two alternatives. On paper, it had seemed clear that a cocktail party would not set them back as much as a barbecue dinner would, because the latter involved an equal amount of liquor with a great deal more food. In coming to this conclusion, they had failed to foresee the toast, proposed by Biff, which included an enthusiastic smashing of cocktail glasses in the fireplace. Or the esoteric dance performed by Roddie on a dining-room table which, surviving the first performance, had given way under the stress of a loudly demanded encore. Or the cigarette burn in the middle of the big chesterfield over which Millicent, always practical, had emptied a full shaker of cocktails.

"You can't be too careful about that kind of thing," Millicent had said. "You have to act at once, or the first thing you know the house has burned down."

When she looked at the house the following morning, Karen had been inclined to wish it had burned down. That way, they would at least have been able to collect some insurance.

From then on, keeping in close touch with the meteorological office on Bloor Street, Karen and Rick had discharged their tribal obligations with barbecue dinners. They felt, and they were probably correct in this, that the cost of the materials Rick had used in building the outdoor fireplace could reasonably be considered as written off after one year, if only because the fireplace was employed for this particular purpose.

In a corner of the basement, in an old steamer trunk of her mother's, Karen kept a store of well-worn cushions and rugs which, added to the garden furniture on the occasion of the annual cook-out, provided all the seating accommodation necessary.

In spite of the fact that they had arrived at the best possible solution to a problem which, Karen realized, had to be solved in one way or another, she was never able to overcome her inward resentment that the problem should exist at all. She had always hated big parties, even though she had met Rick at a big party. For that matter, it had been at a big party that she had met Cyr.

The night when she first met Rick was very clearly before her again when she telephoned Betsey Milner to invite Betsey and Harry to the barbecue. This might have been because, although she had not known it at the time, Harry belonged to the fraternity that had given that particular party. He might even have been at the party. That was one of the things about having lived in Toronto more or less all your life. You practically never met anybody with whom you could not find some common ground, some point of mutual contact. It was only very rarely that you did not, in effect, meet somebody who remembered Bogart in *Casablanca*. In a city of a million and a half people, there were, of course, thousands with whom you had nothing whatsoever in common, but you just didn't meet these people. In a somewhat wider sense, there was a great deal of truth in that bit of doggerel by B. K. Sandwell which—if you remembered correctly—you had first seen in *Saturday Night*:

> Toronto has no social classes,
> Only the Masseys and the masses.

In telephoning to Betsey, rather than going next door in person, Karen knew quite well that she was not saving any time. Betsey would rattle on about nothing for just as long on the telephone as she would if you were with her. But you did spare yourself the necessity of trying to look interested. You could get away with thinking about something else.

Because weather was such an obvious factor in an outdoor party, it was the accepted thing that invitations be issued only a little in advance of the party itself. You alerted your close friends to the possibility a week or more beforehand, but you did not commit yourself to the lunatic fringe until you had obtained the next thing to a Bible oath from the meteorological office that the weather was set fair for the next forty-eight hours.

Sitting at the telephone in the front hall, Karen could see sunlight falling in golden bars across the Chinese carpet in the living-room. As a symbol, the carpet might have become meaningless, but this did not mean she wanted its intrinsic value ruined by spilled drinks and cigarette butts. The buckwheat lawn was, fortunately, more durable. The lawn, now in its eighth year, was still the best lawn in Rowanwood. It would, if they moved to Planesville, add considerably to the price they would get for the house.

"Hello? Betsey?" Karen could hear herself using what she privately thought of as her social voice. It was a warm, interested voice, with just enough but not too much intimacy in it. "Betsey, Rick and I would be so pleased if you and Harry could come over tomorrow evening. Just a friendly cook-out, but we think it will be fun."

"Why, darling, how wonderful!" Betsey said. "Just a minute while I look at my book. Day after tomorrow——no, it was tomorrow you said, wasn't it?"

"Yes," Karen said, "that's right. Tomorrow."

"Let me see. That would make it Wednesday, wouldn't it?"

"That's right," Karen said. "Very spur of the moment, but then for a cook-out you just have to wait for the right weather. The people at Malton have crossed their hearts and hoped to die if it isn't sunny tomorrow. As soon as we heard this, Rick and I said why don't we have some fun, and have our friends in."

Karen hated social lies, but in a situation of this kind the truth was obviously unsuitable. She could hardly tell Betsey that she and Rick had shouldered the burden of what they referred to as "that bloody barbecue" at least ten days earlier, and that they had seen no possible way of avoiding the inclusion of Betsey and Harry.

"Darling! How marvellous! We're free!" Betsey and Harry had never yet failed to accept any invitation, but Betsey always made it sound as if you had, with uncanny foresight, found the one empty crevice in an otherwise crowded programme.

Like everything Betsey did, Karen found this supremely irritating; but she was fair-minded enough to feel that if she herself was telling lies, there was no reason why Betsey shouldn't lie, too.

It would have been nice if that had been the end of the conversation, as it perfectly well could have been. Because she knew that it was, instead, simply the beginning, Karen cradled the phone against her shoulder while she lit a cigarette.

"Did I tell you that Harry and I have been considering a Cadillac?" Betsey asked. "Of course there's a lot to be said for a smaller car, but Harry and I—"

Betsey, Karen knew, was going to say exactly what she had said a year ago when they had turned their Ford Fairlane in on a new Buick. She was going to say that both she and Harry loathed ostentation of any kind. Simply loathed it. But the thing about Harry and herself was that they had this feeling for quality, for good workmanship. It was, she would imply, almost an affliction to be quite so sensitive where the Finer Things in life were concerned.

Harry worked for a very successful brewery. Karen was tempted to ask Betsey if the brewery was also one of the Finer Things in life. She was tempted to hang up—as Susan would probably have done—before Betsey got around to her mink coat, something without which no conversation with Betsey was usually complete. That she should do neither of these things was due to a clear recognition of the fact that Betsey could no more help being what she was, than she, Karen, could. Betsey, born with not too much intellect, on a rising tide of materialism, protected herself from anxiety and self-doubt in the only way she knew how to, behind a constantly reinforced bulwark of mink coats, new cars, and bigger and better TV sets. In a way she was to be envied, as was anybody in the middle of the twentieth century who could not think, or who refused to think. To attack this bulwark would have been wanton cruelty, Karen knew, because she was so much stronger than Betsey, even though she was afraid and Betsey was not. Even though nothing made sense to her any more, and all Betsey had to do was reach for her cheque-book in order to have things make perfect sense.

Betsey was well launched now into a word-for-word account of what the Cadillac salesman had said to Harry and herself, and what they had said to the Cadillac salesman.

If Harry had, as was more than possible, been at that party where Karen had met Rick, he would undoubtedly have been talking about salesmen, too. He would have been saying to anyone who would listen, "Have you heard the one about the travelling salesman who—" Since this was what he did at parties now, it was safe to assume that it was what he would always have done at a party.

Karen could, at any time during the years when Harry had been their next-door neighbour, have asked him if he had been at that party. She had not done so because, if he had been, it was something she did not want to know. To have had to weave Harry, even remotely, into any part of the fabric of her first evening with Rick, would have been horrible.

She had met Rick in the October following her return from Geneva; and if she had still been thinking of Cyr, she never did in the same way again.

She was at the university by then, and Geneva was already a dream she could almost believe had been dreamed by somebody else. A very detailed dream, but not a very credible one. In part this was because very few people at the university knew she had been away unless she told them so, which was something she felt disinclined to do. In those days, if you were wise, you suppressed the fact that you had lived abroad, just as you suppressed the fact that you could speak French. It was all right—in some circles even desirable—to have spent a holiday in Europe, but you set yourself apart if you admitted to having actually lived anywhere but in Toronto.

She had chosen to go to University College because it was the largest and most cosmopolitan of the various colleges that made up the university as a whole, and because, in those days particularly, Waycroft graduates almost never enrolled in University College. At Waycroft one was given to understand, by indirection, that a certain stigma was attached to University College. You could read what you liked into this. You could think that, negatively, Waycroft girls were not expected to turn their backs on their Anglican tradition by failing to go to Trinity. Or you could suspect that, more positively, it was considered undesirable to mix with a group ungoverned by taboos of race, colour, or creed.

She had taken modern languages, and, although she had in the beginning known nobody in any of her classes, had felt totally at home as she had not since she was eleven years old. While she had been at Waycroft her life had been divided into two separate sections as definitely as the city itself was divided by the Hill which was far more than a simple geographical line of demarcation. To live below the Hill was, metaphorically, to live on the wrong side of the tracks, and excusable only if your father was a professional man. Even when this was the case, it was not considered good taste to *like* living below the Hill.

Waycroft was, of course, above the Hill. Rowanwood, when it came into being, was, equally of course, above the Hill.

Karen had always liked living below the Hill, and had never made any secret of this. It was only below the Hill that you came into direct contact with the core of vitality that was the true essence of the city. Here you were acutely and excitingly aware of the steady heart-beat of a really great metropolis, fresh blood continuously pumped into it from the four corners of the globe. Here you felt as if the city belonged to you as much as you belonged to it. The throb of an ever increasing flood of traffic was the audible tempo of your own exhilaration. Chinatown with its wonderful restaurants was your Chinatown. The Royal Ontario Museum, with its three-storey-high totem pole built into the stair-well, was your museum. The biggest hotel in the British Empire was your hotel. The huge department stores, the musty pawnbrokers on Queen Street, the luxury shops at Bloor and Yonge, the street market south of College, the wide sweep of University Avenue leading up to the Provincial Parliament Buildings, and the spreading green oasis of Queen's Park—all these, and hundreds of others, were things that belonged to you as you belonged to them when you lived below the Hill, no more than fifteen minutes' walk from the University campus.

In that the greater must of necessity contain the less, you knew that Waycroft was a part of Toronto, too. But the perspective of a year away had shown you that the two were not, as most Waycroft graduates would have you believe, synonymous.

You realized, of course, as you had not before, that Torontonians were a particular breed unto themselves, as were the residents of most large cities. But you were none the less a Canadian for having been born and bred in Toronto. It was a little the way it would have been if, several centuries earlier, you had been an Iroquois, and within that frame of reference a Mohawk. The fact that the Oneidas and the Senecas were also Iroquois did not rule out intertribal differences, any more than being Canadian ruled out a certain amount of rivalry between Toronto and Montreal. This was why it was just as well not to advertise the fact that you spoke French. Somebody might think you came from Montreal.

After Geneva, you were more critical of Toronto than you had been in the past, but paradoxically you loved it more than you ever had, and you were damn proud of it. It was not London, and it was not Paris, but it *was* Toronto, and that was more than good enough for you. You were terribly excited about this St. Lawrence Seaway thing they had started to talk about, because you could see that if it went through, your city, your Toronto, could become one of the great inland seaports of the world.

Free of the restrictions against which she had rebelled while she was still at Waycroft, Karen was extremely happy at the university.

On that October evening which was to be the most important in her life, somebody had known somebody who knew somebody whose fraternity was having a party. There had been eight of them, and they had gone to the fraternity house uninvited—as you did, when you were a college freshman, to almost any place that was not barred and bolted against you.

The fraternity house was one of those huge Victorian relics on St. George just north of Harbord. Three stories and cupola. In spite of its size, it was already crammed to capacity when Karen and her friends got there a little before nine. Every window was open, and from every window there poured a Niagara of sound.

Several victrolas were playing. A radio, turned on full blast, brought Glen Gray and his Casa Loma orchestra back home from the other side of the forty-ninth parallel. A male quartet, in anything but close harmony, was slaughtering "When Day is Done". And through and under and above these individually recognizable noises rose an unceasing barrage of voices.

Separated from her companions almost as soon as they pushed through the front door into a hall that reminded her of Grand Central Station on an Easter week-end, Karen fought her way towards a corner of what had once been a very elegant drawing-room. The sort of drawing-room where, when she was small, her mother had occasionally taken her to tea at the written invitation of white-haired gentlewomen who wore lace at the necks of their black silk dresses; who sat and stood with beautiful erectness; and who always gave her a little present when she and her mother left.

She finally reached the corner of the room, leaned against the wall to catch her breath, and realized that she was still wearing her coat. Shrugging, more amused than not, she found cigarettes in one of the pockets, and lit one.

"Hiya, honey. What'll it be? Scotch, rye, or gin? Personally, I recommend the gin. Brought over from Buffalo this morning."

He was nobody Karen had ever seen before. She smiled, and said she would love some gin, but she was quite sure she would never see him again.

"Be right back," he said. "Now don't run out on me, honey."

At that time you could not drink in public, but you could, for private consumption, buy anything you wanted at a Liquor Control Board store. Where the Government and the consumer were inclined to differ was in the definition of the word "private". A parked car, for instance, was not considered by the Government to be a private place. Confronted by a policeman with a flashlight, you were inclined to agree with the Government. A policeman with a flashlight could shatter very effectively any illusion you might have entertained that you were in a private place. On the other hand, the underside of a table in the main dining-room of the Royal York Hotel, discreetly curtained by a floor-length white damask cloth, could be turned into a well-stocked private bar without unwelcome interference from the law. And in a fraternity house, its windows uncurtained, as open to the public eye as a goldfish bowl, you could stand upon your rights of privacy as long as you could stand at all.

None of it, as far as Karen could see, made any sense. Any more than bringing gin over from Buffalo made sense, apart from the fact that it had certainly been run through the customs—a saving more than negated by the cost of driving to Buffalo and back.

"Hello, there, puss-in-the-corner. You been waiting for me?"

This was nobody Karen knew either. But she did know the answers. "Patiently waiting," she said. "Why were you so long in coming?"

"Hadn't learned to dream. Flunked the last three semesters. Can I dream now?"

Karen laughed. "If you like."

"Anybody got strings on you for the big party next month, puss?"

"I'm allergic to string," Karen said. But she said it in the right way.

"It should be quite a party," he said. "Strikes me you'd be a nice doll to have around. Did you know we were trying to get Bing?"

"Are you?"

"You're damn right we are."

Karen was quite sure they wouldn't get Bing, but she did not doubt that they were trying and that the tariff would be no handicap. There was unlimited money, as well as unlimited gall, to be found around a great many of the fraternities. One of them, she had been told, had got Sally Rand over for a party the previous year.

"Hey, you haven't got anything to drink!" he said, and he looked really upset. "Personally, I recommend the gin. It's Uncle Sam's best. Guaranteed to make a girl say uncle after one shot. Now, you stay right where you are, and I'll be right back."

"All right," Karen said.

"Don't run away!" He had to shout to make himself heard. "I'll be right back."

At no time was she left alone for more than a minute or so. They all told her to stay right where she was, and they all quite honestly meant to come right back. She was glad there was so much running interference between them and their good—or, as the case might be, bad—intentions. For her, a party like this was a spectator sport. She did not want to get involved.

"Are you enjoying this?"

He was tall, and dark, and his voice was quiet and without emphasis, but Karen heard his words with disturbing clarity. It was as if this man who had spoken was alone with her in some remote place she had always known existed, but which she had never visited before.

She looked up into his face, and saw that although he was smiling, his eyes were intent and serious. Almost frightened, she knew instinctively that, without warning or preparation of any kind at all, she faced one of the major decisions of her life. If she was flippant, he would go away, and he would not tell her that he would be right back. He wouldn't come back at all, ever. If she answered him honestly, she would never be able to go back, herself, to anything as she had known it before. She would be involved not just for this moment, or for this evening, but quite possibly for the rest of her life. And she didn't want to be involved. Not yet. Not for a long time to come. All she wanted was to be Karen Holbrook, herself, with no strings attached. A self which, even as she tried to defend it, betrayed her.

"No," she said. "I'm not enjoying it."

"Shall we leave?"

He was giving her a second chance. It was one of the first things she learned about Rick. He never pressured you into anything. He made his own wishes clear, but where you went from there was up to you.

Karen's answer to his question was almost inaudible, but he must have heard it, because he took her hand and guided her to the door through a throng that parted in front of an authority of purpose that she was to learn was very much a part of him.

When they emerged into the fresh quiet of the October night, the noise behind them something they had already forgotten, he immediately released her hand. And Karen, who had intended to withdraw it, was perversely disappointed.

"Do you feel like walking?" he asked. "Or would you rather go somewhere for coffee?"

"Both," Karen told him. And she was glad that her voice should be so casual. "Walk first. Coffee afterwards."

"Do we go north or south?"

"In the daytime I like to go south. At night, I like to go north," Karen said, even while she wondered why she should have told him something quite so silly, something she had never said aloud before.

"Do you?" he said. "So do I." He sounded very pleased.

The dry rustle of fallen leaves underfoot, they turned north toward Bloor Street, walking in a rhythmical unison that was a physical satisfaction in itself.

"We would dance well together," he said. It was not until nearly a year later that Karen got him to admit, in so many words, that he had meant exactly what she had thought he meant. During that first evening, and for some weeks afterwards, it was the only thing he did say that could have meant anything of the kind.

When he finally left her at her own door it was after one o'clock, and though she still knew very little that was factual about him, she felt she already knew him better than she had ever known anyone before. She had never guessed that it would be like this. But then, she thought, how could she have guessed, because she had never *really* been in love before.

He would not move fast. He had made that perfectly clear, while making it equally clear that there was little likelihood of his changing the direction in which he was moving.

She had known, in advance, that he would make no attempt to kiss her good night. And she had been glad. The warmth and texture of his hand, which had again found hers as they turned up the walk to her house, had been enough, had been a promise that left her light-headed with happiness.

She had had no doubts then about anything. Everything had made wonderful sense.

Betsey was still talking, which meant, Karen realized vaguely, that she herself must have been saying yes, and no, more or less in the right places.

Her mind formed a pattern rather like an equilateral triangle, with Betsey at one corner, her memories at another, and the Chinese carpet—its translucent green still barred with sunlight—at the third.

With the corner allotted to Betsey she listened to Betsey explaining that the Cadillac would not in the long run cost any more than a Buick. This was utterly absurd. But Karen had no doubt that Betsey believed it. Betsey was a sucker for the something-for-nothing sales pitch, particularly when that something was something she wanted. And it wasn't just Betsey. Most of the people on the North American continent, as far as Karen could see, were prepared to play ostrich to this kind of approach. The salesmen and the advertisers, very earnestly and sincerely, assured them that it was indeed so, they could indeed get something for nothing. All they had to do was sign on the dotted line, and keep it in mind that quality was its own reward. And if they were to buy right now, they would actually be saving money.

Anyone unfortunate enough to discover that this was not so, was likely to go into a state of shock. But not too many did, because the something-for-nothing creed was too well established for its devotees to doubt it even when faced with facts—usually in the form of overdue time payments—that flatly contradicted it. In its infancy it was a religion for the most part limited to proselytizing those who could read. With the introduction of radio, the potential adherents who could be captured was doubled more or less overnight. Now, Karen thought cynically, with television in the pulpit, complete imbecility seemed to be about the only human state as yet untapped.

You don't have to give up the idea of that new house in order to go to Europe this summer. You can do BOTH! You can go now, pay later. It won't cost you a thing! And if you want to take the kids along, you will save hundreds of dollars!

You would have been thrown out of school at the Grade III level, if you had produced this kind of reasoning in arithmetic class. And yet Betsey, and thousands of others like her, accepted it as gospel. Betsey believed implicitly that you could actually save money by going to Europe, and by owning a Cadillac instead of a Buick.

Her attention caught as sharply as one's attention is sometimes caught by something on a radio programme to which one has not really been listening, Karen became aware of what Betsey was now saying.

"Harry and I," Betsey was saying, "are considering buying a Chinese carpet. Of course there's a lot to be said for broadloom, but feeling the way Harry and I do about quality and workmanship, we think—"

"Betsey!" Karen cut in. "I've got to go. The telephone's ringing—I mean there's somebody at the door. I am so glad you can come tomorrow. About seven o'clock. Just a friendly cook-out, but it should be fun."

With the abrupt cessation of Betsey's voice as Karen cut the connection, there should have been no sound at all in the sunlit silence of the house. The echoes of her own hysterical laughter were shocking to her in a way that the helpless tears that followed were not.

12 | Just a friendly cook-out

During the next thirty-six hours Karen blotted out all thought of anything but the preparations necessary for the cook-out. With grim determination she refused to think of the implications of laughter that, there was no getting away from it, had been closer to genuine hysteria than she had ever been in her life.

The pain in her side, catching her from time to time, was a piercing bid for attention that she found almost welcome because it was so purely physical. Even so, the fact that she was committed to seeing Dr. Lowe on the day after the cook-out was something she would just as soon not think about either. The appointment with Dr. Lowe stood like a grey wall between her and anything that might follow it, making it impossible now to dwell in any concrete way on the trip to Planesville. Impossible, too, to come to any definite conclusion, one way or the other, about Cyr. By concentrating on what lay on this side of the grey wall, she was still Karen Whitney who, though she had problems admittedly, nevertheless had unlimited time in which to cope with those problems. To look beyond the grey wall was to move into a treeless, blighted area that had never known the sun; an area where there was no sound or movement other than the whisper of sands running out toward a loneliness too terrible to contemplate.

Although a cook-out meant that you entertained outdoors, this did not mean that the whole house did not have to be cleaned in advance. Short of installing outdoor conveniences, something that Karen and Rick occasionally joked about in a semi-serious vein, there was no avoiding what would be, as the evening wore on, a steady stream of traffic to both the downstairs and the upstairs bathrooms. And once people were in your house, even if relatively briefly, they always managed to be in the whole of it. The minute they got inside they would be visited by necessities other than those that had brought them in. They would phone home to make sure the children were all right. They would realize they were out of matches, and start searching for some. They would need pins they had not, for some obscure reason, needed while they were still outside. They would develop a very temporary preference for water in place of hard liquor—water that they themselves ran out of a tap into a glass that they themselves took down from the shelf where you had, you thought, safely hidden your cut crystal.

They might even—and this was something that had shocked you badly on the only occasion when it had happened in your house—make use of the guest bedroom. That was how you had known for sure about Fay and Harry. Fay had tried to straighten up the bed afterwards, but she never had been able to make a bed properly.

Once the house was cleaned, and you had checked on fresh towels and soap, and put out quantities of matches, ash-trays, and Kleenex where, you hoped, people would trip over them without having to go any farther, the preparations ahead of you were still formidable.

You had to bring up the rugs and cushions from the basement and put them out to air. Then you had to wash all the garden furniture, because, although people would come in sports clothes, these would not be the kind of sports clothes they wore at their cottages. They would be more in the line of "just a little Schiaperelli slacks suit that I picked up for nothing, my dear, literally nothing". Karen, herself, planned to wear a pair of dark-blue gabardine slim-jeans, and a full-sleeved blue silk shirt that had cost as much as any of her dresses. She looked very well in sports clothes, and it was one of the most becoming outfits she had ever owned; but her pleasure in it was offset by the knowledge that she had bought it in order to be a properly dressed member of Rowanwood's big, happy family.

The pottery dishes, which had been all they owned when they gave the beer parties back in the days on Gavin Street, were perfect for a cook-out; but they had to be taken down from a top shelf and washed, because now they were never used at any other time. Peg had always been very fond of the pottery dishes, and Karen, before she realized how useful they might still be, had promised Peg that she could have them whenever she got married. It was not a promise that Karen would go back on; but the idea of investing in a whole set of picnic china for a once-a-year party that she did not want to give in the first place was, to say the least, revolting.

It was just another possibility from which they would escape if they moved to Planesville. In Planesville, she was sure, there would be neither cocktail brawls nor mass barbecue dinners. In Planesville there would just be small, quiet dinners that really were informal and friendly, which you could enjoy because they would contain no element of keeping up with anybody or anything. There would probably be euchre and whist parties, too, like the ones her mother used to talk about. Euchre and whist were, she had to admit, pretty dull games compared with bridge; but it would be the atmosphere that would count, jolly and uncompetitive, with prizes like home-made preserves and place mats that people had crocheted themselves. And if she and Rick missed their bridge, they could always have a good, tight game with Susan and Lewis when they visited Toronto.

The food you served at a cook-out was relatively simple. It was the quantity you had to handle, and the cost, that threw you. At least that was the way things were in Rowanwood. In Rowanwood you did not offer your guests hot dogs and hamburgers, as you had on Gavin Street. You gave them the best steaks available, together with those special rolls you could get only at the Patisserie Française. You also made up enormous amounts of tossed salad, done the way you had learned to do it in Geneva, with leaf lettuce and oil and vinegar. You served mustard and catsup because you knew you had to, but ever since Geneva this had been something it really hurt you to do. And then for dessert you had those marvellous little rum cakes that had to be ordered by mail from that store in Stratford.

You were the only one in Rowanwood who knew about the store in Stratford. In your mother's and your grandmother's day family secrets of this kind consisted of recipes handed down from one generation to another. Now you simply tried, whenever possible, to keep people from knowing where you bought things. Both Betsey and Millicent had, you knew, snooped through the kitchen at last year's cook-out in an effort to find the containers in which the rum cakes had arrived. When you found this out, you didn't feel quite such a fool for having hidden them under the bed in the guest-room. You had reasoned, and correctly, that the sort of person who would be interested in the guest-room bed would not be the sort of person who would care where you bought your rum cakes.

Karen had not intended to mention to Rick the possibility that Betsey and Harry might buy a Chinese carpet. They were in their bedroom changing their clothes for the cook-out with, Karen was relieved to know, a clear half hour before anyone might arrive, when she finally told him.

"Rick," she began, "the Milners are thinking of buying a Cadillac."

"It was only a matter of time," Rick said. "Where the hell have you hidden my shirt, sweetheart?"

"I haven't hidden it, darling. It's just where it should be. That's the only reason you can't find it."

"Well," Rick said, "it certainly isn't in my shirt drawer."

"It must be," Karen told him. "Here, let me look. Darling, this is no time to start anything like that. That's odd. Your shirt really isn't here. Now, what on earth could have happened to it? Oh, I remember. I put it in one of my drawers."

"And you don't call that hiding it?"

"As a matter of fact, this time I did hide it. It was because you were wearing it just any old time. A Jaeger shirt like that isn't for wearing just any old time. Here you are, and don't say what I know you want to say. And Rick—darling, please leave me alone or I'll never be ready in time."

"You didn't use to be like this. I can remember a time when—"

"Darling, don't tease me, or I'll get everything on back to front, or put on the wrong shade of lipstick or something."

"What a disastrous thought. Are the Milners going to get a chauffeur with their Cadillac?"

"No," Karen said, "but they are—Rick, they're going to get a Chinese carpet!"

"Are they? Well, what of it?"

"What of it! Rick, don't you see, it spoils—I mean—"

"All I can see is that it doesn't matter a damn what Betsey and Harry do. Not one small sawed-off damn. What Betsey and Harry do has absolutely nothing to do with us, and never has had, and never will have."

He was already dressed, and Karen knew that she really would have to hurry. It was no time for trying to explain that it wasn't what Betsey and Harry did that bothered her. What bothered her was that she and Rick should apparently be doing it too. If she once got started, she would say more than she meant to say. She might even end up in tears. And it was no time for that.

Instead, as some release for her feelings, she said, "Damn this bloody party! I don't see why we should have to do so many things we don't really want to do."

"Everybody has to do things they don't want to do. You should learn to roll with the punches, sweetheart. You make things hard for yourself because you've never really learned to roll with the punches."

Karen got up from her dressing-table and crossed to the bed where she had laid out her slacks and the blue silk shirt. "I don't see," she said, "why people can't be content with simple things any more. Like euchre parties, for instance."

"My God!" Rick said. "Have you ever been to a euchre party?"

"No," Karen said, "but I know all about them. My mother told me all about them."

"She couldn't have," Rick said. And he was laughing now. "If she had, you wouldn't want to go to one. If you ever went to a euchre party, you'd be bored silly."

"I would rather," Karen said, "be bored silly at a euchre party than be bored silly by Harry at a damn Rowanwood barbecue."

"We'll have to talk about this again," Rick said. "Right now I had better get downstairs and set up the bar."

After Rick had left the room, Karen glanced out of the window and saw Pete coming up the drive. She ran downstairs with no other thought than that she must speak to him before any of the neighbours began to arrive. Although she and Rick had given countless parties in Rowanwood, she had never been able to get over an acute sense of guilt because they had never once invited Pete's mother. Useless to tell herself that to have done so would have been to crucify Mrs. Johnson. Useless to remind herself that Mrs. Johnson, working the evening shift in that restaurant downtown, would have been unable to come anyway. Both these things were true, but they did not alter an outward appearance of standing, along with all the rest of Rowanwood, on the opposite side of the fence from Mrs. Johnson. She would have liked to ask Pete himself to something like an outdoor barbecue, but here she was up against a different kind of brick wall. You simply could not ask a boy of his age to a party where several of the guests might drink more than was good for them.

She reached the front door and opened it just as Pete arrived at the steps.

"Hi, Mrs. Whitney," he said. "I was wondering if there were any odd jobs you wanted done this evening?"

"Not this evening, Pete," Karen said. "But it was nice of you to think of it. This evening we have people coming in. We're paying off all our social debts. You know how it is. You keep accepting invitations, and then suddenly you realize it's time you repaid some of them."

"I know what you mean," Pete said. "It's that way at school, too."

Instantly Karen saw all that lay behind the little he had said. Oh, god-damn everything, she thought violently.

Without being told, she knew precisely the position Pete was in, and precisely how uncomfortable he must feel about it. He had, because he was the kind of boy he was, made a place for himself at Upper Canada. It was more than a year since he had come home with a black eye. There could be little doubt that he had been to quite a few parties at the houses of some of the other boys, because boys weren't like girls. Once a boy made a place for himself with his classmates, the fact that his mother was a waitress would not make too much difference any more. For a girl at an expensive private school it would be the kiss of death. At a school like Waycroft, it would be easier to have a father in jail on an embezzlement charge—provided he had embezzled on a sufficiently large scale—than it would be to have a mother who was a waitress. At a boys' private school, even one like Upper Canada, it wouldn't necessarily matter. If you were good at rugby or cricket, and proved, when you had to, that you could take it, you would be all right.

Once this happened, however, you might find yourself facing a different kind of social problem. If, as in Pete's case, you had no home to which you could take your friends, you were in fresh difficulties. Because Mrs. Johnson's house was in no sense a home. Mrs. Johnson could, if she had wanted to, have worked a day shift. Whether she chose the hours she did because of the larger tips she would get, or because she liked to stay in bed all morning, did not actually matter. All that did matter was that she had never given Pete what could be called a proper home. In spite of, perhaps even because of this, Pete was belligerently loyal to his mother. His loyalty was just one of the things that had drawn Karen to him, but it was now an element that made what she did more difficult than it might otherwise have been.

She began very carefully.

"I suppose it is that way at school, too," she said. "I suppose you get asked to parties, and then you have all the bother of having to give one of your own."

"Yeah," Pete said. "That's the thing. It's getting all the stuff, and sort of, well, organizing things."

He sounded very off-hand, but Karen knew he was tense because he had pushed his hands into his pockets, and she could see from their outline that they were clenched.

Nevertheless, she still moved cautiously, working along the

lines that the only real problem in giving a party was the inherent nuisance value, that the practical details of ordering such things as cokes and ice cream were all that ever made the giving of a party in any way difficult. Any criticism of Mrs. Johnson, no matter how oblique or inadvertent, would, she knew, be fatal.

"If you're like me," she said, "you probably put that kind of thing off just because it's such a bother. Like this evening, for instance. We've had to ask more than thirty people just because we've put it off so long. And it's much easier for me than it must be for you and your mother because I don't have to work at two jobs the way your mother does."

"Yeah," Pete said, "it's hard on my mother. It's hard for her to find the time for a silly old thing like a party. Her never being home for dinner, you know."

His freckles, Karen saw, were more noticeable than usual. It could have been the evening light, but she didn't think so. And remembering all that Carol and Peg had had in the way of love, and privilege, and protection, she felt her throat tighten with pity for this boy who had none of these things.

"It is hard for your mother," she said. "In fact, I don't see how she could possibly arrange a party with all she has to do. Pete— I wonder. You're such a help to me, cutting the lawn, and things like that. I wonder if I couldn't be of some help to you. How would it be if you talked this over with your mother, and, if it was all right with her, asked some of the boys up to your house, and then brought them over here to eat. It wouldn't be any trouble for me to pick up some stuff at Loblaw's one morning. You and your friends could take it from there, and do your own cooking on the barbecue at the back of our garden."

She had never, Karen told Rick later, seen anything quite like the expression on Pete's face, unless it was the time when they had given Carol the doll back on Gavin Street. The one they hadn't really been able to afford. The one with the real hair, and the big brown eyes that opened and shut. The expression on Pete's face had made her glad for the first time that they had a barbecue.

"Gee, Mrs. Whitney," Pete said, and he was stammering. Pete, the boy whom Millicent chased off the edge of her lawn. "Gee," he said again, "that would be super. But I couldn't let you—"

"I wouldn't be doing a thing, really," Karen cut in. "It would be a cook-out, and you'd be the cook. I'd just be around, that's all."

That she would be around was, she knew, the thing that would matter most. Mrs. Johnson, one way and another, was never around.

"Hi, Karen, Pete! Are we horribly early?"

Karen looked up to see Susan and Lewis walking up the drive. Lewis was not, of course, wearing a double-breasted grey suit, but even in a dark plaid shirt and flannels, he gave you the impression that he was.

"Hello!" Karen called. "You're not early. But you are the first, which we always hope you and Lewis will be."

"Hello, Karen," Lewis said. "Hello there, Pete."

"Hello, Mr. Preston. Hi, Susan."

Karen, who happened to be looking at Lewis, felt an old memory stir before the sudden inscrutability of grey eyes that might, instead, have expressed some surprise at the familiarity with which Peter had greeted Susan. It was exactly the same lack of expression that she had found odd, even for Lewis, on an afternoon ten years earlier when Mrs. Johnson's name had been mentioned on the terrace behind Susan and Lewis's house. It was an incident, if you could call it that, which she had almost forgotten. I was right, she thought. There was, and still is, some tie-up here. The only obvious conclusion, however, was as untenable on this warm June evening as it had been on that crisp October afternoon when she and Rick had seen the For Sale sign on what was to be their house.

"Pete," Susan was saying, "are you in on this party?"

"Heck, no," Pete said. "Not this party. This is just—I mean this is for grown-ups."

"Pete and I," Karen said, "have been talking about another party. Come September, Pete's going to let me pretend I have Carol and Peg back for an evening. He's going to bring some of his school friends around, and I think it's very nice of him."

"She's the one that's nice," Pete said. "But I guess you know that, because you're friends of hers. I guess I better beat it now. Bye, Mrs. Whitney. Bye, Mr. Preston. Bye, Susan."

When he had gone, Lewis turned to Susan. "I didn't know you and Pete were such friends."

Susan had come all in black. She looked very sophisticated. Flicking an invisible speck from her slacks, she said, "We're not, really. Is Rick in the back garden? Let's go join him."

As they came around the side of the house, Lewis said, "Very nice, Karen. Very nice indeed."

In the gentle light of sunset, it did all look lovely. But Karen would have liked it better if it had not reminded her so vividly of one of those full-page colour advertisements in *Life* magazine. It could, equally well, have been an advertisement for a great many things. For asbestos shingles, the kind that are guaranteed to last a lifetime. For Canadian Club Whiskey, served to the right people at the right time. For what the well-dressed man will wear, because Rick did look both very handsome and very well dressed in his Jaeger shirt. For the kind of weed-killer that frees you from all worry about your lawn, even a lawn as big as this one, which was, really, merely a continuation of the lawns surrounding the house. For Sheridan Nurseries. For informal garden furniture, the Cape Cod style that—if you were prepared to repaint it every year—you could leave out in all weathers. In fact, for any damn thing at all that represented Gracious Outdoor Living.

It was too perfect. Just how they had accomplished this, Karen was no longer quite sure. All she was sure of was that it was much too perfect. The only thing it lacked, if you could call this a lack, was a wire-haired terrier frisking on the lawn, a terrier made vital by Gordon's Special Dog Food. Or, perhaps, a poodle with a ribbon on its head, also made vital by Gordon's Special Dog Food. Advertisers, for some curious reason, seemed better able to picture a family without children than without a dog. This might, of course, be a Malthusian trend, but it didn't seem likely. Neither Carol nor Peg had ever wanted a dog. Julia and Ned, who owned a disastrous creature whose principal activity consisted of scratching itself, had referred to this as "a suppression of natural instincts due to improper environmental conditioning".

In Toronto, if you gave a party, it was surprising if all your guests did not arrive within a few minutes of the specified time. In this respect, with Canadians more than with any other nationality, you knew where you were. Once a party was well under way, however, Canadians were just like everybody else. Anything could happen, and often did.

The first thing Lewis said, when they joined Rick at the fireplace, was, "Let me know when I can give a hand."

"Right," Rick said. "It could be any time now."

The friendship between Rick and Lewis was one that had always puzzled Karen a little, perhaps because it was so purely a man's relationship. As far as she could see, they had very little in common. And when they went hunting for a week in the fall, as they always did every year, she had never been able to discover what they talked about. She sometimes wondered if they talked at all. The first time Rick had gone with Lewis on a hunting trip, she had expected afterwards to know a lot more about Lewis than she had before. But this had not been the case. And it wasn't that Rick was holding anything back.

"But you must have talked about something," she had said. "In a whole week, you must have talked about something."

"I suppose we must have," Rick had said.

"Well then, what?"

"I really don't know," Rick had told her.

During the October week when Lewis and Rick were away, Karen always stayed with Susan. And, although she felt oddly incomplete without Rick, she did have a marvellous time. It was, as she had told Susan, like being back at that hotel in Cannes where they had spent their Easter holidays the year they had been in Europe.

Breakfast was the same; coffee and *croissants* brought to your bedside when you rang for them. And being addressed by the maid as "Madame" was the same. You had not, of course, been "Madame" when you stayed at Cannes. But in those big hotels facing the promenade and the Mediterranean, they always called you "Madame" just to be on the safe side. So that if you did what they fully expected you to do, there need at no time be any embarrassment. Neither she nor Susan had been even remotely tempted to do what had been expected of them. Not that there had not been opportunities. All you had to do was go out and sit in one of those sidewalk cafés with the gaily painted metal chairs and tables, to be surrounded by opportunities. When she stayed with Susan in Rowanwood, it was one of the things they often talked about, that Easter holiday on the French Riviera. She and Susan talked all the time, and, when Rick got back, Karen never had any difficulty in recalling what they had talked about.

Rick had just had time to mix drinks for Susan and Lewis when the rest of the neighbours began to arrive in a steady stream.

"Susan," Karen said, "the salad is in the refrigerator. It's all ready in bowls. Will you be an angel and bring it out later? And, for heaven's sake, in so far as you can, keep Millicent from trying to run things."

Susan's lazy smile was very reassuring. "*Entendu,*" she said.

With a feeling that everything was nicely under control, Karen went forward to greet her guests. Bill and Ruth Newton. Bill was a partner in the firm of Newton, Newton, Morecombe and Fry, the chartered accountants on Bay Street who were branching out into methods engineering, and who had been after Rick for some time. Jane and Fred Coleman. Fred was a vice-president of Canasco Oil, and had yet to discover that he couldn't hold his liquor. Frank and Betty Anderson. Frank was a lawyer, and Frank and Betty were people whom Karen and Rick enjoyed spending time with in a really—not a socially—informal manner. Betty had been two years ahead of Karen at Waycroft. When you were far enough away from it, having been to Waycroft was a passport to friendship rather than a bar to it. Whatever you had thought of the religion of Standing Up Straight while you were being exposed to it, in later years you always recognized with pleasure somebody who had been taught to Stand Up Straight, even when they weren't actually doing so.

"Karen!"

Karen looked up to see Millicent and Biff standing on the terrace. They had, apparently, come through the house rather than around it. Although slightly annoyed by this, Karen could not help thinking that they looked rather splendid there together on what could briefly be imagined as an otherwise empty stage. With her black hair and high colouring, Millicent did, now that you came to think of it, look, as she had described herself, rather like Pallas Athene, perhaps as Epstein might have conceived her. Biff, of course, was pure Epstein, though you were baffled as to just what he might be supposed to represent.

They came down the short flight of stairs to the garden.

"Karen," Millicent said, "I've left your tickets on the table in the front hall. They're right there beside that big vase with the lotus flowers on it. You can pay me for them later."

"What tickets?" Karen asked.

"For the bridge," Millicent said. "The one for the New Canadians."

"Oh, yes," Karen said. "The one for the New Canadians."

"I've fixed you up with a four, too," Millicent said. "I've arranged that you play with some friends of mine from out of town. I could see, when I thought it over, that you had a point in thinking you might not be able to make up a table, because Rowanwood has really rallied this time."

Karen reminded herself that Millicent was her guest. "That was very thoughtful of you, Millicent," she said.

"Well, my dear," Millicent said, "it seemed the least I could do, and since you had agreed to buy the tickets anyway, I knew it wouldn't much matter to you who used them. It is really heart-warming the way Rowanwood has rallied."

"When you want something done," Biff said, "all you have to do is give the ball to Millicent. Millicent certainly knows how to carry the ball."

Karen was relieved to see that Barbara had come across to join them. Barbara was dressed in white, and had a white ribbon in her smooth blonde hair. It was not something everybody could have got away with, but on Barbara a hair ribbon was very becoming.

"How is Arlene?" Barbara asked Millicent. "I heard that the poor child wasn't well."

"Oh, she's all right," Millicent said. "She's still in bed, but she's perfectly all right. It's just some kind of summer flu."

Barbara looked much as she might have done if Millicent had said that it was just some kind of seasonal syphilis. "You have a nurse with her, I suppose?"

"A nurse!" Millicent said. "For God's sake, why?"

"It's all right," Biff said. "We've left Millicent's lap dog with her."

When she heard this, Barbara really did look shocked. Barbara would never dream of criticizing Boris's presence in Millicent's household on any grounds other than that he was not a Mothercraft nurse, and had not kept up his tennis.

"Don't worry, Barbara," Karen said. "Arlene is well looked after. She will be perfectly all right."

Biff laughed. It was rather an overpowering sound. "That's right," he said. "Any female would be all right with Boris."

Biff, like so many large men, was inclined to make the mistake of equating sexual potency with size. In this instance, it was probably as well that he did. Nevertheless, Karen was unreservedly glad when he turned to wander off with Barbara. Biff admired a woman who kept up her tennis.

"Karen," Millicent said, when they were out of earshot, "I've been thinking about what you said. About not going on with it. If I do decide not to go on with it, can I come over and talk to you sometimes? I'll need somebody to talk to if I don't go on with it."

"You can come over any time you like, Millicent."

"Thanks," Millicent said. "I'll let you know. Anyway, I won't do anything definite until the summer is over. Now you won't forget where your tickets are, will you? On that table in your front hall beside the vase with the lotuses on it."

What, Karen wondered, as she watched Millicent walk toward the group around the fireplace, did the summer have to do with it? Millicent, though you would never have thought such a thing possible, was in some ways as wilfully foolish as Fay. Fay, whom she could now see holding what she knew to be a martini—very dry—while she talked to Matt.

Both Fay and Millicent, for reasons completely outside the realm of ordinary comprehension, seemed to think that summer in itself was at one and the same time an excuse and a protection for their actions. Because there was such a thing as loyalty to your own sex—although some people did not seem to believe this—you hoped that nothing would happen to prove either of them wrong. You strongly disapproved of what they were doing, but you did not want either of them to get hurt.

"Darling! When did you put in the lights?"

Betsey and Harry, the last to arrive, were still some yards away, but Betsey's voice had carrying quality.

Betsey was wearing a red matador suit that looked as if it had been custom tailored for her, probably at that special women's department at Squire's. Betsey was one of those anomalies, a woman with a really perfect figure and no sex appeal. She was the kind of girl who would have enjoyed quite a rush at high school. At North Toronto Collegiate, while the boys were still immature enough to let their eyes be their principal guide, she had probably had herself quite a time.

"Hello, Betsey. Hello, Harry," Karen said in her best social voice. "How nice to see you. The lights? Why, Rick put them in last week. It must have been while you two were at that convention in Chicago. We wondered beforehand if lights outside were a good idea, but now they're in we think they're quite effective."

It was true that they had wondered. It was equally true that they had been right in going ahead with the idea. Rick had done the job himself, putting one floodlight on the terrace, and two amongst the pines, with a switch by the French windows, and another beside the fireplace. The lights were not too bright, and Rick had angled them very cleverly. Now that the sun had actually set, and the sky was darkening, they were a definite contribution to Gracious Outdoor Living.

The first time Rick had tried them out, he had said, "*C'est un peu Versailles*. Or if you prefer, *un peu* Bayview." But he had obviously been pleased with his handiwork.

Karen, although of course she hadn't said so, had seen the lights as something else that would improve the price of the house if they moved to Planesville.

"You're quite right, Karen," Harry said. "They're very effective. You've done it with real taste. I always appreciate something that's in really good taste."

Because Betsey and Harry were the last to arrive, Karen went with them to join the others. Rick was still serving drinks, but Lewis had started to grill steaks. Like everything else he did, Lewis did this very well. And Susan had, Karen saw, already brought out the salad. Everything was under control. All she had to do for the present was talk to Harry, which meant, as it always did with Harry, listening to stories as far removed from good taste as social tolerance would permit, and being bored to extinction by an account of the night-club shows Harry had seen on his one visit to Paris. He might, Karen felt, just once have mentioned something he had seen in Paris other than unclad beauties whom he insisted on referring to as "little numbers". But he never did.

"Now there was a little number third from the left," Harry was saying.

With a fixed smile on her face, Karen pretended to listen while thinking, as she often did when forced to listen to Harry for any length of time, of a conversation she had once had with Cyr.

It had been just before she and Susan had gone to Paris for the first time. Cyr, who knew the city well, had been telling her what to see and what not to see. Amongst other things he had advised her to stay away from the Folies Bergères.

"Why?" Karen had asked. "Do you think I would be shocked?"

"Not in the way you mean."

"What other way is there?"

"The show wouldn't shock you," Cyr had said. "But the audience would."

She had gone, of course, just to find out what he meant. He had been quite right. The audience had made her sick. It had been made up principally of Harrys. Susan had not felt the way she did. Susan had just enjoyed the show, and ignored the Harrys.

When she had got back to Geneva, Cyr had not asked if she had gone. There had been no need to. He had known she had, just as he had known in advance what her reaction would be. Cyr always had understood her better than she had wanted him to. Better than she had understood herself.

"Well," Harry was saying, "that little number was really a knock-out, if you get what I mean."

Karen did get what he meant, and had reached the limit of her endurance. "Harry," she said, "I'm sorry to leave you, but there are a few things I must see to."

Rick was working with Lewis at the grill now.

"Oh, God," Karen whispered, as she came up beside them. "Give me something to do. Anything."

"Harry?" Rick asked.

"What else?"

"Couldn't you stop him?" Rick asked.

"Nobody," Karen said, "can stop him. You know that, darling. Here, I'll take those plates."

"There are certain things," Lewis said, "that should not be permitted in decent society." Lewis had very acute hearing.

"In my experience," Karen told him, "that is where one seems most likely to find them."

"That's a very cynical remark, my dear," Lewis said. "It's not like you to be cynical."

"She isn't cynical," Rick said. "She just hasn't ever leaned to roll with the punches. Here, darling, these are for Frank and Betty Anderson. Go and talk to the Andersons, and you'll feel happier."

It was a little after eleven o'clock when Karen saw Susan beckoning to her from one of the two garden lounge chairs close against the hedge that separated their garden from the Willoughbys. Karen always felt a little uncomfortable about not asking the Willoughbys when they had a party, even though they had never, since the Willoughbys built in Rowanwood, exchanged more than the barest civilities with them. Rick was quite happy about not asking the Willoughbys. It was, he said, one of the most satisfactory and civilized relationships he enjoyed with anyone, and he did not want to see it disturbed.

Actually, Karen agreed with Rick in this, but as she approached Susan and Matt, the sight of a glowing cigar through a gap in the hedge was not exactly a welcome one.

"Karen," Susan said, "Matt tells me he hasn't heard the story about how you and Rick went to the Palace. Here, you take my place, and sit down and tell him about it. I'll do my good deed for the day and rescue Barbara from Biff."

A moment later, Karen found herself sitting down while Matt waited expectantly for her to begin what was really rather a long story. Susan, who never gave the impression of moving with undue haste, was already half-way across the garden on her way to the terrace steps and Barbara who, actually no longer with Biff, had just been joined by Rick.

If she had not known Susan quite so well, Karen would have seen nothing odd in any of this. But she did know Susan well. Very well. And with no more to go on than intuition, she knew beyond a shadow of a doubt that Susan was either beginning, or possibly even continuing, a private campaign designed to keep Barbara from going to Cape Cod again. To be left with Matt under these circumstances made her feel acutely embarrassed. She felt rather as she did when Ned produced one of his wretched word-association tests, as if no matter what she did she would betray herself in one way or another. More in order to avoid any possible mention of Fay's name, than to amuse Matt, she began to tell him the story about the Palace. But even as she told it, she continued to be torn between irritation, unwilling amusement, and a quite irrational sense of guilt. Susan might not have been out of place conducting intrigues at the court of Louis XIV. But as far as she herself was concerned, it was an occupation at which she suspected she would not have lasted twenty-four hours.

She was still feeling guilty as she and Rick stacked the last of the dishes in the sink, a little before two in the morning.

"Why did Barbara leave early?" Rick asked. "Was it something to do with children?"

"No," Karen said. "She had a headache."

"That's too bad. It was a pity Matt had to go, too. Of course he would go with her if she wasn't feeling well, but it was a pity he had to leave when he was having such a good time."

"Was he?" Karen asked. She was busy filling highball and cocktail glasses with water, and she had her back to him.

"You should know," Rick said. "You were talking with him. I don't know when I've seen Matt look as if he were enjoying himself more. What were you telling him that made him laugh so much?"

There was one thing to be said for rinsing out glasses. You could, if you wanted to, make it take quite a long time. "I don't know what I was saying," Karen told him. "I really couldn't tell you. I was just being a good hostess and trotting out all my old jokes."

"He laughed at one point in particular. Which one were you telling him then?"

There seemed to be no way of stopping this conversation any more than there had been a way of leaving Matt gracefully. She could, of course, tell Rick the whole thing, but this was something she wanted to avoid if she possibly could. Rick thought little enough of Fay as it was, and he had very strong views about interfering with other people's lives. Any plan to influence Barbara's thinking, even for her own good, would meet with his unqualified disapproval.

"It could have been the joke about first prize and second prize," she said.

"Which one is that?"

"Oh, you know, darling. The one about the Montreal contest where the first prize was one week in Toronto, and the second prize was two weeks in Toronto."

Rick had heard it before, but he laughed. "What other ones did you tell him?" he asked, and he was still laughing.

"Darling, I don't know. You can't remember everything you say at a party. You have too much on your mind. Particularly when it's your own party. I told him about how we went to the palace. I was just being a good hostess."

"Well, sweetheart, you certainly succeeded. You're a wonderful hostess. Susan was saying the same thing. As a matter of fact she was saying a great many nice things about you this evening."

"Was she?" Karen said. "Will you hand me the rest of those glasses, darling? And those forks too, if you don't mind. What was Susan saying?"

"Well," Rick said, "amongst other things she said that although she didn't know how you did it, you had never ceased to be an attractive woman just because you were a housewife. She said that I was very lucky to live with such an attractive woman, and one who was always so interested in everything I did. She said that you were exactly the kind of wife every man wants. Susan really is very perceptive."

Turning, Karen said, "Darling, I love you very much."

Rick was smiling. "Don't ever stop. It's not every man who finds exactly the kind of wife he wants."

Suddenly, Karen wanted to laugh, in part because she was happy, in part because she could no longer feel guilty, and in part because Susan was so completely outrageous.

"Look," she said, "you don't have to hang around the kitchen. I'll only be a few minutes more."

"I like it here."

"All right," Karen said, as she turned back to the sink, "then you can entertain me by telling me what else you and Susan talked about. You can't have spent all your time talking about me."

It was interesting, Karen thought, that though Barbara had most definitely been with them, she had apparently said very little.

"Well," Rick said, "let me see. Oh, yes, she was talking about some research which has been done recently into the various component chemicals in the air in different areas. She was saying that there is a very high iodine content in the air at Georgian Bay. High, that is, for an inland area. It's extraordinary the amount of information Susan picks up on all kinds of subjects."

"Yes," Karen said, "It is, isn't it?" It was all she could trust herself to say.

"She also said that too much iodine in the air could be quite harmful, although most doctors won't admit this; because iodine is, after all, a poison in sufficient quantity, and a rather unpleasant one. It seems that the latest findings point pretty definitely toward a higher death rate near the sea than inland because of the relative quantities of iodine in the air. It would appear that, like most things, the right amount is essential but that it can be overdone."

Stifling laughter, Karen thought that Susan had missed her calling. Susan ought to have been a saleswoman, because, when she tried, she could sell almost anything to anybody. Her way of putting things was so casual and yet so utterly convincing. Even she, Karen, although she knew that Susan had been talking complete nonsense, would probably always feel from now on that Georgian Bay was a particularly healthful spot, with just enough but not too much iodine in the air.

Amused though she was, Karen was at the same time a trifle unnerved by such a precise example of the ease with which almost any individual's thinking could be manipulated by the oblique pressures of suggestion and indirection. It was simply a question of assessing the individual concerned, and then employing the right approach. Certainly Barbara, essentially literal-minded, so sensitive on the subject of health that she believed everything she read in the *Readers' Digest*, would have been influenced in precisely the way Susan wished her to be. Skilfully pricked into doubt of herself both as a wife and a mother, it was not surprising that Barbara had gone home with a headache.

The terrifying thing was the simplicity with which it had been done. Assess the situation correctly, employ the right approach, and you could save a marriage. Or sell a nation on the idea of having a second car in the family. Or spread racial prejudice. Or start a war. . . .

"It was a good party, wasn't it?" Rick was saying. And because he had seen that she was more or less through at the sink, he was beginning to turn off the kitchen lights.

"Yes, darling," Karen said. "It was a very good party."

The only light left on was the one above the sink.

"I had almost forgotten about going to the palace," Rick said. "Even though it was only two years ago. Taken all in all, it was an interesting trip, wasn't it?"

"Yes, darling," Karen said. "It was a very interesting trip."

13 | Nothing definitive ever happens in Geneva

When Rick had come home one evening, in the spring when Carol and Peg had been preparing for their junior matriculation, to say that he had to make a business trip abroad, Karen's heart had sunk in a quite alarming way.

She had, however, been very good about it. This was something that she was always glad about afterwards.

"That should be fun for you, darling," she said. "How long will you be gone?"

"About six weeks," Rick said. "Two months if we decide to go by boat."

This was worse than Karen had anticipated. But she still managed to be good about it. "Is the company sending somebody else, too?"

"No," Rick said, "they're not sending anyone else. That's why it's up to us to decide whether we go by boat or by air. If we go by boat it will mean using some of our holidays."

"You mean I'm going, too?"

"Of course you're going," Rick said. "That is, as long as you want to, sweetheart. I just assumed you'd want to."

"Want to—oh, Rick, of course I want to. But what about the kids? How can we both leave the kids?"

"The trip's scheduled for July and August," Rick said. "They'll be at camp then, as they usually are. And don't forget we'll never be more than eighteen hours away from them once we get to the other side."

Karen knew this was true. They would be no more than eighteen hours away. But knowledge and acceptance were not always quite the same thing. You could know a fact because it was established. You could accept it only with the greatest difficulty, because everything really had moved so fast. So much too fast. Carol and Peg were lucky. They could accept trans-Atlantic flights as no more remarkable than the morning milk delivery. They had never known a world in which you could not call T.C.A. and reserve a place on a flight to London, or Rio, or Karachi. They belonged to a generation prepared to protest if a flight was an hour late in reaching the other side of the world, rather than one that would always be a little surprised that the flight should exist at all. Neither Carol nor Peg, when they were ten years old, had known what it was like to stand in the middle of the street—a small unit in a general hysteria—wildly waving an American flag because a man called Lindbergh had just accomplished the impossible.

Karen had no tendency toward hoarding, but she still had that American flag. Somehow, you couldn't throw out a flag on which you had spent a whole week's pocket money in order to celebrate the achievement of the impossible.

On a more purely personal basis, it took her several days to get used to the idea that going to Europe was possible, from the point of view of the money required. That they were in a position to pay her fare without worrying about it was something to which it was necessary to adjust. Until then she had never properly appreciated the fact that Gavin Street really was a long way behind them, and that, even in Rowanwood, they were no longer struggling simply to keep their heads above water.

"Of course," Rick said, "it will mean putting off the Chinese carpet for another year or so, but that's something I don't mind if you don't."

"I don't mind in the slightest. We'll just have that much longer to look forward to getting it. And I'll adore going to England with you. And we can go any way you choose. We can swim, for all I care, just as long as we're both going."

"I thought you'd be pleased," Rick said. And he looked the way he always looked when he was able to give her something he knew she would really like.

After talking it over, they had decided to go by boat; and since, if they were going to do it at all, they might as well do it properly, they had chosen to take the *Constitution* out of New York to Genoa. That way, as Karen pointed out, it would seem more like a cruise. You were always, she told Rick, seeing advertisements that said if you went to Europe by the Sunlane route you would feel just as if you were on a cruise.

She had worried a little about clothes, but had finally decided that what was good enough for Rowanwood would probably be good enough anywhere. This was an estimate that proved to be exactly right. Actually, she found that she was better dressed than most of the women she saw while they were away, even on the *Constitution,* where you were expected to dress for dinner every night—with the single exception, of course, of the first one. On the one Sunday night they were at sea, she was very sorry for the Englishwomen who turned up for dinner in tweeds, because nobody had told them that on an American ship you dress on Sundays just as you do on any other night of the week.

One of the fortunate things about being a Canadian was that you knew the rules of the game on both sides of the fence. Socially, you were unlikely ever to make a mistake in any English-speaking environment. Even when she made that fuss about what she should wear to the Palace, she had known instinctively what category of dress to fuss about. And when it came to conversation, as a Canadian you could talk equally intelligently about the Dodgers and an Oxford Double Blue. You might not, of course, consider it particularly intelligent to spend much time on either subject. But that was something else again.

She had known enough, too, to save her gold lamé for the night of the Captain's dinner, even though a lot of people had gone around saying that there wouldn't be a Captain's dinner. They had said that with the stop-over at Cannes, and then Genoa, and then Naples, there would be no proper "last night out", and therefore no proper "second-to-last night out".

All she had had to do was get the feel of the ship—and this hadn't taken any time at all—to know that of course there would be a Captain's dinner.

The whole feel of the *Constitution* had been very de luxe; and because being at sea was to be in a never-never-land anyway, she had thoroughly enjoyed this. The coloured lights on the after-deck outside the Marine Bar and the Barbary Tavern would have been meretricious on land. At sea, they created exactly the impression they were supposed to create. The impression that you had briefly stepped into a fairyland where colour and ease and gaiety were all that mattered.

It was marvellously relaxing to lie in a deck chair on the sports deck out of the wind, and do nothing. Absolutely nothing. When you lay in a deck chair like that, you thought of such things as "Roll on, thou deep and dark blue ocean, roll," and "Rule, Britannia! Britannia rule the waves," even though you were on an American ship and the fact had to be faced that Britannia no longer did rule the waves. It was, you thought idly—under those conditions all your thoughts tended to be idle—a pity that the United States had as yet to produce any deathless lines concerning the sea. Neither Hermann Wouk nor Nordoff and Hall had in this respect challenged Byron, or Thomson, or Conrad. When you thought of the sea, you thought first of Conrad, not of *The Caine Mutiny*. Conrad might not have been British by birth, any more than the seven seas were British on a continuing lend-lease supervised by the Almighty; but it would be a long time before, at sea, you would not feel that you were committing trespass when you sailed under something other than the Union Jack.

"Rick," Karen said, "it must have been a good year for refrigerators."

"What?" Rick said. He had his eyes closed, and he was getting quite a tan.

"Stoves can't have done too badly, either," Karen said. "And washing-machines must have enjoyed quite a boom, too."

"Sweetheart, I wish I knew what the hell you were talking about."

"I'm talking about there being so many wives on board," Karen said.

"I still fail to see what you're driving at," Rick said.

Karen laughed. "Do you, darling? I'm just talking about the

way North American wives tend to feather their nests before venturing out of them. They don't seem to feel secure without a new refrigerator behind them."

"Did it," Rick asked, "occur to you that you have a new refrigerator?"

"Oh, my God!" Karen said. "So I have. Well, it just underlines my point." Then she, too, closed her eyes and let herself drift, sun-soaked, thinking about nothing at all. Her line of thought, if she had followed it through, might later have helped her. But she did not follow it through.

The *Constitution* passed her sister ship the *Independence*, westbound, after nightfall near the Azores. The American Export Lines made quite a thing of this. In advance, Karen thought it rather silly. After all, it was nothing more than two ships, one going in one direction and the other going in the opposite direction. She couldn't see why the loudspeaker system was keeping the passengers as closely in touch with the possible time as it might have with the impending results of a presidential campaign.

But when, at 2230 hours, she stood on deck and watched their sister liner, lit up from stem to stern, pass in the limitless darkness of an otherwise empty ocean, she was so moved she couldn't even speak. She could only hold tight to Rick's hand, overcome by the realization of what the phrase "ships that pass in the night" really meant, and how far beyond the present moment that meaning went. And when the two ships saluted one another, their deep voices vibrating through the soles of her shoes, she shivered with an excitement it would have been quite impossible to put into words.

When they got to London, having gone direct from Genoa, they took a room at the Shaftesbury because "doing things properly" did not extend to a six weeks' stay at the Savoy. Actually, although it was a one-price hotel and the rooms were very small, they were well satisfied with the Shaftesbury. It was central, only a short walk from Piccadilly Circus, and it served what were really very good meals in the basement dining-room. That Shaftesbury Avenue might well have been rechristened

Prostitutes' Walk did not bother Karen. Dressed in what was good enough for Rowanwood and more than good enough for London, and holding herself the way she had been taught to hold herself at Waycroft, she never had any mistakes made about her. In the stores which, because she was a Canadian, she knew enough to call shops, she was usually taken for an American. But this was a different kind of mistake.

London, Karen found, had changed considerably since she had last seen it in the thirties. The change lay neither in the bomb damage, still evident in parts of the city, nor in the increase in traffic and neon lights. It lay rather in the atmosphere, or—to use the French word because it better described what she felt—the *ambiance*. Trafalgar Square, the Tower of London, St. Paul's, the British Museum—none of these physical landmarks had changed, but the *ambiance* had. Something—it was impossible to say quite what—that had endured for centuries, had vanished, never to be recaptured. Although, in a sense, this was nothing to her, it nevertheless made her sad, and, by contrast, increased her pleasure in the fact that Geneva did not appear to have changed at all.

She and Rick had intended to fly over to Geneva together, but in the end she went alone because Rick could not spare the time from his business.

She had been very disappointed when it became obvious that Rick could not go, but afterwards she was not entirely sorry. With Rick, she would have seen Geneva, at least in part, through the eyes of a stranger. Alone, she could feel briefly as if she had never been away. She could, as one so seldom can, step back into the past as if it weren't the past at all but simply a suspension of time that had needed nothing other than her presence to go on exactly as it had done before.

The feeling that she had, almost literally, stepped back into the past, claimed her immediately she got off the Swissair plane at Cointrin airport.

Her French, she discovered before she even got out of the airport, was decidely rusty. In Toronto it was good enough to annoy Julia and Ned, but here it was not good at all. Yet, oddly enough, even this sustained the illusion that time had stood still in that it established her memories in some kind of proper chronological order. She had known very little French when she had arrived in Geneva for the first time. At Waycroft they gave you an excellent grounding in grammar, but they did not teach you to speak the language. On that occasion she had arrived at the Gare Cornavin in the heart of the city, and, when she got into a taxi, it had been necessary to write down her destination before the taxi-driver could understand where she wanted to go.

"Ah!" the taxi-driver had said. "Route de Chêne. *C'est entendu, mademoiselle.*"

He had sounded, Karen remembered, as if he had made some quite remarkable discovery, which, from his point of view, he probably had.

By this time Karen had become distinctly averse to the idea of spending a year with a French-speaking Swiss family. And as the taxi had rattled down the Rue du Mont Blanc, and across the Pont du Mont Blanc toward the other side of the Rhone River, she had formed a very unfavourable mental picture of the Monsieur and Madame Dutoit under whose roof it had been arranged that she live.

When the taxi had deposited her before a gate in a grey stone wall, beyond which she could see a large house and an enclosed garden, she had felt very much like telling the taxi-driver to take her away again. Only the fact that she was incapable of telling him anything had prevented her from doing so.

She had been totally unprepared, as she reached into her purse for money as foreign to her as the language, for a voice behind her, saying, "Are you the other boarder? Can I help you with that?"

Later, she and Susan had often laughed about this, because Susan really hadn't been able to speak French any better than she could, herself. Susan's method of paying the taxi-man had been very like those card tricks where you are asked to "pick a card, just any card." With all the assurance in the world, Susan had plucked a bill from the sheaf in Karen's hand, and handed it to the taxi-man. From the look on the man's face there could be little doubt that she had picked the equivalent of the Ace of Spades.

Now, on arrival from London, things were not quite as bad as this, because when she told the taxi-man to take her to the Hôtel de la Paix he seemed to have no trouble in understanding her. However, to her own ear her French was certainly not what it had been.

She could have taken the airport bus into the city, but this would have meant changing to a taxi outside the Gare Cornavin, and, since it was such a short distance anyway, it seemed simpler to take a taxi the whole way. It was when the taxi-driver addressed her as mademoiselle that the neither-past-nor-present feeling took full possession of her. She had forgotten that in Switzerland, if you were young at all, you were always addressed in this manner as long as you were wearing gloves or your rings were otherwise hidden. In Switzerland, unlike France, you were always given the benefit of the doubt.

It was as if nothing had changed at all, and when she signed in at the De la Paix, she almost registered as Karen Holbrook. Mrs. Richard Whitney seemed like an impostor she had conjured up on the spur of the moment.

Actually, for Karen, those two days in Geneva never existed in their own right at all. Everywhere she went, she encountered a past that was just as real and just as vivid as it had been eighteen years earlier.

She felt that if she were to walk into the grounds of the International School—something she chose not to do—Susan would be there where they had always met after school, in the shade of "Alexandre", the ancient American black walnut that was as much a part of the school as any of its buildings. Everybody always met under the spreading branches of Alexandre. It was, in its own way, as important a landmark as the Statue of Liberty.

And when she sat, as she did do, drinking Cinzano at a sidewalk table in front of the Casanova restaurant, it seemed perfectly possible that Cyr might join her at any moment. If anything at all had changed—the mountains on the farther side of a lake dotted close at hand with swans, and farther out with sail-boats—the open carriages with their beribboned horses, waiting for tourists in the heavy green shade of the plane trees—the traffic, still mainly composed of bicycles, sweeping past in a broad right-angled stream as it turned off the Quai du Mont Blanc on to the Pont du Mont Blanc—if any of this had changed, she might not have felt as if she were actually once again waiting for Cyr to join her.

Cyr had never approved of her sitting outside the Casanova, because he felt it improper for her to sit on the street unescorted. He had felt, too, that men might think she was there because she wanted to be picked up.

"What of it?" Karen had asked him. "I don't want to be picked up. That's all that matters, isn't it?"

Cyr had not thought it was all that mattered. For some reason, he had always felt he had to look after her.

"Why are you always trying to look after me?" Karen had asked him more than once. "I'm not a baby, you know."

"I know," Cyr had said. "If you were, I wouldn't need to worry about you."

Cyr had, she remembered, had his way about rather a lot of things, but the Casanova had not been one of them, and they had spent a great deal of time sitting outside the Casanova in the late afternoon sunlight because he had known that, whatever he thought, it was a likely place to find her.

"I don't see," he had said, "what you find so fascinating about this place."

"Look," Karen had said, "if you don't think it a suitable setting for a member of the diplomatic corps, you can always go somewhere else."

She would not, of course, have said this if she had thought he would take her up on it. She had, right from the beginning, been oddly sure of her hold on Cyr. Even though she had never been able to determine the exact extent of his interest in her. Even though, as Susan had put it, it had been the damnedest relationship.

"Anyway," Karen had told him, "you don't look like a diplomat. You look more at home here than you do at the Consulate, if you want my opinion."

"If I don't look like a diplomat, what do I look like?" Cyr had asked.

"Do you really want to know?"

"Yes," Cyr had said, "I really want to know."

He had, Karen knew, been laughing at her. But she had never seemed to mind when Cyr laughed at her. "All right," she had said, "but don't forget you asked for it. You look like a newspaperman."

"My God!" Cyr had said. "Don't tell me I look as disillusioned as all that."

"Well," Karen had told him, "you do. But in a nice kind of way. You don't give any impression that absinthe will get the better of you."

"As long as it's in a nice kind of way, I suppose I can stand it," Cyr had said. "As long as I look as if I could hold my absinthe." And he had been laughing at her again.

"Cyr," Karen had said, "go on and admit it for once. Admit that you like this place as much as I do."

"I never said I didn't like it," Cyr had replied. "I simply said it wasn't a proper place for you."

"Do you have to apply a double standard to everything?"

For a moment he had not replied. When he did, he was completely serious. "Where you are concerned, I admit to only one standard."

"How am I to interpret that?" Karen had asked.

"You can interpret it any way you damn well please, darling. But however you interpret it, you will still know perfectly well what I mean."

"All right. I know what you mean. Now will you please act like a gentleman instead of my keeper, and order me another Cinzano?"

Cyr, when he replied, had been laughing again. "A double or a single, darling?"

She had never, she realized afterwards, told him why the Casanova had such a fascination for her. She had never told him that it was the location, rather than the place itself. Sitting outside the Casanova you could watch the most fabulous collection of pedestrians in the world. It was a mixed parade of harlotry and aristocracy, of statesmen and entrepreneurs, of semi-nudity and costumes straight from the great French ateliers, of skin colours ranging through all the nuances between pure black and pure white, of nationalities as varied and polyglot as the individuals representing them.

When you sat outside the Casanova, you didn't just sit where the Pont du Mont Blanc divided Lake Geneva from the Rhone River; you sat at the crossroads of the world, at the core of an oasis that, though always crowded, was, like all oases, peculiarly detached from any definitive reality. In a broad sense, people came to Geneva to talk, to exchange views, but not to take action. Any action that was taken was always taken somewhere else. What you thought and said in Geneva might very well have a close bearing on what you did later somewhere else, but it would never be definitive in itself, any more than her relationship with Cyr had been.

Not to see and accept this condition of a sojourn in Geneva, was to be foolishly unrealistic. It did not do, however, to underestimate the subsequent effects of such a sojourn.

Certainly what she had thought and said on the night when Cyr took her away from the dance at the Hôtel des Bergues might, under certain circumstances, have altered the whole course of her life after she left Geneva.

It had been in February, she remembered, and for weeks there had been no sun at all. Nothing but a quiet, grey fog that blotted out all sight of the mountains encircling the lake. A grey shroud against which the pollarded plane trees had stood out in cruelly dismembered ugliness, a purposefully stunted black frieze that could, she felt, have served as an illustration for a dark, medieval fairy tale.

It could have been the weather that had engendered her reckless mood on that night when she went to the Hôtel des Bergues. Or it could have been a hurt she had not wanted to admit even to herself.

When Cyr had gone away on mission three weeks earlier, he had said nothing about writing. She had simply taken it for granted that he would. He had not written, and she had gone to the Hôtel des Bergues in a disgracefully low-cut evening dress determined to prove to the whole world, but to herself in particular, that she didn't give a damn if she never saw or heard from him again.

If Susan had been there, Susan might have been able to make her see a little sense. But Susan had been in bed with the flu, and Karen, when she went in to say good-bye to her, had been careful to keep her coat done up.

"Is there anything I can get you?" she asked Susan.

"Not a thing, darling," Susan said. "In the morning you can cancel the order for the hearse. I think I'm going to live."

"You look much better."

"I feel much better, thank God. Whom are you going with tonight?"

"Maurice," Karen said.

Susan could raise her eyebrows in a most expressive way. "Interesting," she said. "I hope you're taking your roller skates along."

"I can look after myself," Karen told her.

"I'm sure you can, darling. It's just that it's easier if you have your roller skates along."

The people who said that the Swiss were a very reserved race, and most people said this, had indubitably never been to a large Swiss party. Karen, who had been to one or two Swiss parties before the one at the Hôtel des Bergues, knew what to expect. And although she had never before gone out with Maurice, she knew as well as Susan did what could be expected of Maurice, too, because that kind of thing got about.

From the moment when she walked into the huge ballroom, she knew she was going to have a busy evening, and not only with Maurice. She was, as usually happened in a strange group, taken for an American; and in the thirties—before Europe started saying "Americans, Go Home"—this did one no harm at all. European men, taking their cue from Hollywood rather than from generally contradictory fact, seemed to have fixed ideas about American girls that were as difficult to dislodge as they themselves sometimes proved to be.

Afterwards, Karen could remember very little about that dance up until the moment when Cyr cut in. In her new black dress, what there was of it, she simply got on the roller-coaster. And you never do remember much about a roller-coaster.

She was, she remembered, dancing, and the music was going round and round. To be perfectly honest, everything had, by that time, begun to go round and round, because it wasn't in any sense a dry party.

Cyr's voice, formal, expressionless, took her completely by surprise, because until he spoke she had not known he was in Geneva, let alone beside her on the dance floor of the Hôtel des Bergues.

He did not speak to her. Instead, he addressed the man with whom she happened to be dancing just then.

"*Est-ce que je puis avoir l'honneur, monsieur?*"

Karen's partner came to a stop, but she could sense his resistance to the idea of letting her go. "*Monsieur—*" she heard him begin, and then he didn't go on.

"Go ahead," Karen said, but she forgot to say it in French. "Tell him to go away. Tell him he can't have the honour."

"*Pardon, mademoiselle?*"

"Oh, hell," Karen said. "*Dites-lui qu'il ne peut pas avoir l'honneur.*"

The Swiss would have liked to do what she asked. It had been his own initial intention. She could understand, however, why he did not.

Cyr looked very tall, very quiet, and somehow very dangerous. And for some odd reason he was the only thing in the room that was not going round and round.

"*Monsieur—*" Karen heard her partner begin again.

"*Merci, monsieur,*" Cyr said. "*Vous êtes bien gentil.*"

Then she was dancing with Cyr to the rhythm of "Street of Dreams", and trying not to cry.

"What the devil do you think you're doing?" Cyr said. He had never spoken to her like that before.

"Minding my own business."

"I don't like the way you're doing it."

"I don't give a damn what you like or don't like," Karen told him. "That's something I want you to have quite clear."

"You've been drinking," Cyr said.

"How observant of you."

"Not very."

Too angry now to feel like crying, Karen nevertheless knew that she would be just as well pleased if she never heard "Street of Dreams" again.

"If you came here to be unpleasant," she said, "you'll be happy to know that you're doing a very good job of it. How did you know where I was, anyway?"

"I dropped in at the house. One of the maids brought down a message from Susan."

"I can imagine what must have been in that message for the marines to rush to the rescue like this. Why don't you and Susan take up social service? Why don't you find yourselves a few starving Armenians, and concentrate on them instead of interfering with my life?"

"Come on," Cyr said. "We're getting out of here."

Short of actually fighting with him on the dance floor, Karen found she had no choice but to do what he wanted. And things weren't going round and round quite fast enough for her to start a fight. Almost, but not quite. And not in front of the Swiss.

As they came down the short flight of stairs to the front lobby, Cyr said, "Where is your coat?"

"I don't know," Karen said.

"In that case we'll go without it."

"I'll catch pneumonia," Karen said.

"I wouldn't wonder," Cyr told her. "In that dress. Worse things than that could happen to you in that dress."

The night air was raw and damp, and Karen was shivering violently by the time they reached the car even though it was no more than a few yards away.

Without a word, Cyr unlocked the doors, reached into the back and took out the leather windbreaker he often wore while driving. "Put this on," he said. "Before I take you home you're going to have some coffee, black and strong."

"I don't want to put it on," Karen said. "I don't want coffee."

Cyr did not bother to argue. He placed the windbreaker around her shoulders, worked the sleeves on to her limp bare arms, and did the zipper all the way up to her chin.

Karen looked down at herself in disgust. The windbreaker was much too large, and the long black velvet skirt below it was completely absurd. "I look like a floozie," she said.

"No, you don't," Cyr said. "You did. But you don't now. Now you look just what you are, a nice little girl."

"I'm not going anywhere like this," Karen told him. "And the hell with being a nice little girl. Did you hear what I said? I said the hell with being a nice little girl."

"I heard you," Cyr said. "The doorman probably heard you, too. Now either get into the car, or get pushed in. Take your choice."

They had gone to the Bavaria café on the other side of the lake, as Karen had expected they would.

Almost two decades later, as she walked across the Pont du Mont Blanc in the warm sunlight of a beautiful July morning, Karen told herself that she was not going to the Bavaria. It was one thing to sit outside the Casanova. It was quite another to go back to the Bavaria, and she was not going to do it.

She would, she told herself, go to the Ours de Berne and buy some presents to take back to Toronto with her. Then she would cross over to the restaurant in the Jardin Anglais. Susan had said she wanted one of those carved wooden Madonnas. Some people might find it odd that Susan would want a Madonna. When you really knew Susan, there was nothing odd about it at all. For Carol and Peg, Karen decided, she would buy some of that lovely ivory jewellery, also hand-carved. Then she would go over to the Jardin Anglais, although even the Jardin Anglais had memories of Cyr attached to it.

Cyr had approved of the Jardin Anglais as a place for her to idle in the sun. And it was certainly a beautiful spot, cut off from the traffic on the Grand Quai by wide lawns, ancient shade trees, and rainbow-hued flower beds. You could look out over the lake toward the mountains on either side, and a blue distance that, if you followed it far enough, would take you to Lausanne, and Montreux, and Chillon. It was the kind of place, Cyr had said, where men would not think she might like to be picked up. Which went to show how much he knew about it. Which went to show that he wasn't always right about everything.

When she reached the gift shop, Karen spent some time looking at the show windows on both sides of its corner location. Half the fun of going to the Ours de Berne lay in studying its quite irresistible window display.

But in spite of the strong temptation embodied in some silver and amethyst earrings, her mind wandered, and she found herself thinking that there were very few restaurants in Geneva to which she had not gone with Cyr. Their time together seemed to have been divided between his car and a series of restaurants and cafés, probably because even in Geneva there had been no real meeting point between their two worlds. Cyr would not have fitted with her friends at the International School. And he had appeared to want to get away from the Consulate people whenever he could.

"My God," he had said once, "if they dig up some of those people a few centuries from now they'll find them perfectly preserved. They'll find them mummified with red tape, and embalmed in the oil of their own diplomacy."

"Why do you stay there, if you feel that way?" Karen had asked.

"Why does anyone ever do anything?" Cyr had replied.

They could, of course, have used one of the living-rooms in the house on Route de Chêne where she and Susan lived. Like all large Swiss houses, it had an over-supply of living-rooms, and the Dutoits had been only too willing that she and Susan ask their friends in. There had been two maids in the house, so there had been no question of extra work as far as Madame Dutoit was concerned. She and Susan had given one or two very nice parties there for the school crowd, and had been grateful that they could do this. But as a place in which to spend an evening alone with someone, particularly someone like Cyr, it had been quite impossible. Lost in a sea of furniture, all of it uncomfortable, depressed by high ceilings and the drab browns and greens so popular with the Swiss, chilled by bead-fringed lamps which, though numerous, were still inadequate, you simply could not be yourself. It was an atmosphere that impelled you to talk, while at the same time rendering you incapable of saying anything with any real meaning.

So they had spent their time together, she and Cyr, either driving to nowhere in particular, or in restaurants and cafés. And if the Casanova had been the one to which they went most often in the daytime, the Bavaria was where they most often wound up in the evening. Therefore it wasn't surprising that they should go there on the night when he took her away from the Hôtel des Bergues, or that it should have been from there that they left on their last evening together.

No more surprising than that Karen, when she finished her shopping at the Ours de Berne, should, as she had known perfectly well she would, go there instead of across to the Jardin Anglais.

The minute she walked through the front door of the Bavaria she was again wearing a black velvet evening dress and Cyr's leather windbreaker. There must, she knew, have been some changes made between then and now, but if there had been they were not noticeable. The walls, of course, were hung with many more autographed drawings of the famous, who had used this place as a rendezvous, than they had been in the past. But this was more an expected continuation of the stream of history than a change. That Roosevelt, Molotov, General Montgomery, and Mendès-France should—amongst many others—have joined a unique gallery, added rather than took away from the illusion that all time was existing simultaneously.

Feeling as if she were in the middle of an unfinished dream, Karen walked along the single narrow aisle, between tables at that hour almost deserted, to the same place where she had sat with Cyr and drunk coffee she had said she did not want. She had had three cups, although the second and third had not been necessary.

That night the Bavaria had been crowded to capacity, as it nearly always was toward midnight; but they had been alone there, she and Cyr, in a way that would not have been possible if the people around them had been talking one language rather than a dozen or more. Even her own odd costume had been unremarkable, as it could only have been in a city long since indifferent to such incongruities as gold-embroidered saris worn with fur-lined overshoes.

Until they had finished their first cups of coffee, and Cyr had ordered more, they did not talk at all.

Karen broke the silence between them, saying the last thing she had wanted to say. "Cyr," she said, "why didn't you write?"

"Did I promise to write?"

"No."

"Then don't sound so much like a discarded mistress."

"For your information," Karen said, "I have never been a mistress, discarded or otherwise. Although I wouldn't want you to think this was due to any lack of opportunity."

"I don't," Cyr said. "There's plenty of opportunity for you right across the way. Even with that zipper done up."

"You mean the man who looks like a Spanish grandee?"

"That's right," Cyr said. "Though, on the evidence, he is more probably a South American. However, don't worry, he won't look at you again."

"I'm not worrying," Karen said. "And how do you know he won't?"

"Because I looked at him," Cyr told her.

"My God, you're conceited!"

"No, I'm not," Cyr said. "I just happen to know under most circumstances where I stand, which is something you don't. Not yet. That's what I want to talk to you about. I want you to promise me that you will never go looking for trouble again the way you did tonight. Anyone who looks for trouble of that kind usually finds it. With some girls it might not matter too much, one way or the other. But with you, darling, it would be bad afterwards. Very bad."

Her hands tightening on one another under the edge of the table, Karen thought of an ugly, sombre house on Lowther Avenue and another night on another continent when she had been an unsuspecting, rather than a deliberate fool. Was she never going to learn to know herself as well as Cyr apparently knew her?

Slowly she let her gaze wander across the scene around her. In the Bavaria the predominant colour was brown, and usually she did not like brown, but here it was just right. It was traditional, and she hoped it would never change. It was an unobtrusive and suitable background for the heterogeneous collection of people who, in spite of their differences in race and colour, here achieved a homogeneity that was universal. This was perhaps why it was such a suitable background for herself and Cyr, why they could talk more freely here than anywhere else. If the League of Nations, she thought, had ever achieved anything like the atmosphere you found in the Bavaria, things might have been better all round.

"Anything you ask, Cyr," she said quietly.

"This isn't for me," Cyr told her. "This is for you. I'm not asking you to make any promise for my sake. It is for your sake. Some day you will meet a man who really matters to you, and when that happens you won't want anything on your conscience."

"Perhaps I've already met him."

He made no pretence of misunderstanding her. "There's no future for you and me, darling. You know that as well as I do."

"Give me a cigarette, will you, Cyr?"

He took a package of Du Maurier's from his pocket, lit a cigarette, and gave it to her. He smoked Gaulois himself, but he always seemed to have her brand with him. And he always lit a cigarette and then gave it to her, something she had never allowed anyone else to do.

"Why are you so sure there's no future for us?" she asked.

"There are a lot of reasons," Cyr said. "To take just one, it's never any good to get yourself involved with somebody you meet on a vacation."

"But we're not on vacation, either one of us."

"Yes, we are, darling," he told her. "Everybody in Geneva, with the exception of the Swiss, is on vacation. That's just something one has to realize about Geneva. As long as you live in Geneva you're on vacation, and if you have any sense you won't get really involved."

"All right," Karen said, "then why don't we go somewhere else and see how things look from there?"

"Is that a serious suggestion?"

"I—I don't know."

Cyr was having trouble getting his own cigarette to light properly. When he looked up, his eyes were narrowed against a cloud of smoke. "That's exactly what I mean, darling. In Geneva, you can't know."

"Even in Geneva," Karen said, "you could try to find out."

In the Bavaria you said things you would never have said anywhere else. Which was perhaps the reason why Cyr mentioned his father. It was the only time he ever said anything even remotely personal about either of his parents.

"Karen," he said, "will you just this once face the fact that you know nothing whatsoever about me?"

"I know all I need to know."

"No, you don't," Cyr said. "You don't know that I'm getting out of this damned diplomatic racket before the year is over. You don't know that I hate it more than I ever hated any goddamned thing."

"Then how did you get into it in the first place?" Karen asked.

"God knows," he said. And that would probably have been all he would have said, if they had not been at the Bavaria, and if it had not been by that time long after midnight. You could almost tell the hour by the density of the smoke in the air.

"If you must know," Cyr said, "it was a follow-in-the-footsteps idea of my father's that hit him while we were living in Washington."

Karen had wondered before, and was to wonder again if she

and Cyr would have established such an immediate rapport if he had not been able to speak her language as well as she could herself. It was one of those things you wonder about from time to time as long as you live, although no positive conclusion is possible. Because he had been brought up in the States, Cyr *could* speak her language as well as she could herself, and it was quite impossible to imagine him as incapable of doing so.

"And you're sure your father wasn't right?"

"My father," Cyr said, "has virtually never been right about anything in his life."

Years later, on an occasion when Ned was holding forth about how important it was for a son to respect his father, Karen remembered very vividly the way Cyr had looked when he said that his father had virtually never been right about anything.

"What are you going to do?" she asked him.

"I really don't know," he told her. "And, frankly, I don't much care. Which is something you would never understand, darling. You would make a charming wife for a career diplomat. You would fit in very well at Buckingham Palace. But, to use your own comparison, you'd be a hell of a wife for a newspaperman."

"I don't see why you should think that," Karen said. "And, anyway, I didn't say you looked like an unsuccessful newspaperman, which is what you are inferring. I wouldn't have dreamt of saying anything like that, because you have the look of a man who could do whatever he wanted to do."

Cyr had suddenly seemed very tired. "I told you that you wouldn't understand, darling. It isn't a question of what I can or cannot do, it's a question of what I might or might not want to do. Let's just skip it, shall we, and get back to the point. Will you promise me not to go looking for trouble again until you know where you're going?"

"I told you, Cyr. Anything you ask."

"You know what you're promising, don't you?"

"You don't have to spell it out for me," Karen said. "With one possible exception, I promise."

At the Bavaria you said things you would never have said anywhere else.

Cyr had looked directly at her for what had seemed a very long time. Then he had said, "I hope you'll keep that promise, Karen. And just to have the record clear, the question of an exception will not arise."

Without dropping her eyes, Karen had said, "It must be nice to be so sure of yourself. Is that why you've only kissed me once, Cyr? Because you're so sure of yourself?"

"Quelque chose d'autre, mademoiselle?"

For a moment Karen stared blankly at the waiter who stood politely beside the table, her empty coffee cup already in his hand. It needed the presence of her neatly tied packages from the Ours de Berne, with their flowering rosettes of ribbon, to convince her that she was here rather than there.

She shook her head. She had no desire to linger any longer in the Bavaria, no desire just then to remember the last time she had been there, because it was also the last evening she had spent with Cyr. She had already remembered too much as it was.

"Merci," she said. *"L'addition, c'est tout."*

"Un instant, mademoiselle."

While she waited for the bill, Karen tried desperately to bring the previous forty-eight hours into focus as some kind of reality that could be recognized as such. But nothing she had seen or done since her arrival at the Hôtel de la Paix was any help to her in this.

The service in the hotel was just the way it had always been, perfect as it could only be in a Swiss hotel. Any North American hotel that might have tried to get away with the kind of furniture you found in a room at the De la Paix, would have gone into immediate bankruptcy. But no North American hotel ever achieved the comfortable perfection of service, without the slightest trace of obsequiousness, that you found in Switzerland.

On the streets at least, she had expected to orient herself to the present rather than the past. But, wherever she had gone and whatever she had done, Geneva had defeated her purpose. The Lux flakes she had bought for washing out her nylons had turned out to be those large flakes she had not seen at home for years and years. The swans on the lake could have been the same swans she had watched so often when she was at the International School. The open-air flower markets were still there, and the people of Geneva still thought it worth while to have iron baskets of flowers high up on the tall light standards along the quais. The plane trees were still pollarded to the exact height at which she remembered them. In the parks she again saw nursemaids pushing those enormous, old-fashioned baby carriages. Cars were still very much in the minority amongst the bicycles on which people still carried anything from a rocking-chair to a funeral wreath. And bathtubs were apparently still regarded as private possessions, to be moved along with the rest of the furniture, because she had seen one on a lawn amongst some gilt and damask French chairs.

But the one thing more than any other that had made it impossible to believe that she was here rather than there was that they were still playing the same popular tunes. She had heard, not once but several times, both "My Silent Love" and "Night and Day", songs that she had never been able to dissociate from the evening when she had first met Cyr.

Those two songs had been played over and over at the dance at the Parc des Eaux Vives to which she would not have gone if Susan had not more or less dragged her. It had been Susan, too, who had almost literally pushed her into the Paul Jones that, when the music stopped, had left her facing a tall, loose-limbed man with disturbing eyes.

When the music had started again, he had made no move to dance with her. He had said, "Do you like big parties?"

"No," Karen had said. "I hate them."

"If I tell you that I don't go in for etchings, will you come for a drive with me?"

The orchestra had been playing "My Silent Love" when they left, and the park had been bathed in quiet moonlight. Moonlight that had flowed down across long, sloping lawns to silver a lake beyond which rose the Juras, a dark rampart against the night.

That had been the beginning, because what he had said had been perfectly true. He was not a man who went in for etchings.

Karen, when she got back to the house on Route de Chêne, found Susan there ahead of her. Susan was ready for bed. Even as far back as that, Susan had worn devastating negligees. She was sitting in Karen's room reading Proust and smoking. She was not, of course, reading Proust in French.

"Well?" Susan said.

"Well, nothing," Karen said.

"Nothing at all?"

"Nothing at all," Karen told her.

"How disappointing," Susan said. "He's very attractive looking. Are you going to see him again?"

"I don't know."

"Do you want to?" Susan asked.

"Yes," Karen said. "I want to."

Susan lit another cigarette. "In that case you indubitably will."

Susan's calm confidence in her ability to get what she wanted, where and as she wanted it, had already done a lot for Karen. Right from the start, Susan had seemed to take it for granted that Karen was a girl who could write her own ticket, and this really had done a lot for her.

"What did you do?" Susan asked.

"We drove."

"Is that all?" Susan asked.

"That's all."

"Well, what did you talk about?"

"I don't know," Karen said. "Nothing in particular. Actually we didn't talk much at all."

Susan closed her book and put it down. "If you didn't talk, and if there were no advances, to put it delicately, then what in the world did you do?"

"I told you," Karen said. "We drove."

"This," Susan said, "is the damnedest thing I ever both heard and believed."

It was not long after this that Susan began calling it the damnedest relationship.

The waiter, Karen realized, must have put the bill for the coffee on the table without her noticing that he had come back at all. With a curious mixture of impatience and reluctance, she stood up. Impatience to free herself from a spell she had thought broken long ago. Reluctance to leave the Bavaria because she was unlikely ever to drink coffee there again, and a last time, even one without any great significance in itself, is always upsetting.

Her beautifully wrapped packages from the Ours de Berne held carefully in one arm, she walked back across the Pont du Mont Blanc with the certain knowledge that she had had more than enough of being neither here nor there. She had planned to stay another day in Geneva. Now she knew that if she could get a plane out that afternoon she was going back to London at once. She was going back to Rick as fast as she could go. You couldn't compare the Shaftesbury Hotel with the Hôtel de la Paix, but the Shaftesbury Hotel was where Rick was, which made it the only place in the world where she really wanted to be.

The people at Swissair were, as always, very obliging. Certainly, they said, they could give her a seat on the early afternoon plane. No, there was no question of any waiting list. All she had to do was be at the Gare Cornavin forty minutes before take-off time, or, if she preferred, at the airport itself a half hour before take-off time. Everything was at the convenience of Madame. Since they already had her name, it was natural and proper that they should address her as madame.

It was also oddly comforting.

14 They're very informal at the palace

Karen had not, although she had sent him a telegram, expected Rick to be at London Airport when she got in.

As soon as she saw him, waiting for her outside the customs inspection, she knew that she had never been quite so glad to see anyone in her life.

"Rick," she said, as she kissed him, "darling, I missed you so."

"I missed you, sweetheart." And he sounded as if he really meant it, which made her very happy.

"It was such a long journey," she said.

"It's less than two hours, isn't it? Though, of course, when you fly, there's always the waiting around ahead of time."

He had not, Karen realized, understood what she meant, which was just as well. "I wonder why they've made it so that you have to walk such miles to get out of this place," she said.

"You think it's farther than at Idlewild?" Rick asked.

"Miles farther, darling."

"Well," Rick said, "that's something to be said for the Toronto airport. You don't have to walk far. I hadn't realized before that there was anything to be said for the Toronto airport. The car's over this way."

They had rented a Ford Zephyr from the Hertz people for the duration of their stay in England, and it had proved a very good idea. They had already been able to get down to Canterbury, and, though it had been rather a rush, to Cornwall. To think of a week-end in terms of the run from Toronto to New York was, they had discovered, a mistake in England. The conditions under which you drove weren't comparable in any way. In England you found a courtesy on the road with no parallel anywhere; but if you expected to get on with it, you could think again.

"Look, Karen," Rick said, as he started the motor, "I made an engagement for dinner tonight before I knew you would be back. But if you're tired it would be perfectly easy to call it off."

He was obviously still thinking about her remark that it had been a long journey.

"I'm not really tired," Karen said. "Who is it? Anyone I know? You're wonderful the way you remember to stay on the left-hand side of the road, darling."

"Yes, it's someone you know," Rick said. "Jim Evans. You remember, he used to live on Warren Road and was in my year at college."

"Of course I remember him," Karen said. "How nice. What is he doing over here?"

"He's with the diplomatic corps."

"Which diplomatic corps?" Karen asked.

"The Canadian, naturally. What other one would you expect him to be with? You must be tired, sweetheart."

Annoyed with herself, Karen saw that she had not yet apparently made a complete transition from there to here.

"Perhaps I am a little tired," she said. "But it's nothing that a good drink won't cure. Oh, Rick darling—darling, I'm so glad to be back with you."

"That's nice."

"You don't know just how nice it is. Will I have time for a bath when we get back to the hotel?"

"Plenty of time."

By the time she had had a bath, and changed, Switzerland and Cyr had retreated into the past again where they belonged.

The only thing in the Shaftesbury to which Karen had not adjusted easily was the business of having to go down the hall to take a bath. In a hotel corridor, she could not help feeling, in her dressing-gown, peculiarly exposed, more naked than if this had actually been the case. It was silly of her, she knew, but there was something unpleasantly intimate about an encounter in a hotel corridor with someone also equipped with what in

England were called bath-robe and sponge-bag. It made you think of false teeth and depilatories, which were not things you normally thought about. You could, of course, if you wanted it badly enough, get a room with a private bath; but the English set a very high premium on this kind of eccentricity. A premium which both she and Rick had decided was, under the circumstances, too high for value received.

They had not, however, been in London two days before Karen said, "The next time we discuss a decision of this kind we're going to discuss it in a public bathroom. We're not going to be in our living-room at home the next time we make up our minds about anything like this."

Rick had laughed. "Have you any idea where you would look for a public bathroom in Toronto?"

"The wash-room at the Union Station will do. We don't actually have to have a bathtub staring us in the face."

"Sweetheart, you've been over here too long. You're out of touch already. At the Union Station we wouldn't be allowed into the same washroom. My God, what have you got there?"

"Bon Ami Powder," Karen told him. She had been getting her things together before taking a bath. "And I've got a cleaning rag, too, if you really want to know."

"My God!" Rick said again. "Do you scrub the floor, too?"

"Never mind what I do. If you were any kind of a gentleman you wouldn't be spying on a lady when she's collecting her things before having a bath."

She wished she had not let Rick see the Bon Ami Powder, because he knew as well as she did that the bath was invariably immaculate, and that she was being perfectly idiotic about the whole thing. Which did not prevent her from always cleaning the bath out twice, not only before but also after using it. There was something about a public bathroom which made you wish to remove, when you left it, all trace of yourself, to erase the scent of your soap, your perfume, and your tooth paste.

The way she felt about the WC was quite different. Apart from the occasional inconvenience this might entail, she did not care how many other people used the WC. It was a difference she had not been able to make Rick understand.

"Darling," she had said, "if you can't see the difference for yourself, I can't explain it to you. It just isn't the same, that's all. Maybe it's that you don't climb right into the damn thing. I don't know. It just isn't the same, that's all."

Jim Evans had said he would be along at half-past six, and while they were waiting for him, Rick asked Karen where she thought they should have a before-dinner drink.

"We can always go downstairs, of course," he said. "But I rather thought we might serve them up here. It's more informal, and it isn't as if Jim weren't a Canadian."

"I'd just as soon stay here," Karen said. "If you don't mind sitting on that straight chair, Jim can have the arm-chair, and I'll sit on the bed."

"You don't think it will be too cosy?" Rick asked. "This room is damn small, really."

"It's fine," Karen said.

While Rick got Scotch, rye, and soda-water from the clothes closet, Karen took glasses of their own from the bottom bureau drawer and polished them with a clean hand towel from the towel-rail on the back of the door. It also occurred to her to put out a pack of Camels that she happened to have. Jim, she thought, would probably enjoy an American cigarette. It was a pity that they did not have a view of anything in particular from their window, like the dome of St. Paul's, for instance; but after several years in London, Jim had undoubtedly grown a little tired of such views.

Jim, when he arrived, was wearing a dark suit, and carrying a bowler hat and an umbrella. He looked, Karen thought, very distinguished. Rather unnecessarily English, but still very distinguished.

"Well, hello, Karen," he said. "Terribly nice to see you, but I wouldn't have barged on up if I'd known you were back."

"Why ever not?" Karen asked. "Do come in, Jim. It's wonderful to see you again."

"How are you, Jim?" Rick said. "It's great to see you. Here, give me those things, and I'll throw them in the closet."

Jim, it seemed to Karen, was a little taken aback when Rick relieved him of his bowler and his umbrella. He looked much more natural, but rather as if something had been amputated.

"Sit down, Jim," Rick said. "What will you have to drink? Scotch or rye?"

"I don't think I quite follow you."

"He's offering you a drink," Karen said. "You know, the stuff that hurts but does you so much good. You're not on the wagon, are you, Jim?"

Because the arm-chair was set with its back to the dressing-table, Jim had evidently not seen the bottles and the glasses.

"Oh, I see," he said. "No, I'm not on the wagon. You just caught me on a bad wicket. I'd forgotten that you Toronto people were in the habit of drinking in hotel bedrooms. Scotch and soda will be fine, fine."

"Jim," Karen said, and even though she was sitting on the bed, there could be no doubt at that moment that she was a girl who had been taught to Stand Up Straight. "Jim, were you, or were you not brought up in Toronto?"

"What's that? Of course I was."

"And have you, or have you not lived most of your life in Toronto?"

"Certainly I have. Damn fine city, too. But I don't quite see what you're getting at, Karen?"

"I just wanted to be sure I had all the facts straight. I just wanted to be sure that you'd brought your bowler and your bumbershoot to the right room."

She was smiling when she said it, but she did not mind letting him see that she was annoyed by the patronizing way he had said "you Toronto people". She didn't mind a bit.

Jim Evans suddenly stopped looking like Alec Guinness. It was extraordinary how little he looked like Alec Guinness after that.

"Sorry, sorry, old girl! I mean, I'm sorry, Karen. One gets so used to being in Rome, one forgets sometimes that one isn't a Roman oneself. Now that you've put me to rights, as I deserved,

I don't know when I've felt so much at home. It's just like being back in the Royal York Hotel."

"Well, Jim," Karen said, "just as long as you feel at home, that's wonderful, because we really are glad to see you."

Now that he had stopped playing the part of Alec Guinness playing the part of a Torontonian in London, Jim started to have a good time.

They were having a second drink all round when Rick and Jim started to talk about some of the men they had known at college, and Karen, briefly no part of the conversation, found her mind wandering to an evening she had once spent with Cyr. She had not meant to think of Cyr, but Jim's remark about drinking in hotel bedrooms had led her, in spite of herself, back to a discussion of the same topic with Cyr.

She had never realized, until that evening with Cyr, that there was anything at all odd about drinking in a hotel bedroom.

They had been having dinner at Chez Eve, in the Old Town in Geneva, and Cyr had ordered cocktails with the meal, and later, wine.

"You don't know how delightfully sinful this feels," Karen said. "To be drinking a cocktail right out in plain view in a restaurant, instead of hiding things under the tablecloth."

"What do you mean?"

"I mean you'd practically get a life sentence in Toronto if you had liquor on top of the table instead of underneath it. And it pretty well has to be a hotel table, too. A restaurant isn't much good because then there isn't any bedroom upstairs where you can finish off what is left."

"Darling," Cyr said, "you can't really mean what you appear to mean. You aren't telling me that *you* drink in hotel bedrooms, are you?"

"Why, of course. Of course I do. There just isn't anywhere else, really, except at home."

"I'm afraid I still don't understand."

"Well," Karen said, and by this time she had been laughing, "you can't drink in Canada unless you are drinking where you are 'in residence'. If you have a hotel room, you are 'in residence'. You see, in Canada, people think that drinks and bedrooms are a safer combination than drinks without bedrooms."

"That is not what people of other countries tend to think."

He had thought she was joking, and even after she had explained the whole thing to him very carefully, he had not believed her.

Now, in a bedroom at the Shaftesbury, Karen could appreciate his lack of comprehension as she had not at the time. If you were an Eskimo, you saw nothing odd about living in an igloo, and if you lived in Toronto in the thirties, you quite honestly could not see anything odd about having a party in a hotel bedroom. It was all in what you were used to.

Only half listening to what Rick and Jim were saying, she realized that the heritage of that grey era that had been neither honest prohibition nor reasonable licence was embodied in drinking habits that, from the outside looking in, must appear dubious at best. Because Torontonians, having discovered through necessity that it was cheaper to bring your own and drink upstairs, rather than down in the bar, were still drinking upstairs. Whenever you were invited to anything at a hotel—a dance, a business dinner, a charity affair—you said "Thank you" first, and immediately after that, "What room number?" You knew that somebody would have taken a room, because somebody always did. You didn't ask if you should bring a bottle; it was understood that you would. And when you arrived, you just put it down on the dressing-table, if there was still room on the dressing-table.

It had been that way when you went to fraternity dances, and it was still that way. It probably always would be.

The window was wide open, because it was a warm night, and in the distance Karen could hear Big Ben striking, and this, oddly enough, also reminded her of Toronto.

"This is the BBC news coming to you direct from London—"

You might pick up news from other sources, but in Toronto it was not considered either official, or really reliable, until you had got it direct from London, with the deep tolling of Big Ben in the background to assure you that there had been no mistake, that it was indeed the horse's mouth.

On a summer day in Toronto, when the windows of the houses were all open, you heard Big Ben over a wider area than you would have done if you had actually been in London.

"I've just realized something!" Karen said.

Both Rick and Jim looked startled, and she saw that she must have interrupted them in the middle of something. But she went on, anyway. "I've just realized," she said, "that we don't listen to the BBC newscast as often as we used to."

"You don't mean you get your news from NBC?" Jim asked. He looked really shocked.

"No," Karen said. "No, I've just realized that we get it, more often than not, from the Canadian Broadcasting Corporation."

"Even at noon?" Jim asked.

"Yes. Even at noon."

"And you find that satisfactory?"

"*Very* satisfactory," Karen said. She was tempted to say more, but there was no point in getting annoyed with Jim again for not understanding something that she had not, herself, fully understood until now.

That Toronto should now look to the CBC for world news coverage was so significant, and in so many ways, that she needed time to consider that significance. Jim, when he left home, had left an English stronghold. He would return to something very different. And a good thing, too, she thought, as she stood up and suggested that it was time they went down to dinner.

During dinner, which was surprisingly good, they talked about a variety of subjects, most of which seemed to be amusing. It was not until they were having coffee that Jim started asking questions. And it was apparent, when he did, that he had recognized the need to readjust some of his ideas.

"Tell me," he said, "are we still living in our basements back home?"

"There is," Rick said, smiling, "a definite trend toward coming up out of the basement."

"I'm glad to hear that. I never could understand why Toronto people should spend a fortune on a house and then go live in the basement. Quite frankly, I was never able to understand it."

Ned, Karen remembered, had once said that a society that went underground when it sought amusement was definitely sinister. He had said that the fact had to be faced that there was something very sinister about a sect that reverted to the cave in its leisure hours. He was not, he had said, going to draw a positive parallel between the cave and the womb, although one undoubtedly existed, because in this case it was more complicated than that. There was, Ned had said, more than a little evidence of schizophrenia in an attitude of mind that could accept the goldfish bowl of picture windows on the one hand, and the sunless depths of the recreation room on the other. It indicated conflicting urges and repressions that, when examined closely, were a matter for the gravest concern. He was not going to go into those urges and repressions in detail. He was simply going to say that until Torontonians had the courage to bring their caves up into the sunlight, he would continue to be extremely concerned about them.

Ned, as usual, had been exceedingly annoying, because as usual he had mixed some sense with no sense at all.

"The explanation," Rick was saying to Jim, "in so far as I can give you one, is that the basement seemed to be the only place where Toronto people felt free to express themselves uninhibited by mores with which they were no longer actually in agreement. There are now, I think, rather strong indications that they are ready to enjoy a somewhat wider freedom."

"You mean," Jim said, "that they are no longer as afraid of letting their hair down in public as they once were?"

"Precisely. As my brother-in-law once suggested they should, they are bringing their caves up into the sunlight."

"That's a very interesting way of putting it. I must say I would not have thought of it myself, but that doesn't make it any the less interesting."

"Of course," Rick added, "you understand that in using the word 'mores' I was using it in the general social sense, rather than in the narrow sense."

"Naturally. I didn't for a moment think in terms of orgies."

"Jim," Karen said, and she could not help laughing, "you're quite right not to think in terms of orgies. Still, I think it's time you came home for a while. If you stay away too long, I think you're going to be caught a little off-base when you do come back."

The night when Roddie had danced on the dining-room table, and somebody had set fire to the lounge, had most certainly not been an orgy. And it was Biff's own business if he wanted to do two hundred dollars' worth of damage to his own living-room replaying a rugby game. Nevertheless, it was rather surprising, when you came to think of it, that this sort of thing was no longer confined to downstairs recreation rooms. Biff had as yet, of course, to bring his Petty drawings and the ash-trays shaped like chamber-pots upstairs. But if he did, there was a fair chance that even Biff might see that sunlight did not go well with these things, and that a general compromise between the "downstairs" outlook and the "upstairs" outlook would produce a more satisfactory way of life than anything else.

It was when Jim was leaving that he said, "Look here, are you going to be in London on the twenty-first? There's a garden-party at the Palace on the twenty-first, and it might amuse you to go."

They were standing in the lobby of the Shaftesbury when he said this, and the lobby of the Shaftesbury simply was not the kind of place where you could take a reference to the Palace at all seriously.

"Do you mean Buckingham Palace?" Rick asked.

"Of course," Jim said. "What other palace is there?"

"I wouldn't know. But don't carry the joke any farther, Jim."

"I'm not joking," Jim said. "Her Majesty is receiving Commonwealth people at a garden-party on the twenty-first. The only reservation is that you must represent some group or other. Is there anything you could represent, Rick?"

"How about the Toronto Tennis Club?"

Rick still thought it was a joke, but Karen saw, in spite of their being in the lobby of the Shaftesbury, that Jim was perfectly serious.

"Would the Canadian Manufacturers' Association do?" she asked.

Jim bit his lip. "It's borderline, but we might get away with it. You'd be surprised who goes to these parties. The first thing to do is to see if the C.M.A. will agree to your representing them. I'll cable Toronto first thing in the morning, and let you know as soon as I have anything for you. As far as this end of it is concerned, you can consider it settled. The relations between Canada House and the Palace are very cordial. Very cordial, indeed."

"Jim," Karen asked, "what would I wear?"

"Wear anything. They're very informal at the Palace these days."

"That's nice. As long as I know they're informal at the Palace I won't worry at all about going in my sweater and slacks. My better slacks, of course. Will there be anybody there whom I could trust with my shopping-bag, or shall I just keep it with me?"

"It's nothing to be funny about. You *were* just being funny, I hope, Karen?"

"Up to a point, Jim. But only up to a point. After all, it was you who said I could wear anything."

"Well, I meant a dress. Some sort of nice dress."

"Jim, you should get together with the people at Dior's. The people over at Dior's would be mad about you. You have that *je ne sais quoi* when it comes to couture. Look, you've got to come right upstairs again and show me which of my dresses come under the heading of 'nice'."

Some people who were waiting for the elevator were obviously listening. The desk clerk was taking an interest, too.

"Karen," Jim said, "don't be so difficult. I'm sure all your dresses are nice."

"That is where you are wrong. Some of them are not at all nice. They were especially designed *not* to look nice."

"Jim," interposed Rick, and he was smiling, "you really

haven't a hope. The best thing you can do is to come upstairs and get it over with."

"I really am sorry, Jim," said Karen, "but if you were married you would know that a woman has to have some pretty definite idea of what's right for her to wear to a place that matters. I've got white gloves, and a terribly smart hat. That part of it is all right. And I know you shouldn't wear anything sleeveless. But that still leaves—"

"All right, Karen," Jim said, and he wasn't even sounding like Alec Guinness any more. "We'll go back up. And if there's anything left in that Scotch bottle, I won't mind thinking I'm at the Royal York for a bit longer."

As Karen said to Rick afterwards, it really was one of the nicest evenings they had ever spent with Jim, even if they didn't get to bed until after three. In all ways, it had been a great deal like an evening at the Royal York.

The Canadian Manufacturers' Association proved, naturally enough, to have no objection to being represented at the Palace.

"Well," Rick said, when they heard this, "it's nice to know that it's definite. What do you think I should wear?"

"Darling," Karen said, and she was laughing so hard she could hardly say it, "just wear anything. They're very informal at the Palace these days."

Afterwards, when people asked Karen what the palace had looked like, she was never able to tell them much, because along with everybody else she and Rick had been ushered through a series of large reception rooms directly to the garden. There had not, of course, been any signs in the reception rooms reading "Do Not Loiter" or "Hands Off Unless You Wish to Be Prosecuted"; but subtly there were restrictions on your behaviour about which you were left in no doubt at all, with the result that you emerged on to an immense stone patio with no more than a vague impression of heavy, ornate furniture that, you felt, must be the accumulated sum of a great many unsolicited "presentations". The kind of furniture that, once Graciously

Accepted, would leave the grateful monarch with still another problem on his or her hands.

They had been permitted—or at least there had been no indication that they should not do this—to pause for a moment on the patio from which a flight of steps led down to acres of lawn that, you could not help feeling, would have made a quite remarkably superior golf course.

There must, Karen and Rick decided later, have been over two thousand people spread out across these lawns on which were set up, at some distance from one another, two very large marquees—one for the multitude, and the other, in effect, the Royal Box. Everybody seemed to be smiling and having a very nice time. There was, inherent in the whole scene, an oddly secure feeling that Karen could never, then or later, define in any other way. And, seeing what appeared to be as many nationalities and national costumes as she had once seen on the Pont du Mont Blanc in Geneva, she was struck as never before by the extent and variety of the Commonwealth. Somehow, you tended to equate "British" with "Anglo-Saxon", which, of course, was quite wrong.

They had not actually been presented to the Queen, which was something Jim had told them to expect.

"You may or may not be presented," Jim had said. "Her Majesty, as I am sure you'll understand, can't speak personally with everybody. So it's just a matter of chance. However, you will certainly see her, because she will circulate. Her Majesty is very good about circulating."

The Queen had strolled around, accompanied close at hand by an equerry, and a lady-in-waiting, and the Archbishop of Canterbury. An apparently loose, but consistent outer circle composed of two or three more ladies-in-waiting and possibly eight more equerries, made up the balance of her entourage.

It had all been very informal, as Jim had said it would be; but you could not help noticing that the equerry, and the lady-in-waiting, and the Archbishop of Canterbury were never more than a few feet from the Queen. It would, you felt, have been disrespectful to refer to this as a bodyguard. Bodyguards tended to make you think of Chicago. But this was, nevertheless, exactly what it had been, although you were morally certain that neither the equerry, nor the lady-in-waiting, nor the Archbishop of Canterbury was armed.

It had all been very smooth. The Archbishop, with an air of choosing people at random, had presented them to the Queen, and in this way made it seem that the choice was his rather than hers. Which, in fact, it probably had been. At any rate, if you had wanted to feel snubbed, you would have had to feel that it was the Archbishop rather than the Queen who had snubbed you, which was not something you would have been likely to feel strongly about.

And, anyway, your injured feelings, if you had had any, would have been healed by a word with either the Duke of Edinburgh or the Prime Minister. The Duke, or Mr. Macmillan—and you couldn't help admiring the organization this implied—managed to speak to everyone to whom the Queen had not spoken.

Karen felt that it was quite good enough for anyone representing the Canadian Manufacturers' Association to have had a short conversation with the Prime Minister. And the fact that she had once, a long time before, been responsible for seeing that he had a sufficient number of cucumber sandwiches and did not feel too lonely, had done nothing to take the edge off this occasion.

When they left the Palace, both she and Rick agreed that an immediate return to the Shaftesbury Hotel would be a little in the nature of an anticlimax. It was not at all difficult to decide that they would have cocktails and dinner at the Savoy.

Karen always remembered that dinner at the Savoy, because it reminded her of the first time she and Rick had ever had dinner together. Dinner at the Savoy had the kind of festive feeling that you always hope, in advance, to achieve when dining out, and that you so rarely do. It had the gay, relaxed, this-night-will-never-end feeling they had experienced on the night when they went to Winston's a week after they met.

Rick, in his last year at College, had not really been able to afford to take her to Winston's. But when he invited her, she had known enough not to protest. For some years, if they were to eat out at all, they would, she knew, do so at such places as Murray's or Child's. And so she had realized she ought not to protest.

By that time, Winston's had dropped its initial advertising gambit of private keys to the dignified, panelled door on King Street, because it was already established as one of the best supper clubs on the continent, and had become the place to which people like Katherine Cornell and Orson Welles would go automatically for late supper after leaving the theatre. It was where, long after that first time, Karen and Rick one evening found themselves sitting next to Vladimir Horowitz. Winston's, candle-lit, the walls lined with autographed pictures of celebrities, had the same kind of internationally recognized *cachet* that the Bavaria had. Impossible to say just how a place achieved this kind of distinction, but it was as undeniable at Winston's in Toronto as it was at the Bavaria in Geneva.

The Savoy was not really in any way similar to Winston's, but in both places Karen and Rick felt the same—with the one very important difference that now, dining at the Savoy, they knew there would be nothing to stop them, later, from having what they both wanted.

And the Shaftesbury, they decided when they got back there, was quite as good, for some things at least, as the Savoy. Or, for that matter, as the Palace.

15 Only a routine check-up

On the morning after the cook-out, Karen thought that straightening things up and washing the dishes would keep her occupied until noon, would leave no time for thinking about her appointment with Dr. Lowe in the early afternoon. But at eleven o'clock she found herself still with an hour to fill before she would need to have lunch and change.

She could, she knew, do some baking, or wax the front hall, or put a few things through the washer; but in any of these directions lay madness, because neither her mind nor her body would be in any sense really occupied.

If she had used her head at all, she thought, she would have washed the dishes by hand, rather than putting them in the electric dish-washer while she put away rugs and cushions and cleaned up the house.

At an earlier stage in her life, she could have lost herself for a little while in a book, or distracted herself with a visit to the museum or to the art gallery. As avenues of escape these were now closed to her, because they no longer possessed the small accompanying habits of familiarity that in themselves would have provided comfort, would have drawn her out of her miserable preoccupation with herself.

Standing in the middle of the sunlit kitchen, staring helplessly at hands whose emptiness was painfully symbolic, she decided suddenly that she would scrub the kitchen floor.

Ten minutes later, in a red shirt and a pair of faded jeans, she was down on her knees, an old-fashioned scrubbing-brush in her hand, working hard and methodically at a job that did not need doing but was nevertheless extraordinarily satisfying. She had heard about women who scrubbed floors as a form of mental anaesthesia, and had thought it a very silly thing to do. Now she saw that it wasn't silly at all.

She and Rick had laid the green and white rubber tiles themselves. When they had asked the people down at Aikenhead's about laying tiles on their own, the people at Aikenhead's had said there was nothing to it. If your floor was level, they said, it was really a very simple job. You just had to use a little care in spreading the cement. You mustn't use too much, they had said. And then again, you mustn't use too little. Just a nice, even coating. You would know instinctively when it was right. And now that you knew all about the job, they would like to advise that you buy a really good quality tile. They found it necessary, they said, to carry quite a range quality-wise, because not all their customers were people of taste and discernment. However, when their advice was asked, they always considered the best interests of the customer and recommended their top quality. At first glance, they had said, you might think that the top quality cost rather a lot, but when you thought of a kitchen floor in terms of a lifetime—possibly even longer—you would see at once that you were making an excellent investment. Another point to consider, they had said, was that it was not a job you would want to do twice.

The people down at Aikenhead's had undoubtedly been right in everything they said, but they had really hit the mark when they had said that it was not a job you would want to do twice. Before they were through, Rick and Karen had discovered that it was a job they didn't even want to do once. It had not, of course, been anything like as bad as the buckwheat lawn, even with something that was obviously not "just a nice, even coating" oozing up between tile after tile. But it had been bad enough.

"This," Karen had said, as they had neared the end of the undertaking, "is the last do-it-yourself job I ever take on, so help me. When I'm dead, I'm going to have Do-It-Yourself put on my headstone. It will be my final message to anyone who wants to read it. It will mean, go lay an egg, go lay rubber tiles, go cut your throat. Go do anything you damn well please, but do it yourself, don't ask me to."

She sat back on her heels and looked at the area of floor she had already scrubbed, while she thought, death was an idea I could joke about then. I was not only healthy in body, I was healthy in mind. I may still be reasonably healthy in body. In a few hours I will know about that. But this other thing—this terrible, inner discontent that is slowly engulfing everything I see, and do, and touch—where has it come from? What are its causes?

There must, she though, be specific causes that are individual to me. There must also be a wider frame of reference, because I am not alone in this. I may not sleep around like Fay, or transfer my affections to an expatriate Polish Count as Millicent has done, or expend myself on my children like Barbara, or hide in a castle built of dollar bills like Betsey, but I have this much in common with them—I am, in my own way, as off balance as they are.

Slowly she picked up her scrubbing brush, dipped it into the pail of water and detergent beside her, and set to work again.

Fay had always been headed for trouble. Only a miracle could have kept Fay on an even keel. But the others had had every opportunity to make pretty much what they wanted of their lives. They had all, she knew, been given an excellent start. That, in itself, could be part of the trouble, contradictory as this might seem at first glance.

Because she was reasoning objectively, and because her hands were occupied, temporarily she was able to forget her dread of the afternoon ahead of her.

We were all right, she thought, until we were around twenty, Barbara and Millicent and Betsey and I, because until then we were thinking for ourselves, we were growing mentally as best suited us within our individual limitations. Even Betsey, though you wouldn't guess it now, had done quite well at the university.

They had all, she realized, got married between the ages of twenty and twenty-three, as most girls do if they are interested in getting married at all. According to the book, you ought at this stage to have been able to write "and they lived happily ever afterwards" under each case history.

It had not been as simple as that. And the fault, she was becoming more and more convinced, lay in the one thing they all had in common—a "good home", as it was envisaged and striven for in their particular era.

She had made a big mistake in arguing this point with Ned recently. It was always a mistake to argue with Ned, because you never reached a conclusion.

"Let's face it," Ned had said, "you women of today have a pretty easy time of it."

"For your information," Karen had told him, "we women of today have a hell of a time of it."

"Your difficulty, Karen—not that it's one you couldn't overcome if you faced it—is that you don't know when you are well off."

"Ned, can you honestly believe that anyone is well off shut up in an air-conditioned box with a lot of shiny little contrivances so fool-proof a moron could get good results with them?"

"Would you prefer the old homestead with a wood-burning stove, and cows to milk before breakfast? Not after breakfast, mind you, Karen, but before."

"Yes, I would. At least the cow would kick the bucket over occasionally. And there would be times when the stove wouldn't draw properly. You just have no idea, Ned, how satisfying it would be to have a stove that didn't always draw properly."

"Karen, you really are not talking sense."

"Aren't I? You try staying home and pushing buttons all day in order to produce laundry that is 'whiter than white', and cakes a hell of a lot better than anything Grandma ever baked, and see how much satisfaction you get out of it."

It was at this point that Ned had become sententious. At some point or other in any discussion Ned always became sententious. "Karen," he had said, "you are overlooking the fact that woman's place is in the home, and that the stability of our present society depends on this. I would be gravely concerned, very gravely concerned, if women were taken out of the home."

Karen had been really irritated, "That is not what I'm talking about. What I'm talking about is the kind of home that our society is putting women into today. Julia should be thankful that at least she doesn't live in a place like Rowanwood. Just the same, look at this damned house of yours. Three floors and a basement. Because Julia has a washing-machine and a vacuum-cleaner you probably think it's easy for her to keep up a house that was designed for not less than two servants and a weekly laundress. Well, give me the honest-to-God leisure you had when there were servants, rather than the kind of so-called leisure you see in the advertisements now, and you can have your damned washing-machines and vacuum-cleaners."

"Now, Karen, don't get excited. There's no reason to get excited about this."

"Ned, if you ever tell me again not to get excited, I'll throw one of your precious Picasso ash-trays at you. I'll miss, because I never went out for basketball, but it will be the end of the ash-tray anyway."

"Now, Karen," Ned had begun again. But he must have realized that she had meant what she had said, because instead of going on, he raised his voice and called out to Julia.

Julia had been in the kitchen, because even if you are a poor cook the kitchen is where you do your poor cooking. When you came to think of it, it was quite a spectacular accomplishment on Julia's part to remain such a terrible cook in face of the forces aligned against her to prevent this state of affairs.

"Julia," Ned had called, "don't you think you're fortunate to have a washing-machine and a vacuum-cleaner?"

"Certainly I do," Julia had answered.

"Julia," Karen had called out, "don't you think you're lucky to have such a big house to look after?"

Julia had not replied.

"She didn't hear you," Ned had said. "She has the electric beater going, so she didn't hear you, Karen."

It had been interesting, Karen thought, as she knelt on the floor in her own kitchen, to discover that, whatever their other differences, she and Julia had something very basic in common. They both thought that the home, as it had become, was a hell of a place for an educated woman. Because Julia had pushed the button on her electric beater after, and not before, Karen had asked about the house.

Scarcely noticing that she was doing so, Karen abandoned pail and brush, got up, and crossed to the sink counter to get a cigarette. The electric dish-washer, with sunlight falling across an enamelled top of almost impossible purity, looked even better than it did in the advertisements. Deliberately, she raised the lid, and dropped a burned-out match into it.

There could be no doubt about it, she thought. What she had said to Ned had, by and large, been the absolute truth. The modern mechanized home was a hell of a place for an educated woman. There was something horribly wrong with a system that insisted first on compulsory education, and then lured you into a full-time occupation that any reasonably intelligent illiterate could have handled without a qualm.

But this, she thought, although it is a general truth that could apply equally well to any woman of my approximate age and income level in any residential suburb from here to Los Angeles, is neither an answer nor the whole truth. On the basis of this truth, I could offer myself a good many "cures", but they would be negative rather than positive, and in the long run would not be likely to do me much good, because I still can not be sure in what capacity I am upset.

She might not, she saw, have recognized the infinite number of possibilities that could lie behind that phrase "in what capacity", if it had not been for the question which Ned had put to her just after Julia had pushed the button on the electric beater.

"Karen," Ned had said, "just answer this question with one or two words. The question is—what are you?"

"What am I?"

"Yes. Just answer in one or two words. Just say the first thing that comes to your mind."

"There isn't any first thing. Even for you, Ned, that's a very silly question. I know you probably got it out of a book, but still it's a very silly question because it couldn't be answered with a hundred words, let alone one or two. I'm not any one thing, as you know perfectly well. I'm dozens of things."

"Beginning with?"

"No, Ned, I'm not beginning with anything, because I wouldn't know where to begin."

She could not, in all honesty, think of herself as any one particular thing more than any other. But Ned had made her see just how complicated she actually was, and the infinity of answers she could have given.

"I find this very significant," Ned had said. "Very significant indeed. I cannot offhand remember anyone who has answered that question in quite that way."

"I didn't answer it."

"Exactly the point I was making. And I find that very significant indeed."

At the time she had simply been annoyed, as she so often was with Ned. Now, leaning against the edge of the sink watching the smoke curl upwards from her cigarette, she wondered uneasily if it had not, as Ned had said, been significant that she should refuse to put the emphasis on any one facet of herself.

So many things, all of them true.

I am me. I am a woman. I am a human being. I am Mrs. Richard Whitney. I am a Canadian. I am forty. No matter who you were, you could go on almost indefinitely, but you would have to be a very smart cookie, a really *very* smart cookie, to get all these things in their proper order of importance to you, and in addition to this recognize in which capacity you would be most affected in any given set of circumstances.

And, although on the surface her problems were primarily those of a woman, Karen found herself becoming more and more certain that her present emotional troubles were tied in with her capacity as an individual rather than her capacity as a woman.

It was the first time in many months that she could feel she was really thinking constructively, that she might just possibly be getting somewhere. And she might have experienced a definite lightening of spirit, if she had not glanced up at the clock on the pale-green kitchen wall.

Fear again a constriction around her heart, she saw that in a few minutes it would be time to go upstairs to bathe and change before having a sandwich and a glass of milk. Before going out, and getting into the car, and driving downtown. Before finding out if she would ever have the time in which to resolve her problems.

She steadied herself against the sink, and wondered for a moment if she were going to be sick. It was one thing to think vaguely about suicide. It was a very different thing to suspect that your days might be arbitrarily numbered.

If the telephone had not rung, she might very easily have been sick. She was extremely grateful that the telephone should ring at that moment, even when she found that it was Fay, and not, as she had hoped, Susan.

She took the call in the front hall, and sat down before lifting the receiver. "Hello?" she said.

"Karen," Fay said, "I'm worried sick."

Karen felt like saying that she was worried sick, herself. But, if she had been going to share her anxiety with anyone, it would not have been with Fay. She had never taken her worries to Fay. It had always been the other way round.

"What's the matter, Fay?"

"Well, it may be nothing," said Fay. "It may be nothing at all, angel."

"What may be nothing?"

"Well, I was just out in the garden, and I happened to see Barbara. You know the way there's no fence between their place and ours, don't you?"

"Of course I know. But what has that got to do with it?"

"Not a thing. I was simply explaining how I happened to talk to Barbara."

"While you're at it, you might as well explain how you happened to be in the garden at all."

"Angel, that simply isn't relevant. It simply isn't relevant in any way."

"I was only trying to find out what is relevant."

"Don't be like that, angel. I told you I was worried sick."

"Yes, you did. But you still haven't said what about."

"I'm getting to that," Fay said. "Karen, Barbara may not be going to Cape Cod with the children this summer. You'll have to believe me, because she told me so herself. That's why I explained about the garden, so that you would know she told me so herself."

"Well, that's just what you wanted, isn't it?"

"Not precisely," said Fay.

"Look, when I ran into you at Loblaw's, you said most distinctly that you intended to stay away from Matt. If Barbara doesn't go to Cape Cod, it will make things easier all round. You won't even have to make up your mind not to chase Matt again this summer, because you won't have the opportunity."

"I didn't chase him."

"Fay," Karen said, "this is me. Tell that to somebody else if you like, but don't tell it to me."

Fay dropped this issue. "Angel, you don't seem to see the real reason why I'm so upset."

"Frankly, I don't."

"Just a minute while I get a cigarette."

Fay was never so upset that she couldn't take time out to get a cigarette. That night when Karen had cleaned the blood off the bathroom floor, Fay had, she remembered, been sitting up in bed smoking when she came back to the bedroom.

"There," Fay said a few moments later, "that's better. I couldn't get the damn lighter to work. None of the lighters around here ever seem to work. Now, where was I? Oh, yes, I had just told you that Barbara may not be going to Cape Cod this summer. And I'm absolutely terrified that she suspects something. I can't think of any other reason why she should stay home."

"Didn't she give you any reason?"

"Well, yes, in a way she did. But it just didn't seem valid to me. She said that she was worried about the amount of iodine in the air at Cape Cod. She said she was considering Georgian Bay instead, because the iodine was in perfect balance in the air at

Georgian Bay. Doesn't that sound a little improbable to you, angel?"

"Well," agreed Karen, "it does, a trifle."

"I was sure you would see that. And Barbara was talking about Matt, and you know she never talks about anything but her children. She was saying that she thought it would be good for Matt to get away to a place where there was just the right amount of iodine in the air. She said that if she could find a cottage at Georgian Bay, then they could all have a holiday together, and that this would be very good for Matt, much better than staying in the garden. She said she thought he hadn't been looking too well recently. Do you think he looks unwell? I don't."

So Susan had managed to make Barbara concerned about Matt's health. This being the case, Matt would almost indubitably find himself back in his own bed, which would make him very happy. He might also find himself back in his tennis shoes. This would not make him quite so happy. But then you could never have everything, and Matt, she was sure, was balanced enough to recognize this. He would have Barbara—as she had been when they were first engaged—really absorbed in him, and there could be no doubt that this was what he wanted and needed above all else. He must, Karen thought, have been lonely beyond endurance during the warm, slow passage of summer after summer alone in that big house.

A common loneliness was the only thing that could have made the liaison with Fay possible. A glamour girl would never have got to first base with Matt. But a tiny, pathetically confused wisp of a girl, with haunted eyes and a closer acquaintanceship with loneliness than he had himself—that was a combination of appeals that, almost without his knowing it, would have aroused first his sympathy and then his senses. And he would never at any time have realized that he was seeing only one side of a picture. He would never at any time have seen that Fay had chased him with desperate, perhaps, but nevertheless coolly deliberate intent.

"Angel," Fay was saying, "can you honestly believe that there's any validity in this iodine business?"

"Well," Karen replied, and she was choosing her words very carefully, "I don't think that is exactly the point. I think the point is that Barbara could very well believe there was. In my opinion, there is no reason for doubting that Barbara was saying what she believed, no more and no less. You know how Barbara is about health, and exercise, and vitamins."

"You really think that's all there is to it?"

"Yes, I do. I'm reasonably certain that you have nothing to worry about at all. Just the same, it would be a very good idea if you were to stay right away from both Barbara and Matt."

"Angel, I feel so much better. I can't tell you how much better I feel. I really was worried sick. I don't know why it is, but you always seem able to help me the way nobody else ever does."

"I'm glad if I've made you feel better," Karen said. It was all there was to say until the next time.

"Karen," said Fay, "do you remember the way things used to be at Waycroft?"

Surprised, Karen answered, "Yes. Very well."

"It could have been worse there, couldn't it?"

"It could have been a whole lot worse." And Karen didn't know when she had ever felt quite so sad about anyone.

It was a sadness that lingered with her after Fay had rung off. It belonged with the kind of sadness that, she knew, lay on the other side of a door through which she might have to pass that afternoon.

Karen was always punctual, and it was exactly quarter past one when she closed the front door behind her, and crossed the gravel drive to the car. She would probably, she realized, get to Dr. Lowe's office ahead of time, but some allowance had to be made for striking a great many traffic lights the wrong way. You were constantly reading statements in the newspapers to the effect that they had at last synchronized the lights, but if you could get downtown without having to slam on the brakes at half a dozen intersections, it was something to talk about at the next party you went to.

When she was in the car, she took off her white pumps and put them on the seat beside her white gloves and white handbag.

You felt, when you went to the doctor's, that you had to be inhumanly clean. So a mark from the brake pedal on a white shoe could be quite upsetting. This was perfectly absurd, you knew, and you could rationalize it only on the basis of symbolism. If, when you went to the doctor's, everything about you appeared to be perfect, then perhaps everything *was* perfect. Or at least good enough to go on with for some years.

She opened the glove compartment and took out the nylon socks she often wore while driving.

The street, she saw, looked almost exactly as it had three days earlier when she had gone across to apologize to Millicent about the New Canadian bridge business.

The shadows of the elms now fell in dark, quiet pools directly beneath them, rather than slanting across the road. Pete's bicycle no longer lay against the verandah steps of his house, because Rick had already helped him to put it together again. And today it was unlikely that any man reminding her of Cyr would walk, his hands in his pockets, along the heat-drenched, dusty road.

Apart from these things, time might have stood still.

Boris's car again stood in the driveway of Millicent and Biff's house. The blind was again down in Mrs. Johnson's bedroom. The street itself again lay quiet and undisturbed under the hot summer sun. This time because the women were all shut up in their boxes having lunch. Perhaps with their children. Perhaps alone. Returned from shopping, or a morning coffee party—if any of them had done either of these things—they were again shut up in their boxes because it was lunch time. Hungry or not, you went back into your box at lunch time because it was expected of you. And if you lived in Rowanwood, you did what was expected of you.

On Monday, before she had picked up the three letters that were each to mean something different to her, the street had been, if no longer well loved, at least pleasantly familiar. But now, as she pressed gently on the accelerator and the car began to move forward, it was as if the scene before her were one from which she was already separated by an immeasurable distance.

Desperately she tried to think of something, anything, with which she might anchor herself to a living reality. But things past might never have been. Any future seemed unlikely. And a wall of glass seemed to stand between her and the present.

A block from the house she passed Pete, walking his bicycle because it was so hot. She smiled, and waved to him. And though he returned both her smile and her wave, he seemed to her to be as alone on his side of the glass wall as she was on hers.

She attempted to think about Planesville, to really believe that she and Rick were actually going there tomorrow. Instead she felt as if she were starting on a long, long journey in exactly the opposite direction. The only time in her life when she had experienced a feeling even remotely like it had been on the day when she had left Canada for the first time, *en route* by ship to Europe, Geneva her eventual destination.

She had not, after she reached Geneva, been even briefly homesick. But, if it had been feasible, she would have got off that ship before it left the St. Lawrence River.

Driving down to the Medical Arts Building, she felt very much as she had on that occasion. If there had been any reasonable way of getting off the ship, she would have done so.

Some people, she knew, would have been ashamed to admit weakness of this kind even to themselves. These were the people who believed that fool thing about a coward dying a thousand deaths, and a brave man only one. If you were capable of one death only, the actual one, you were nothing better than a living or—as the case might be—dead proof of a total lack of imagination. If you had any imagination at all, you were possessed of an instrument that, by its very nature, was honed to equal sharpness on either edge, and would exact a price in direct proportion to the pleasures it afforded you.

This was a truth that Karen acknowledged and accepted, but even so she did not think she would ever go through another day quite as bad, in its own way, as this one. The experience through which she was going was, though created by her imagination, an actual one, and as a result, no matter what Dr. Lowe told her, she would have got a little of her dying over and done with. The peculiar brassy quality that she had never seen in sunlight before, the terrible helplessness, the feeling of being irrevocably separated from anything and anyone she had known and loved—these things, like everything else in life and death, had a greater impact on first recognition than they would ever have again.

She had not expected to find a place for her car in the Medical Arts parking space. When she did, she chose to look on it as a good omen. That to do so was unutterably foolish, she quite realized; but when you were dying any one of your deaths, from the first to the last, you had a right to be foolish if you wished.

She left the car unlocked, and turned away from it toward a back door in the angle of the building. The corridor inside was comparatively dark. She was glad of this, because the brassiness of the sunlight outside had been rather horrible. She never had liked afternoon sunlight. In the future, if there was to be any future, she would like it less than ever.

The lobby at the front of the building was quite full, as it usually was. The lobby at the Medical Arts was a place where you could not help feeling that people were rather wonderful. Although most of the people you saw there must, you knew, be suffering in mind or in body—or they would not have been there at all—you could never remember having seen any positive emotional proof of this. And here, the individual was allowed the dignity of complete privacy. Even at close quarters in the elevators, people did not speculate about one another.

Anywhere else, an elevator was usually a socially uncomfortable spot. In an elevator in the Royal York Hotel, for instance, even a Waycroft girl could not remain ignorant of the kind of speculation she was arousing. It was invariably a relief to get out of a crowded elevator in the Royal York.

There was nobody in Dr. Lowe's waiting-room other than his secretary, Miss Bolton.

"Good afternoon, Miss Bolton."

"Good afternoon, Mrs. Whitney. How are you?"

"I'm fine, thank you."

For a moment Miss Bolton looked surprised, and Karen realized that probably Dr. Lowe's patients did not come in to see him when they were feeling fine. Well, she certainly wasn't feeling fine, herself, but it was nevertheless the natural thing to say.

"Oh," Miss Bolton said, finding a different explanation, "it's only your routine check-up today, isn't it, Mrs. Whitney?"

Karen sat down in one of the two rows of armchairs arranged rather like those in a club car on a train. Her hands felt clammy, and if Miss Bolton had not been there, she would have taken a piece of Kleenex out of her purse and wiped them off.

"Yes," she said, "that's right. It's only a routine check-up."

"How are your girls?" Miss Bolton asked.

"They're fine."

"I really can't believe they're grown up. They're both in the States, aren't they, Mrs. Whitney?"

"Yes, Carol is in California, and Peg is in New York. We expect Peg home for holidays this summer."

"Are they liking it down there?"

"They just love it down there."

"You must miss them."

"I do, yes," Karen said. While she talked, she had been trying to hear if there was a patient already with Dr. Lowe behind the closed door of his consulting-room. It was difficult to hear if there was anyone in the consulting-room. You regretted this when you were on the outside. You were glad of it when you were on the inside.

"Of course both the girls will be coming back to Canada eventually, won't they?" Miss Bolton was asking.

"Of course," said Karen, although this was something she did not necessarily believe. Carol and her husband were almost certain to come back. She could not be as sure that Peg would.

"It has been very hot, hasn't it?" Miss Bolton said.

"Yes, it really has been very hot. Have you had your vacation yet, Miss Bolton?"

"No, not yet. I still have that to look forward to."

After this, Miss Bolton redirected her attention to her desk with its typewriter, two telephones, and shaded desk lamp.

Whenever you came in you had a short conversation with Miss Bolton, which in view of the circumstances got neither of you anywhere, and which always ended with the weather being either very hot or very cold.

Karen looked at her wrist-watch. It was still only twenty past two, and Dr. Lowe might or might not have come back from lunch. He might or might not have a patient in the consulting-room with him. And she, Karen, might or might not go crazy if she didn't have a cigarette while she waited.

She was always determined, in advance, not to smoke while waiting to see Dr. Lowe. There was nothing to stop you smoking while you waited, but eight chairs and only one ash-tray could not be regarded as strong encouragement to do so.

She opened her purse and surreptitiously wiped her hands off on some Kleenex as she took out cigarettes and matches. At least she had learned across the years to sit in a chair next to the ash-tray. And there was no reason, just because she smoked in his waiting-room, for Dr. Lowe to jump to the conclusion that she smoked too much.

Miss Bolton, just as Karen lighted her cigarette, got up, crossed to the door of the consulting-room, opened it, and then said, "You can come in now, Mrs. Whitney. Dr. Lowe is ready to see you."

Karen saw that her timing had as usual been terrible, because Miss Bolton was saying, "I'm sure Dr. Lowe won't mind if you take your cigarette in with you, Mrs. Whitney."

Damn, Karen thought, and double-damn. He'll notice that my hand is shaking. She did not want him to see that her hand was shaking, any more than she wanted him to notice that her hands were damp, because she had decided not to tell him that there was anything the matter with her. If he did not find anything the matter when he examined her, then they would not need to talk about the pain in her side at all. He was an excellent doctor, and if he found no cause for pain, then it would mean that there was nothing really serious behind it, and they wouldn't have to talk about it at all.

I am, Karen thought, as she got up and walked into the consulting room, behaving like Carol or Peg, aged six. Except that neither Carol nor Peg would ever, at any age, have been as childish as I am being right now.

Dr. Lowe was sitting at his desk, with the window, of course, behind him. He got up immediately.

"Hello, Karen," he said. "Nice to see you. How are you?"

"I'm fine," Karen said. There really *was* nothing else to say.

"Well, you look fine," Dr. Lowe said. "Sit down. We'll just talk for a minute or two while you finish your cigarette. Perhaps I'll have one, too."

Dr. Lowe always smoked a cigarette when you came in with one, and you were morally certain he seized the opportunity with an addict's enthusiasm. This, however, was something you could only guess at, because he invariably managed to make it sound like an indulgence he rarely allowed himself.

Now that she was finally at the vortex of the whirlpool, Karen no longer felt much of anything. Perhaps this was the way people felt when they took the last step toward the guillotine. Perhaps it was numbness rather than courage that made the last step possible.

Dr. Lowe had a ledger open in front of him, and had casually picked up a pen. Whenever he said that you would just talk for a minute or two, you knew perfectly well that he was not going to waste time. But it was very nice the way he brought his statistics on you up to date while apparently carrying on an idle conversation.

Karen liked Dr. Lowe very much. And, up until this moment, he had never failed to make her feel curiously safe as soon as she stepped into his consulting-room.

Ned at one time had made a study of the relative ages of doctors and their patients. Women under fifty, Ned had said, always choose doctors who are older than they are themselves. The manner in which he had said this had made it sound, if not actually neurotic, at least dangerously abnormal. To have pointed out to Ned that you usually tended to have more confidence in the judgment of someone older than yourself, would have been a waste of time. As a conclusion, it would have been far too obvious for Ned to find it acceptable.

"You must miss the girls," Dr. Lowe was saying.

"I do. Very much," Karen told him.

"Feel a bit at loose ends these days without them?"

He had, without her really noticing it, already disposed of headaches, and cold frequency, and so on. She must have answered these questions automatically, because the answers were simple and satisfactory from her own point of view as well as the doctor's. He was now exploring a different area, again in a very casual manner. He was actually asking her if she ever felt depressed.

"No," said Karen, "I don't feel at loose ends without them." Which was the truth. She was at loose ends all right, but not because Carol and Peg were on their own. It went deeper than that. Much deeper.

"I imagine you have enough to do with a big house to look after. You're still in Rowanwood, aren't you?"

"Yes, we're still in Rowanwood."

"Well," Dr. Lowe said, "suppose you just slip into the examining room now. No need to take off more than your dress, and your stockings and shoes. You don't wear a girdle, do you? I'll be with you in a minute, and we'll check your heart and blood pressure. But off-hand I would say there's nothing much the matter with you."

The Canadian way of doing these things was, Karen thought, as she had thought many times before, infinitely preferable to the way they did them in Switzerland. In Switzerland the doctor was usually right there when you took off your dress, which gave the operation a strip-tease flavour that was most inappropriate. Once your dress was off, everything was perfectly all right again, even in Switzerland. It was very typical of the European mind not to perceive a distinction so apparent in North America that if you went to your doctor with a cut finger, he would, you felt, as likely as not look the other way while you took your glove off.

It was not until Dr. Lowe had tested her heart, blood pressure, and lungs, and noted that her weight had not changed, that he said, "Now just put your arms above your head, and bring them down to see if you can touch your toes."

"Of course I can touch my toes," Karen said.

"I'd just like to have you do it, anyway."

Her fingers were still several inches short of the floor when the pain caught her. Clenching her teeth, she laid the palms of her hands flat on the floor before straightening up again. If the pain had been as bad as it sometimes was, she could not have done it.

Dr. Lowe made no direct comment. "Just lie down on the couch there for a minute, will you, Karen."

Short of throwing away the last shreds of her self-respect, there was no escape. Dr. Lowe already knew she had a pain, and exactly where that pain was.

"That hurt?" he asked.

"No."

"Or that?"

"No."

It was quite true that the fairly strong pressure he was exerting on the muscles of her waist and stomach was not painful in any way.

"All right," he said. "You have a wrenched muscle in your left side. That sort of thing can be acutely painful, but since, in this case, it doesn't seem to have caused you much discomfort, I don't think we need to bother with strapping it up. Have you some liniment of any kind at home?"

"You mean—" Karen began, and couldn't say any more.

Dr. Lowe smiled. He had a very nice smile. "Yes," he said, "that's all it is. You'll live for a while yet. I knew there was something on your mind. It was just a question of finding out what it was."

Karen sat up, swung her legs off the couch, took a deep breath, let it out again, and said, "I owe you an apology, don't I?"

Dr. Lowe smiled again. He already had his hand on the door to his consulting-room. "I'll be in here. Come out when you're ready."

Alone, Karen stood up and looked out of the window at the city eight stories below. It was, of course, still early afternoon, but in spite of this she thought she had never seen the sky so blue, or sunlight so softly warm and beautiful. It couldn't have been a nicer day for coming home from a long journey.

And when she again sat on the other side of the desk from Dr. Lowe, she knew she was very, very glad to be alive. She still had major problems to sort out, but for the moment she could not think beyond the simple, wonderful fact that she had all the time in the world to do it. Given enough time, you could do anything. And tomorrow they were going to Planesville, she and Rick. Excitement building in her, she thought, perhaps tomorrow it will be all wrapped up, and I can start out on a whole new life that really satisfies me. And because this was what she wanted to believe, she made herself believe it.

"Now," Dr. Lowe said, "just as a matter of purely academic interest, how much pain do you get with that side of yours?"

"None, most of the time," Karen said. "But when it does come, it can be—well, it's often pretty bad."

"I thought so," Dr. Lowe said. "What kind of liniment have you?"

"Absorbine Junior," Karen told him.

"That will do very nicely," Dr. Lowe said. "Massage your side with it gently, two or three times a day. Take care how you move from one position to another, and don't twist when lifting things. If it shows no sign of improvement in a week to ten days, come in again, and we'll show you how to strap it up."

"That won't be necessary," Karen said. "I don't mind pain, as such."

"No," Dr. Lowe said, "I know you don't. Not as such. Well, I guess that's all. Don't forget you can call me any time. I'm right here, any time you want to call me."

Karen had collected her gloves and purse, and was already standing up, when she said, "Dr. Lowe—sometimes I think about suicide."

She had not known she was going to say this until she had said it.

"Oh?" Dr. Lowe said. "How do you think of going about it?"

Karen stared at him. "I hadn't thought," she said. "I hadn't thought about that at all."

Dr. Lowe actually laughed. "Well," he said, "when you've decided on a method, drop in again and we'll talk it over."

He was, Karen thought, probably the sanest man she had ever met. In addition to this, he knew her in some ways a great deal better than she knew herself. He would not, she was quite certain, have let many patients leave so casually on that particular note. With her, he knew it was the best thing he could possibly do, because, as Cyr had once done, he understood her better than she understood herself.

When she passed through the waiting-room on her way out, there were three people there, two men and a woman, none of them smoking. And, briefly, she had what amounted to a need to stop and say, "Don't worry. Whatever brings you here, it probably isn't as bad as you think."

It was one of those times when you loved people you had never seen before, and would never see again. To have told them so would only have embarrassed them. So you said nothing. You left them as you had found them, to live alone, and perhaps before long to die alone. As some time you yourself would die. But not today.

16 | It could have been a whole lot worse

The glass wall shattered, her horizons once again infinite, Karen had fully expected to concentrate during the drive home on the now unencumbered prospect of the trip to Planesville. Instead, and perhaps because her emotions were still very close to the surface, she could not help thinking of Fay and her pathetically revealing question about Waycroft: "It could have been worse there, couldn't it?"

In a sense it was a pity that the past could not be precisely and exactly that: the past—things done and seen and thought that you could not remember and were therefore finished with, rather than a series of experiences irrevocably woven into the present by memory, which would not, perhaps could not, leave them alone. Both waking and dreaming, day and night, the past was always with you, provoking comparisons that you would as often as not have been better off without.

That Fay should now look back with nostalgia on something that she had really hated was heart-breaking, because it showed so clearly how unhappy she must be with her life as she found it.

And yet Fay was right. It could have been worse at Waycroft. It could have been a whole lot worse.

From the vantage point of maturity and the passage of years, Karen realised that the Waycroft Way had, in spite of its many faults, the rather rare virtue of discipline. Discipline of a kind that was likely to be of most use to you later on, if you had the breadth of outlook to discard the particular for the general, if you had the wit to see that Standing Up Straight could be something more than just a physical exercise.

That she should not at the time have seen any virtue at all in the Waycroft Way was because she had, from the beginning, run head on into its faults by continuing, in spirit if not in fact, to remain a New Girl for as long as she went to Waycroft.

New Girls were those who had as yet to comprehend that there was nothing quite as important in life as the Waycroft Way; who had as yet to shed the undesirable habits, views, and convictions that had been theirs before they were lucky enough to be exposed to the only right way of doing anything.

The dignity and beauty of the stone building, with its vaulted Gothic corridors, mullioned windows, broad stairways, and atmosphere of being a tradition in itself encouraged an initial belief that Waycroft, in its less tangible aspects, would be equally deserving of admiration. As a New Girl, you very quickly learned that this was not the case, because there was no getting away from the fact that a New Girl always had a hell of a time there. Of course, if you came in at the kindergarten level, with nothing to shed but your diapers, you were all right. Any later in life than that, and you had a hell of a time.

Waycroft was already many years behind her before Karen fully understood that New Girls had been alternately patronized and ignored, not so much on personal grounds, but because they had represented a threat to a kind of security that was fast vanishing, not just from Toronto, but from the world. The security of having been there first; of being able to feel especially privileged; of being wholly and utterly convinced that your place in the sun was yours by right of inherited merit.

While she was at Waycroft, Karen had not recognized the scope of the social changes in which she was involved; but, oriented by temperament and outlook toward the future rather than the past, she had had some insight within her own periphery.

"Thank God," she had said to Fay on one occasion, "thank God, they didn't catch us when we were really young. I would hate to be staying at Waycroft for the rest of my life."

"Angel," Fay had said, "nobody stays all their life. It may seem like it. It does to me. But really nobody stays all their life."

"Oh, yes, they do. Just take a good look around you some time.

Toronto is full of people who have never left Waycroft. That's one of the things that's wrong with Toronto. It's riddled with people who have never left Waycroft."

"Don't you like Toronto? I always thought you liked it, angel."

"I love it. But that doesn't prevent me from seeing that it isn't perfect. That doesn't prevent me from seeing that where you were educated still counts for too damn much here. And it isn't a question of 'whether' but 'where'."

"Well, angel," Fay had said, "it will probably all come out in the wash. There's no need to get excited about it, because it will probably all come out in the wash."

The drive home from the Medical Arts Building to Rowanwood was a fairly long one, and there was enough traffic that Karen, forced to give some attention to her immediate surroundings, found it easier to continue with a train of thought in itself concerned with the city, than to think of a small town that she had so far seen only in imagination.

Fay's rebellion had always been a very personal thing, and therefore, in a larger sense, passive. Her own rebellion, she decided, had been more symptomatic of her times than individual to her. If it hadn't been, she would not at this stage be qualifying it at all.

With definite evidence that it was already all beginning to come out in the wash, she discovered she had a surprisingly strong desire for some assurance that there would be something left. She could not help feeling that any brave new world would be better off for some leavening from the past, and that even the Waycroft Way contained elements that were well worth salvaging. With more and more of everything within the reach of more and more people all the time, it was inevitable that a new set of social values would emerge to fit the times, and they would emerge first where there was the greatest accumulation of deadwood to be got rid of, in the large urban centres.

Toronto—and you could sense this everywhere except on the Hill—was becoming increasingly restive under the yoke of traditions that it had outgrown. Traditions represented in their most concrete form by the large private schools. The general opinion now seemed to be that the large private schools, Waycroft among them, were Imperial British islands floating on the surface of a community to which they no longer belonged. You could, Karen thought, say with truth that they no longer belonged to the times and that changes were in order; but if you had any understanding at all of the roots from which these schools had sprung, you could no more divorce them from the community than you could disown your own grandmother simply because she had preceded you.

Without Fort York, a literal English fortress, Canada might never have survived on the North American continent as an entity in itself. Both the Americans, to whom it had been such a thorn in the flesh, and French Canada, for whom it had been a bulwark to the west, were prepared for the most part to recognize this. What had been harder for everyone to recognize was that Fort York, when it emerged as the city of Toronto, had been an equally essential metaphorical English fortress. In order to maintain the most astonishing, and most mutually profitable division of lands ever achieved anywhere, the existence of a powerful, English-speaking city north of the forty-ninth parallel had been an absolute necessity. Only the Torontonians had really seen this, and, seeing it, beleaguered whether they liked it or not, had closed their ranks.

Thrown back on their own resources, they had proceeded to shape a way of life based on a heritage that included not only the world's last real aristocrats, but also the world's most efficient shopkeepers. Because practicality was natural to them, they prospered. Because they would have been uncomfortable without an aristocracy, they fashioned one. They won recognition, in doing these things, but not liking. They earned a grudging admiration, but no gratitude. None of which mattered to them. Like the shopkeepers and the aristocrats behind them, as long as they could think well of themselves, what other people thought of them did not matter a damn.

The city, growing steadily outward from Lake Ontario in concentric half-circles, became an enlargement rather than an evolution of its original pattern.

With autocratic benevolence, for which a precedent had not been hard to find, it had shaped an increasingly homogeneous population into the image which it had first created for itself. In its own eyes, as much as in the eyes of others, it continued to wear the mantle of Toronto the Good—an illusion so powerful it could incorporate within itself, and still ignore, a strip tease beginning at noon directly across from the City Hall, and the fact that nowhere in the western world was a girl of good family more likely to be accosted than on the streets of Toronto.

To the shopkeepers these things did not matter.

The aristocrats turned their backs on them, and retreated to the Mount Olympus of the Hill, taking their prestige clubs and their prestige schools with them. That the city as a whole should bow to the supremacy of the Hill, and those who lived in its more rarefied atmosphere, was tacitly acknowledged by the solid fact that neither to the east nor to the west, although population growth in these directions was as great or greater than to the north, was any attempt made to establish either a prestige school or a prestige club in competition with those on the Hill.

To Karen, the most fantastic thing of all was that until very recently Torontonians should not only have tolerated, but supported, a prestige bus which, whether by accident or design, followed the exact route of the retreating aristocracy who had first lived on Queen's Park Circle, and then moved on to St. George Street, and then on up to the Hill. When you had taken the Hill bus north from downtown, you had felt, as Susan had once put it, a little as if you were following the Trail of '98. It took courage, Susan had said, but if you just stuck with it, you'd find gold in that thar Hill.

The Ladies' Club, when it finally surrendered its downtown holdings, did not, it is true, go quite as far north as the Hill, because to have done so would have been to negate its purpose. In moving to Bloor Street near Yonge, it did, however, move in the proper direction while at the same time establishing itself well within the limits of what was to become known as the Mink Mile. It was even possible that this choice of location might have been a determining factor in the growth of the Mink Mile, because the purpose of the Ladies' Club was to provide a place where a lady, while shopping, might lunch without rubbing shoulders with just anybody.

It was, Karen thought, wholly typical of Toronto as it had been, that it should at one time have thought of a lady in terms of someone who refused to rub shoulders with just anybody, while underwriting civic receptions for Hollywood personalities who, if rumour was correct, were not averse to doing something more than just rub shoulders with anybody.

It was just like the long-established contradiction of a strip tease more or less on the City Hall steps. You would have to go far afield to find anything as dull as the Toronto City Hall, a fact that Mayor Phillips seemed to be more sharply aware of than anyone else. You would have to go even farther to find a North American city, if you could find one at all, that approved of noon as a suitable hour at which to start stripping down.

Even when the police in many of the downtown areas had been forced, for their own protection, to go on patrol in pairs; even when switch knives had begun to outsell water pistols by more than three to one; even when murder and rape and robbery had become, and been accepted, as part of the daily scene, the city, through some hypnosis known only to itself, had contrived to cling to its threadbare disguise of Toronto the Good.

That it should, finally, be throwing off the disguise—if it had not already done so—was, in Karen's opinion, desirable in every way, even though the last thing she would ever wish for was that it either be, or become known as, Toronto the Bad. On the whole, this did not seem likely, in spite of the fact that a crisis was fast approaching in which the Waycroft Way, and everything it stood for, was in danger of being swept away entirely.

A long-overdue twilight of the gods had already fallen across the Hill, allowing the focus to shift downtown again where it belonged, and from where it never should have strayed. The whole atmosphere was now one in which a New Girl would feel right at home.

In spite of herself, Karen experienced a swift regret that she should be planning to leave just when a New Girl would be likely to have such an interesting time.

It was a regret, however, which vanished as quickly as it had come, because getting out of Rowanwood was a great deal more important than staying in Toronto. With the promise of a long life once more ahead of her, getting out of Rowanwood had become, if possible, even more important than it had been before.

She might be able to look back at Waycroft, and think that it could have been a whole lot worse.

She was, she decided, unlikely ever to think the same thing about Rowanwood.

17 | And how do you like our little town?

There had never been any doubt in Karen's mind that the sun would shine on their trip to Planesville. And when she woke to a cloudless sky, she experienced—and was able to keep throughout the entire day—a frame of mind rarely achieved except by a child. An adult, at one level of consciousness or another, is almost always concerned with either the past or the future as it must relate to the present moment. Total absorption in the present, to the exclusion of old doubts or the projection of new ones, becomes almost impossible.

Karen's thoughts did, of course, wander backwards and forwards, but at no time during that Friday did they touch on any area that disturbed her personal equilibrium.

They were to start out at two in the afternoon, and Rick, when he left for the office, told Karen that he would pick up some lunch downtown and be ready to take off as soon as he got back. He ought, he said, to be in the clear well before two o'clock, but she must keep it in mind that you could never be quite sure in advance how things would shape up downtown.

Karen told him that she understood perfectly, and that he wasn't to worry if he was held up. Nevertheless, she was quite sure he would not be.

She felt just the way she used to feel when she was small and had taken care not to step on any cracks in the sidewalk. As long as you didn't step on the cracks, you had, when you were small, all the assurance you could possibly need that everything was going to be just the way you wanted it to be. There were, of course, no sidewalks in Rowanwood, but it had still been possible, in her own way, to avoid the cracks, and so she was quite sure that everything was going to be all right.

Although she had left the packing until the morning, she had been subconsciously preparing for the week-end for several days. She had ordered the new slip she had been needing, and had made sure that the clothes they might take were sent out to the cleaners. In spite of this, when the suitcases were lying open on the bed, she found that she was not at all sure what to put in them.

She had asked Rick about it, and he had been much the same as Jim Evans on the occasion when she had asked what she should wear to the Palace.

"The usual sort of thing, I guess," Rick had said.

"Rick, darling, you know perfectly well there isn't any usual sort of thing. Can't you be a little more helpful?"

"Well, I imagine you would be safe with just what you would wear to a luncheon here. That French dress, for instance."

"A French dress? In Planesville?"

"Why not?"

"Because it's not that kind of place."

"How do you know what kind of place it is?"

"It's obvious. After all, you don't play—" She had been about to say that you didn't play euchre in a French dress, but considering the way he had reacted the last time, it had not seemed an entirely good idea to mention euchre to Rick again. So she had just said, "Thank you, darling. I'll work it out."

Now, looking at the empty suitcases, she knew that it was something she had not yet worked out.

In Rowanwood clothes fell into two categories only, and they seemed equally unsuitable for Planesville. In Rowanwood your clothes were either strikingly smart and expensive, or strikingly casual and beat-up. In Rowanwood you either wore, in effect, a dress by Dior, or a pair of three-ninety-eight blue jeans.

What I need right now, Karen thought, is a nice sensible print and a cardigan that somebody in the family knitted for me.

Because she had neither of these, she finally decided that her black linen sheath, the one that really was crease-resisting, and her white cashmere cardigan, would be the best bet. Nobody would be able to see the label in her dress, she told herself, and black was conservative. As far as the sweater went, it probably wouldn't be recognized as quality cashmere, any more than her pearls would be recognized as real pearls.

Shoes presented no problem, if only because loafers were so obviously out of the question. And anyway, her I. Miller pumps were about as simple-looking as shoes could be.

Once she had made up her mind, she packed quickly and efficiently, using quantities of tissue paper, and not forgetting to put in such things as Rick's new blue tie and his best cuff links. And as she did so she was aware of a quality of excitement she could not remember experiencing since the days when she used to pack for summer camp in her early teens.

The camp always sent you a list of the articles you were expected to bring with you: two bathing-suits, two pairs of tennis shoes, three pairs of shorts, two pairs of slacks, a sweat-shirt with the camp crest on it, two single blankets (not white), three towels—the list covered two pages, and there was a note at the bottom of each page reminding you that your name must be clearly marked on every item.

You never used half the things the camp insisted you bring, but even so, there were a great many extras you added yourself, each one of which had to be discussed with Barbara. You spent as much time on the telephone with Barbara as you did in sewing on name tags and putting your things in blue canvas bags that also had the camp crest on them.

"Barby? Listen, how many films are you going to take for your camera? Well, do you think four is really enough?"

"Barby, it's me again. Listen, if I take twelve packets of chewing gum, will you take some Sweet Marie bars? I know they have a tuck shop, but last year they didn't have any Sweet Marie bars, and they were always running out of gum. Don't you remember the way they kept running out of gum?"

"Hello, Barby, were you able to get any you-know-whats? . . . Barby, don't be so dumb! You know what you-know-whats are. Well, think of a camp fire. . . . Barby, honestly! . . . Well, you're making me take an awful chance. If anyone hears me it will be all your fault for being so dumb. C-I-G-A-R—Well, thank heavens! Well, did you get any?"

When the special camp train had pulled out of the Union Station, there had always been a sense of almost unbearable excitement, engendered by the quite unwarranted conviction that this was the kind of journey on which nothing could possibly go wrong.

It was, Karen realized, exactly the mood in which she set out for Planesville with Rick at two o'clock. A mood unmarred by delay. And unmarred by the feeling that you might—although this had never really seemed likely—be struck down from on high for having hidden cigarettes in with the Kotex in one of the canvas bags with the camp crest on it.

"What a lovely day," Karen said, as they swung out of their driveway. "Darling, did you ever see a more lovely day?"

"It is nice," Rick said. "But it's a good thing we'll be driving away from the sun. I wouldn't want to be driving into the sun today."

"Aren't you excited, darling?"

"Not particularly," Rick said.

"But you're going to make up your mind this week-end, aren't you?"

"I imagine so," Rick said.

"Then why aren't you excited?" Karen asked.

"Because I don't know enough about the set-up yet. There may be nothing to get excited about."

He was, Karen knew, being perfectly reasonable. Much more reasonable than she was. But he was missing something, and it was the same thing that Barbara used to miss when the special train pulled out of the Union Station. He was missing the very real pleasure that could be derived from something that had yet to happen—that, conceivably, might never happen at all.

Once the city lay behind them, they still had several miles to go before they reached open country.

Whichever route you chose in order to get out of the city, you saw the same kind of thing. You saw the untidy, exploratory tendrils of a vine that, in this stage of its development, had none of the powerful beauty that distinguished its tap root. You saw excrescences which seemed to bear no relationship to the clean, tall shafts of steel and concrete that constituted the heart of this steady outward growth.

"I thought France, as seen from a highway, was about as tatty as you could get," Karen said; "but at the rate we're going, Beautiful Ontario is soon going to look worse than La Belle France."

Because France had come to her mind, she tried, when the last clusters of hot-dog stands, gasoline stations, and Insul-Bric houses lay behind them, to see the countryside as a cultured European might be likely to see it. The wind-shaped pines, the rocky pasture-lands, the dense stretches of bush, the low-lying patches of swamp, the occasional glimpses of blue lake water—all these things were repeated again and again and again, until she felt (as was in a sense true) that they would continue unconquered toward a horizon she could never hope to reach.

To a European it was a country that might be quite terrifying. And she saw for the first time that its promise of limitless space, of untrammelled freedom—qualities so dear to a native-born Canadian—ought, if reason were applied, to be just as frightening to the average Canadian as to a European. For what, when you came right down to it, did a city-bred Canadian know about survival in the wilderness that was unknown to a European? Not much. How to take longer in dying would be about the sum of it.

"Rick," she said, "can you light a fire by rubbing two sticks together?"

"No. Should I be able to?"

"I was just asking. Could you by any chance snare a rabbit?"

"Not by any chance at all."

"Well, I don't suppose it's likely to matter. And, anyway, I wouldn't like to think of you eating it raw."

"I wouldn't either. It's a thought I've managed to avoid up until now."

"I wasn't trying to be funny," Karen told him. "Actually I was being quite serious. I was thinking that our woods lore was pretty limited. We can make a balsam bed, and we can tell the difference between blueberries and deadly nightshade, and not much else. Which would only be a help in the blueberry season. And a balsam bed doesn't keep the rain off. All we know, really, is how to take longer in dying, which is scarcely an asset of lasting value."

"This is, I am sure," Rick said, "a very interesting conversation, but I wish I knew more precisely what it was about."

"Skip it, darling. If you live in Toronto, it doesn't really signify. It's nothing that would be likely to signify to a Torontonian. And if it ever did, it would be too late. Once you've learned how to mix a dry martini, it usually is too late. Rick, you'd better watch that car ahead. They've got those damned dolls on strings in the rear window."

Ned had a theory about people who hung things in their car windows. Only a psychologist could have accepted it, yet it was difficult to dismiss entirely.

The dolls were not, Ned said, either infantile good-luck charms or tasteless decoration. They were, of course, tasteless, but this was beside the point. The point was that they were the exact opposite of what anybody, including their owners, thought them to be. Far from being good-luck symbols, they were disaster fetishes. Christianity, Ned said, had, amongst other things, robbed its adherents of a very basic need. The fact had to be faced that Christianity, in demanding that all guilt, whether careless or premeditated, be shouldered by the unfortunate individual concerned, took from that individual the ancient right to place the responsibility for his actions on some other person or thing.

You would find, according to Ned, if you studied as many primitive religions as he had, that the need to shift guilt responsibility was very basic. Very basic indeed. This was something that primitive peoples had the instinct—you couldn't call it wisdom—the unerring child-like instinct to recognize as a need equally important as, for instance, sexual satisfaction. He had used this particular comparison, Ned said, because this was another need to which Christianity had failed to attach the proper significance. This was beside the point, of course, but he had just thought it worth mentioning.

The point he wanted to make was that primitive religions

attached almost as much importance to disaster fetishes as they did to sex symbols. The civilized approach to guilt was as immature as the civilized approach to sex. Which was very immature indeed.

There was, Ned said, a bearable limit of guilt just as there was of pain. Beyond a certain point, the human animal was incapable of tolerating any more guilt than he had already assumed, and it was at this stage that it became absolutely necesssary for him to place some of it elsewhere. If he could not do this, he became neurotic, quite dangerously so. It was to guard against such an eventuality that primitive peoples created evil spirits expressly designed for the purpose of absorbing guilt in any given quantity. This was the chief reason why uncivilized peoples were so much better balanced than their civilized counterparts.

To get back to the dolls in car windows—though if you had been following him intelligently you would know he had never really left them—they were no more or less than evil spirits ready at a moment's notice to accept the responsibility for any accident that occurred. The fact that they themselves caused accidents was merely a proof of their fitness as disaster fetishes. It was also proof, Ned said, that their owners had a primitive, childlike instinct where basic human need was concerned. As to whether or not primitive, childlike people ought to be granted driving licences, he was not prepared to say. And anyway, that was beside the point.

It was not, Karen was quite willing to admit, a theory that she would have liked to hear expounded to Lewis, for example. At the same time, once you had heard it, you found you could not forget it simply by telling yourself that it was sheer nonsense.

"Rick," she said, "you will be careful when you pass those people, won't you?"

"Yes, sweetheart. I'll be careful."

It was just like being on the special train that took you to camp. You talked, and thought, about inconsequential things, but this was no denial of the secret excitement you carried with you, that made you feel as if you were on a magic carpet travelling toward a journey's end where everything would be just the way you wanted it to be.

"The car's riding very nicely, isn't it?" Rick said. "It seems almost a pity to think of turning it in this fall."

"You know how I feel about a car in," said Karen.

It seemed that no sooner did you get fond of a car than it was time to part with it. As soon as it became something more than just another way to get from here to there, as soon as it acquired a personality of its own, you had to give it up.

Karen had, a few years earlier, set out to prove in terms of dollars and cents that the idea of turning a car in every two years simply established them as victims of the cult of obsolescence. She had been both frustrated and annoyed to find that in this case, at least, it actually was more economical to turn in a used article on a new one than to continue with the old one. And not so old at that. She would, she felt, like to have a Rolls Royce, not because it was the most expensive car you could buy, but just because you could, if the ads were correct, keep it for eleven years. It would not matter to her that at sixty miles an hour the loudest noise would come—according to the ad—from the electric clock, or that every nut and bolt, every cotter pin and washer, would be chromium or cadmium plated to guard against corrosion, or that by moving a switch on the steering-column you could adjust the shock-absorbers to suit road conditions. She didn't really give a damn about any of these things. All she wanted was a car that you could keep for eleven years, that you could love without having it snatched away from you.

"Rick," she said, "why don't we get a Rolls-Royce?"

Rick laughed. "Which reason do you want me to give first? I think it's time we stopped for gas. We'll stop at the next gas station we come to."

You went on making casual conversation, but your pleasure in the countryside, like your excitement, was a constant obbligato to everything you said. You kept on noticing individual trees and rocks—a birch tree, silver-white against a stand of maple; a clump of pines in sharp, beautifully proportioned silhouette against what was now a reflected sunset light; an outcrop of red rocks, surprising amongst the more general grey of granite and yellow of sandstone. And all the time you were aware of the freedom and space around you. Even if you couldn't snare a rabbit, you would not, you knew, have traded this particular kind of freedom for all the gold and myrrh and frankincense of an overcrowded East. You would, you knew, rather die in this country than live in any other.

When they turned off the highway, to come to a stop beside a combined gas station and restaurant—something that was becoming increasingly prevalent—Karen said, "Rick, will you ask if I need a key, darling?"

Rick, who always got out of a car if only to stretch his legs, spoke to the attendant who had already come out of the gas station. "Fill her up, will you, please," he said. "And it might be a good idea to check the oil."

"Okay, sir," the man said. "Lovely evening, isn't it?"

"Couldn't be nicer," Rick said. "Do we need keys to get into the washrooms?"

"They should be unlocked," the man said. "If they're not, just let me know. Right around to the left there. You've got a nice car here. As it happens, I drive a Buick myself, and I don't think you could find a nicer car."

Rick, apparently, was not interested in washrooms at the moment, because, as Karen went around to the left, he was still talking with the man who also owned a Buick.

In the distance, across two fields, Karen could see trees, but there were none anywhere near the gas station. Four-square, architecturally unprepossessing, it stood open to the four winds, its white-painted western wall broken only by two angle signs above two identical doors. There was a sign that said "Ladies" and one that said "Men".

The door beneath the sign that said "Ladies" was unlocked, and Karen went in, to find to her relief that the place was neat and clean, and that there was actually soap in the dispenser above the wash-basin.

Her thoughts as inconsequential as they had been when she was in the car, she considered the two signs outside. "Ladies." "Men."

The distinction amused even while it irritated her. Gentlemen, if you were to believe the plentiful evidence on washroom doors, had vanished from the North American scene. It wasn't just in Canada. The same was true in the States. There were no gentlemen on the New York Thruway either.

You could remember a time when the signs almost invariably read "Ladies" and "Gentlemen". This had been followed by a more forthright era of "Men" and "Women". A down-to-earth, let's-call-a-spade-a-spade approach, that, in your opinion, had been much better suited to washroom doors than the euphemistic gentility that had preceded it, or the self-conscious cuteness that followed it. A cuteness that, frankly, made you sick, descending as it did to such vulgarities as "Cows" and "Bulls", and "Hers" and "His".

Recently, however, it seemed as if Ladies were making a comeback, though the Men were still Men.

In England, the simplicity of the desgination had, she remembered, equalled the simplicity of the plumbing. There was never more than one door and one sign, "WC", and you were lucky if you found that much. What English people did, when faced with a need certainly equal to and quite as primitive as the need to shed responsibility, was something she had yet to learn.

In France, there had usually been two signs, "Messieurs" and "Mesdames", and two doors, but only a single destination. Which, on reflection, was very French.

Somebody, Karen thought as she left the washroom, ought to do a monograph on the subject. In a perfectly nice way, of course. It was the kind of thing that Ned might do, in a perfectly nice psychological way.

The hood of the car was still raised, and Rick and the gas-station man were still talking. Probably about Buicks. Owning the same make of car could be quite a bond, particularly if it was the same year and model. In fact it could make you a blood brother with almost anyone, and without the trouble of learning a special handshake, or cutting the throat of something or other at midnight on the Ides of March. You could leave all the throat-cutting to General Motors and Ford, which was not only convenient but sensible, because they were so much better at it than you were.

With nothing else to do, Karen lit a cigarette, and strolled around to the other side of the building. Which was how she happened to see the bears. As soon as she saw the bears, she realized that this was not the first time she and Rick had stopped at this place for gasoline.

The first time, she recalled, had been on a July week-end three years before, and they had been on their way to Millicent and Biff's summer place.

A week-end spent with Biff at his summer place was not something you forgot, or something you would ever expose yourself to again if you could help it.

Biff had three hundred acres, and when you asked him how in the world he had been able to get hold of that much land in that particular neck of the woods, he told you it was just a matter of getting the ball and running with it.

The house had reminded you of the Seigniory Club, and you never had found out how many rooms there were in it. You had been too tired to even try and find out, because it wasn't the house that had thrown you as much as the athletic equipment. There was a tennis court, and a badminton court, and a horse-shoe pitch, and an archery range, and a high diving-tower, and a low diving-tower, and water skis, and aquaplanes, and speed-boats, and sailing-boats, and row-boats, and canoes. All of which you, as a good guest, were expected to use. And if you couldn't finish the course in daylight, there were floodlights so that you could go right on committing hari-kari into the small hours of the morning.

It really had been a lot like the Seigniory Club, the chief difference being that you could not pay to be left alone.

"Biff," Rick had said, "you've got a very nice little place here."

It was the kind of thing that Rick could say with a perfectly straight face.

Biff had tried to look modest, but the materials with which he had made this attempt had proved inadequate. "Well," he had said, "Millicent and I are very pleased with it. Millicent and I both feel we've scored a touch-down with this place. Now, how about another game of badminton, or would you rather get out the water skis again?"

Just thinking of that week-end was enough to make Karen feel stiff all over. But even without this reminder, she knew she would not have forgotten the bears.

They were black bears, and there were two of them, caged on a concrete block walled on three sides with steel netting. On the fourth side, at the back, was a covered retreat so contrary to anything nature might provide that hibernation was a seasonal escape denied them as unequivocally as any wider escape.

One of the bears was lying down. One of them had known enough to give up. The other paced to and fro, and to and fro, his characteristic rolling gait confined to twenty feet in one direction, and twenty feet in the opposite direction. He had, Karen remembered, been doing exactly the same thing three years previously. Perhaps he had never stopped. Perhaps in all that time he had never ceased to search—twenty feet this way and twenty feet back—for the long-lost resilience of leaf mould and spruce needles, and the cool shade of a thick forest. The heavy, powerful body, so beautifully controlled it could move without a whisper of sound through deadfalls and bogs and the high tree-clad slopes of its choice, defied concrete and steel in the only way left to it—twenty feet this way and twenty feet back. Some time, inevitably, he would give up the terrible, hypnotic rhythm of his fruitless search. Some time he would lie down. But only to die. Some time, in the only way left to him, he would cease to be a proof to American tourists that some Canadians were as barbarous as their predecessors who had walked quiet forest aisles, bird songs in their ears, bleeding scalps at their belts.

Slowly, Karen raised her eyes from the cage to the television aerial on the roof of the restaurant, and saw, instead, as if it were again hung before her, a painting of Eric Aldwinkle's from which the walls of his Toronto studio had seemed to fall away. A painting of an Indian crucified on a telephone pole.

Abruptly, she turned and walked back to the car.

"Do you want to eat here?" Rick asked. "It's almost six o'clock, and we could have dinner here."

"No," Karen said. "No. Anywhere but here."

Again on the highway, the long shadow of the car, in never-ending flight ahead of them, seemed to Karen a projection of her own ardent desire to reach a destination from which she wished they need never return. And it was not, as was actually the case, as if she were on her way to an unknown place, but rather to one she had known and loved all her life.

Impatient now, as she had not been earlier, she said, "Don't let's take a lot of time out for dinner, darling. Let's just stop at some hamburger stand. There's no point in taking a lot of time out, because the food is almost bound to be terrible. I wish I'd made up sandwiches to eat in the car. I wish Howard Johnson would hurry up and discover this country."

"I didn't know you were so crazy about the Howard Johnson places," Rick said.

"Everything," Karen said, "is comparative. And I just wish Howard Johnson would pull up his anchor and set sail in this direction. He wouldn't be risking anything. Nobody who knows how to travel on other people's stomachs ever risks anything."

They ate, finally, just after seven o'clock at another gas-station restaurant. Rick did not like the look of it, but, as Karen pointed out, he wasn't going to like the look of any of the places along this particular stretch of highway, so they might as well eat and get it over with.

It was dark when they drove into Planesville, but there was still a trace of afterglow in the sky. A luminous frame for the tops of tall old elms, and unfrosted street lights that cast a flickering, shadow-struck light on uneven pitted asphalt and small houses surrounded by shrubbery.

In the past, when she had gone to camp, journey's end for Karen had been the white glimmer of tents through dark tree trunks, and sunset reflected from the windows of a log dining-room in a pine grove by a lake.

That had been beautiful. And this, too, was beautiful. This, too, as the other had been, was exactly as she had hoped it would be.

And because it was all so exactly as she had pictured it, she knew no disappointment when they exchanged the elms and the small frame houses for a main street lined with little stores, and an intersection with a red brick post office, and a red brick bank, and a red brick hotel. A square, three-storey hotel with a hanging sign above the entrance, and the inevitable neon sign farther along that promised you a "Ladies' Beverage Room".

"I never," Rick said, as he pulled into the curb in front of the hotel, "thought I would look back on the Shaftesbury with quite such acute regret. Are you sure you're not going to mind this too much, sweetheart?"

"Mind it?" Karen said. "Why, I'm going to be crazy about it."

"You're a good sport," Rick said.

Karen felt like telling him that being a good sport had nothing to do with it. Absolutely nothing at all. She felt like telling him just what Planesville meant to her. But it was not, she saw, the right moment for it. Saturday afternoon, on their way back to Toronto after everything was settled, would be the right time. When everything was settled, she could tell him how happy she was about it all. She could tell him just how sick she was of Rowanwood, and how glad she was that they were going to get away to the kind of simple life that, deep down, suited them so much better than Rowanwood ever could.

"Do you want to come in while I register?" Rick asked. "Or would you rather wait in the car?"

"I'd like to come in," Karen told him.

"All right, then I might as well take the suitcases in now, too. I imagine the car will stay right where it is. I don't seem to have blocked any hitching posts."

"Rick," Karen said, "I wish you wouldn't be so patronizing. I wish you'd stop being so Toronto, and just relax now that you've got away from it all."

Rick laughed. "I'm more concerned about what I may be getting into, than what I might be getting away from."

The lobby of the hotel was small, and it smelled of varnish, and there were three men, one of them picking his teeth, sitting in chairs tilted back against the wall opposite the desk. As she stood beside Rick at the desk, Karen could feel the eyes of all three travelling up and down her back, which, she told herself, was nothing she ought to object to. It was, she told herself, perfectly natural in a small, close-knit community for a stranger to be an object of interest. It was not the kind of thing that would continue when you were no longer a stranger.

The desk clerk was in his shirt sleeves, and his hands, Karen noticed, were not very clean. But to judge a town by the condition of a desk clerk's hands was obviously as wrong as to judge it by the calendars on the walls. The calendars had undoubtedly been presented by some of the commercial travellers who stayed regularly in the hotel. It was not the hotel's fault that it was forced into accepting calling cards whose signatures were all spelled "Bikini".

"There you are," the desk clerk was saying. "Two-eleven. Second up, fourth on your right. Lavatory at the end of the hall."

"Will you get somebody to carry up the bags?" Rick asked.

In not carrying up the bags himself, Rick had, Karen saw, struck the wrong note. It was evident that the desk clerk did not like people who were not prepared to carry their own bags. In a small, close-knit community you did these things for yourself if you were able.

The desk clerk hesitated, then he said, "Horace, you want to carry these here bags up?"

Horace, it appeared, was the man who had been picking his teeth.

"Okay, Gus," he said, "you got my number, all right. You know I never mind taking a bag upstairs."

He must, Karen realized, have meant something other than what he seemed to mean, because the two men with him began to snicker. She might have become quite uncomfortable, if Rick had not taken things in hand.

Rick did not do much. He just looked at the three men. But it was enough. They stopped their snickering at once. And the man called Horace got up and took the bags much faster than might have been expected.

"Two-eleven. Second up. Fourth on your right," Rick said. He said it very pleasantly, but for some reason the man called Horace almost ran up the stairs.

The stairs were steep, and it was difficult to tell whether you were taking the smell of varnish up with you, or whether it had got there ahead of you.

"Bastard," said Rick, still pleasantly, as the door closed behind the man called Horace, leaving them in a room with a scratched oak dresser, a white-painted iron bedstead, two straight chairs, and a narrow window covered by a sagging green blind. From the centre of the ceiling an unshaded bulb hung on a length of brown electric cord.

"Well," Karen said. "We're here."

"Yes, there seems to be no doubt about that. Did you pack any whiskey, sweetheart?"

"Yes. There's a bottle in the big suitcase. You'll find it right on top of our dressing-gowns," Karen told him. Then she laughed. "It isn't even hidden in with the Kotex. It's right there on top of our dressing-gowns."

In the morning Rick seemed a little concerned about leaving her alone in the hotel. They had already been down to breakfast, which they had eaten, not in the hotel dining-room, but across the street at a Chinese restaurant. The hotel dining-room had been, after one look, more than even Karen had felt like facing.

"I don't like to walk off and leave you," Rick said. "What will you do with yourself until Mrs. Holmes comes to pick you up for the luncheon?"

"Darling, you make it sound as if you were leaving me in a log cabin about to be attacked by wolves."

"I'm afraid you'll be attacked by boredom."

Karen, who was standing by the window, could see a T. Eaton Company order office a little farther up the main street. It made her feel right at home. "Bored? Here?" she said. "I couldn't possibly be bored here. It's a beautiful day, and I'm going out for a walk."

"Well, as long as you won't feel lonely."

"Run along. They'll be expecting you at the factory, and you don't want to keep them waiting. You don't have to worry about me at all. I couldn't be happier."

She was still feeling that she couldn't be happier as she strolled first up one side of the little main street, and then down the other. It was, she thought, much like being back on Elmdale Avenue, because the stores were just like the ones where she and her family had done their shopping when they lived on Elmdale Avenue.

There was a dry-goods store, with smocked dresses, teddy bears, bolts of printed cotton, and knitting supplies in its overcrowded show window. There was a plumber's with a rather terrible bathtub on display. And a grocery, with fruits and vegetables on racks outside. There was a Chinese laundry, and from the open door she could smell the same curious odour in which Fu Manchu had swathed himself when she was very young. And on a corner was just the kind of small Loblaw's she had expected to find in a town like Planesville.

That she was attracting some attention, Karen knew. She encountered an occasional direct stare, and was aware that after she had passed anyone she was being watched. But none of it really added up to anything more than you might expect in a small, close-knit community.

She enjoyed her walk, but the luncheon to which she had been asked could be quite important to their future, hers and Rick's, so she was careful to be back at the hotel in plenty of time to change into her black linen, which had come out of the suitcase without a crease in it.

She was still a little uneasy about the black linen, and the cashmere sweater, and the real pearls, but Mrs. Holmes, who would probably be a friendly, comfortable person in a good print, would not be likely to notice anything out of the way. And once she had been able to tell Mrs. Holmes, quite casually of course, that she liked canning fruits and putting up preserves, everything would certainly be all right between them. With anybody, it was just a question of establishing the fact that you had some interests in common.

It had been agreed that she meet Mrs. Holmes in the lobby of the hotel at half-past twelve, and when she came downstairs at half-past twelve exactly, Mrs. Holmes had just come in.

"Mrs. Richard Whitney, please," Mrs. Holmes was saying to the desk clerk.

Afterwards, Karen could never remember what she had said to Mrs. Holmes during those first minutes, or what Mrs. Holmes had said to her. She must, she knew, have said the correct things in the correct way, or she would not have found herself sitting beside Mrs. Holmes in the front seat of a grey Cadillac, apparently on terms of the greatest cordiality.

"My dear," Mrs. Holmes was saying, as she pushed the drive button with a casual white-gloved finger, "so silly of me to have doubted for a moment that we would be the best of friends. So silly of me to think, in advance, that we might, just conceivably, not have too much in common."

Exactly what Mrs. Holmes might think they had in common, Karen could not, of course, guess. Certain surface details, however, did not require conjecture, because Mrs. Holmes was wearing what was indubitably a French dress, and a sweater that was indubitably quality cashmere, and pearls that were indubitably real.

"My dear," Mrs. Holmes said, "do you mind if I say that your hair is fabulous. Really fabulous. And I don't need to ask if you do anything to it, because I know quite well that you don't."

To have questioned the sincerity of this remark would have been stupid, if only because Mrs. Holmes was a woman who obviously knew all that was worth knowing about the cosmetician's trade. Her cameo-perfect features were undoubtedly made up in a variety of ways, but it was difficult, if not impossible, to say what those ways were. Her pale blonde hair might or might not have been touched up. You simply couldn't tell, any more than you could tell whether or not her slender, almost too thin figure was natural to her or the result of the Stauffer System.

The Cadillac had left the main street for a side street lined with large, old, white clapboard houses.

"What lovely houses!" Karen said.

"Picturesque, aren't they?" Mrs. Holmes said. "But, of course, nobody lives in them."

"They look lived in," Karen said.

Mrs. Holmes had a very musical laugh. "Oh, my dear, that's marvellous! Really marvellous. How nice that you should have such a sense of humour."

Karen was virtually never obtuse. When she was, it usually resulted in complete misunderstanding, as was now the case. And very fortunately. She was better prepared for the Holmes's house, when they passed it a few minutes later on the crest of a wooded hill just outside the town.

"That's our little place," Mrs. Holmes said, with a small flick of her hand.

"It's charming," Karen said. Rick might be able to talk about "little places" with a straight face, but it was something she knew better than to try, herself.

The Holmes's house, as seen in passing, might have been a replica of Millicent and Biff's cut-stone residence in Rowanwood, with the addition of a tree-lined drive, and what Karen, quite correctly, assumed to be separate servants' quarters.

"I'm sorry not to be taking you to the house, my dear," Mrs. Holmes said, "but even with servants it didn't seem quite possible to have lunch at home. You know how it is, I'm sure."

"Yes," Karen said. "I know how it is." This was not what she would have liked to say, but she was being very careful.

"At least, we do have servants," Mrs. Holmes said. "That's something our benighted village can offer. They're French Canadians. You do speak French, I suppose, my dear?"

"Yes," Karen said, "I speak French." And she had a hysterical desire to laugh because it should matter in Planesville whether or not she spoke French. She had passed the first test by wearing the clothes she had on. She had passed the second test by being able to speak French, and she could not help admiring the smooth way in which Mrs. Holmes had established this. Because speaking French really had nothing to do with having French-Canadian servants. The country girls who crossed the Quebec-Ontario border to do housework until they tired of it and moved on to something else, spoke a patois that could be understood only if one learned it as a separate language in itself. It was not the French of Montreal or Paris.

Mrs. Holmes had at no time been driving fast, but now she slowed down to no more than twenty miles an hour. She was allowing herself a few more minutes before they arrived at the Country Club where, she had told Karen, they were to lunch.

"Of course, my dear," she was saying, "it's an awful bore to keep up a house the size of ours, even with help. Paul and I would move into something smaller tomorrow, if we felt free to do so. I suppose you and your husband are lucky enough to live in one of those adorable bungalows they build so well these days."

The hell with her, Karen thought. The hell with her.

"No," she said, "I'm afraid we don't. I'm afraid my husband and I are old-fashioned enough to like space."

The houses and grounds they were passing could only be called estates. There simply wasn't any other word for houses and grounds of that size. None of them were as large as the Holmes place, but they were all large.

"Do you really?" Mrs. Holmes said. "Well, quite confidentially, my dear, and don't pass this on, I do rather like a sense of space, myself. But don't tell me you have more than one storey?"

The hell with her. "As a matter of fact, we do," Karen said. "It just wouldn't be possible to have a library, if we didn't have two storeys. And really I don't feel that a house is a home without a library."

"Exactly the way I feel, my dear," Mrs. Holmes said, and a slim, well-shod foot increased its pressure on the accelerator.

There was, Karen thought, a great deal to be said for having been to Waycroft when you were faced with in-fighting of this kind. At Waycroft, although it had not been on the curriculum, you learned all you would ever need to know about the subtle, but not at all gentle, art of of social fencing.

"Well," Mrs. Holmes said, as they swept up the long gradient of a gravel drive to a cut-stone building surrounded by pines, "there it is. It's not the Rosedale Golf Club, of course, but it is rather nice, don't you think?"

"It's charming," Karen said. "Charming" was really a very useful word. When you said "charming" you combine approval with just the smallest hint of patronage in a way that you could not with any other word in the English language. And then, because it was something she had to know, she said, "Do you come from Toronto, Mrs. Holmes?"

"Of course, my dear," Mrs. Holmes said. "Didn't you know that?"

"No," Karen said, "I didn't actually know it."

It had been the way in which Mrs. Holmes had referred to the Rosedale Golf Club. She had referred to it as if she owned it, and you did not do that unless you either were, or had once been, a member.

"We'll just leave the car right here, my dear. Somebody will put it away. I do hope you like this little place. We call it the Annex. Just jokingly, of course."

"What is it the annex to?" Karen asked, but she had a horrible feeling that she already knew the answer.

"Why, the Planesville Chemical Company, of course," Mrs. Holmes said. "What else?"

"Of course," Karen said. "What else."

As she followed Mrs. Holmes across a wide, flagged patio and into a combined bar and solarium, she felt as she imagined a a drowning man must feel who has just lost his last, desperate hold on a life raft. Planesville, rather than being a better place to live in than Rowanwood, would without a doubt be infinitely worse. Far worse. My God, she thought, the Annex! Oh, my God, the Annex—

"Well, isn't this nice," Mrs. Holmes was saying. "The others are here ahead of us."

As if they had dared do anything else, Karen thought.

The two women who rose from chairs in a casual grouping of expensive modern Danish furniture, were both very smartly dressed, and both very slim. They were, Karen guessed, about her own age, perhaps a little older.

"Merle, my dear," Mrs. Holmes said, "I would like to present Mrs. Whitney of Toronto. Mrs. Whitney, this is Merle Harden, wife of our first vice-president, and on your left, Lucille Curtis, wife of our second vice-president. Lucille, my dear, how well you're looking."

All very protocol, Karen thought as she shook hands—first, of course, with Mrs. Harden, and second, of course, with Mrs. Curtis.

"And how do you like our little town?" Mrs. Harden asked.

"I think it's charming," Karen told her. "Perfectly charming."

"I'm so glad you like it," Mrs. Harden said.

"It's charming," Karen said again.

"Well, my dears," Mrs. Holmes said, "why don't we sit down and have a cocktail? I think a cocktail would be just right, don't you?"

Everybody agreed, of course, that a cocktail would be just right. They also agreed, of course, that a martini was the perfect thing for a warm day.

Mrs. Holmes did not need to ring for a waiter. A waiter, in a white coat, was already standing beside her.

"Michel," she said, "we would like four martinis. And don't let them get too close to the Vermouth bottle. Just close enough, but not too close."

Everybody laughed. Everybody except Michel, who permitted himself merely an appreciative smile.

"Have you always lived in Toronto, Mrs. Whitney?" Mrs. Curtis asked.

"More or less," Karen said. It was not a particularly illuminating reply, which was exactly what she intended. They would, she knew, all three of them, prefer to throw curved balls, but if they were to get anything out of her they would have to lay them directly across home plate, and even then they would not, if she could help it, get much.

"Do tell us about the less," Mrs. Holmes said. "I always think it's the little things about one's friends that are of most interest. No, my dear, you must smoke one of mine. I think they're rather special. They're English. I suppose you've been to London?"

"Thank you," Karen said, as she accepted one of Mrs. Holmes's cigarettes, which she was reasonably certain had been produced simply in order to guide the conversation. "Yes, I know London quite well."

"It's an interesting city, isn't it?" Mrs. Harden said.

"Very interesting," Karen said.

"Were you lucky enough to catch a glimpse of any of the Royal Family?" Mrs. Curtis asked.

"Yes," Karen said, "I caught a glimpse of some of the Royal Family."

The way in which Mrs. Curtis had said "Royal Family" indicated that she might very well be from Toronto, too. Either that, or she was an American.

Michel was already putting their cocktails down in front of them. In the time, this could only have been possible if they had been ready and mixed in advance. She had, Karen saw, been given a choice that had been axiomatically regarded as no choice at all. It was this realization, rather than Mrs. Holmes's next question, that was actually the last straw as far as she was concerned.

"Don't," Mrs. Holmes said, "tell me that you, too, had to go through all the silly fuss and feathers of being presented at Court?"

The hell with all of them. "No," Karen said, "I didn't. I'm afraid that I've never been to the Palace except by invitation."

After that, it was just a question of getting through lunch with as much speed as was decently possible. After that, there could be no doubt that shrimps Creole, and sweetbreads cooked in white wine, would agree with her companions as little as they did with her.

And when, still in the early afternoon, Mrs. Holmes dropped her off at the hotel again, she got to the second floor, and the lavatory at the end of the hall, just in time to be sicker than she could ever remember being.

Then she went to room two-eleven, locked the door behind her, and stood at the window looking out at the little main street of Planesville while tears ran silently down her face for more than an hour.

At five o'clock, when Rick came back, she was sitting on one of the straight chairs, her back to the window, quietly reading.

"Karen," Rick said, "sweetheart, would you be disappointed if we were to pack up and leave more or less right away?"

"No," said Karen, "I wouldn't be disappointed."

"Well, in that case, I think we'll push off. You see, I've turned the offer down, and though Holmes tried to insist that we stay over for dinner, I felt it would be awkward both for him and for me."

"Why did you turn it down, Rick?"

"I just didn't like the set-up."

"Then that makes two of us. I just didn't like the set-up either."

"There's nothing you want to do here before we go, I suppose?"

"No," Karen said, "there's nothing I want to do here now."

18 | A once smooth, grey cube

Wrapped in a terry-cloth robe although the night was warm, Karen sat in the armchair by the bedroom windows as she had on so many other nights during the six months just past. In the darkness of the room behind her, Rick slept undisturbed by the soft movements she had made when she got up.

Outside, the white, depthless brilliance of moonlight lay across the empty street; a soundless reshaping of a pattern of light and shade more often determined by the street lights.

There was little outward and visible difference between this night and the many sleepless nights that had preceded it. There had been little difference between this Sunday, spent working in the garden, and any other summer Sunday in Rowanwood. They had, perhaps, got up somewhat later than usual because the drive back from Planesville the evening before had been tiring, the roads heavy with week-end traffic. But once they were up, it had been a very ordinary day, unaccented by anything other than the most casual mention of a trip that Rick had dismissed from his mind because it had contained nothing of importance to him. And which she, herself, had not talked about because it had been of such vital importance that she could not trust herself to discuss it until she had had time to think about its many implications.

Tonight, she sat alone by the open windows neither to cry, nor to play with a deadly toy that, although its promise had been no empty one, she was unlikely ever to play with again.

Memory brought the grey cube, smoothly evil, between her fingers once more. With a quick, convulsive gesture, she rubbed the palms of both hands hard against her thighs, feeling the flesh firm under the rough terry-cloth. Not that, she thought. Not that ever again, so help me, God.

Her eyes fixed on the sleeping street, both seeing it and yet not seeing it, she thought dispassionately of her other toy, now irretrievably smashed.

It had been such a bright-hued block, that other one, its sides painted in so many glowing colours, its single legend, "Planesville", open to so many interpretations, all of them apparently rich with possibilities. As she had fashioned it, it had been beautiful. It had also been as fragile as a Christmas-tree ornament bought at the five-and-ten, and as worthless. Now all that remained of it were dusty fragments, drained of every vestige of colour. Fragments undeserving of honest grief, because she knew —as she must really have known all along—that they had never been made of anything better than tinsel.

Her tears in the hotel room at Planesville had not been shed for a dream that had been no more than that. They had been shed for all the years that she had at last realized could not be recaptured, even in essence.

In fabricating her illusion of Planesville, she had been trying to do what her mother had warned her could not be done. She had been looking for a way back to something that no longer existed. A way back to the relatively uncomplicated problems of extreme youth. Refusing to accept the fact that life as she had known it on Elmdale Avenue had ceased to exist anywhere, she had wilfully transplanted it in time and space while turning her back on reason, which would have told her, if she had allowed it to, that she was attempting the impossible.

Even if it had existed, it would not, she saw now, have suited her, because she was no longer nine, or nineteen, or for that matter twenty-nine. How she had managed to persuade herself that euchre parties and home-made preserves would, either literally or metaphorically, be satisfying to a modern city-bred woman like herself, she really did not know. The very absurdity of such a concept, and the fierceness with which she had clung to it, underlined, as little else could have done, her genuine need to get away from Rowanwood at almost any price. That this was a need, and not a whim, she could not doubt, even while she accepted the unpalatable knowledge that all she had done so far was to look for an avenue along which she could run away.

Running for the wrong reasons, and in the wrong direction, she had been so concerned with her own miserable dissatisfaction that it had never once occurred to her to wonder why Rick should have considered the Planesville offer. She knew that he found his work at ChemCon both satisfying and challenging, and he had said nothing to make her think he had changed his opinion in this respect. So why had he gone to Planesville at all?

Briefly distracted by the sound of a car coming up the hill, the first to pass since she had taken up her solitary vigil, she guessed that it was probably Mrs. Johnson. From where she sat, she had a view, unobstructed by trees, of the Johnsons' dilapidated frame garage and the small space of unkempt grass between the garage and the house. Scarcely aware that she was doing so, she absorbed the rhythm of sights and sounds that comprised Mrs. Johnson's homecoming, now almost as familiar to her as they must be to Mrs. Johnson herself.

The old green Chev, looking black in the moonlight, came to a stop a few feet from the garage doors, and Mrs. Johnson got out to open them. Karen could not, of course, see either her hard blue eyes, or her tired, over-painted face; but even at that distance and in that light, it was as obvious that Mrs. Johnson bleached her hair as it was that she carried a remarkably large chip on her shoulder. There was, in the way she held herself, something truculent that told you to mind your own damn business.

The garage doors opened with a grating whine of unoiled hinges, a sound harsh and unpleasant in the quiet of the night, and one that was repeated when Mrs. Johnson closed the doors behind her after having driven the car inside.

Although Mrs. Johnson was of very little interest to her, Karen, caught as one always is by any movement, or promise of movement, in an otherwise motionless scene, shifted her gaze to the small side door of the garage from which Mrs. Johnson would emerge in the next minute or two. On a moonless night she would have been unable to see the side of the garage, much less distinguish the side door. Tonight, in the flat white light, she could see it clearly.

Her thoughts reverted to Rick, and her startling realization that he had grown to dislike their present living environment, if not as bitterly as she did, at least to an extent that had led him to consider moving right away from it. It was not his job that he had thought of leaving, so much as Rowanwood; and she should have known this, even though he had done a very good job of keeping it from her. The amount of work he had done recently on the house and garden should have given her a clue if she had not been so preoccupied. Do-it-yourself undertakings were for Rick, as they were for herself, something you did only if you felt you had to, or as a release for tension and restlessness. There was not, and had not been for some time, any economic necessity for them to do-it-themselves. Rick, when he had set up the floodlights in the garden, must have done so in somewhat the same spirit as that which had moved her to scrub the kitchen floor before seeing Dr. Lowe.

Rick, she thought, Rick—darling, why didn't you talk about it? And she would have waked him and asked him, if she had not already known the answer. With no idea of how she felt, believing her as interested in the house as on the warm October day when they had first thought of buying it, he had kept his feelings to himself for her sake.

When she had gone to Planesville, she had been running away, and nothing more.

Rick, in going to Planesville, had been searching for an actual way of life that he could think might be better for both of them. He had thought of it, in all probability, as a modification of Rowanwood, and had been closer to the truth than she had.

Absently, Karen realized that Mrs. Johnson was staying in the garage much longer than she usually did. Offhand, there didn't seem to be much that one would want to do in one's garage at two in the morning, but then people were funny.

When Rick had come back to the hotel room in Planesville, he had said, "Would you be disappointed—" At the time, she had thought "disappointed" an odd word for him to use. Now she saw it as an unguarded expression of personal disappointment.

It was frightening how much two people who loved one another could conceal within themselves when they really tried. Under certain circumstances, the presence of love could be a real hindrance to any wholly honest exchange of ideas. In your attempt to go along with what you thought the other person wanted to do, you were more likely to get things crossed up than if you were dealing with someone you didn't like as much.

Very quietly, and without taking her eyes from the moon-whitened side door of the Johnsons' garage, she reached for a cigarette and lit it with a small gold lighter Rick had given her on her fortieth birthday. There was an engraved inscription on it, so fine it was necessary to use a magnifying glass to read it. "Life begins—darling." She had been both touched and amused, as Rick had intended. Neither she nor Rick had ever believed that life began at any point in particular other than at birth. He had simply been telling her that for him life began with her. It was wonderful that he should say this, but of course it wasn't true. Not really. You could not live for a single person, or even a group of persons. Not if you were to feel that you were a positive, if small, force for good in the whole world of which you were, whether you liked it or not, a part.

And the word "good", as she saw it, must of necessity relate to the evolutionary aspects of life. What she needed—in fact what she *had* to have—was some recognizable identification with the forward movement of an era that, to date, had left her floundering, out of her depth, contributing nothing. In Rowanwood, she was in a backwater, suffering from frustration that went far beyond the immediate futility of competitive materialism.

She was sufficiently absorbed in thoughts that she felt instinctively were leading her toward a specific goal, that she might quite easily have forgotten all about Mrs. Johnson. That she should, instead, become suddenly acutely worried about Mrs. Johnson to the exclusion of anything else was due to an association of ideas rather than to any outside cause. If she had not so often sat in this way by the windows after midnight, playing with the thought of death, she would not now be so concerned about Mrs. Johnson.

She could not be sure how long Mrs. Johnson had been in the silent garage across the road, but at this time of night it was too long.

Half rising, with the intention of waking Rick, she sank back, telling herself that she was an over-imaginative fool. There were any number of things that Mrs. Johnson might be doing. She might have fallen asleep. She might be doing something or other to her car. She might be having a quiet drink. Whatever she was doing, it was none of her, Karen's, affair.

Yet, even as she told herself these things, Karen knew that she was applying the kind of false, self-protective logic that you employed when you heard what could have been a scream in the night. When you hesitated, wondered if you might not have been mistaken, and decided to wait and see if you heard it again, while all the time knowing that the opportunity to scream twice was, more often than not, denied in any absolute crisis.

Mrs. Johnson had not, of course, screamed. All she had done was go into her garage between two and three in the morning, and fail to come out again. But in a black-and-white silence oppressive in its lack of any disturbance, Karen could not get rid of a mounting apprension.

Again she began to get up, and again sank back, her cigarette burning down unnoticed between her fingers. This, she thought, is what living in a place like Rowanwood does to you. You become so afraid of what your neighbours may think of you that you would rather die—or let someone else die—than take the risk of appearing even slightly ridiculous.

Her cigarette was burning her fingers. Without looking away from the Johnsons' garage, she put it out in an ash-tray on the small table beside her, while she remembered how, again and again, on a suburban street at night, she had scanned the houses she was passing, and known that even though there were people, and plenty of them, in those houses, it would be over-optimistic to expect help if she were to need it. In the suburbs at night, you were far more alone than you ever were downtown. In the suburbs at night, togetherness, like the palsied wraith it was, ceased to exist.

Why am I thinking like this? Karen asked herself. Mrs. Johnson isn't in need of my help, or anyone else's, and there is no earthly reason why I should think she is. I'm going to get back into bed, and stop being such a damned fool.

Seconds later, moving very quietly but very fast, she had stripped off her terry-cloth robe and her nightgown, and, leaving them on the floor between the windows and her clothes closet, was pulling on a dark sweater and a pair of slacks. Her left hand feeling for the side zipper of her slacks, she pushed her feet into moccasins, opened and closed the door of the bedroom, and ran swiftly downstairs.

In the front hall she paused just long enough to find a small torch in the drawer of the telephone table. Then she was outside in the moonlight, her soft moccasins making scarcely a sound on the gravel drive, and no sound at all on the dusty surface of the road.

And as she moved across the road, and up the short, weed-grown length of the Johnson's driveway, it was as if she were still at the bedroom window watching a projection of herself crossing the usually empty stage of the sleeping street. She saw herself lost from sight in the deep, black shadows of the elms bordering the road. Saw herself emerge again, a figure that had nothing to do with reality as it applied to her, that, losing substance in the deceptive moonlight, became the *doppelgänger* of legend.

It needed the metal knob of the side door to the Johnson's garage, cold under her hand, to shake her free from a fantasy almost as compulsive as the apprehension that had brought her out into the night.

The door was fastened on the inside. Giving herself no time to reconsider, she went around to the front, and, setting her teeth against the rasping noise the hinges would make, lifted the catch of the double doors and pulled them open far enough that she could slide between them.

Afterwards, she was to wonder why she had neither knocked nor spoken Mrs. Johnson's name. At the time, the quality of the silence enveloping the small, ugly frame structure had been a sufficient reason for not doing so. It was a silence quite unlike that surrounding either Millicent and Biff's great house behind thick shrubbery on her left, or that which encompassed the house, close on her right, in which Pete Johnson was sleeping.

It was the thought of Pete which, more than anything else, sustained Karen through the next hour, and helped her to face death quietly and with controlled efficiency.

She used her torch only to locate the light switch inside the double doors.

Mrs. Johnson lay huddled on the cinder floor between her old green Chev and the side door. The fingers of one hand, stretched at arm's length from her twisted body, were embedded in the cinders, a last terrible clutching at life, which had brought her no great gifts. Her face, turned in against a plump shoulder, was shielded by a fall of brassy hair, dark at the exposed roots.

Karen felt a single, awful shudder run through her. For what seemed like an infinity, she stood by the light switch, incapable either of going forwards or backwards. That Mrs. Johnson was dead, she had no doubt at all. And if she had not been braced for this, she would probably have turned and fled. But she had been prepared for it, if only by her own imagination, and so she held her ground until she was able to think rationally.

She had come expecting suicide. But it did not look like suicide.

Gingerly, wincing as the cinders creaked beneath her feet, she moved slowly toward the dead woman. She stooped, and briefly, very briefly, touched an arm left bare by a flimsy summer dress. The arm was already colder than the door knob had been.

"Thank God," she whispered. "Thank God."

Mrs. Johnson's death must have occurred within minutes after she had driven into her garage for the last time. She, Karen, need feel no guilt for not having come sooner.

"Thank God," she murmured again.

She straightened up, and looked around her, dismissing as unimportant a clutter that was no more than she might have expected. A small window at the back of the garage was partially open. There was no odour of carbon monoxide, and the car engine was not running.

It was probably a heart attack, Karen thought. I don't think she killed herself. I must get a doctor, and get one quickly. Is there anything I should do before I call the doctor? Keys to the house. I must have keys to the house because Pete has to be taken away from this. I must go home, call Dr. Lowe, wake Rick, and then come back for Pete. But I don't want to come in here again. Not in here again.

Abruptly, she rubbed the back of her hand across eyes pricked by tears, not for the dead woman, but for a boy who had no single living relative, who was now utterly alone.

The keys should be in her purse, Karen thought. Oh, God, where is her purse?

Mrs. Johnson's purse, a large white patent-leather shoulder-bag, was lying beside her, half hidden by her skirt.

Shaking in spite of herself, Karen picked up the purse and undid the clasp so awkwardly that the contents fell out in a pathetic heap at her feet. Compact, lipstick, pencil, wadded handkerchief, mirror, cheque-book, a loose bank cheque, a gilt charm bracelet, and two key-rings.

Still shaking, she picked up the key-rings, put them in her pocket, and began to replace the other articles while she fought distaste for the need to touch them at all.

The loose cheque was the last thing she picked up, and she had already dropped it back in the purse before she realized its significance.

Her breath a sharp, audible gasp, she pulled it out again and looked at it for more than a minute before she folded it with precise care and put it deliberately in her pocket with the key-rings.

If Mrs. Johnson's death was not a natural one, there would be a police investigation that would probably render her suppression of the cheque useless. It might even go farther than that. She might find herself in serious trouble. All she could do was pray that this would not be the case, that the cheque could remain her own private problem. A problem from which she shrank in prospect even as she turned off the light and went out into undisturbed moonlight to set in motion the complicated, depressing mechanics with which her society attempted to civilize death itself.

And as she crossed her empty stage again, her shadow woven, interwoven, and unravelled from the static shadow patterns of the windless night, she felt as if she were leaving, in a corner of a dark garage, the broken pieces of a once smooth grey cube.

19 | I'm sure you'll understand

The cheque, pale blue, bearing the letterhead of the Royal Bank of Canada, and Lewis's forceful signature, lay on the breakfast table between Karen and Rick. It was not until they had finished eating, however, that they discussed it directly.

"We could just tear it up," Karen said slowly. "We could pretend we had never seen it."

"Do you think that would help anybody?" Rick asked.

"No," Karen said. "I'm afraid I don't."

"Neither do I," Rick told her. "Which means that one or the other of us will have to see Lewis this morning. As soon as possible, in fact."

I should be relieved that it was a heart attack, that we are free to handle this as we see fit, Karen told herself. But the thought of facing Lewis with that cheque was not conducive to feelings of relief.

She pushed back the sleeve of her dressing-gown, and looked at her watch. "It's almost nine o'clock," she said. "Lewis will already have left for his office. He always leaves the house at a quarter to nine."

Her watch, quite naturally, did not tell her that this was Monday, did not remind her that today she had, if she wished, a luncheon engagement at the corner of Holton and Yonge. For the present, her mind was wiped clean of anything and everything that did not directly concern Susan. Mrs. Johnson, lying for the last time in her bedroom across the street behind a drawn yellow blind; Lewis, at the wheel of his dark-blue Lincoln, somewhere between Rowanwood and downtown Toronto; even the exhausted boy, at last asleep in the guest-room upstairs—none of these entities counted except in so far as they might affect Susan's future happiness.

"It would probably be easier for Lewis if I were to see him," Rick said.

"Yes," Karen said, "it probably would. But this is not a time when I feel inclined to consider what would, or would not, be easy for Lewis. I think our only hope of getting anywhere with him is to make things as difficult as possible. He has to be forced out into the open, for his own sake perhaps as much as for Susan's, but particularly for Susan's."

"Have you any idea what you might say to him?"

"No," Karen said. "That's not something I could know in advance."

"You feel up to it?"

Briefly Karen envied Mrs. Johnson. Mrs. Johnson's troubles were over. "I can try," she said. "You see why it has to be me, rather than you, don't you, Rick?"

"Yes," Rick said.

"Darling—" Karen said. There was no need to say any more. She did not have to thank him in so many words for an understanding that made it possible for him, against his own inclination, to leave her free to do what she could for Susan, that allowed him to see that she was the only one with any real chance of accomplishing anything.

"Oh, God," she said, "I wish it wasn't so hot again. I wish I wasn't so damn tired. Darling, will you call Lewis's office, and make an appointment for ten-thirty? You had better try for it in your name. You're more likely to get it, if you say it's for you. When you've done that, I'll call Susan and get her to come over and stay with Pete."

"Susan?"

"Yes," Karen said. "Susan."

"Are you sure that's a good idea?"

"I'm not sure of anything any more," Karen said. "But if you're going to gamble at all, in my book you might as well push all your chips into the middle of the table at once. Pete gets on with

Susan even better than he does with us. When he wakes up, she can take him over to her house."

Rick was chain-smoking, something he practically never did. "Pete may want to go home when he wakes up."

"He may," Karen said. "But unless he breaks a window, he can't get in. And I don't think he will want to do that."

"How do you know he hasn't got a key?"

"Because I went through his pockets," Karen said. "And there's no point in looking at me like that. I know you wouldn't have done it, but then you aren't me, darling. You wouldn't have taken the cheque, either. You would have seen it in terms of money rather than people. Men are trained to think that way."

Rick smiled for the first time that morning. "Aren't women?"

"Perhaps they are," Karen said. "But it doesn't take in the same way."

While Rick was telephoning Lewis's office, Karen cleared the breakfast dishes from the table and put them into the electric dish-washer. She felt, doing this, rather like the lady called Charlotte who, her lover "borne before her on a shutter, went on cutting bread and butter". It was, she thought, curious how, if you were brought up in a certain manner, you always went on cutting bread and butter, no matter what was happening. As long as you went on cutting bread and butter, you knew you were not likely to lose your grip.

She heard Rick come into the kitchen behind her, and swung round at once, her eyebrows raised in a mute question.

"It's laid on," he said.

"Ten-thirty?"

"That's right," he told her. "And I'll drive you down on my way to the office. That still doesn't leave you much time to dress, though."

"I don't need much time," Karen said.

"It could matter," Rick said. "The way you're dressed could matter."

For a moment Karen looked at him in silence, and knew that they were both thinking of the same thing. They were thinking of the impressively modern, thirty-three-story Preston Building, and Lewis, invariably immaculate in a double-breasted grey suit. Any emissary, regardless of his or her purpose, would, in those surroundings, and vis-à-vis Lewis, be at ease only if properly dressed.

"Thanks, darling," Karen said. "You were a jump ahead of me on that one. Do you think you could call Susan? It would give me more time to hunt up white gloves and so on. There's no need to break anything gently to her. She didn't really know Mrs. Johnson. Just ask her to look after Pete as a favour to us. Tell her it's because of Pete that I have to go downtown. She won't ask questions. Susan never does."

Rick had already gone out to the garage when Karen came downstairs half an hour later. She was at the front door when the telephone rang.

Undecided as to whether to let it ring unanswered, or go to it, she hesitated. Then, because she was afraid it might wake Pete, she turned back, thinking, I should answer it anyway. It could be Dr. Lowe. It could be the undertaker.

Without laying down her handbag or gloves, she lifted the receiver.

"Hello?" she said.

"Angel," Fay said, "I have something to tell you."

"Fay, I'm sorry, but I simply haven't time now. I'm just on my way out the door."

"That's all right," Fay said. "It isn't something I would want to say over the telephone, anyway."

Fay often behaved as if she thought her telephone wire was tapped. She could discuss her private life freely in the middle of Loblaw's, but on the telephone she was often absurdly circumspect. She was no more consistent about this than she was about anything.

"I think it will please you," Fay said. "It won't please everybody, and there's one person it won't please at all. But I think you'll be quite happy about it, angel."

"Fay," Karen said, "I can't stay, and I don't know what you're talking about."

"Of course you don't," Fay said. "I haven't told you yet, and it's not something I want to say on the telephone. As I said, there is somebody who is not going to be pleased at all."

It was impossible not to be curious. When Fay said she had something to tell you, she usually meant it. Whatever it was, you could be sure it had nothing to do with the Home and School, or the Garden Club. At this particular moment, however, Karen felt as if she would scream if Fay did not get off the line.

"The wonderful thing about you, angel," Fay was saying, "is that you're so broad-minded."

Oh, God, Karen thought, whose husband is it this time?

"Fay," she said, "Rick is waiting for me in the car. I'll talk to you tomorrow."

"Angel," Fay said, "you're always rushing around so. It isn't good for you to be always—"

In the act of replacing the receiver, even though she knew that Fay would never understand how such a thing could be necessary, Karen saw Susan coming in through the front door.

Susan was wearing a plain grey linen dress. No slacks. No bright colours. But nothing that could be thought of as even remotely funereal. She looked exactly as she ought to look, and her decision must have been made in a matter of seconds or she could not have arrived so quickly.

Covering the receiver with the palm of her hand, Karen said, "Fay. Deal with her, will you, darling. I can't. You were wonderful to come. I'm sorry to leave you with all this."

"I'll look after it," Susan said, and took the receiver from Karen's hand. "I'll look after everything. And don't worry about getting back at any special time. Do whatever you have to do, and don't worry about when you get back."

With a sense of enormous relief, Karen thought, there's nobody like her anywhere. Lewis must know that. He must. Oh, God, I hope I'm not making a really horrible mistake.

The traffic on King Street was too heavy for Rick to stop any longer than was necessary for Karen to get out of the car at the nearest corner to the Preston Building. By the time she reached the curb, and turned to wave to him, he was already too far away to see her. It was a very small thing, not being able to wave to Rick and have him wave in return, but this was a day and an hour when small things mattered.

Feeling very much alone, she walked across a crowded pavement, moving from sunlight into the shadows cast by the massive buildings that lined the south side of the street. Here she took out her mirror, and looked carefully at her face and hair. Neither her eyes nor her skin reflected any trace of the strain she had undergone, and her hair lay in the same smooth waves she had seen in the mirror at home. This was, she thought, one occasion when she could be grateful that any visible aftermath of stress was always delayed. By tomorrow she would almost indubitably look and feel like the wrath of God. Today, she was looking her best.

Although, for one reason and another, she had quite often been in the Preston Building, Karen had never been up to the thirty-third floor and the offices, occupying the entire floor, that Lewis kept for the exclusive use of the Preston Trust Company. In coming here she was forging a link between the social and business sides of Lewis's life that Lewis himself had been at some pains to avoid. Even Susan rarely came to Lewis's office.

As she crossed the black marble floor of the main lobby toward the bank of elevators on the far side, she quickly debated with herself the advisibility of taking the express elevator directly to Lewis's suite. She would, if she did this, have to announce herself to the elevator operator, with the possible risk of being, at least temporarily, refused at a level that would do nothing to bolster her self-confidence. On the other hand, if she took one of the ordinary elevators to the general offices, she would have to run the gamut of Lewis's outer as well as inner defences.

The express elevator, standing open at the ground floor, its uniformed attendant smartly at attention beside it, decided her.

Her head up, grateful to Rick for having seen how important it was that she be particularly well dressed, she approached the attendant.

"Mrs. Whitney," she said pleasantly but firmly. "I have an appointment with Mr. Preston for ten-thirty."

"Yes, Mrs. Whitney. Just a moment."

Moving as smartly as he had stood, he stepped backward into the elevator to consult written instructions which, Susan had once told Karen, it was as much as his job was worth to ignore. The elevator, Susan had told her, had its own telephone so that any discrepancy could be checked with as little delay as possible. Occasionally, Susan had said, someone like the president of the Chartered Trust would drop in to see Lewis without making an appointment in advance, and it didn't do to keep people like that standing around indefinitely while you vetted them.

"Excuse me, madam, but did you say *Mrs.* Whitney?"

It was, Karen thought, the most ridiculous yet sublimely tactful way of being told something was not quite right, that she had ever encountered. Under any other circumstances, she would have laughed outright.

Instead, she smiled. "I would hardly have said 'Mister', would I? Yes. Mrs. Richard Whitney. At ten-thirty. I see it's just ten-thirty now. And, as of course you know, Mr. Preston does not like to be kept waiting, does he?"

Still smiling, she stepped into the elevator. If there had been even the slightest trace of hesitation in her voice or manner, the attendant would, she was certain, have started a chain of calls that would have gone all the way through to Lewis.

As the elevator began its swift ascent, she said, "You must be Miguel?"

He turned, white teeth flashing in a quick smile. "If I may ask, how did you know that, Mrs. Whitney?"

"Mrs. Preston has spoken of you," Karen said, and she was glad to see that he was now, as she had intended, perfectly happy about taking her up.

Much the same tactics got her past the platinum blonde who presided over a perfectly appointed private lounge that preceded the office of Lewis's private secretary, Miss Carlisle. They did not get her past Miss Carlisle unchallenged.

Susan had once described Miss Carlisle as one part policewoman, one part watchdog, and one part granite. There was little doubt that this was true, but Miss Carlisle's appearance denied all of it. She was slim, grey-haired, elegant, and had a very soft voice.

"Mrs. Whitney? But wasn't it your husband who called?"

"Yes," Karen said. "He called to make the appointment for me."

"Oh, dear," Miss Carlisle said. "I seem to have misunderstood what your husband said."

This, Karen knew, was another brand of tact. Every member of Lewis's staff had probably taken a Ph.D. in tact.

"Well," Karen said, "as long as Mr. Preston has set the time aside, it isn't very serious."

"I'm sure it isn't," Miss Carlisle said. "But if you'll forgive me, I'll just check with Mr. Preston. I'm sure you'll understand, Mrs. Whitney, that it's just a formality. I suppose there isn't any way in which I could help you, is there?"

"Not in this instance, Miss Carlisle. Another time, perhaps, but this is rather personal. I'm sure you'll understand."

They understood each other perfectly, Karen thought. There was nothing complicated about it. She, Karen, wished to get into Lewis's office. Miss Carlisle wished to keep her out.

"I quite often look after Mr. Preston's personal matters for him," Miss Carlisle said. "He's such a busy man he finds it necessary to entrust me with what are really quite personal matters."

In a way, Karen could not help being sorry for Miss Carlisle. She could guess the kind of directives under which she operated. Lewis would want to know not only whom he was scheduled to see, but also their business.

"I'm sure Mr. Preston is entirely justified in the confidence he places in you, Miss Carlisle. My reason for wanting to see Mr. Preston, however, is personal to me."

Miss Carlisle knew how to be graceful in defeat. "In that case, Mrs. Whitney, I quite understand why you would like to see Mr. Preston personally. If you would be kind enough to sit down for a moment, I'll just check with him before you go in."

"Thank you, Miss Carlisle."

"Not at all, Mrs. Whitney."

When Miss Carlisle had left the room, her high-heeled shoes noiseless on the thick broadloom, Karen could not help thinking that the conversation they had just had resembled a ballet. You took two steps forward, and two steps back. You leaned first to one side, and then to the other. You did these things with a very nice dexterity, but it was a frantic waste of time.

Instead of sitting down, Karen walked over to the windows. Miss Carlisle probably earned every cent of her salary, but she did it in what were unusually pleasant surroundings. Karen thought she had rarely seen such a magnificent view of the city. And she was struck, as she always was when she looked down on the city from a height, not by the increasing number of skyscrapers, but by the green, interlaced design of tree-tops. Toronto was still, fortunately, a city of trees.

She had expected Miss Carlisle to come back immediately, and as the minutes passed without any sound or movement from beyond the soundproof door through which Miss Carlisle had disappeared, she found herself becoming almost as nervous as she had been in Dr. Lowe's waiting-room. Of all the people she had ever known, Lewis was the last into whose private life she would willingly have chosen to intrude.

"You can come in now, Mrs. Whitney. Mr. Preston is ready to see you."

It was unfortunate that Miss Carlisle should have taken her by surprise, just as Dr. Lowe's secretary had done, and that Miss Carlisle should have used exactly the same phraseology. It was a common enough formula. But still the coincidence was not a happy one. At least this time she was not tangled up with a cigarette. Holding her chin high, as she had done in the lobby downstairs, and still wearing her elbow-length white gloves, she was able to walk into Lewis's office with reasonable poise.

"How are you, Karen?"

Lewis, as immaculate as she had known he would be, stepped forward from behind a large mahogany desk set in an angle between two huge windows.

"I'm very well, thank you, Lewis," Karen said. "You have a beautiful office here."

"I'm glad you like it, Karen."

"Your view is superb."

"It is rather nice, isn't it," Lewis said.

"I see you patronize the Canadian artists here, as well as at home, Lewis."

"Yes," Lewis said, "I do. Canadian scenery is very much to my taste."

To want to wipe your hands off with a piece of Kleenex when you had gloves on was palpably absurd. But it was exactly what Karen wanted to do. She had never seen Canadian landscapes set off to as great advantage as they were against the dark panelling of this large, well-lit room, but she had not come to Lewis's office to discuss pictures. She felt as if the cheque, made out to Sybil Johnson, was a time bomb that might, with further delay, go off in her hand-bag, blowing both herself and Lewis to perdition with nothing gained at all.

Lewis, apparently, had also had enough of this particular *pas de deux*, because he gestured toward a large red leather armchair beside the desk. "Won't you sit down, Karen?"

Karen was glad to sit down, and glad to accept the cigarette that Lewis offered and then lit for her. Through the window opposite her she could see the top of the Bank of Commerce Building. She had never really admired the Bank of Commerce Building, but now it had a very solid and comforting familiarity.

"Well, Karen, what can I do for you?"

Lewis had seated himself in the chair behind the desk. Lewis got down to cases faster than Miss Carlisle did.

Looking at him, Karen suddenly realized what he must be thinking, and she felt a slow, hot flush rising from her throat to her face. Lewis thought she had come here to borrow money from him. From his point of view, it was the only possible explanation for her presence in his office. He had not said, or in any way indicated, that she was unwelcome, but beneath the surface of his unfailing good manners she sensed that she most definitely was.

It had been impossible to plan what she would either say or do, once she and Lewis were face to face. Even so, she had never imagined doing what, in her anger and embarrassment, she now did.

Without a word, she opened her hand-bag, took out the pale blue oblong of paper, and laid it on the darker blue of Lewis's blotter.

Lewis's cool gaze dropped to the cheque in front of him. With no change in expression, he looked at it. Still without any change in expression, he looked up again.

"How did this happen to come into your possession, Karen?"

"Mrs. Johnson died last night," Karen said. "I found her."

"How did she die?" The question was unaccented. There was neither surprise nor any great interest in Lewis's quiet voice.

"A heart attack," Karen told him. And she had to remind herself forcibly that this remote, well-dressed stranger was Susan's husband, and, until now, her own friend. Because Lewis had never seemed quite so much of an enigma. The wall, of which she had always been aware, had never been so high between them.

With one finger of a long, beautifully kept hand, Lewis flicked the edge of the cheque. "Do you expect me to explain this to you, Karen?"

"I don't expect you to explain anything, Lewis."

"Then why are you here, Karen?"

This is it, Karen thought. My answer to this question may determine not only Susan's future, but my own relationship with Lewis for the rest of our lives. I may antagonize him for good, or I may know him as I have never known him before.

"I'm here because I love Susan—and Susan loves children."

Lewis was still looking at her, but his eyes were opaque, unreadable.

"Lewis!" Karen said. "Lewis, I'm not asking you why you've looked after Pete, why you've paid his school bills and probably other bills, too. All I'm asking is that, whatever you do for him, you share it with Susan."

Lewis's eyes sharpened into focus on her again, and Karen knew that she had rarely, if ever, been so frightened.

"Do you think Pete is my son, Karen?"

"No. I don't."

"Then why do you think I have looked after him?"

Karen took the final hurdle because he had left her no choice. "I think," she said, "I think you have done it—because you are, for some reason, afraid to have children, yourself."

Unable to look at him now, she dropped her gaze to white gloves whose palms were wet. Oh, God, she thought, what have I done? Right or wrong, what have I done? Why couldn't I have minded my own damn business? Only an imbecile would have said such a thing to any man, let alone Lewis.

Lewis's voice reached her from what seemed like a great distance. "You're quite right, Karen. But how did you know?"

Karen's head jerked up. "We're still on speaking terms, Lewis?"

Lewis's smile was singularly sweet. Susan must have seen him smile like that, but to Karen it was a revelation. It was a smile that made him look, for the first time in her experience of him, vulnerable, human as previously she had only guessed he might be.

"Perhaps," Lewis said, "we have never really been on speaking terms to quite the same degree before. I think we could both possibly use a drink before we go any farther with this. Could you use a small drink, Karen?"

Because he was no longer a stranger, because he was suddenly someone with whom she was completely at ease, Karen sighed, peeled off her gloves, and said, "Yes, Lewis, I could use a drink."

Lewis got up and crossed the room to an inlaid mahogany cabinet. "You prefer Scotch and water, I believe, Karen?"

"Thank you, Lewis."

"Ice?"

"No ice, thank you."

"My preference, too," Lewis said. "I think, Karen—in fact, I have always thought—that we have a great deal in common. I believe I owe you an apology for the manner in which I received you this morning. You have a great deal of courage."

Karen's laughter was spontaneous. "It was the Bank of Commerce Building, Lewis. I don't think I could have done it without the help of the Bank of Commerce Building."

As he set her drink down on a corner of the desk near her, Lewis glanced out of the west window. "I can see what you mean," he said, and he was still smiling.

"Now," he said, when he was again sitting behind his desk, "you haven't answered my question. How did you know?"

"That you were afraid rather than incapable?" Karen asked.

Lewis nodded.

Incredible to be talking to Lewis on a subject so intimate, and with no embarrassment or hesitation on either side. He was, Karen decided, one of the most wholly civilized men she had ever known.

"I knew," she told him, "because I knew you better than I realized I did. When I found that cheque—everything suddenly added up. I knew you could never have been intimate with Mrs. Johnson. Under no circumstances would such a thing have been possible. Your interest in Pete was not the result of either conscience or outside pressures. It represented a—a need of your own which, for reasons of your own, you felt you could not satisfy in any other way. You could, I believe, have adopted him outright years ago, if you had wanted to. Mrs. Johnson, I am reasonably certain, would have exchanged what was really an unwanted burden for a life income, if the suggestion had ever been made to her."

"You might be interested to know, Karen, that she herself at one time made such a suggestion."

"Thank you for telling me."

"Go on, Karen," Lewis said. His voice was remarkably gentle.

Karen looked at the glass in her hand, and thought, this is the first time I have had a drink in the morning since the summer when Rick and I planted the buckwheat lawn. On that occasion, Susan was with me. And she saw this memory not as irrelevant, but as a way station on the road back to the days when Rowanwood had been an almost untenanted paradise in which a man, his inner loneliness well concealed, must often have encountered a small boy whose loneliness was only too obvious. There had, she remembered, been no more than three houses in Rowanwood then. Lewis and Susan's big split-level. The empty farmhouse with the fanlight. And Mrs. Johnson's small frame house.

"If you had been incapable of having children, Lewis, you would have taken him, and brought him up. Feeling as you did about him, there would, in this case, have been no reason why you should not have done so. I asked myself what possible reason you could have had for limiting your relationship with Pete to financial help of which he, himself, was unaware." She paused, and then went on slowly, "Lewis, what makes you think of yourself as unfit to be a father, even by proxy?"

Lewis stood up with what, for him, was startling abruptness, and walked across to the north window. "Come here, Karen," he said. And when she was standing beside him, he asked, "When you look out there, what do you see?"

"Toronto," Karen told him. It was, she knew, a fatuous reply, but she guessed that any reply was better than asking him what he meant.

"And it's familiar to you?" Lewis asked. "You feel you know it well?"

"Yes," Karen said.

"Pick out a few specific landmarks which mean something to you personally."

With no idea where he was leading her, Karen realized it was intensely important that she follow as well as she was able to, and it seemed natural to begin with a close perspective, and move out from there.

"The T. Eaton Company," she said. "The General Hospital. The Canada Life Building. The Museum. Casa Loma. Do you want any more, Lewis?"

"No," Lewis said. "No, that's enough, Karen. Your family always had a charge account with Eaton's, didn't they? And you were born in the Private Patients' Pavilion of the General Hospital, weren't you? And when you were quite young your father took out both life and education insurance for you with the Canada Life, didn't he? And your mother, or your father, or both, used to take you to the Museum on Saturday afternoons rather than turning you loose on the streets? And you not only always expected to go to the University, because that had been insured, but actually did go? And you went to dances at Casa Loma, and leaned on the parapet outside, looking very pretty in a variety of evening dresses on a variety of occasions, as you gazed out over a moonlit and apparently peaceful city? Substantially, this is all correct, isn't it, Karen?"

"Yes, Lewis. Substantially, it is entirely correct."

"Now, will you come over here, Karen, and tell me what you see."

In silence, Karen went with him to the west window. She knew where he was leading her now, and, in advance of any details, the knowledge was acutely painful.

"What do you see?" Lewis asked.

"The city," Karen said, and was fully aware of her difference in designation.

"And this, too, is familiar to you?"

Earlier, Karen would, almost without thinking, have said yes, simply because she could see the Bank of Commerce Building and, to the south, a part of Lake Ontario.

"No, Lewis," she said. "It's not familiar to me."

Lewis's voice, quiet, almost casual, warned her that he was not asking for, and would not accept, sympathy. "Approximately half a mile from here, between King and Queen Streets, is the house where I was born, Karen. Opinions may differ as to whether or not it stands in what could technically be called a slum. There can be no doubt, however, that when I lived there, as I did for fifteen years, mine was a slum existence. There were, at one time, seven of us in the family, and we lived in two rooms on the third floor. In all, there were thirty-one people living in a nine-room house. There was only one bathroom, the dubious privilege of its use denied to the occupants of the third floor. Those who lived on the third floor were expected to use what is, I believe, known as an outside convenience. We had another name for it, and I leave it to your imagination to judge just how convenient it was, and what alternatives were resorted to. Can I freshen your drink for you, Karen?"

"No, thank you."

"Cigarette?"

"Please."

Her hand, Karen noticed, was not quite steady as Lewis lit her cigarette for her. Lewis's hand was sure and firm.

"Are you beginning to get the picture, Karen?" he asked.

"Yes," Karen said, "I'm beginning to get the picture, Lewis. But there is more to it than privation, isn't there?"

"You're quite right, Karen. Privation alone does not necessarily leave scars. As the youngest in the family, I was the most unwanted, which was in a sense fortunate. In order to get me out of the way my parents allowed me to keep the clothes given to me by the Neighbourhood Workers. In that way I could be sent to school. I could be got out of the house for seven hours a day."

"What do you mean? Allowed to keep your clothes? They wouldn't have taken your clothes away from you, surely?"

"They took them away from my brothers and sisters," Lewis said. "You see, Karen, both my parents drank, and even rotgut costs money. On Queen Street, if you know where to look, there are places where whiskey is bartered for almost anything, even a child's survival."

"Oh, God," Karen said.

"I don't believe in God," Lewis said. "But that is beside the point. You mustn't let this disturb you too much, Karen. You must remember that it is all in the past now."

For Lewis, on the air-conditioned thirty-third floor of the Preston Building, it might be in the past. But for hundreds of others, still living in an area which Karen could not believe had improved during another thirty years of actual and moral degradation, it must be the living present. For her, this was going to be knowledge that would be difficult to live with unless she could, in some way, do something about it.

For no better reason than that one could see the feathered green of foliage amongst sharp-angled roofs and broken brick chimneys, she had imagined decency in conjunction with poverty. Completely blind to the squalor in what was metaphorically her own back yard, she had gone on thinking that where there were trees everything must automatically be more or less all right. In accepting this city as her city, she must now accept the whole of it.

As if he had read her thoughts, Lewis said, "One does what one can, Karen. One does what one can. But as long as there are human beings who behave like animals, just so long will there be human beings who live like animals."

"Haven't you got it the wrong way round, Lewis? Isn't it the living conditions which come first, and the behaviour afterwards, as a result?"

"I don't think so, Karen. I may be wrong, but I'm afraid I don't think so. Both my father and my mother came from decent, hard-working English stock, and proceeded to create a little hell on earth for their own children. My younger sister was raped when she was eleven. I won't go into the details of that. She died of pneumonia when she was twelve. My other sister went on the streets when she was fifteen. She enjoyed her work, and did quite well until she was killed in a rooming-house brawl on Jarvis Street. Of my two brothers, one died of what was known in the area as natural causes. Actually, it should have been called malnutrition; but under such circumstances this is quite natural. It was not long after this that I became a ward of the Children's Aid Society."

A slight breeze was moving through the tree-tops to the west. Even from this height, the movement of the leaves could be seen quite clearly.

"Are any of your family still living?" Karen asked.

"Yes," Lewis said. "My mother, and one brother. They are both in mental institutions. I imagine that it is quite obvious to you now, Karen, why I do not consider myself good parent material."

Karen turned away from the window, and returned to her chair before she replied. Her gloves, which she had laid across one arm of the chair, had dried without leaving any marks on the palms.

"I can understand," she said, "why you might not think it wise to have children of your own, Lewis. Though, even here, I feel you are probably wrong. But I can see no reason whatsoever for not adopting a child, if you were so inclined."

"Don't you, Karen?"

"No, I don't."

"I've told you where my only two remaining relatives are. Perhaps I should add that they are incurable, and that they are not suffering from anything as simple as the results of alcoholism."

"What difference does that make?" Karen asked, and she was aware of a rising impatience that she made no attempt to check. "How old are you, Lewis?"

"I am about forty-five," Lewis told her.

"Well—" Karen began, before the impact of what he had said really hit her. With the kind of truths he had been revealing, he would hardly have suppressed his exact age if he had known it. "But your birthday parties?" she said.

For several years she and Rick had gone to Susan and Lewis's house for dinner on Lewis's birthday. They always had steak, done as Lewis liked it. There was always a birthday cake with three token candles. And after dinner they always played bridge. It had become an established pattern, quiet but gay, and an occasion to look forward to for a week or more in advance.

That Lewis should have no known birthday was, ridiculous as it might seem, harder to accept than anything else he had told her.

Lewis's expression had the cool, slightly quizzical flavour with which she most often associated it. "One picks up certain amenities as one goes along, Karen. At a certain stage in one's career it becomes socially necessary to have a birthday."

"Oh, Lewis—" Karen said. And then, because she felt herself dangerously close to tears, she went back to the point she had been about to make. "Lewis, do you seriously expect, at your age, to go out of your mind?"

"If you put it like that, Karen, the answer is no."

"Have you ever in your life needed a psychiatrist?"

Lewis smiled. "If you mean have I ever been to one, then the answer to that is also no."

"May I have another cigarette, please?"

Karen had cigarettes in her purse, but Lewis was the kind of man who did not like you to smoke your own cigarettes when you were with him.

"You're sure you won't have a little more Scotch?" Lewis asked.

Karen shook her head. "Contrary to present evidence, I'm not really a drinking woman. Not in the morning, anyway. Lewis, how often do you change your business directives? How often do you take stock?"

"I see what you're driving at, Karen. But it's not quite the same thing, you know."

"Isn't it?" Karen said. "I think it is. You and Susan have been married for seventeen years, and you haven't taken stock again since. You gave yourself, and Susan, a directive seventeen years ago, and you haven't reconsidered it since. Does that make sense, Lewis? Looked at objectively, does that make any sense at all?"

"Karen," Lewis said, "you can't make that kind of comparison. There are some things that are basic, that never change, and a bad heredity is one of them."

How often had Susan argued this point with Lewis? How often had Susan come up against this barrier with nothing to show for it but invisible bruises? Not too often, probably, because Susan was careful to avoid one's tender spots, which was generally—but not always—a good thing. Occasionally a person had to be hit where it hurt.

"Lewis," Karen said, "has it never occurred to you that you are robbing Susan of something she wants terribly, simply in order to protect yourself? Have you ever seen that you have—I'm sorry, Lewis—been cheating her completely of something that you have taken, in part, yourself?"

With one swift motion, she gathered up gloves and hand-bag, and rose to her feet. "I've said all I'm going to say. All I can say. Except that Pete is with Susan at your house now, and that she knows nothing of my visit to you or its cause."

"Karen."

"Yes, Lewis?"

"I will need a little time to think, but I feel it is safe to say now that I owe you a debt I am quite unable to pay. If you felt like doing me a further favour, you might pass on to Rick what I have told you this morning."

They were already moving toward the door of the office.

"That isn't necessary," Karen said. "It really isn't."

"For me, it is," Lewis said. His smile again contained the sweetness that had earlier come as such a surprise to her. "You see, Karen, I have never, before today, had real friends of my own. It is very comforting to have friends from whom one has no secrets."

Unable to trust her voice, Karen laid her hand briefly on his arm before opening the door and walking quickly through Miss Carlisle's office.

She should, she knew, have stopped to say good-bye to Miss Carlisle. It would have been the proper thing to do, but she was incapable just then of doing the proper thing. And anyway, Miss Carlisle was talking into the telephone. She could hear Miss Carlisle saying, "I'm so sorry to have had to put you off, Mr. Armitage, but Mr. Preston has been in conference much longer than he expected to be. It was something rather urgent that came up at the last minute, Mr. Armitage, and I'm sure you'll understand—"

20 | Good-bye in the afternoon

King Street, when Karen walked out of the Preston Building, was, at a little before noon, sultry with heat, filled with crowds moving slowly in sunlight that struck directly into a canyon whose uneven stratification of brick and granite recorded more than a hundred and fifty years of architectural trial and error.

Becoming one with the crowd, letting it carry her at its own pace toward Yonge Street, she was aware of a sense of anticlimax that made the thought of going home, and picking up her housework where she had left it, extraordinarily depressing. Ever since the previous Monday she had had a sensation of increasing momentum that must of necessity be taking her somewhere. That it should stop here, leaving her aimless, wandering without any urgent destination along a downtown city street, was something she fought against accepting.

Through a slow, late spring, and the sudden heat of summer when it finally came, her everyday life with its obbligato of mounting depression had been one without significant punctuation until the previous Monday, when the three letters—

Abruptly stock still in the middle of the pavement, unaware of being jostled, she pushed back the cuff of her glove in order to look at her watch.

A second later, she was at the curb signalling to a cruising taxi.

"Where to, miss?"

As the taxi turned back into the traffic, she said, her voice carefully controlled, "Holton and Yonge, please."

I can still change my mind, she thought. I haven't committed myself yet. I may be on the verge of doing something unutterably foolish, but I haven't committed myself yet. But even as she told herself this, she realized that—below the surface of consciousness, divorced from reason, which might have denied it—the possibility that she might, after all, go to meet Cyr must have been there from the moment when she read his letter. If it had not been, she would not have reacted so fast to conscious memory, her timing would not have been precisely right. Because, in spite of the noon traffic, she would arrive at the corner of Holton and Yonge within minutes of the time Cyr had specified.

The letter from Planesville had served a purpose. The letter from Dr. Lowe had served a purpose. What possible purpose could there be for her in Cyr's letter, after more than twenty years?

Karen had, quite naturally, expected that when she left Geneva, Cyr would still be there. In spite of what he had said about both of them being on vacation, and the sense of impermanence this inferred, she had thought of him as much more of a fixture in Geneva than she was herself.

She should have known, even then, that nothing is ever exactly as you expect it to be.

Looking back later, she could see that she had still had a lot to learn about a great many things on that June afternoon when one of the maids had come up to her room in the house on Route de Chêne to tell her that there was "a monsieur" downstairs to see her.

The maid had told her this in English, because both the maids were Danish and both spoke English much better than they spoke French. Something she had seen no reason to mention in her letters to her parents.

When she had returned to Canada, her parents had been very pleased with the progress she had made with her French. That she would have made a great deal more progress if she and Susan, and Madame Dutoit, and the maids, had not invariably conversed in English because it was so much easier for all of them, was something that she had simply seen no point in mentioning at any time.

Monsieur Dutoit was the only member of the household with whom she had spoken French, and her conversations with him had been limited to such unexacting remarks as *"Bon jour, monsieur"*, and *"Au revoir, monsieur"*, and *"Le beurre, s'il vous plaît, monsieur"*.

That she had learned to speak French at all was due chiefly to her addiction to uncensored French films, and the disproportionate amount of time she spent in the Geneva restaurants and cafés. Unlike Waycroft, the International School operated on the principle that education was for those who wanted it, and so kept no very precise check on class attendance. Which was why she had been able to pass so many afternoons drinking Cinzano at the Casanova with Cyr.

The last thing she had anticipated, however, was that Cyr would ever come to the house on Route de Chêne in the afternoon, if only because he had never done so before.

"What kind of monsieur?" Karen had asked the maid. "What does he look like?"

"He is tall, mademoiselle."

"What else is he?" Karen asked.

"He is dark, mademoiselle."

"Can't you tell me any more than that?" Karen asked. "Is he someone you remember seeing before?"

"Oh, yes, mademoiselle, but never before in the afternoon. He has come to call for you in the evening, and he is not, mademoiselle, a monsieur one forgets easily."

Karen had known then that it was Cyr. It was a very good description of Cyr—a monsieur one did not forget easily. Also, there was the fact that he had not apparently given his name. Cyr never gave his name. He just said it was unpronounceable, and let it go at that.

"All right," Karen said. "Tell him I'll be right down, will you? Tell him I'll be down in a minute."

She had found Cyr in the larger of the two reception rooms, the one at the back of the house, and it had been just the way she had always known it would be if, for any reason, they tried to talk amongst the bead-fringed lamps, dark oil paintings, and Swiss furniture. They had exchanged words, and no more. It had been quite impossible to communicate with one another in any real sense. She had told Cyr that it would be like that. It was not as if she hadn't warned him. When he explained why he had come, however, she realized that he had chosen this place on purpose. Intending to be impersonal, he had chosen the Dutoits' house in which to achieve and maintain his intention.

"Hello, Karen," he said.

"Hello, Cyr. Won't you sit down?"

"I'd rather stand, if you don't mind."

"I don't mind, but won't you get rather tired?"

This was not the way in which she and Cyr usually talked to one another. Usually they dispensed with any greeting at all, simply coming together as if there had been no time lapse at all between meetings. She ought to have guessed that there was more to it than the Swiss furniture.

"I'm not staying long," Cyr told her.

"Oh. Are you on your way somewhere?"

"Karen," he said, "I'm going away."

Glad that she had, herself, sat down on the arm of a chair, Karen said, "Will you be gone long?"

Cyr had not answered at once. He had tried to find an easy way of saying what he had come to say. He had failed to find one, because there simply wasn't one. "I'm not coming back, darling," he said.

Very little light ever got through the two layers of curtains with which Madame Dutoit kept the windows shrouded, but for Karen even this much light was briefly blotted out by a swirling wave of darkness. She had never experienced anything quite like that moment, and she was never to experience anything like it again.

As the darkness receded, and she got herself in hand, she could hear her own voice, detached, betraying nothing. "I'll miss you, Cyr," she was saying. "But since I'll be going home so soon, myself, I suppose it doesn't make that much difference now."

"No," Cyr said. "It doesn't make that much difference now."

"When do you go?" Karen asked. She even managed a smile.

"Tomorrow," Cyr told her. "Tomorrow morning. Quite early. I will have to pack this evening. That's why I came around to say good-bye to you this afternoon."

"It was nice of you to take the time," Karen said.

For an instant he looked as if he might say something that really meant something, even if they were in the Dutoits' reception room. That he didn't was due only, Karen guessed, to the fact that he had had himself well in hand right along. He had had the advantage, as he usually did, of knowing what he was, and was not, going to do.

"You know I couldn't have left without saying good-bye to you," he said. "Without seeing you."

"I'm glad you felt that way, Cyr."

"We've had a good time. I won't forget that."

I can't, Karen thought, stand any more of this.

She stood up, and held out her hand. In Switzerland, she had got into the habit of shaking hands. It was a useful custom, because it put a definite period to any encounter. In holding out her hand now, she was saying good-bye to Cyr. Period. Because she really couldn't stand any more.

"Good luck, Cyr," she said. She was still smiling.

That was when Madame Dutoit came into the room and reduced the situation to a shambles. Not that it hadn't been pretty much of a shambles from the beginning. Nevertheless, if Madame Dutoit had not come in, Karen would probably not have seen Cyr again. No matter how unsatisfactory their good-byes might have been, they would have concluded them, and she would not have been left with such an immediate and shattering sense of unfinished business.

"Oh," Madame Dutoit said. "I didn't know anyone was here. Forgive me."

If she had not been Swiss, Madame Dutoit would have retired again at this point, because she really was very tactful. Being Swiss, however, she felt compelled in the name of good manners to shake hands.

So, instead of shaking hands with Karen, Cyr shook hands with Madame Dutoit, and after that there was no going back for any of them. It wasn't a matter of choice. There just didn't seem to be any way of going back.

"A pleasure, monsieur," Madame Dutoit said, as Karen introduced her to Cyr.

"The pleasure is mine, madame," Cyr said.

"You, too, are from Toronto, monsieur?" Madame Dutoit asked.

"No, madame," Cyr replied. "I am not from Toronto."

Karen could not help laughing. She was, she told Susan later, feeling more than a little hysterical.

"I have said something amusing, then?" Madame Dutoit asked.

"Yes," Karen said. "I mean, no, madame."

Madame Dutoit smiled. "Is it then yes or no, *chérie*?"

"It isn't either," Karen said. "It's Toronto."

This was when Cyr, she told Susan, had come to her rescue. He had known that if she went on laughing, it would be only a matter of time before she began to cry. He had, she told Susan afterwards, known perfectly well that it was all his fault, with his damned good-bye in the afternoon and his high-handed way of doing what he considered best for her.

"What mademoiselle Karen means," Cyr said, "is that Toronto is a very entertaining place."

"*Hélas*!" said Madame Dutoit. "If only my poor Geneva were more entertaining!"

"You do not," Cyr told her, "do your beautiful city justice, madame."

Madame Dutoit brightened at once. "You like it, monsieur?"

"It is entirely fascinating, madame."

It was, Karen told Susan, the first time she had realized that diplomacy was an art with which Cyr, whatever he thought of it, was more than familiar. Before he was through, she said to Susan, he had complimented the city, the canton, the country, Madame Dutoit, Monsieur Dutoit whom he had never met, and most of Madame Dutoit's ancestors whom, as far as she knew, nobody had ever met.

Karen could never remember afterwards how they managed to arrive in the front hall, or the precise manner of Cyr's leave-taking. She had a confused impression that, at one stage, even she and Madame Dutoit had shaken hands. This would have been the height of absurdity, but, in Geneva, not at all impossible.

The only thing that was quite clear, as she stood under the heavy crystal chandelier with Madame Dutoit, was that he had gone, and without really saying good-bye at all.

"*Mais il est charmant, chérie!*" said Madame Dutoit. "*On ne l'oublierait pas facilement, cet monsieur.*"

"No," Karen said, "he is not a man one would forget easily. If you will excuse me, madame, I'll go upstairs and change for dinner."

In her high-ceilinged bedroom, with its ordinary brass bedstead and rich Oriental carpet, Karen realized that it was quite impossible for her to leave things as they stood between herself and Cyr. Her heart was not breaking, but something was happening to her that was equally bad. If this thing, whatever it was, was not to go on happening for some time to come, there would have to be a more clear-cut break between them than they had so far accomplished. And she was as sure as she had ever been of anything in her life that Cyr, himself, must feel as she did.

If Madame Dutoit had not interrupted them, Cyr might have been able to persuade himself that the farce they had been playing out was still the only safe—and therefore only possible—way in which he could say good-bye to her.

As it was, he must be as dissatisfied as she was.

But what, if anything, would he do about it?

Using only a fraction of her mind with which to select a dress and accessories, she concentrated on a problem that she was certain she would have to solve for herself.

He would not come back to the house. She could rule that out completely.

He might telephone her later in the evening. But she did not think he would.

If their good-bye, hers and Cyr's, was to be anything other than a good-bye in the afternoon, her guess was that he would not accept more responsibility for this than was implicit in meeting her half-way. And there was only one place in the world where he could be absolutely sure that she had, in fact, come to meet him half-way.

Between eight-thirty and nine would be the right time for her to arrive at the Bavaria, Karen decided.

There was no need to make any other decision.

It was not until three weeks later, not until she was on the ship on her way back to Canada, that she wondered why she had at no time questioned the assumption that their parting, whatever form it took, would be a final one. Neither then nor later was she able to find a wholly satisfactory answer to why she had, without protest, accepted this as inevitable.

At a quarter past eight, she left the house on Route de Chêne, to walk without haste through a dream city in the dream-like tranquillity of a warm, windless summer evening.

There might be times in the future when she would not know where she was going or why, but on that June evening in Geneva she knew exactly where she was going and why. And, in memory, she would see Geneva more often as she saw it then, than in any other of its many guises, even though all were beautiful. Across thousands of miles and many years, it would remain with her, like a scene looked at through the wrong end of a telescope, tiny, remote, perfect in every detail, and eternally changeless.

Gentle shadows lay in the streets, seeming to muffle the footsteps and laughter of the passers-by, softening the sombre grey of stone buildings, muting the colours of café tables and chairs and the striped awnings above them.

Following one of the steep streets that wound down toward the lake, she looked up to see the last of the sun's rays merge with the golden spires of the Russian church, briefly visible at an oblique angle on a height above her. But when, having chosen a route longer than she need have done, she reached the Quai Gustave-Ador and the lake, the city lay completely enfolded in the premature twilight of a mountain-encircled valley.

Strolling, a part of the dream, toward a rendezvous that might not exist, yet never doubting that it did, she identified herself with a scene from which she would never be entirely severed. The plane trees, no longer the tormented witches' trees of winter, but soft bouquets of foliage limned in tenderness against water silvered by the dying day. The swans, a snowy unreality, floating toward darkness on the lake's quiet surface. The gulls, patterned in flight against the cloudless sky. The mirrored reflection of lights on the farther shore. The people, drifting past in lazy, sensual enjoyment of freedom from need to do anything else. The spires of the cathedral, beyond and above her objective, as severely serene as an interior long since stripped of Catholic splendour by a Calvinist denial of all sensory indulgence.

With no break in the fabric of her waking dream, she reached the Bavaria, and went slowly but without hesitation into the bright, moving vitality of another but equally vivid facet of a trance from whose soft, tenacious embrace she would not have torn herself for anything else the world could offer.

He was there. She saw him at once, sitting near the back talking to a man she did not know.

She chose an empty table, neither near him nor so close to the door that he would feel forced to acknowledge her presence if he chose to leave without speaking to her. To further underline the fact that he had a choice, she sat, not on the banquette against the wall, but in a chair with her back to the long, narrow aisle separating the two rows of tables.

Without seeing it, she gazed at a sketch of Ramadier on the wall in front of her. Then she looked down at her hands, palms up, shaken by a tremor too slight to disturb the folds of the skirt against which they lay.

She had come half-way. The initiative was no longer hers.

She ordered coffee, conversations in many languages no more than a blurred backdrop for her own peculiarly detached thoughts. Curious, she thought, that she who disliked brown so much should find it so pleasing in this one place. Here, brown was entirely right, was warm and reassuring, helped to still the tremor in her hands. She hoped they would never change it, that the Bavaria would remain the same in fact as it would in memory. She did not expect ever to come here again. But still she would like to believe that it would remain unchanged.

When Cyr stood beside her, he did not have to speak to make her aware of his presence.

Without haste, she raised her gaze from her empty hands.

He spoke very quietly. "*Tu viens avec moi?*"

"*Si tu veux.*"

They had never spoken French to one another before.

He placed a franc on the table beside her untouched cup of coffee.

"In that case," he said, "shall we go?"

21 You never get something for nothing

Karen had not been nervous when she went to the Bavaria on that evening, so far removed in time but now so close in memory.

That she should be indisputably nervous as, the taxi paid off, she stood on the corner of a busy Toronto intersection, was a direct legacy of her long refusal to part with a dream she had wished to keep as such. In memory, she had always up until now chosen to separate Cyr from the long chain of experiences that, stretching back across her life, in sum represented a continuing reality. That this arbitrary distinction between what she was prepared to interpret as real or unreal, was in itself unrealistic, she had known well enough. She had even recognized the theoretical element of dishonesty in it; but since it was so purely her own business, this hadn't seemed to matter.

There was, she saw, only one corner restaurant. It was diagonally opposite her, its plate-glass windows sun-struck mirrors reflecting a distorted duplication of cars and pedestrians that moved, and stopped, and moved again, like pull-toys operated by the same mechanism that controlled the traffic lights.

With a green light alternately on her left and then on her right, there was no practical need for hesitation. Yet she did hesitate, fighting not only nervousness but a sudden and very unpleasant feeling of guilt. It was not a sensation to which she was accustomed. As Cyr himself had once said, there was no such thing as definitive virtue or definitive guilt, or in most cases even an approximation of these extremes. Nevertheless, there *was* a dividing line, and a very clear one, between what you could and could not do with a clear conscience. A dividing line established not by logic, but by your background, experience, and training; by the accepted mores of the particular society to which you belonged. If, either literally or metaphorically, you lived on a certain side of a certain street, you took ice off the back of the iceman's cart at your own risk.

It was then that she saw him.

His head bent, he was walking along Holton toward the restaurant. A tall, loose-knit man in a grey suit, whose broad shoulders rolled to his easy, slightly rolling gait because he walked with his hands in his trousers pockets.

Immobile, she stared—not across a busy Toronto intersection, but across a span of more than twenty years. Torn between an almost overwhelming desire to reach back across that gulf in time, and the immediate certainty that it was the last thing she should do, she experienced a stabbing mixture of emotions she would not have analyzed if she could have. She had been a girl when she last saw him. She was a woman now, and one who finally understood the components of a relationship that, up until this moment, she had wilfully chosen to misunderstand. The dream, as she had preserved it, had been a romantic one. The truth was that they had shared, she and Cyr, a powerful attraction, and little else of any real consequence. The contradictory element in what had been, as Susan had called it, the "damnedest relationship", had been her own long refusal to commit herself on what she had known by instinct would be essentially physical terms. If he had thought her grown up enough to know what she was doing, Cyr would have found such terms perfectly acceptable. He had refrained at all times from putting any pressure on her because he had known that she was not grown up enough. Only now was she doing this part of her growing up. And for any number of reasons, it was hurting like hell.

Still without moving, she watched him reach the door of the restaurant, and disappear through it. And a French phrase she had not thought of for years came back to her. *On ne peut pas être et avoir été*. One cannot *be* and *have* been. Not at one and the same time.

Her eyes fixed on the door through which he had gone, Karen

knew that she had again, as she had so often recently, tailored a situation in advance to suit her own wishes. Dismissing fact in favour of fancy, in favour of a romantic dream she had created herself, she had deluded herself into believing that they could meet again, in effect, outside the Casanova, with Cyr still primarily concerned with protecting her. Which would be all she could possibly want from him now. There were not, fortunately, many situations in which it was possible to betray everyone involved, yourself included. But this happened to be one of them.

She continued to stand where she was for a full minute. Then she turned and walked quickly away from the corner of Holton and Yonge—from the Casanova in the sunlight—from the Bavaria—from a part of her past that was no more than that.

She walked for three blocks, scarcely seeing where she was going, and without knowing precisely where she was, before going into a drug store. There was a pay telephone just inside, as she had expected there would be.

She opened her handbag, took out a coin, put it in the correct slot, dialled a familiar number, spoke to a switchboard operator, to a secretary, and then to Rick himself.

"Rick," she said, "are you free to have lunch with me?"

"Yes, I am."

In spite of herself, Karen said, "I couldn't have borne it if you hadn't been."

"Is anything the matter, Karen?"

She hesitated, and then said, "Not really. Not now, darling."

"Are you still downtown?"

"More or less."

"The Park Plaza roof be as good a place as any?" he asked.

"Better than most."

"Good. I'll meet you there in, say, half an hour?"

"That should be just right, darling."

He could not, Karen thought, as she left the drug store, have chosen a better place to meet her, and not only because it was within walking distance of where she was.

Although they would never have dreamed of having lunch in the roof dining-room of the Park Plaza when they lived on Gavin

Street, it belonged to the section of the city that she had known best, both during that period, and when she had lived on Elmdale Avenue.

It gave her confidence to be on such familiar ground, made it easier than it might have been to accept, and forget, that it was chance more than anything else that had allowed her to withdraw in time from what could not have been other than a very bad mistake. To speculate now or later about Cyr's reasons for wanting to see her would be both futile and rather silly, because the obvious one was in all probability the correct one. That it should seem obvious to her now, when it had not a week earlier, served to underline both her present clarity of thinking, and the previous confusion of mind that had prevented her, for a time, from seeing anything clearly. She had much, she thought, to be grateful for. So much, that it would take a lifetime to appreciate it fully.

Walking north on Yonge amongst a stream of people, half of whom Millicent would probably have called foreigners in spite of her present preoccupation with New Canadians, Karen thought, I've missed this more than I knew. This vivid turbulence that, while denying homogeneity, nevertheless contrives a cohesiveness to which I can attach myself without loss of personal identity. And, sunlight warm on her uncovered head, she realized that she always thought of the core of the city in sunlight, as, conversely, she always thought of Waycroft in the rain. Factually it was ridiculous. Figuratively, she could not see it as other than valid.

Turning on to Bloor and walking west along the Mink Mile, she found herself remembering all the things she and Rick had done when they had lived on Gavin Street. Even though they had, at the time, been relatively poor, they had gone to concerts and hockey games, had spent many hours in the Art Gallery, had seen the latest plays from London and New York.

There had, of course, been nothing to prevent them from doing these things during their twelve years in Rowanwood. But somehow, even though they often made plans, the effort of coming downtown usually seemed too high a price to pay for a change of scene. You forgot, living in Rowanwood, what a lift you could get just from being a part of a diverse cross-section of the population. It could be a renewal of vitality. A renewal, too, of your basic faith in humanity—something that, in suburbia, tended to become a trifle frayed at the edges.

And thinking of faith, when you lived right in the city you weren't tied by social pressures to any particular church. You could choose the brand of rhetoric to which you exposed yourself. Because the chances were that if you went to church you would go on a Sunday—which, in general, was not the case in Rowanwood, where Sunday was one of the busiest days in the week. It was the day when you cleaned out the basement, or clipped the hedge, or had people in for drinks because in that way you avoided spending a whole evening with them. Somehow, in Rowanwood, church was a mid-week activity revolving around the Girls' Club, and the Boys' Club, and the Senior Members' Club, and the indoor badminton court. Biff played badminton every Thursday night, without fail. He said he owed it to himself to do so, though quite what he meant by this was never really clear.

Ahead of her, Karen could see the tall shaft of the Park Plaza, and on the opposite corner the Royal Ontario Museum. How long, she wondered, is it since I went into the museum? Only that morning, although it seemed much longer ago, Lewis had made her pinpoint it from the top of the Preston Building as a place that had been a definite part of her childhood. There could, she thought, be worse places to spend your childhood than one of the world's great museums. Rowanwood might offer you a Lady Ellis Store, and a United Cigar Store, and a Loblaw's where, if you bought enough canned sweet potatoes and corn flakes and frozen spinach, you could earn a complete set of Shakespeare; but that was just about all it did offer. Of course, you could not say that a community with a Loblaw's that supplied Shakespeare was entirely devoid of culture. But damn near. Damn near.

If she had not been looking at everything and anything, Karen might have failed to notice the occupants of a car that passed her as she approached the corner.

For a moment she thought she must be mistaken. Then she saw that she was not, and, before she could stop herself, she was laughing. Because here, for all the world to see, was the answer to what Fay had made such a mystery of on the telephone. In a way it was not funny at all. In a way it was almost tragic. Yet, initially, Karen could not help being amused.

For it was Boris's car, and in it, sitting beside Boris, was Fay.

Sobering, as she crossed Avenue Road and went through into the panelled lobby of the hotel's south block, Karen wondered why she should not have foreseen something which, under the circumstances, had been quite so inevitable. For Fay and Boris had a potential bond stronger than most, in that they were equally lost, equally the victims of chance, which had not been kind to either of them. Drifting at loose ends on the fast-moving tides of a fast-changing era, they were, apart, a threat to almost everyone with whom they came in contact. Together, they might just conceivably keep clear of ultimate disaster. Roddie wouldn't care. Roddie was not Biff. And though Rowanwood would gossip, and do so interminably, both Fay and Boris were immune to gossip; it had no power to hurt them as it could have hurt Barbara and Millicent.

It had been an overstatement on Fay's part to say that she, Karen, would be pleased by this turn of events. Negatively, however, she could not find it in herself to disapprove. Where Fay was concerned, she had never felt that she was in any position to cast stones, if only because chance had favoured her as it had not favoured Fay. And not just today, but always. From the beginning, she had been well equipped to shape her own destiny, something she was now more sharply aware of than she ever had been before.

Waiting for an elevator, she was glad that this lobby, which had once been the main one, had not been modernized. As it stood, it provided an authentic rather than a studied link with the past, and she hoped that it would remain unchanged.

Both elevators arrived at the ground floor at once, and she chose the right-hand one, as she usually did when given a choice. Ned had once said that she was oriented to the right, psychologically speaking. He did not, he had said, want her to think he was speaking politically. Politics and psychology simply did not mix. They were like oil and water. However, as Mackenzie King had said to him—

When she stepped out of the elevator at the eighteenth floor, Rick was not yet there. Without any need for a conscious decision, she turned past the receptionist's desk and walked out on to the terrace, drawn to its southern parapet as if by a magnet.

In one sense, the perspective was different from that which she had seen when in Lewis's office. In another sense, it was identical because it encompassed the same values, the same challenge. A challenge infinitely broader in its implications than any you would be likely to find in Rowanwood. Civilization, when it took you beyond the necessity to know how to snare a rabbit, moved you into an area where you fought for mental and moral survival. And whether or not you won this particular kind of battle depended to a great extent on where you fought it, and with what weapons. That is, if you fought at all. If you did anything beyond labelling yourself "I, the victor"—while stripping cellophane from fresh-frozen rabbit beside a suburban barbecue.

Far below her she saw two little girls in bright summer dresses, slowly climbing the broad sweep of steps leading up to the museum entrance. Fore-shortened by distance and height, they appeared pathetically small and vulnerable; two tiny human beings on their way to meet all the ages that had brought them to this moment. Even though the building was immense, it would be impossible for them to lose their way while actually inside, because nothing they saw would be irrelevant to the creative pattern of which they themselves were a part. When they came out again—they could very easily lose their way, as she herself had done.

"Hello, sweetheart."

Rick had known where to look for her, as she had expected him to. And though normally she would never have thought of kissing him in public, today she did. And, oddly, he seemed as unsurprised as he was unembarrassed.

"Hello, darling," she said.

"I hope I haven't kept you waiting?"

Karen shook her head. "No. I just got here."

"Feel like a cocktail before lunch?"

"But—" she began, because Rick rarely, if ever, took anything to drink at noon.

"No buts," he said, taking her hand as he had once done—was it long ago, or only yesterday?—in a crowded St. George Street fraternity house.

The cocktail lounge was almost empty, as it was likely to be on a Monday at noon, and they were able to sit beside a window that commanded a view to the south.

"Martini?" Rick asked.

"A martini would be wonderful."

As she drew off her gloves, Karen noticed that her hands were trembling. The previous twelve hours had not been easy ones. For that matter the whole of the preceding week had, she realized, been a period of almost uninterrupted strain. Here, high above the city, to all intents and purposes alone with Rick, she could feel the beginning of a relaxation that, if not yet peace of mind, was a closer approach to it than she had been able to make for a long time. Rick, in suggesting this place, had as usual done the right thing at the right time. And when the bartender brought the martinis, she knew he had been right about this, too.

"Rick," she said, "I feel at home here."

They had dined or lunched at the Park Plaza roof perhaps not more than a dozen times all told, but he knew at once what she meant.

"Yes," he said. "I do, too."

She had turned her head toward the window. When she looked back at Rick, he was watching her intently.

"Tell me about it," he said.

"About Lewis?"

"If that's what is bothering you."

"It isn't," Karen told him. "I'll tell you about that tonight. For the moment, I'll just say that Susan and Lewis and Pete will be all right."

"You speak of them as a unit?"

"They will be. I'm certain of that now. Darling, why do people have to get so unnecessarily mixed up?"

"You're talking about yourself, aren't you, Karen?"

She nodded. "How did you know?"

"In the same way that you would have known if I had been troubled."

"But you haven't said anything?"

"It was you who had to say something, sweetheart. Until you were ready to talk about it, we would have got nowhere." He smiled. "For someone who is, basically, almost painfully honest, you nevertheless have a quite remarkable talent for evasion when you think it advisable."

Where should she begin? Karen wondered. Not with Cyr, certainly. Cyr had nothing to do with her life with Rick, and never had had, even though he was an inescapable factor in a process of growing up that would not, really, be finished in her lifetime. The mistakes you made, and the mistakes you avoided making, all in their own way contributed to whatever degree of maturity you managed to achieve.

"Karen."

"Yes, Rick?"

"Don't go into anything that isn't necessary. Don't confuse the issue."

Could he have known what she was thinking about? Not possibly. He was simply giving her some very good objective advice.

Slowly turning her cocktail glass around and around between her fingers, unaware that she was doing so, she said, "No, darling. I won't confuse the issue."

Not with Cyr.

And not with the grey spectre of self-destruction that would be unlikely ever to threaten her again, if only because she now knew that there were some toys you didn't even play with if you wished to stay sane and healthy. Like a loaded gun, a toy of that kind needed no more than one moment of real desperation to become actively lethal.

"The best thing to do," Rick said, "is to jump right in, even if the water *is* cold."

He was right. There was no way in which she could lead up gently to what she wanted to say. And the water was not as cold as it might have been if he had not agreed with her so immediately when she had said that she felt at home in this place.

"Darling," she said, "it's Rowanwood. Or perhaps I should say it's myself in conjunction with Rowanwood."

"I thought that was probably it."

"You always help me, don't you, Rick? Well, here's where I really jump in. Darling, I can't go on living in Rowanwood, or in any other place even remotely like it. For me, it's a dead end where, in time, I think I would go out of my mind. It isn't the city, and it isn't the country. I don't know how to describe it other than to say that it's an impossible compromise between the two, and totally lacking in the best features of either."

She had been more vehement than she had intended, and it was with immeasurable relief that she saw him begin to smile. Ever since the previous night when she had guessed why he had gone to Planesville, she had been morally certain he shared her feelings. But it was still the most profound relief to *know* it.

"Go ahead, sweetheart," he said. "Get it all off your mind while you're at it."

In projecting this conversation, Karen had thought of it as taking place on the terrace in Rowanwood at dusk, the last rays of sunlight gilding the tops of the poplars, a quiet breeze stirring amongst the pines. Their terrace, at the end of the day, was an extraordinarily pleasant place, and for this very reason, would, she realized now, have been entirely the wrong setting. A setting that would have blunted objectivity, that would have once again distorted values she was only now getting straight. Here, she could be dispassionate, could accept without regret the inescapable truth that you never get something for nothing, that there is always a price tag attached to anything worth having.

When she spoke, she did so slowly, but without hesitation or uncertainty. "I can't get it all off my mind now. There isn't time. But I can sum it up in general. Rick, we have a beautiful house full of beautiful and expensive things, but it's smothering us because it has become an end in itself, and because it epitomizes a way of life that is essentially trivial. As long as we go on living in it, we won't really be living at all. We have too much of everything, and we are paying the wrong price for the wrong things. Rowanwood may be a wonderful place to grow trees and flowers and buckwheat lawns, but it's not a place where people can grow. Or, at any rate, very many people. It's—it's an evolutionary *cul-de-sac*."

Rick was really smiling now. "Those are big words."

Karen, grateful to him for easing what could have been an over-emotional moment, smiled too. "They are rather, aren't they? But you agree with me, don't you?"

"Yes. I do."

With unnecessary care, Karen set her cocktail glass down on the table in front of her. "How did we let it happen to us? Darling, how did it happen? We never intended to live the way we're living. We didn't start out with the idea of putting so much emphasis on purely material possessions, on power mowers, and home freezers, and all the other damn things we have."

"We took the line of least resistance, sweetheart."

"But we've fought all the way."

"It was still the line of least resistance."

Beyond the museum, Karen could see the wide green circle of Queen's Park, and farther to the south the downtown skyline of the city, blurred a little by haze and smoke. Looking at that skyline, she was caught up by the quick excitement—quite unlike any other—that was the measure of her own spontaneous identification with its growth. A city with a future, like an individual with a future, could never remain static for long, could not afford to expand indefinitely along the lines of least resistance. The suburbs, as they now existed, were the city's lines of least resistance. The towering buildings to the south were the real yardstick of its stature.

I would, she thought, be more at home on any one of those streets lying between me and the lake, than I ever have been in Rowanwood. How did I come to forget it?

Rowanwood might be all right for individuals like Susan and Lewis, who were insulated both by temperament and circumstance from their immediate environment. It could continue to be a pagan paradise for permanent adolescents like Betsey and

Harry. But for people like herself and Rick, it could never be anything other than a *cul-de-sac*.

She felt Rick's hand close over hers, bringing a familiar strength and reassurance. "It won't be all you think it's going to be. It won't be a complete solution."

"You don't need to tell me that. Last week, perhaps. But not now."

"We will still, in a great many ways, have too much of everything."

"I know," Karen said. "But here we may be able to make it work *for* us rather than against us. We will know where we are going, and why. That's what really matters. To know where you are going, and why. Even if you never get there."

People, Places, and Things

The *Torontonians* is full of contemporary references that ground the novel firmly in a particular place and time. While a work of fiction, it is sprinkled with actual people, places and things, providing what Phyllis Brett Young referred to as "an outer framework of fact for an inner core of fiction" (Author's Note).

Real people salt the novel with cultural and political connections. American musicians, BENNY GOODMAN, DUKE ELLINGTON, GLEN MILLER, ARTIE SHAW, and BING CROSBY along with actors such as KATHERINE CORNELL, MAE WEST, JOAN CRAWFORD, and RONALD COLMAN provide a general context. The interwar period is sketched with wide-ranging references to the JOE LOUIS – MAX SCHMELING 1936 boxing match, hockey stars RED HORNER and CHING JOHNSON, fan dancer SALLY RAND, and "Jazz Age" writers such as WARNER FABIAN, HAVELOCK ELLIS, VINA DELMAR, and F. SCOTT FITZGERALD. Post-war international culture is acknowledged with the mention of screenwriter and director ORSON WELLS and PIERRE LE MURE's 1950 bestselling novel *MOULIN ROUGE.* Popular novelists such as HERMAN WOUK, JAMES NORMAN HALL, and CHARLES NORDOFF are dismissed as not challenging "Byron, or Thomson, or Conrad." (180) One of the most famous piano virtuosos of the twentieth century, ARTHUR RUBINSTEIN, represents high or at least sophisticated culture, along with actor ALEC GUINNESS, the prints of French painter RAOUL DUFY, and the ceramic ashtrays of PABLO PICASSO.

Politicians such as US Presidents FRANKLIN DELANO ROOSEVELT and HARRY S. TRUMAN alongside former British Prime

Phyllis Brett Young and husband, Douglas Young, feeding the pigeons in Milan, mid-1950s. Courtesy Valerie Argue.

Minister WINSTON CHURCHILL remind the reader that Torontonians in the late 1950s lived in an international context. But a large number of the references to specific individuals were Canadian. Canadian Prime Ministers WILLIAM LYON MACKEN-

ZIE KING and LOUIS ST LAURENT (but not John Diefenbaker!) appear in the pages with D. C. ABBOTT, the federal finance minister who presided over the creation of the 1947 Income Tax Act. Diefenbaker, the Conservative prime minister between 1957 and 1963, was not the sophisticated, cosmopolitan Canadian Young was attempting to present to the world.

Canadians associated with interwar mass culture include orchestra leader GUY LOMBARDO and the swing band GLEN GRAY and the CASA LOMA ORCHESTRA. Post-war public figures linked to high culture and science are also mentioned, such as Canada's foremost child development specialist DR WILLIAM E. BLATZ, painter and insulin discoverer DR FREDERICK BANTING, essayist and longtime editor of Saturday Night B. K. SANDWELL, author ROBERTSON DAVIES, and photographer YOUSUF KARSH. Indeed, the full range of Torontonians appear in the novel, from the anonymous immigrants referred to as NEW CANADIANS to one of Toronto's most prominent families, industrialists and philanthropists the MASSEYS.

Places also play a central role in this novel – the city of Toronto itself might be considered a major character. ROWANWOOD, PLANESVILLE, and WAYCROFT SCHOOL did not exist but other districts and institutions were identified by name. Neighbourhoods such as FOREST HILL, the ANNEX, and CHINATOWN appear alongside UNIVERSITY and TRINITY COLLEGES at the UNIVERSITY OF TORONTO, UPPER CANADA COLLEGE, and ST MICHAEL'S. The HILL, the escarpment created by the ancient shoreline of glacial Lake Iroquois, marks residential status as living above the hill connoted economic success. Landmarks such as MASSEY HALL, the ROYAL ONTARIO MUSEUM, the ROYAL YORK HOTEL, the ROYAL ALEXANDRA theatre, the PARK PLAZA roof, the CANADA LIFE BUILDING, the ROSEDALE GOLF CLUB, UNION STATION, QUEEN'S PARK, and the LOBLAWS grocery chain are familiar to present-day city residents. The BANK OF COMMERCE BUILDING was the tallest building in Canada from 1931 to 1962, even if it is now dwarfed by other buildings in the Commerce Court complex.

The shopping area west of Yonge Street along Bloor is no longer referred to as the MINK MILE but high-end stores still grace this district. Large downtown department stores EATON'S and SIMPSON'S and the hardware chain AIKENHEADS are gone, as is the US-based chain of CHILD'S Restaurants. SHERIDAN NURSERIES continues but DALE'S NURSERIES have closed. The Toronto Airport has not been known as MALTON since 1960 and it is difficult to imagine the city and its traffic before the YONGE SUBWAY line opened in 1954. Canadian historical reference occurred with reference to FORT YORK and the Klondike Gold Rush's TRAIL OF '98. Beyond Toronto, there are detailed references to the elegant MONTREAL MOUNT ROYAL HOTEL and descriptions of London and Geneva. GEORGIAN BAY, the popular cottage country for Torontonians concentrated both around Go Home Bay and Point Au Baril, receives passing mention, as does the SEIGNIORY CLUB at Montebello, Quebec.

Things also take a major part in the novel. Domestic consumption is apparent in the description of cars and appliances. FRIGIDAIRE and MIXMASTER still have contemporary resonance but BENDIX is no longer a major manufacturer of televisions, radios, phonographs, and washing machines. Brand-name clothes such as a JAEGER shirt or a DIOR dress were meant to convey a particular style status, as was the class contrast between the card games of Rowanwood – BRIDGE – and Planesville – EUCHRE and WHIST. T.C.A. stood for Trans-Canada Airline, the original English-language name for Air Canada. A reference to ERIN HODGE'S 1946 bestseller (and later movie) *Mr Blanding Builds His Dream House*, about a New York couple who transform their lives through a country house renovation, would have been difficult to resist.

To contemporary readers references to cigarettes and liquor laws are particularly striking. Scientific research, which established a connection between smoking and lung cancer in 1950, is acknowledged but Karen does not stop smoking. Rather, she occasionally feels that she should. This is a world where it was possible to smoke in the doctor's waiting room and have your physician share a cigarette during a consultation. This is also a milieu where attitudes toward alcohol are complex. Alcohol is both intensely regulated in its public consumption but ubiquitous in private drinking. The LIQUOR CONTROL BOARD OF ONTARIO stores, where customers did not see actual bottles, private hotel room parties, packed bottles, and LADIES BEVERAGE ROOMS (which restricted admission only to women and their male escorts to deter casual fraternization) are contrasted with martinis and scotch before noon, whiskey in the suitcase, and cocktail brawls.

The use of particular names of public figures, precise locations, and specific articles and artifacts helps provide the novel with a realist orientation. In an interview published in June 1960, Phyllis Brett Young described *The Torontonians* as "social history." She mourned the absence of Canadian novels set in the thirties and forties, stating "If we're not careful the fifties and sixties will be lost too. Our ancient history can be written at any time. What our writers should be doing is reflecting ourselves as we are now."[1] The careful attention to detailed context and customs means that upper middle-class Toronto suburban life of the late fifties endures in fiction and *The Torontonians* helps prevent this important transitional moment from being lost.

Nathalie Cooke and Suzanne Morton
2007

1 Dorothy L. Bishop, "Phyllis Brett Young: Without the Canadian Slur," *Ottawa Journal*, 4 June 1960.